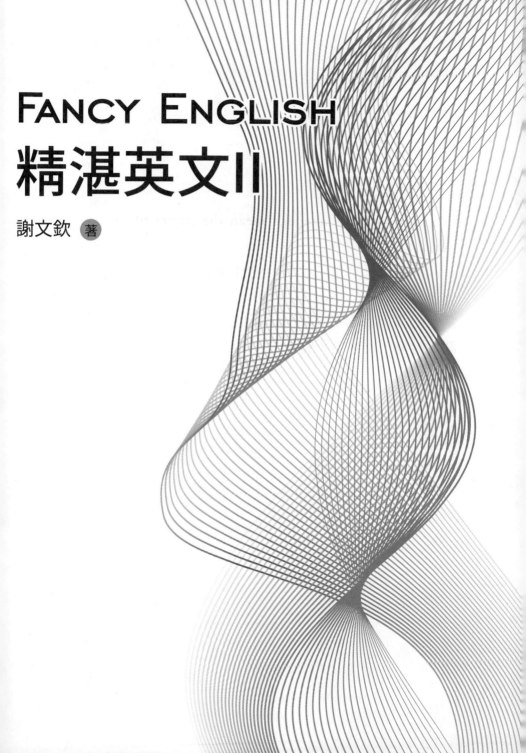

FANCY ENGLISH
精湛英文 II

謝文欽 著

The limits of my language mean the limits of my world.

——Ludwig Wittgenstein

語言的能力與我們的世界觀息息相關，學會更多語言能夠拓展你的視野。

——奧地利哲學家維根斯坦

給喜歡這本書的你

Hi there, don't forget to nurture yourself regularly. You're blossoming, evolving into another level.
You possess an unwavering resilience. Allow yourself to dream big and act upon those dreams.
Remember, the most critical believer in your vision is none other than yourself.

別忘了呵護自己，綻放、進化成更好的自己。用堅韌的精神，付諸行動、完成夢想。記住，一直支持著夢想最重要的人就是自己。

作者序及導讀

承襲第一冊的「FancyEnglish‧精湛英文」高效實用與世界
接軌的作品風格，第二本「FancyEnglish‧精湛英文」仍然
與時俱進，跟著時代潮流欣賞及學習英文，讓英文的學習有
趣、生動，不再單調乏味。本書英語的學習除了針對單字的
解釋、例句及說明，還有英文時事或精彩的英文短文，讓讀
者沈浸在英文的世界，熟悉單字、片語在英文文章中的應
用，享受英文的內容、閱讀及寫作樂趣。除了單字的同義字
詞及相關片語都有例句及釋義，針對需進一步瞭解的字彙，
還有相關單字使用細節的介紹及比較，讓您一目了然。這次
第二冊的「FancyEnglish‧精湛英文」特別針對重要字詞彙
加上音標，希望對於讀者發音瞭解能有所幫助。筆者要強調
的是學習英文的關鍵不僅僅在於擴充詞彙量，還要掌握每個
字詞片語的正確用法。透過廣泛閱讀和吸收文章中的句子，
瞭解應用方式，方能夠顯著提升個人的英語水準與能力。這
正是《精湛英文FancyEnglish》出版的核心宗旨之一，致力
於提詞彙量外，還要透過大量閱讀，讓讀者能夠深入理解、
運用各種詞組與片語，達到流暢運用自如的目標。

本書羅列了許多生動、有趣及重要的單字像是：找到
自己生命的節奏Find your groove、獨特風格Shtick、變
遷Vicissitude、暗示Adumbrate、拐彎抹角Circumlocution
／Beat around the bush、無傷大雅Innocuous、漫不經心

Insouciant、泰然自若Aplomb、口若懸河Grandiloquent、目瞪口呆Flabbergasted、內外兼具的美人Pulchritude、堅毅不拔Fortitudes、變化多端Mercurial、閃爍其詞Prevaricate、指桑罵槐Make a veiled attack等重要的英文字詞片語；還有實用的句子及字詞，如：別頂嘴Don't sass me、欺騙Beguile、輕視／輕蔑Precatory、敏銳Perspicacious、謹慎的Prudent、欠人情Beholden、掩飾Belie、矯情Unctuous、深不可測Unfathomable、防患於未然Nip in the bud、眾所矚目、泰然自若、自吹自擂、沾沾自喜、好事多磨、垂頭喪氣等字詞語、英文短文，還有日常需了解的英文。

此外，本書還包括重要的財經法律用語，如：撤資Divest；政治社會用語，如：譴責Opprobrium、應受譴責的Reprehensible、狹隘觀點Parochial perspective、本質Quiddy、可行性Tenable、亦敵亦友Frenemy、特權Prerogative、變遷等，並提供了這些詞彙在例句和文章中的用法。同樣地，醫學用語如：失樂症Anhedonia、陣痛舒緩Anodyne也一併羅列在本書的詞彙。

一些重要的流行語，像是低頭族Phub／Pedestrians、黃牛Scalper、秒殺be snapped up in no time的用法、裝病偷懶Swing the lead、滿足渴望Slake、慾望激情派對Zingy Party、旅行狂熱Wanderlust、宅度假Staycation、標題黨／釣魚網站Clickbait、怪癖Foible、精疲力盡I'm running on fumes、閒差Sinecure、食言Renege、頓悟Apiphany、泰然自若Unfazed、搖錢樹Cash cow、掃興的人A buzz-husher、腹肌Abs、放我一

馬Cut me some slack、水逆、馬甲線的說法，糾葛、糾結、口誤、卽興發言卽興處理等不一而足，絕對能豐富您的「英文字彙銀行」English Vocabulary Bank，應用解說及例句詞條上千筆，同義字詞及短文應用，絕對讓您英文學習高效有成就感，耳目一新。

當然閱讀實用的文章更是訓練英文閱讀培養實力的好辦法，本書也特別羅列精彩專文包括：iPhone 15值得觀察的成功關鍵Apple iPhone 15's Success: Key Factors to Watch、捍衛人權：正義的支柱Safeguard Human Rights：The Pillars of Justice、一次意外驚喜An unexpected surprise、米酵菌酸毒素警訊：台灣首次發現Taiwan's First Encounter with Deadly Bongkrekic Acid— Emphasizing the Importance of Food Safety and Storage Practices.、科學家復活史前巨獸向復育猛瑪象幹細胞邁進、一生一次跨越星際的味蕾之旅：太空米其林用餐體驗、馬斯克、OpenAI奧特曼大鬥法：開源碼與AI未來之爭、美加州消費者對愛馬仕Hermès獨家銷售策略，發起反壟斷集體訴等優文，結合最新時事讓您滿足求知的慾望與閱讀樂趣。

還有很多重要字彙的「超級比一比」像是「僞善」與「正直」的比較，Prudery vs Rectitude，Scrappy和Eristic都是「愛爭吵的」有甚麼不同？Remiss及Amiss還有Nip in the bud和A stich in time saves nine在意思、用法示例的解釋比較等。透過《FancyEnglish·精湛英文》系列書籍，讀者一定能享受英文閱讀樂趣，及提升英文實力，期待您的閱讀及欣賞。

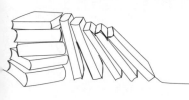

目錄

作者序及導讀 4

A watched pot never boils｜好事多磨 12

Abrasive｜粗魯／魯莽 15

Abs line／Six-pack abs｜馬甲線 19

超級比一比｜**Acrimonious vs Benevolent** 21

Adumbrate｜暗示 25

超級比一比｜**Adulterate vs Tamper with** 30

Aholic & Shopaholic｜購物狂 35

Aloof｜冷漠 38

Anodyne｜鎮痛舒緩 43

Arcane｜奧祕 47

Aplomb｜泰然自若 51

Balk｜猶豫／恐懼不安 54

Beguile｜誘騙 57

Beholden｜欠人情 60

Behoove｜必要 63

Belie｜掩飾 67

Cantankerous｜易怒暴躁 70

Capacious是什麼意思？ 75

Capitulate｜屈服 79

Cash cow｜搖錢樹 83

Circumlocution｜拐彎抹角 86

Clickbait｜標題黨、釣魚式標題 90

Copacetic｜令人滿意的 94

Corroborate｜證實 98

Crestfallen｜垂頭喪氣 101

Cut me some slack｜放我一馬 107

Cynosure｜眾所矚目的焦點 110

Deleterious｜有害的 114

Deprecatory｜譴責／鄙視／輕蔑的 118

超級比一比｜**Dilettante vs Layperson** 121

Dissipate｜褪去 125

Divest｜撤資 128

超級比一比｜**Engender、Effectuate、Transpire** 131

Engross｜引人入勝 134

Enthrall｜著迷 137

Epiphany｜頓悟／靈感 140

Esoteric｜深奧 144

Encomium｜讚美 147

超級比一比｜**Fathom vs Unfathom vs Unfathomable** 150

Feign｜假裝／偽裝 160

Flabbergasted｜目瞪口呆 164

Flummox｜困惑啊！ 167

Foible｜怪癖 169

超級比一比｜**Fortitudinous vs hellbent** 172

Frenemy｜亦敵亦友 175

Frivolous｜輕浮 178

Gasconade｜自吹自擂 181

Gaslight & PUA英文是什麼意思 185

Grandiloquent & Pompous｜誇誇其談 190

Groove｜自己舒適的節奏 194

His words are a self-fulfilling prophecy｜一語成讖 197

Hush the buzz｜掃興 200

I'm running on fumes｜精疲力盡 203

超級比一比｜**Imbroglio vs Entanglement** 207

Inadvertent｜不經意 211

Inimical 敵意／對立 216

Innocuous｜無傷大雅 220

Insouciant｜漫不經心 223

Intoxication levels｜酒醉程度的英文應用 228

超級比一比｜**Lackadaisical vs Obsequious** 230

Make a veiled attack｜指桑罵槐 236

超級比一比｜**Mercurial vs Mercury Retrograde** 239

Myopia｜近視度數怎麼說？ 244

Nip in the bud 防患於未然 245

Nonplus｜不知所措 249

Opprobrium｜譴責 252

Parochial perspective｜狹隘觀點 255

Perspicacious｜敏銳 257

超級比一比｜**Phubbing vs Petextrians** 261

Prerogative｜特權 264

Prudent｜謹慎 267

超級比一比｜**Prudery vs Rectitude** 271

Pulchritude│內外兼具的美人 275

超級比一比│**Purloin vs Peculate** 279

Quiddity│本質 284

超級比一比│**Remiss vs Amiss** 287

Reprehensible│應受譴責 290

Safeguard Human Rights：The Pillars of Justice捍衛人權：正義的支柱 295

Sass│挑釁、頂嘴 302

Scalper│黃牛 305

超級比一比│**Scrappy vs Eristic** 308

Shtick│獨特風格 312

Sedentary│久坐 316

Sinecure│高薪閒差 318

超級比一比│**Slip of tongue vs Off-the-cuff remarks vs Ad hockery** 322

Slake│滿足你的渴望 326

Smug│自以爲是／沾沾自喜 330

Soporific│昏沉沉 333

超級比一比│**Sore loser vs Gracious winner** 336

Staycation│宅度假 341

Suave & Deferential 優雅、殷勤 344

Swing the lead│老闆來了還「偷懶」 349

Tenable／Untenable│可行不可行？！ 352

Terricolous 陸生及各種生態介紹 355

To throw a sprat to catch a herring│拋磚引玉 360

超級比一比│**Unctuous vs Fulsome** 362

Unfazed｜泰然自若　　　　　　　　　　367

Vicissitude｜變遷　　　　　　　　　　370

Vindictive｜報復　　　　　　　　　　375

Wanderlust｜旅行狂熱者　　　　　　　377

Zingy party｜激情派對　　　　　　　379

專文｜**Apple iPhone 15's Success: Key
Factors to Watch** 蘋果 iPhone 15 的值得觀察成
功關鍵因素　　　　　　　　　　383

專文｜**Taiwan's First Encounter with Deadly
Bongkrekic Acid— Emphasizing the
Importance of Food Safety and Storage
Practices.** 米酵菌酸毒素警訊：台灣首次發現！　390

專文｜**Scientists Nurture Mammoth Stem
Cells, Edging Closer to Resurrecting the
Prehistoric Giant.** 科學家復活史前巨獸：向復育
猛獁象幹細胞邁進！　　　　　　　393

專文｜**Culinary Journey Beyond the Stars:
The Space Michelin Dining Experience.** 一生
一次跨越星際的味蕾之旅：太空米其林用餐體驗！　396

專文｜**Musk vs OpenAI: A Legal Battle Over
AI's Ethical and Open-Source Future** 馬斯
克、OpenAI奧特曼大鬥法：開源碼與AI未來之爭　400

專文｜**California Consumers Launch
Antitrust Class Action Against Hermès
Over Exclusive Birkin Bag Sales.** 美加州消費
者對愛馬仕Hermès獨家銷售策略，發起反壟斷集體訴 404

A watched pot never boils
好事多磨

A watched pot never boils
心急水不沸／好事多磨

一句英文諺語，字面上的意思是「盯著的鍋永遠不會煮沸」，出自美國開國元老班傑明・富蘭克林Benjamin Franklin發表的《窮理查的年鑑》（Poor Richard's Almanack）一書。有沒有這樣的感覺，當你越想某事情快點發生，你會覺得時間過得越慢。就像你想鍋裡的水快點煮沸，一直盯著鍋子，可是感覺水好像煮了好久都不滾，可能還會懷疑火爐是否壞掉？

1. The idiom means that focusing too much on waiting for a result can seem to make the process drag on longer. 所以有些事情是需要耐心等待的，尤其是美好的事情是急不來的。

2. Checking my email nonstop for the job offer is like a watched pot. 不停地檢查我的電子郵件等待工作錄取通知，就像是盯著的鍋永遠不會煮沸一樣。

來看一下這句諺語在短文中的應用：

In life, as in the kitchen, "a watched pot never boils." Emily learned this the hard way. Eagerly anticipating her promotion, she fixated on every email, meeting, and casual remark from her boss. Yet, days turned to weeks with no news. It wasn't until she shifted her focus to improving her skills and helping her team that the long-awaited promotion announcement came. It seemed that when she stopped watching, her pot finally boiled.

在生活中，正如廚房裡的「盯著的鍋永遠不會沸騰」。艾蜜莉終於學到這個「好事多磨」的硬道理。她急切地期待著自己的晉升，非常關注在每一封電子郵件、每次會議和老闆的日常言語。然而，隨著日子一天天過去，卻依然沒有任何消息。直到她把焦點轉移到提升自己的能力和團隊的協助上，那個期待已久的晉升公告才來臨。這不就是好事多磨嗎？

Patience is a virtue和A watched clock never moves都與A watched pot never boils有相似的概念和效果

Patience is a virtue
強調了耐心的重要和價值，提醒人們等待過程中要保持耐心。

1. When learning a new language, remember that patience is a virtue; it takes time to become fluent. 在學習一門新語言時，請記住耐心是一種美德；要運用流暢需要時間。

2. She waited calmly for her turn to speak, showing that patience is a virtue, especially in heated debates. 她平靜地等待著講話的機會，顯示出耐心是一種美德，尤其在激烈的辯論中。

A watched clock never moves
強調當你焦急地等待某件事情時，時間似乎過得特別慢。

1. During the last few minutes of the workday, he found that a watched clock never moves, making the time seem endless. 在工作日的最後幾分鐘，他發現盯著的鐘表似乎從不動，時間顯得特別漫長無休止。

2. As she waited anxiously for the test results, she realized that a watched clock never moves, and each second felt like an hour. 她焦急地等待測驗的結果時，她意識到盯著的時鐘永遠不動，每秒鐘都像一小時一樣長。

Abrasive｜粗魯／魯莽

Abrasive（形容詞），形容那些表現出粗魯、刺激或令人不悅的特質或行爲。用來描述某人的態度，言語或舉止，通常是指他們的互動方式不夠溫和或友善，可能會引起摩擦或矛盾。在工業上，abrasive也可指磨損用的材料，如砂紙或磨輪，用於去除表面的不規則性。

The word "Abrasive", as an adjective, is often used to describe qualities or behaviors that are rough, irritating, or displeasing. It can be used to characterize someone's attitude, language, or conduct, typically implying that their manner of interaction is not gentle or friendly, possibly causing friction or conflict. In the industrial context, "abrasive" can also refer to abrasive materials such as sandpaper or grinding wheels used to remove surface irregularities.

再一起來閱讀如何將Abrasive運用在以下這篇有關「一個粗魯性格的人和與他人互動關係」的文章之中，如何運用的：

An abrasive personality can have a detrimental impact on relationships and interactions. When someone is consistently abrasive in their communication or behavior, it can wear down the patience and goodwill of those around them. An abrasive individual tends to come across as harsh, rude, or unkind, making it challenging to establish positive connections. It's essential to recognize the importance of effective and respectful communication to avoid unnecessary conflicts. Treating others with kindness and understanding, rather than adopting an abrasive approach, can lead to more harmonious and productive interactions.

一個粗魯的個性可能會對關係和互動產生不利影響。當某人在溝通或行為上一直表現出粗魯時，可能會消耗身邊人的耐心和善意。粗魯的個體傾向於顯得嚴厲、無禮或不友善，這使得建立正面的聯繫變得困難。認知有效和尊重的溝通的重要性是必要的，以避免不必要的衝突。對待他人時時保持善良和理解，而不是采取粗魯的態度，才能實現更和諧和更有成效的互動。

閱讀一篇新聞有關「粗魯對待兒童的托兒所」相關新聞，學習及如何應用abrasive這個單字：

April 2023, a childcare center in New Taipei's Linkou faced accusations of child abuse when the director was seen roughly handling and even hitting a toddler's thighs four times for struggling during a diaper change. Despite complaints to the social welfare department, the center's director claimed surveillance malfunctions, leading to a delayed investigation. The city-imposed fines of NT$150,000 on the individual, who was also barred from childcare employment for three years, and NT$180,000 on the center for its failure to provide evidence and improper management. The abrasive behavior and scabrous neglect highlighted a severe lapse in care and oversight.

2023年4月，新北林口的一家托嬰中心因為中心主任在換尿布時對一名幼童進行粗魯的處置，甚至因孩子掙扎而連續四次打擊孩子的大腿，而面臨虐童的指控。儘管對社會福利部門提出了投訴，中心主任卻聲稱監控故障，導致調查延遲。市政府對個人處以15萬新台幣的罰款，並禁止該個人三年內在托嬰中心就業，對中心因未能提供證據和管理不當處以18萬新台幣的罰款。這種粗魯的行爲和粗鄙的疏忽凸顯了在照顧和監督上的嚴重失誤。

註：Scabrous / skæbr s/粗鄙的、爭議的。He is known for his scabrous sense of humor, which is not to everyone's taste. 他以其粗鄙的幽默感著稱，這並不合每個人的口味。

Abrasive的例句應用

1. Her abrasive comments during the meeting offended many colleagues. 她在會議中的粗魯評論冒犯了許多同事。
2. The abrasive tone of his email makes communication difficult. 他電子郵件的刺激語氣使溝通變得困難。
3. Using an abrasive substance, he smoothed the rough edges of the wooden table. 他使用拋光的材料來修整木桌的粗糙邊緣。

Abrasive的同義詞及例句

1. Rough粗糙的（形容詞）
   The surface of the rock was rough to the touch. 這塊岩石的表面摸上去很粗糙。
2. Harsh嚴厲的（形容詞）
   His harsh criticism left her feeling hurt. 他嚴厲的批評讓她

感到受傷。

3. Acrimonious 尖酸刻薄的（形容詞）

Their acrimonious exchange of words escalated the argument. 他們尖刻的言辭交鋒加劇了爭論。

4. Caustic 腐蝕性的、尖酸刻薄的（形容詞）

Her caustic comments left a lasting impact on his self-esteem. 她的刻薄評論對他的自尊心產生了長期的影響。

5. Gnarled [na:ld] 多節的、粗糙扭曲的，常用來形容老樹的樹幹或老人的手指。（形容詞）

The old man leaned on his gnarled walking stick as he moved slowly down the road. 那位老人依靠著他那根多節的手杖，緩緩地沿著道路前行。

6. Scabrous [skæbrəs] 粗糙的、難以處理的，引起社會爭議或不適的。（形容詞）

His weather-beaten face and scabrous skin belie his true age. 他歷經風吹雨打的臉以及粗糙的皮膚掩飾了他實際的年齡。

The novel was notorious for its scabrous depiction of the underbelly of society. 這部小說因其對社會底層的粗糙描繪而聲名狼藉。

（註：1. Belie（動詞）掩飾、與…不一致。通常指外表或某種表達掩蓋了真實的性質或情況。2. Underbelly（名詞）意指脆弱的部分、弱點或指社會、組織等的陰暗面或最脆弱的部分。）

Abs line／Six-pack abs
| 馬甲線

「馬甲線」的英文最常見的說法是six-pack abs，指的是腹部有明顯的「六塊肌肉」。Abs則是abdominal muscles的縮寫，意思是「腹部肌肉」。不過，馬甲線的特色是腹部兩側有兩條明顯的肌肉線條，因此也可以說是two-line abs或ab lines。也有人用corset line來稱呼，因爲馬甲線的形狀與馬甲的線條相似。

Chiseled [tʃɪzəld] 在英文中則是「雕刻的」意思，通常用來形容身材非常健美、肌肉線條明顯的人。He has a chiseled physique with well-defined muscles and a strong jawline. 他有一副鑿刻般的體格，肌肉和下巴的線條分明。因此，chiseled 也可以用來形容有馬甲線的人，因爲馬甲線代表著腹部肌肉的鍛鍊程度。

「馬甲線」的例句及應用

1. She has a perfect six-pack abs. 她的腹肌線條完美，就像六塊肌一樣。
2. I'm working hard to get two-line abs. 我正在努力訓練，希望可以練出兩條腹肌線。
3. My corset line is starting to show. 我的馬甲線條開始隱約可見了

4. He has a chiseled six-pack. 他擁有雕刻般的六塊腹肌。

5. She has chiseled abs. 她擁有雕刻般的腹肌。

6. My abs are starting to look chiseled. 我的腹肌開始變得像雕刻般明顯。

超級比一比｜Acrimonious vs Benevolent

Acrimonious [əˈkrɪmənɪəs]
激烈的、尖酸刻薄的、對立的

（形容詞）常用來描述關係或討論，當一場辯論變得激烈且充滿敵對情緒時，我們可以使用這個詞來形容。它強調了人際關係或爭論中的尖銳和敵意。

Benevolent [bəˈnɛvələnt] 仁慈的、慈善的、善良的

（形容詞）用來描述具有善意和仁慈心腸的人、組織或行爲。這個詞通常用來形容那些樂於幫助他人，無私奉獻，並關心他人福祉的人或事物。

當我們將兩個對立意思的單字，應用在一篇關於政治的善惡的文章，來看看是如何運用的：

In the world of politics, we often witness acrimonious debates and contentious disagreements. However, it's a refreshing change when a benevolent leader emerges. Acrimonious discussions filled with harsh words and animosity can leave a nation divided. On the contrary, a benevolent leader's compassionate actions and commitment to the welfare of their citizens can unite a country.

在政治世界中，我們經常目睹尖銳的辯論和爭議的分歧。然而，當一位具仁慈心腸的領袖出現時，這將會是一個令人耳

目一新。充滿尖刻的言詞和敵意可能會使一個國家分裂。相反，一位仁慈的領袖的憐憫行為和對公民福祉的承諾將可以團結一個國家。

Acrimonious的例句應用

1. The acrimonious debate between the two politicians left no room for compromise. 兩位政治家之間的針鋒相對毫無妥協的餘地。

2. Their acrimonious divorce proceedings lasted for months, causing emotional distress to both parties. 他們激烈的離婚訴訟持續了幾個月，給雙方都帶來了情感上的困擾。

3. The acrimonious exchange of words during the meeting only deepened the divisions within the team. 會議期間的尖銳言詞只是加深了團隊內部的分歧。

Benevolent的英文例句

1. The benevolent billionaire donated a significant portion of his wealth to various charitable causes. 這位仁慈的億萬富翁將他財富的一大部分捐贈給了各種慈善事業。

2. The benevolent teacher always went out of her way to help her students succeed. 這位善良的老師總是不辭辛勞地幫助她的學生取得成功。

3. The benevolent actions of the community brought hope and relief to those in need. 社區的善行為那些需要幫助的人帶來了希望和寬慰。

Acrimonious的同義字詞

1. Contentious（形容詞）有爭議的、引起爭論的

   The contentious debate over the proposed law lasted for hours. 有關提議法律的爭論持續了數小時。

   Their contentious relationship often led to heated arguments. 他們之間有爭議的關係常常導致激烈的爭論。

2. Hostile（形容詞）敵對的

   Their hostile relationship made cooperation difficult. 他們敵對的關係使得合作變得困難。

3. Spiteful（形容詞）惡意的

   Spiteful comments were exchanged during the debate. 在辯論中惡意的評論交鋒。

4. Caustic（形容詞）刻薄的

   His caustic remarks hurt many people. 他刻薄的言論傷害了許多人。

5. Vitriolic [vɪ'tri,ɒlɪk]（形容詞）尖酸刻薄的

   The article was a vitriolic attack on government policy. 這篇文章對政府政策進行了尖酸刻薄的攻擊。

Benevolent的同義字詞

1. Compassionate（形容詞）富有同情心的、憐憫的

   The compassionate nurse comforted the grieving family members. 富有同情心的護士安慰了悲傷的家庭成員。

   Her compassionate nature led her to volunteer at the local homeless shelter. 她憐憫的天性使她成為當地無家可歸者收容所的志願者。

2. Kind-hearted（形容詞）心地善良的

The kind-hearted nurse cared for her patients tenderly. 心地善良的護士溫柔地照顧她的病人。

3. Altruistic [ˌælˈtruː.ɪs.tɪk]（形容詞）無私的

He is known for his altruistic service to the community. 他以對社區的無私服務而聞名。

4. Magnanimous [məgˈnænɪməs]（形容詞）寬大的

He was magnanimous in victory, praising his opponent. 他勝利時表現得寬宏大量，稱讚了他的對手。

5. Munificent [mjuːˈnɪfɪsɛnt]（形容詞）意指極其慷慨的，用於形容給予或捐贈大量的金錢或資源

The munificent donation from the philanthropist helped to build the new library. 那位慈善家慷慨的捐款幫助建立了新圖書館。

Her munificent support of the arts has benefited many local artists.她對藝術的慷慨支持惠及了許多當地藝術家。

Adumbrate | 暗示

Adumbrate [əˈdʌm.brɪ.eɪt] 暗示、預示

一詞源自拉丁文，詞性爲動詞，是以模糊、簡略或提要的方式描述或描繪事物，通常是爲了暗示或預示未來的事件或情況。這個詞彙常用於文學、藝術和政治領域，有時也可用於日常對話中，以強調某事物的輪廓或主要特點。

The word "Adumbrate" is derived from Latin and is a verb that means to describe or outline something in a vague, brief, or summary way, often to imply or foreshadow future events or situations. This term is frequently employed in literature, art, and politics and can also be used in everyday conversations to emphasize the outline or key features of something.

這是一篇有關夢境及潛意識預示著自己會獲得一比鉅額金錢，一起來看看如何將Adumbrate運用在文章之中：

Last night, in my dream, I experienced an intriguing moment that seemed to adumbrate a future windfall of immense wealth. In the dream, I found myself surrounded by symbols of prosperity— gleaming gold coins, opulent mansions, and endless luxury. It felt as if the dream was trying to adumbrate the possibility of a significant financial gain in my waking life. Though dreams can be enigmatic, this one left me with a sense of hope and anticipation, as if it were a subtle message from my subconscious, hinting at potential wealth awaiting me.

昨晚，在我的夢中，我經歷了一個迷人的時刻，似乎預示著未來將會有一筆巨額財富。在夢中，我發現自己被財富的象徵所包圍—閃閃發亮的金幣，豪華的豪宅，以及無盡的奢華。這感覺就像夢想試圖暗示我在現實生活中可能會獲得龐大的財富收益。儘管夢境可能充滿謎團，但這個夢給了我一種希望和期待的感覺，仿佛它是我的潛意識發出的微妙訊息，暗示著等待我的潛在財富。

說明：1.Opulent mansion意思是豪華的大宅或華麗的宮殿式住宅。這個詞組通常用來形容非常富裕或奢華的人所擁有的宏偉建築，具有大量的精緻裝飾、寬敞的空間和高度的舒適度。

Adumbrate的應用例句

1. The politician's speech seemed to adumbrate a major policy change, leaving the audience speculating about the government's intentions. 政治家的演講似乎在預示一項重大政策變革，讓聽眾對政府的意圖產生猜測。

2. Her dream adumbrated a future filled with success and happiness, inspiring her to work harder to achieve her goals. 她的夢想預示著一個充滿成功和幸福的未來，激勵她更加努力地實現自己的目標。

3. The professor used diagrams and charts to adumbrate the complex scientific concept, making it easier for the students to understand. 教授使用圖表和圖表來簡要說明這個複雜的科學概念，使學生更容易理解。

4. The mysterious letter seemed to adumbrate a hidden message,

leading the detective on a quest to uncover its meaning. 這封神祕的信似乎隱含著一個隱藏的訊息，引領著偵探踏上一場揭示其含義的探索之旅。

Adumbrate的同義詞和片語

1. Foreshadow（動詞）預示或預兆，通常是指暗示未來的事情

   The dark clouds foreshadowed an impending storm. 黑暗的雲預示著即將來臨的風暴。

2. Presage ['prɛs.ɪdʒ]（動詞）預示或預兆，常常伴隨著不祥之兆

   The raven's presence in the courtyard seemed to presage bad news. 庭院中烏鴉的存在似乎預示著壞消息的到來。

3. Portend [pɔːr'tɛnd]（動詞）預示或預兆，通常涉及到重要事件或巨大的變革

   The sudden stock market fluctuations may portend an economic crisis. 股市的突然波動可能預示著經濟危機的到來。

4. Foretell（動詞）預言或預測未來事件，通常涉及超自然力量或直觀

   The ancient oracle was believed to foretell the fate of individuals. 古老的神諭被認為可以預言個人的命運。

5. Hint at（片語）暗示或示意，通常是以不明顯的方式提到或顯示

   She subtly hinted at her upcoming surprise birthday party. 她巧妙地暗示了她即將舉行的驚喜生日派對。

6. Forecast（動詞）預測或預報未來，特別是天氣、經濟或趨勢等方面

Economists forecasted a growth in the country's GDP for the next year. 經濟學家預測了明年該國的GDP增長。

7. Suggest（動詞）提出或暗示建議，也可以表示對某事物的模糊說明

Her smile suggested that she was pleased with the outcome. 她的微笑暗示她對結果感到滿意。

8. Foresee（動詞）預見或預知未來的情況，常涉及到有洞察力的觀察

She could foresee the challenges that lay ahead and prepared accordingly. 她能預見前方的挑戰，並做好了相應的準備。

9. Augur（動詞）根據徵兆或預兆來預測未來，通常與超自然信仰或神祕主義相關

The ancient priest would augur the outcome of important events by observing the flight of birds.
古代的祭司會觀察鳥的飛行來預測重要事件的結果。

10. Betoken（動詞）預示或象徵，通常指某事物具有象徵性或象徵某種含義

The dark clouds betokened an approaching storm. 黑暗的雲預示著一場即將來臨的風暴。

11. Forebode（動詞）意指預兆或預感未來不祥的事件或不好的結果

The eerie silence in the haunted house seemed to forebode something unsettling. 在那所鬼屋裡的陰森寂靜似乎預示

著某種令人不安的事情。（註：Eerie的中文意思是「怪誕的」或「令人不寒而慄的」，通常用來形容一個地方、情境或感覺帶有不尋常或令人不安的氛圍，可能讓人感到毛骨悚然。Unsettling的中文意思是「令人不安的」或「使人感到困擾的」，用來形容某事物或情境引起不安、擔憂或疑慮的感覺。這個詞通常指的是一個讓人感到不安定或不安心的情況。）

12. Presuppose（動詞）假設或預先假定某事是真實的，通常是為了進一步的討論或分析

    To understand the argument, we must presuppose certain basic principles. 要理解這個論點，我們必須預設某些基本原則。

13. Anticipate（動詞）預期或預見未來的事件，可能是基於信息或直覺

    We anticipate a significant increase in demand for our product next year. 我們預期明年我們的產品需求將大幅增加。

超級比一比 | Adulterate vs Tamper with

Adulterate摻僞、摻雜（動詞）

指的是在某物質中摻入其他不純的或劣質的成分，通常是為了降低品質或增加量而這樣做。這個詞彙經常在食品、藥物或其他產品的上下文中使用，強調了不正當的改變或混淆。

Adulterate的英文例句

1. Some unscrupulous producers adulterate their olive oil with cheaper oils to maximize profits. 一些不道德的生產商會在橄欖油中摻僞較便宜的油以極大化利潤。

2. It's illegal to adulterate prescription medications with non-approved substances. 將處方藥物與未經批准的物質混合是違法的。

3. The restaurant was fined for adulterating its premium coffee beans with filler additives. 這家餐廳因將優質咖啡豆摻雜填充劑而被罰款。

Tamper with干涉、操縱、篡改（動詞片語）

意味著以不正當的方式干涉、改變或操縱某物，通常是為了欺騙或破壞。這個詞彙可以用在多種情境中，包括數據安全、選舉、證據等。

Tamper with英文例句

1. Someone tried to tamper with the security camera footage to hide their involvement in the break-in. 有人試圖干預監控鏡頭影像為了隱瞞他們參與入侵。

2. Election officials take strict measures to prevent anyone from tampering with the voting machines. 選舉官員採取嚴格措施，防止任何人干涉投票的機器。

3. Tampering with evidence can lead to serious legal consequences in a criminal case. 在刑事案件中對證據進行篡改可能導致嚴重的法律後果。

這兩個單字的差別在於它們的意義和使用情境，Adulterate（摻偽、摻雜）是一個動詞，指的是在某物質中摻入其他不純的或劣質的成分，通常是為了降低品質、增加量或欺騙消費者。這個詞通常用於描述食品、藥物或其他產品的不當改變或混淆。而Tamper with（干涉、操縱、篡改）則指以不正當的方式干涉、改變或操縱某物，通常是為了欺騙、破壞或達到不正當的目的。這個詞彙可以用在各種情境中，包括數據安全、選舉、證據等。

參閱以下這兩個字詞及片語在「產品的摻偽與竄改數據的影響」一文中的演示：

When discussing the quality and reliability of products, it is essential to rigorously prevent any form of "adulterate" or "tamper with." If manufacturers "adulterate" products during the production process, it can jeopardize consumer health and trust. Similarly, when someone attempts to "tamper with" data or documents, it can compromise the integrity and credibility of information, posing risks to both businesses and individuals. Therefore, we should emphasize the preservation of the purity of products and information to ensure the healthy functioning of our society and economic life.

當討論產品的品質和可靠性時，嚴密防止任何形式的「摻假」或「篡改」是至關重要的。如果製造商在生產過程中「摻假」產品，可能危及消費者的健康和信任。同樣地，當有人試圖「篡改」數據或文件，可能破壞訊息的完整性和可信度，對企業和個人都構成風險。因此，我們應強調保護產品和訊息的純度，以確保我們社會和經濟生活的健康運作。

說明：雖然這兩個詞都涉及到處理或改變，但它們的重點和使用情境不同。Adulterate更強調品質的降低，而Tamper with則強調不當的行為或干涉，可能包括任何類型的改變或篡改。

Adulterate的同義字詞

1. Contaminate [kən'tæmɪneɪt]（動詞）污染、污染

   The river was contaminated with chemicals from the factory. 河流被工廠的化學物質污染了。

2. Taint（動詞）污損、玷污

   The scandal tainted his reputation beyond repair. 這場醜聞污損了他的名譽，無法挽回。

3. Dilute（動詞）稀釋

   They dilute the wine with water before serving. 他們在上菜

前將酒與水混合稀釋。

4. Pollute（動詞）污染

Industrial activities can pollute the air and water. 工業活動可能會污染空氣和水質。

5. Sully ['sʌli]（動詞）玷污、損害

The scandal sullied the company's image. 這場醜聞損害了公司的形象。

6. Spoil（動詞）損壞、破壞

Leaving food out overnight can spoil it. 把食物放在外面過夜會讓它變壞。

7. Vitiate ['vɪʃɪeɪt]（動詞）損害、削弱

Errors vitiated the credibility of the report. 錯誤損害了報告的可信度。

Tamper with的同義字詞

1. Interfere with [ˌɪntərˈfɪr wɪð] 干涉

It's illegal to interfere with the operation of a flight. 干涉飛行操作是非法的。

2. Meddle in [ˈmɛdəl ɪn] 插手

She was accused of meddling in her colleague's affairs. 她被指控插手同事的事務。

3. Manipulate [məˈnɪpjuleɪt] 操縱

The suspect was charged with manipulating the evidence. 嫌疑人被控操縱證據。

4. Fiddle with [ˈfɪdəl wɪð] 擺弄

He was nervously fiddling with his keys during the interview.

面試期間，他緊張地擺弄著鑰匙。

5. Tinker with ['tɪŋkər wɪð] 修補、篡改

He spent the afternoon tinkering with his car. 他花了一個下午時間修補他的車。

6. Meddle with干預、干涉，非法或不當地干預或觸碰

The detective warned the suspect not to tamper with any evidence at the crime scene. 偵探警告嫌疑犯不要在犯罪現場干預任何證據。

7. Alter ['ɔːltər] 改變

The document had been illegally altered. 這份文件被非法修改了。

8. Mess with [mɛs wɪð] 亂動、亂調

You shouldn't mess with those settings without proper knowledge. 你不應該在不了解的情況下亂動那些設定。

Aholic & Shopaholic
| 購物狂

-aholic和Shopaholic是兩個有趣且常見的單字。前者以aholic結尾，通常指的是某人對某事物上癮，例如：Workaholic指工作狂，Chocoholic指巧克力迷。後者Shopaholic則特指對購物上癮的人，他們總是追求購物的快感，無法抑制購物的慾望。

"Aholic" and "Shopaholic" are two interesting and common words. The former, ending in "-aholic," usually refers to someone addicted to something, such as a "workaholic" who is addicted to work or a "chocoholic" who is addicted to chocolate. The latter, "Shopaholic," specifically refers to someone addicted to shopping, constantly seeking the thrill of making purchases and unable to control their shopping desires.

來閱讀一段-aholic的文章及相關字詞變化：

"Aholic" is a versatile word ending that describes various forms of addiction. Whether it's a "workaholic" who's obsessed with work, a "chocoholic" who can't resist chocolate, or a "shopaholic" addicted to shopping, these "-aholics" all share a common trait: an insatiable passion or craving for something specific. It's fascinating how this simple suffix can encapsulate the essence of being consumed by one's desires. So, whether you're a "foodaholic," "bookaholic," or any other kind of "aholic," remember moderation is key to maintaining a balanced life.

「Aholic」是一個多用途的字尾，用來描述各種上癮的形式。無論是工作狂、巧克力迷還是購物狂，這些「-aholic」都有一個共同的特點：對某種特定事物的不可滿足的熱情或渴望。令人著迷的是，這個簡單的字尾如何能夠概括人們被欲望所吞噬的本質。因此，無論你是「食癮者」、「書癮者」還是其他任何一種「-aholic」，請記住，保持平衡生活的關鍵是節制。

Shopaholic、Workaholic Chocoholics的英文例句

1. She's a real shopaholic; she can't resist buying something every time she goes to the mall. 她眞是個購物狂，每次去商場都忍不住買東西。
2. John is such a workaholic that he rarely takes a day off, even on weekends. 約翰是個工作狂，連週末都很少休息一天。
3. My friend is a total chocoholic; she keeps a stash of chocolate bars in her desk at all times. 我朋友完全是巧克力迷，她隨時在辦公桌上放著一些巧克力棒。

除了上述的單字變化以外，使用-aholic單字結尾的變化還可以這樣使用

1. She's a sleepaholic, always seeking the perfect quality of sleep every night. 她是一個嗜睡者，每天晚上都追求完美的睡眠品質。

2. This musicaholic always follows her favorite bands on tour. 這位音樂迷總是追隨著她最喜歡的樂團巡迴演出。

3. He's a sportaholic, participating in different sports activities almost every day. 他是一個運動迷，幾乎每天都要參加不同的運動活動。

4. She's such a coffeeholic that she can't start her day without at least three cups of coffee. 她是咖啡迷，每天至少需要喝三杯咖啡才能開始一天。

5. My friend is a travelaholic; she's always planning her next trip to explore new destinations. 我朋友是個旅遊狂，她總是在計劃下一趟旅行，探索新的目的地。

6. He's a techaholic, constantly upgrading his gadgets to have the latest technology. 他是個科技迷，不斷升級他的各種裝置，以擁有最新的科技。

Aloof | 冷漠

Aloof一詞形容一種「冷漠的」態度，通常指某人避免參與或保持距離，不參與他人的活動或交流。這個詞通常用來描述那些選擇維持疏離感的人，他們可能不願意參與社交場合，或者只是對外界保持冷淡的態度。在某些情境下，這種冷漠可能是一種自我保護機制，但有時也可能被視爲冷酷或不友好的表現。

The word "Aloof" describes a kind of indifferent attitude, usually indicating that someone avoids involvement or maintains a distance, refraining from participating in others' activities or communication. This term is often used to depict individuals who choose to keep a sense of detachment; they may be unwilling to engage in social gatherings or simply maintain a distant demeanor towards the external world. In some contexts, this aloofness can be a self-protective mechanism, but at times, it may be perceived as cold or unfriendly behavior.

一起來閱讀這篇「冷漠不一定是無情」，有可能只是個性內向Introvert，學習單字在文章裡的使用方式：

She stood in the corner, aloof from the bustling crowd, lost in her thoughts. Her aloofness often led others to perceive her as distant, but in reality, she was just introverted. Despite appearing aloof, she longed for meaningful connections.

她站在角落，遠離熙攘的人群，陷入了沉思之中。她的冷漠常常讓人覺得她遙不可及，但實際上，她只是內向。儘管看似冷淡，她渴望建立有意義的連結。

閱讀一篇醫療知識的文章有關「牙痛怎麼辦」？如何將Anodyne套用在文章之中應用：

For immediate toothache relief, consider anodyne methods such as non-alcoholic mouthwash or warm water rinses, avoiding direct ice application which can exacerbate the pain. Panadol, containing ①acetaminophen, can offer temporary alleviation but beware of potential liver damage from excessive use. It's imperative to consult a dentist for severe discomfort to address the root cause rather than solely relying on temporary measures. Incorporating foods like dragon fruit and bananas can also aid in inflammation reduction, complementing medical advice for a holistic approach to dental pain management.

爲了立即緩解牙痛，可以考慮使用無酒精漱口水或溫水漱口等止痛方法，避免直接使用冰塊，因爲那可能會加重疼痛感。含有①乙醯胺酚的普拿疼可以提供暫時的緩解，但要注意過量使用可能會導致肝損傷。對於嚴重的不適，必須諮詢牙醫，直接處理痛症的根本原因，而不僅僅依賴暫時性的措施。同時，食用如火龍果和香蕉等食物也有助於減少炎症，結合醫生的建議，對牙痛管理採取全面性的方法。

說明：①Acetaminophen，一種用於治療疼痛和發燒的藥物。例如：Acetaminophen is recommended for fever reduction and to alleviate minor pains without causing stomach upset. 建議使用acetaminophen來降低發燒及緩解輕微疼痛，而不會引

起胃部不適。

Aloof的例句應用

1. He remained aloof from the office gossip, preferring to focus solely on his work. 他對辦公室的八卦保持冷漠，更喜歡專注於自己的工作。

2. Despite being at the party, she felt aloof and disconnected from the lively conversations around her. 儘管身處派對，她仍感到冷漠且與周圍熱烈的對話格格不入。

3. The manager's aloof attitude towards his team members created a sense of distance and mistrust among them. 經理對待團隊成員的冷漠態度在他們之間造成了疏離感和不信任。

Aloof的同義詞或片語及例句

1. Distant遠離的，不親近的

   She kept a distant attitude towards her coworkers, rarely engaging in conversations. 她對同事保持著遠離的態度，很少參與對話。

2. Reserved保守的，寡言的

   He is often reserved in social gatherings, preferring to observe rather than participate. 他在社交場合中常常保守，更喜歡觀察而不是參與。

3. Detached疏離的，超然的

   After the argument, he became more detached from his friends, needing time to cool off. 爭論之後，他對朋友更加

疏離，需要時間冷靜下來。

4. Standoffish [ˈstændˌɒfɪʃ] 冷漠的，不友好的

Her standoffish demeanor often intimidated people, making it hard to approach her. 她冷漠的態度常常嚇到人，很難接近她。

5. Remote 遙遠的，遠離的

The cabin was remote, surrounded by miles of wilderness. 那個小屋遙遠，四周都是幾英里的荒野。

6. Unapproachable [ʌˌnəˈproʊtʃəbl̩] 難以接近的，不易親近的

Her stern expression made her seem unapproachable, but she was actually quite friendly. 她嚴肅的表情讓她顯得難以接近，但實際上她非常友好。

7. Isolated 孤立的，隔離的

The small village was isolated from the rest of the world, accessible only by a narrow mountain road. 這個小村莊與世隔絕，只能通過一條狹窄的山路進入。

8. Indifferent [ˌɪnˈdɪfərənt] 冷漠的，漠不關心的

His indifferent response to the news of the accident shocked his friends. 他對事故消息的冷漠反應讓他的朋友感到震驚。

9. Reclusive 隱居的，避世的

The famous author became reclusive in his later years, rarely appearing in public. 這位著名作家在晚年變得隱逸，很少公開露面。

10. Phlegmatic [flɛgˈmætɪk] 冷淡的、冷漠的，情緒穩定的；不易激動的

Despite the chaos around him, his response was phlegmatic, showing no sign of panic. 儘管周圍一片混亂，他的反應卻是冷靜的，沒有顯示出任何恐慌的跡象。

11. Apathetic [ˌæpə'θɛtɪk] 無感情的，缺乏興趣或熱情的

He was apathetic about the issues facing his community, showing little interest in participating in any discussions. 他對他社區面臨的問題漠不關心，對參與任何討論顯示出很少的興趣。

12. Stolid ['stɒl.ɪd] 不易激動的，感情麻木的；表情淡漠的

Despite the uproar in the meeting room, her expression remained stolid, unaffected by the chaos. 儘管會議室內一片喧囂，她的表情依然淡漠，不受混亂影響。

Anodyne ｜ 鎮痛舒緩

Anodyne [ˈæn.ə.daɪn] 源自希臘文「ἀνωδύνη」，意指舒緩的、能夠減輕痛苦或令人感到舒緩的事物。形容詞，用來形容那些能夠帶來舒適或平靜感覺的事物。例如，一杯溫暖的茶可以成爲一種anodyne，幫助你放鬆身心。在醫學上，某些藥物也可以被描述爲anodyne，因爲它們能夠緩解疼痛。

Anodyne, derived from the Greek word "ἀνωδύνη," refers to something that can alleviate pain or provide soothing relief. This term is typically used as an adjective to describe things that bring comfort or a sense of tranquility. For instance, a warm cup of tea can be an anodyne, helping you relax. In the medical field, certain medications can also be described as anodynes because they can relieve pain.

Anodyne的英文例句應用

1. The soft, soothing music played in the spa was an anodyne for the stressed-out clients. 細緻柔和的音樂在水療中心播放，對於壓力過大的客人來說是一種舒緩劑。

2. Her words of encouragement served as an anodyne for his troubled mind. 她勉勵的話對於他的心煩意亂起了舒緩的作用。

3. The painkiller prescribed by the doctor acted as an anodyne, easing his chronic back pain. 醫生開的止痛藥充當了舒緩劑，緩解了他的慢性背部疼痛。

Anodyne意涵近似的同義字詞

1. Soothing舒緩的（形容詞）

   The soothing music helped him relax after a long day. 那舒緩的音樂幫助他在漫長的一天後放鬆。

2. Palliative緩解的（形容詞）

   The palliative care provides comfort and relief to the terminally ill patient. 緩解照護給予了末期病患舒適和緩解。

3. Alleviating減輕的（形容詞）

   The medication had an alleviating effect on her migraine. 這種藥物對她的偏頭痛有減輕的作用。

4. Calming平靜的（形容詞）

   The calming presence of the ocean always brought her peace. 大海平靜的存在總是給她帶來平和。

5. Relieving緩解的（形容詞）

   The relieving sensation of a hot bath after a long hike was amazing. 長途跋涉後熱水浴的舒緩感覺真是令人驚嘆。

6. Comforting令人安慰的（形容詞）

   Her mother's comforting words reassured her during the storm. 她母親安慰的話語在風暴期間讓她感到安心。

7. Easing緩解的（形容詞）

   The easing sensation of a gentle massage relaxed his tense muscles. 輕柔按摩舒緩的感覺讓他的緊張肌肉放鬆。

8. Mitigating（緩和的）形容詞

   Planting more trees can have a mitigating effect on urban pollution. 種植更多樹木對城市污染有緩和的作用。

9. Tranquilizing鎮定的（形容詞）

The tranquilizing medication helped him sleep peacefully through the night. 鎮定藥物幫助他整夜安然入睡。

10. Assuaging緩和的（形容詞）

Her kind words were assuaging his grief over the loss of his pet. 她溫暖的話語正撫慰了他因失去寵物而感到的悲傷。

上述同義詞都可以用來描述能夠減輕痛苦、提供安慰或緩解不適感的事物，而其詞性通常都是形容詞。

有關鎮靜的單字sedative、anesthetic

主要與藥物和醫療程序有關，分別用於鎮定和麻醉，anodyne則更廣泛，可用來描述任何能夠減輕痛苦或提供舒適感的事物。有相似之處，但它們的意思略有不同。

Sedative

是一種藥物或事物，用來平靜或鎮定人的情緒或神經系統，通常用於治療焦慮、不安或失眠。常見於醫學上，也可用於一般語境中，描述能夠使人感到鎮靜或冷靜的事物。

The doctor prescribed a sedative to help the patient relax before the surgery. 醫生開了一種鎮定劑，以幫助病人在手術前放鬆。

Anesthetic

是一種麻醉劑，用於使人失去感覺或麻木，通常在手術中用來防止病人感到疼痛。主要用於醫學領域，以形容用於麻醉手術的藥物或技術。

The anesthetic administered to the patient ensured a painless surgical procedure. 給予病人的麻醉劑確保了無痛的手術過程。

Anodyne
是一種能夠減輕痛苦或帶來舒緩感的事物，通常用作形容詞，描述能夠提供舒適或平靜感覺的事物。可用於醫學或一般語境，描述任何能夠減輕不適或提供安慰的事物。

A warm cup of tea can be an anodyne for a stressful day. 一杯溫暖的茶可以作爲一天舒緩壓力的慰藉。

Arcane ｜ 奧祕

Arcane是一個多義的單字,它既可以是形容詞,表示神祕或難以理解的,也可以是名詞,指的是深奧或祕密的知識或實踐。在詞性上,它可以描述某物的性質,也可以指代一個特定領域的特殊技巧或知識。這個詞常常用於描述魔法、科學或藝術等領域中的祕密性質。

"Arcane" is a versatile word that can function as an adjective, denoting something mysterious or difficult to understand, and as a noun, referring to esoteric or secretive knowledge or practices. In terms of its part of speech, it can describe the nature of something or refer to specialized skills or knowledge in a particular field. This word is often used to describe the secretive nature of fields such as magic, science, or art.

說明:Esoteric深奧的、神祕的。通常用來形容知識、教義、或理念,對大多數人來說難以理解或難以進入。強調某些知識或信息的限制性,只有少數特定的人或團體能夠理解或使用。

從一篇與有關罕見疾病治療的文章,引用Abstruse艱澀難懂的、Arcane深奧的到文章中,一起來看看怎麼應用:

In the field of medicine, there exists an arcane and abstruse knowledge of rare diseases and their intricate diagnoses. These conditions are often so abstruse that only a handful of specialists possess the expertise to unravel their mysteries. Imagine a patient presenting with a set of symptoms that defy conventional diagnosis, leading doctors into the arcane realm of medical literature and obscure case studies. It is within this abstruse domain that the relentless pursuit of answers becomes paramount, as physicians strive to bring light to the most arcane medical enigmas, offering hope to those who suffer from the rarest of ailments.

在醫學領域中，存在著一種關於罕見疾病及其複雜診斷的古怪和深奧知識。這些狀況通常蘊含深奧，以至於只有少數專家具備解開其神祕的專業知識。想像一下，一名患者出現了難以進行傳統診斷的症狀，醫生只能從醫學文獻的古怪和晦澀的案例研究。正是這個深奧的領域，對解答的不懈追求變得至關重要，醫生們努力爲最古怪的醫學謎題照亮一盞明燈，爲那些患有罕見疾病的患者提供希望。

Arcane的例句及示例

1. The ancient scrolls contained arcane incantations known only to a select few. 這些古老的卷軸包含了只有少數人知曉的神祕咒語。（註：Incantation [ˌɪn.kænˈteɪ.ʃən] 一種通常被用於咒語、祈禱或儀式的詞句或言辭。通常，這些詞句被認爲具有神祕或超自然的力量，用來引導或改變某些事物的命運或性質。）

2. She delved into the arcane world of quantum physics, exploring its perplexing mysteries. 她深入研究了量子物理學這個深奧的領域，探索其中令人困惑的奧祕。

3. The artist's work often incorporated arcane symbolism, leaving viewers intrigued by its hidden meanings. 這位藝術家的作品常常包含深奧的象徵，讓觀眾對其中隱藏的含義感到好奇。

Arcane的同義字詞

1. Obscure晦澀的（形容詞）

The book contained obscure references that were hard to understand. 這本書包含了難以理解的晦澀引用。

2. Esoteric深奧的（形容詞）

He was known for his expertise in esoteric knowledge. 他以深奧知識的專業而聞名。

3. Mysterious神祕的（形容詞）

The old mansion had a mysterious aura about it. 那座老宅散發著神祕的氛圍。

4. Enigmatic謎樣的（形容詞）

The artist's paintings were often enigmatic, leaving viewers puzzled. 這位藝術家的畫作常常充滿謎樣，讓觀眾感到困惑。

5. Cryptic神祕的，難以理解的（形容詞）

His cryptic message left everyone wondering what he meant. 他的神祕訊息讓所有人都好奇他的意思。

6. Recondite ['rɛk.ən,daɪt] 深奧的，艱深的（形容詞）

The professor's lectures were filled with recondite concepts that challenged the students. 教授的講座充滿了艱深的概念，讓學生們感到挑戰。

Arcane和Abstruse

兩者都表示難以理解或深奧的性質，但Arcane更強調某事物的神祕性質，而Abstruse更強調某事物的晦澀難懂。來看看例句：

1. The ancient manuscript contained arcane knowledge of alchemy that few could decipher. 這份古老的手稿包含了極少人能解讀的神祕煉金知識。

2. The professor's lecture on quantum physics was so abstruse that most students struggled to follow it. 教授關於量子物理學的講座如此的晦澀，大多數學生都難以跟上。

以上這兩個詞都用來描述難以理解或深奧的事物，但arcane帶有一點神祕的色彩，而abstruse則更強調晦澀和難懂。

Aplomb｜泰然自若

Aplomb [əˈplɑːm]（名詞）沉著自信、泰然自若

Despite the intense pressure, the surgeon performed the complex procedure with aplomb. 儘管極大的壓力，這位外科醫生仍然泰然自若地執行了複雜的手術。

來看一下aplomb泰然自若在以下短文中的應用。

In the face of shipping disruptions in the Red Sea, TSMC showcased remarkable aplomb. Their composed assurance highlighted minimal operational impact, underlining their robust approach to risk management and global supply chain preparedness. Such a response is vital in the worldwide chip industry, where TSMC's consistent production and supply chain are crucial. Their skillful navigation of geopolitical challenges in the region reinforces their leadership in the semiconductor field and showcases their extraordinary crisis management abilities.

面對紅海的航運中斷，臺積電（TSMC）泰然自若，在全球晶片產業中至關重要，因為TSMC的持續生產和供應鏈對國際電子市場至關重要。臺積電巧妙應對紅海地緣政治挑戰，進一步鞏固了他們在半導體領域的領導地位，展示了非凡的危機管理能力。

Aplomb的英文例句及應用

1. She delivered her presentation with such aplomb that the audience was completely captivated. 她進行演講時泰然自若的，使得觀眾完全著迷。

2. She handled the difficult situation with aplomb, showing great confidence and composure. 她以極大的自信和沉著應對了困難的情況。

3. Despite the unexpected challenges, he delivered his presentation with aplomb, impressing everyone in the room. 儘管遇到了非預期的挑戰，他還是以非凡的自信、鎮定進行了他的演講，給在場的每個人留下了深刻印象。

4. The young gymnast performed her routine with aplomb, earning high scores from the judges. 這位年輕的體操運動員沉著鎮定地完成了她的表演，獲得了裁判的高分。

Aplomb的同義字詞

1. Sangfroid [ˌsɑŋˈfrɔɪd]（源自法語）指在極端壓力或危險情況下的冷靜和自制。這個詞帶有一定的優雅和從容不迫的含義

   The spy handled the dangerous situation with remarkable sangfroid, never showing a hint of fear. 這名間諜以非凡的冷靜應對了危險的情況，從未顯露出一絲恐懼。

2. Unflappability [ˌʌnˈflæpəbɪlɪti] 描述在壓力或挑戰面前不輕易慌亂或失去控制的特質，強調穩定和堅定

   Her unflappability during the crisis reassured the entire team. 她在危機中的鎮定自若讓整個團隊感到安心。

3. Poise（名詞）鎮定、泰然自若

The speaker showed remarkable poise during the heated debate. 在激烈的辯論中，演講者表現得非常鎮定。

4. Composure（名詞）鎮靜、沉著

Despite the pressure, he maintained his composure throughout the interview. 儘管壓力很大，他在整個面試過程中都保持了沉著。

5. Imperturbable [ˌɪm.pəˈtɜːr.bə.bəl]（形容詞）沉著冷靜的

Despite the chaos around him, the monk remained imperturbable, lost in meditation. 儘管一片混亂，那位僧侶仍然保持著平靜與鎮定，沉浸在冥想中。

6. Nonchalant [ˌnɒnʃəˈlɑːnt]（形容詞）漠不關心或冷淡的態度

He gave a nonchalant shrug, seemingly unaffected by the bad news. 他不在乎地聳了聳肩，看起來似乎不受那條壞消息的影響。

7. Level-headed [ˈlevəlˌhedɪd]（形容詞）冷靜的

In times of crisis, it's important to remain level-headed and make rational decisions. 在危機時刻，保持冷靜和做出理性決策是非常重要的。

Balk | 猶豫／恐懼不安

Balk是一個動詞，指的是由於恐懼不安、猶豫、拒絕或反對而拒絕採取行動或接受某種建議、計劃或要求的情況。這個詞可以在各種情境中使用，通常表示對於某事感到不安或不願意。

"Balk" is a verb that refers to the act of refusing to take action or accept a suggestion, plan, or request due to fear, hesitation, reluctance, or opposition. This word can be used in various contexts, often indicating uneasiness or unwillingness about something.

閱讀一篇有關「是否參選猶豫不決」短文，瞭解Balk的應用：

The potential presidential candidate found himself in a quandary. He had been contemplating a run for the highest office for months, but now he was hesitating. The weight of the decision felt like a heavy ball and chain around his neck. On one hand, he had a burning desire to make a difference in his country, but on the other, the intense scrutiny and responsibility that came with the role made him balk at the idea. The pressure to make a choice was mounting, and he knew he couldn't juggle this decision forever.

這位潛在的總統候選人陷入了困境。他已經考慮參選最高職位幾個月了，但現在他猶豫不決。這個決定的重要性就像是一個沉重的鐵球，壓在他的脖子上。一方面，他渴望在國家做出改變，但另一方面，伴隨著這個角色而來的激烈監督和責任使他對這個想法感到不安。做出選擇的壓力不斷增加，他知道他不能永遠拖延這個決定。

說明：1. In a quandary [ˈkwɑːn.dər.i]（英文片語）陷入困境、猶豫不決、不知道該怎麼辦或作出決定。這個片語通常用來描述一個人面臨困難或複雜的情況，感到迷茫或不確定該如何應對。2. Juggle在生活或工作中同時應對多個事情或責任，處理多項任務，保持平衡；試圖同時維持多個不同的事物，如多個關係、承諾或利益。描述一個人試圖平衡不同方面的生活。

Balk英文例句應用

1. She balked at the idea of speaking in public and declined the invitation to give a speech. 她對於公開演講的想法感到不安，因此拒絕了發表演講的邀請。

2. The company's employees balked when they were asked to work overtime without additional pay. 公司的員工被要求加班而不支付額外加班費時感到不滿。

3. He often balks at trying new foods, preferring to stick to his familiar and comfortable choices. 他經常對嘗試新食物感到猶豫，更喜歡堅持他熟悉且愜意的選擇。

Balk同義詞及英文例句

1. Hesitate（猶豫）動詞

   She hesitated to accept the job offer. 她猶豫是否接受這份工作邀請。

2. Resist（抗拒）動詞

   He resisted the temptation to eat the chocolate. 他抗拒了吃巧克力的誘惑。

3. Recoil（退縮）動詞

   The loud noise made her recoil in fear. 大聲的噪音讓她因害怕而退縮。

4. Shy away from（迴避）動詞片語（Phrasal Verb）

   Don't shy away from challenges; embrace them as opportunities. 不要迴避挑戰，將其視爲機會。

5. Dodge（閃避）動詞

   The athlete managed to dodge the defender and score a goal. 運動員成功閃避防守者，進球得分。

Beguile | 誘騙

Beguile有幾個不同的字義

1. 欺騙：意指用詭計或花言巧語欺騙某人，尤其是誘使他們相信不實之事。

   He tried to beguile her into investing in a fraudulent scheme. 他試圖欺騙她投資一個詐騙計劃。

2. 吸引：表示吸引、迷惑或引誘某人，使他們感到愉悅或沉浸其中。

   The beautiful scenery of the countryside never fails to beguile tourists. 美麗的鄉村風光總是能吸引遊客。

3. 消磨時間：意味著用輕鬆愉快的方式度過時間，通常是在等待或無所事事的情況下。

   She beguiled the long hours of the train journey by reading a captivating novel. 她透過閱讀一本引人入勝的小說來消磨漫長的火車旅程的時間。

Beguile的同義詞及例句

1. 欺騙：同義詞有Deceive、Mislead、Cheat

   a. She tried to deceive her friend by pretending to be someone else on the phone. 她試圖通過假裝成別人打電話來欺騙她的朋友。

   b. The salesman misled customers by promising features that the product didn't have. 那位銷售員透過承諾產品沒有的功能誤導了顧客。

c. He cheated in the game by peeking at his opponent's cards. 他在遊戲中作弊，偷看對手的牌。

2. 吸引：同義詞有Entice、Charm、Captivate
   a. The fragrance of fresh-baked bread enticed people into the bakery. 剛出爐的麵包香氣吸引著人們走進了麵包店。
   b. Her charming smile won over everyone at the party. 她迷人的微笑贏得了派對上所有人的喜愛。
   c. The magician's performance captivated the audience with its stunning illusions. 魔術師的表演以令人驚嘆的幻覺迷住了觀眾。

3. 消磨時間：同義詞Pass (the) time, Amuse oneself, Kill time
   a. He read a novel to pass the time while waiting for the delayed flight. 他讀小說來消磨等待延誤的飛機時間。
   b. The children amused themselves by playing in the park all afternoon. 孩子們整個下午都在公園裡玩耍，自得其樂。
   c. We played card games to kill time during the long train journey. 在長途火車旅行中，我們玩撲克牌來打發時間。

閱讀一篇有關「以廣告誘騙消費者購買商品」的文章，了解Beguile的用法：

In the world of advertising, companies often employ tactics to beguile consumers. They use clever slogans and enticing visuals to beguile people into buying their products, sometimes even exaggerating the benefits. While these strategies can beguile customers temporarily, they may also leave them feeling deceived if the product doesn't live up to the hype. On a more personal level, individuals can beguile someone with their charm and charisma, drawing them into a captivating web of allure. However, it's essential to distinguish between beguiling someone genuinely and using deception, as honesty and authenticity should always prevail.

在廣告業界中,公司常常使用策略來欺騙消費者。他們使用巧妙的口號和誘人的視覺效果來引誘人們購買他們的產品,有時甚至會誇大產品的優勢。儘管這些策略可以暫時欺騙消費者,但如果產品無法達到宣傳效果,也可能讓消費者感到被欺騙。在更個人層面上,個人可以以自己的魅力和魅力來吸引某人,將他們引入一個迷人的誘惑網絡。然而,有必要明確區分真正吸引某人和使用欺騙之間的差別,因為誠實和真實始終應該占上風。

Beholden | 欠人情

Beholden欠人情的、受惠的、感激的

（形容詞）感到負有一種道義或感情上的責任，因爲別人對他們有幫助或於他們有影響。當一個人感到beholden時，他們可能會感到需要回報或感謝，因爲他們知道自己受到了恩惠。

The word "Beholden" is commonly used as an adjective, indicating that someone feels a moral or emotional obligation because someone else has been helpful or influential to them. When a person feels "beholden," they may feel the need to repay or express gratitude because they recognize that they have received a favor.

閱讀一篇有關「父母恩情深似海」的短文，瞭解beholded在文章中的運用：

We are beholden to our parents for their unwavering love and guidance. Throughout our lives, they have selflessly supported us, and their sacrifices are immeasurable. It's crucial that we acknowledge the debt of gratitude we owe them. Being beholden to our parents means recognizing the profound influence they've had on our lives. It's a reminder that we should cherish and care for them as they age, just as they cared for us in our youth. This sense of being beholden serves as a powerful motivation to show our appreciation through actions, not just words."

我們對父母的無私的愛與教導感到感激。在我們的生命中，他們一直無私地支持我們，他們的犧牲是無法衡量的。我們必須承認我們對他們應該抱持的感恩之情。對父母感激意味著認識到父母親對我們的深遠影響。提醒您，我們應該在他們年老時珍惜、照顧他們，就像他們在我們年輕時照顧我們一樣。這種受惠的感覺是一種強大的動力，讓我們通過行動而不僅只是用言語來表達我們的感激之情。

Beholden的英文應用例句

1. She felt beholden to her mentor for guiding her throughout her career. 她感到對她的導師很感激，因為導師在她的職業生涯中一直給予指導。

2. They were beholden to their neighbors for helping them during the tough times. 他們欠鄰居們一份人情，因為在困難時期得到了幫助。

3. The organization was beholden to its dedicated volunteers for their unwavering support. 構對於堅定不移奉獻志工的表達感激不已。

Beholden的一些同義詞

1. Indebted [ɪnˈdɛt.ɪd] 欠債的，感激（虧欠）的，負有義務的（形容詞）
   She felt deeply indebted to her friend for lending her money when she needed it. 她對朋友在她需要時借錢給他深感歉意。

2. Obligated有義務的，受約束（形容詞）

He felt obligated to help his colleague with the project because they had worked together in the past. 因為他們過去曾一起合作，所以他感到有義務協助他的同事完成這個專案。

3. Grateful感激的，感謝的（形容詞）

She was grateful to her mentor for all the guidance and support provided during her career. 她對她的導師在她的職業生涯中提供的所有指導和支持感到感激。

4. Appreciative感謝的，欣賞的（形容詞）

The team was appreciative of the extra effort put in by their colleague to meet the deadline. 團隊感謝他們的同事為達到截止日前要求的額外付出。

Behoove｜必要

Behoove [bɪˈhuːv] 必要，必需的動詞型態

在某種情境下是合適或有必要的。通常用來表示某人應該或應當做某事，以符合社會規範或符合他們自己的最大利益。

"Behoove" is a verb that means it is appropriate or necessary in a certain context. This word is typically used to indicate that someone should or ought to do something to conform to societal norms or for their own best interests.

以下是一個環保議題應用behoove的文章：

It behooves us to be mindful of our environment. The world faces unprecedented challenges due to climate change and pollution. To ignore these issues would be detrimental to our planet and future generations. It is our duty to reduce our carbon footprint, conserve resources, and protect endangered species. Every small action counts, from using reusable bags to supporting renewable energy initiatives. Let us remember that we are stewards of this Earth, and it is in our best interest, as well as our moral obligation, to preserve its beauty and diversity.

我們有義務謹慎對待我們的環境。由於氣候變化和污染，世界面臨前所未有的挑戰。忽視這些問題對我們的星球和後代將會有害無益。我們有責任減少碳足跡，節約資源，保護瀕臨絕種的物種。每一個小小的行動都很重要，從使用可重複使用的袋子到支持可再生能源計劃。讓我們記住,我們是這個地球的管理者,保護它的美麗和多樣性既符合我們的最大利益,也是我們的道德義務。

Behoove的英文例句應用

1. It behooves employees to regularly update their skills to stay competitive in the fast-changing technology sector. 員工應該定期更新他們的技能,以在快速變化的科技領域保持競爭力。

2. As a responsible citizen, it behooves you to vote in every election to have a say in your country's governance. 作為一名負責任的公民,你應該在每次選舉中投票,以對你國家的治理發表意見。

3. In a team project, it behooves each member to contribute their expertise to achieve the common goal. 在團隊專案,每位成員都有必要貢獻他們的專業知識,以實現共同的目標。

Behoove的同義詞例句和應用

1. Benefit好處、利益(動詞)

   It would benefit us to exercise regularly. 定期運動對我們有好處。

2. Behoof利益、幫助(名詞)

   His actions were for the common behoof of the community. 他的行為是為了社區的共同利益。

3. Serve服務、幫助(動詞)

   Volunteering at the shelter would serve a noble purpose. 在收

容所做義工將貢獻於崇高的目的。

Behoove與Necessitate以及Be decorous for

在某些情境下可能有相似之處，雖然意思接近，這些同義詞都可以用來表達類似的概念，即某事對某人或某事情有好處或幫助，但它們在用法和含義上仍然有差異。以下是它們的意思、使用情境以及例句

Behoove指的是某事對於某人或某情況是明智或有益的，但不一定是絕對必要的。用於建議或強調某事是明智的選擇，但不一定不可或缺。

It would behoove you to study for the upcoming exam. 你最好為即將來臨的考試做好準備。

Necessitate表示某事是絕對必要的，不能避免或省略。用於強調某事是不可或缺的，通常指的是需要采取行動來滿足某需求或達到某目標。

The complexity of the project necessitates a skilled team. 這個專案的複雜性需要一個熟練的團隊。

Be Decorous For是得體的意思，表示某行為或情況對於特定情境或場合是適當和得體的。用於描述符合一定社會、文化或場合規範的行為。

Wearing formal attire would be decorous for a black-tie event. 在正式的場合穿著禮服是合適的。

Behoove指的是某事是明智或有益的，但不一定必要；
Necessitate則強調某事是絕對必要的；而be decorous for強調
某行為或情況在特定情境下是合適的。

Belie｜掩飾

Belie是一個動詞，意思是掩飾或遮蓋真相，通常是指透過行為或外表來誤導或使人誤解。這個詞語通常用來描述一個情況或一個人的行為與他們真正的內心想法或狀態不符的情況。

"Belie" is a verb that means to disguise or conceal the truth, often by actions or appearance, to mislead or create a false impression. This word is typically used to describe a situation or someone's behavior that contradicts their true thoughts or state.

參照以下有關專家提出「中國可能為掩飾經濟的放緩，轉移焦點冒險動武」短文來瞭解Belie在短文中的應用：

Amid concerns about China's domestic economic woes, including sluggish growth, currency tightening, and local debt issues, American scholars warn that Beijing may attempt to shift the focus by belying the economic downturn by venturing the risk of war with the United States over the Taiwan Strait situation.

在對中國國內經濟困境感到擔憂，包括經濟增長緩慢、貨幣緊縮和地方債務等問題的情況下，美國學者警告稱，北京可能試圖在台海局勢上冒著與美國開戰的風險，以轉移焦點，從而掩飾經濟衰退。

Belie的英文例句應用

1. His cheerful demeanor belied the sadness he felt inside. 他愉快的態度掩飾了他內心的悲傷。
2. The calm surface of the lake belied the strong currents underneath. 湖面的平靜掩飾了水下的強大洪流。
3. Her confident words belied her nervousness before the important presentation. 她自信的言談掩蓋了在重要簡報前的緊張情緒。

Belie（掩飾）的同義詞及相關例句

1. Disguise（動詞）偽裝，掩飾

   She used makeup to disguise her true appearance. 她使用化妝品來偽裝她的真實外貌。
2. Mask（動詞）遮蔽，掩飾

   He tried to mask his disappointment with a smile. 他試圖用微笑掩飾失望。
3. Conceal（動詞）隱藏，掩蓋

   She tried to conceal her emotions from others. 她試圖隱藏自己的情感不讓其他人看出來。
4. Camouflage（動詞）偽裝，掩蓋

   The soldiers used natural materials to camouflage their positions. 士兵們使用天然材料來偽裝他們的位置。
5. Veil（動詞）遮蓋，掩飾

   Her smile veiled her true feelings. 她的微笑掩飾了她真正的感受。

6. Fabricate篡改，偽造

It's illegal to falsify official documents. 偽造官方文件是非法的。

7. Misrepresent（動詞）歪曲，不正確地描述

The article misrepresents the facts. 這篇文章歪曲了事實。

Cantankerous | 易怒暴躁

Cantankerous [kæn'tæŋ.kər.əs] 是一個形容詞，用來描述一個人或事物的脾氣古怪、易怒和不合作。這個詞通常用來形容那些常常發脾氣、愛抱怨且難以相處的人或物品。

"Cantankerous" is an adjective used to describe a person or thing with a irritable, quarrelsome, and uncooperative temperament. This word is typically used to characterize individuals or objects that are frequently bad-tempered, prone to complaining, and difficult to get along with.

閱讀一篇短文，瞭解一下cantankerous的應用方式：

In a bustling city, there was a cantankerous old shopkeeper who ran a small, cluttered store. He was known for his irritable disposition and constant complaints about the noise and mess in the neighborhood. Despite his cantankerous nature, loyal customers continued to visit his store. One day, a group of local kids decided to help clean up the area around his shop. They planted flowers and painted a mural on a nearby wall. The cantankerous shopkeeper was initially grumpy but gradually warmed up to the positive changes. His heart softened, and he began to appreciate the community's efforts. This transformation showed that even the most cantankerous individuals could change when shown kindness and goodwill.

在一個繁華的城市中，有一位脾氣古怪的經營著一家小又雜亂商店的老闆。他以易怒的性格和對社區噪音和混亂的不斷抱怨而聞名。儘管他脾氣古怪，忠實的顧客仍然繼續光顧他的店鋪。一天，一群當地的孩子決定幫助清理他店鋪周圍的地區。他們種植了花朵，並在附近的牆壁上繪畫了一幅壁畫。脾氣古怪的店主起初抱怨不已，但逐漸對這些積極的改變產生好感。他的心變得柔軟，並開始欣賞社區的努力。這種轉變表明，即使是最脾氣古怪的人，在受到善意和友好的對待時也可以改變。

說明：1. Run a cluttered store經營一家雜亂的商店。2. Disposition用來描述一個人的性格特徵、情感傾向或態度。

Cantankerous單字在句子中的應用

1. My cantankerous neighbor always finds something to complain about, whether it's the weather or the noise. 我那位脾氣古怪的鄰居總是能找到抱怨的事情，無論是天氣還是噪音。

2. The cantankerous old printer in the office seems to jam every time I need it the most. 辦公室裡那臺老舊的電腦印表機似乎在每次我最需要它的時候都會卡住。

3. Dealing with a cantankerous customer on the phone can be quite challenging, but it's essential to remain patient and polite. 與電話中的一位脾氣古怪的客戶打交道可能會很具挑戰性，但保持耐心和禮貌是很重要的。

Cantankerous同義字詞應用

1. Irascible易怒的（形容詞）

His irascible temperament made it difficult to work with him. 他易怒的性格使得和他一起工作變得困難。

2. Quarrelsome好爭吵的（形容詞）

The quarrelsome neighbors argued loudly every night. 這對好爭吵的鄰居每晚都大聲爭吵。

3. Cranky易怒的（形容詞）

Don't bother him when he's feeling cranky; he needs some space. 當他感到易怒時不要打擾他，他需要一些空間。

4. Cross脾氣壞的（形容詞）

She's always cross in the morning until she has her coffee. 她早上總是脾氣壞，直到喝了咖啡才好一點。

5. Argumentative好爭辯的（形容詞）

He's so argumentative that he can't have a civil conversation. 他太好爭辯了，無法進行文明的對話。

6. Irritable ['ɪr.ɪ.tə.bəl] 易怒的（形容詞）

Lack of sleep made her irritable and hard to please. 睡眠不足讓她變得易怒，難以取悅。

7. Crotchety ['krɒtʃ.ɪ.ti] 易怒的，脾氣壞的（形容詞）

The crotchety old man would shout at the kids playing outside his house. 那個脾氣壞的老人會對著在他家外面玩耍的孩子們大喊大叫。

8. Grouchy ['graʊ.tʃi] 易怒的，抱怨的（形容詞）

He woke up feeling grouchy after a restless night. 經歷了一個不安穩的夜晚之後，他醒來時感覺很煩躁。

9. Grumpy ['grʌm.pi] 脾氣暴躁的，易怒的（形容詞）

My neighbor is grumpy in the mornings before his coffee. 我

的鄰居在喝咖啡前的早晨總是脾氣暴躁。

10. Ornery ['ɔː.nə.ri] 難以處理的，脾氣差的（形容詞）

The ornery mule refused to move, no matter how much they coaxed. 那匹脾氣差的騾子無論怎麼哄都拒絕移動。

這些同義詞都描述了一種易怒、好爭吵或脾氣不好的特質，可以用來描述某人的性格或情緒狀態。

脾氣不好的英文單字

1. Feisty好鬥的：指個性強烈、勇敢、有活力的特質，通常是正面的評價。

The feisty young girl wasn't afraid to stand up for herself. 這個好鬥的小女孩不怕為自己辯護。

2. Cranky易怒的：指情緒不穩定，容易生氣或發火。

I try to avoid talking to my coworker when he's feeling cranky. 我嘗試避免在我的同事情緒不穩定時與他交談。

3. Crabby脾氣暴躁的：與cranky相似，形容一個人容易發脾氣或情緒不穩定。

She's always crabby in the morning before she has her coffee. 她在喝咖啡之前的早上總是脾氣暴躁。

4. Eristic好爭辯的：形容一個人喜歡爭論或辯論，通常有貶義。

His eristic nature makes it hard to have a calm conversation with him. 他好爭辯的性格使得和他進行冷靜的對話變得困難。

5. Choleric ['kɒl.ə.rɪk] 易怒的：類似cranky和crabby，形容一

個人容易生氣或發火。

His choleric temperament often leads to conflicts with his friends. 他易怒的性格常常導致與朋友之間的衝突。

6. Scrappy好鬥的、好強的：表示某人具有強烈的決心和意志，通常是正面的評價。

Despite facing many challenges, she has a scrappy attitude and never gives up. 儘管面臨著許多挑戰，她有著好鬥的態度，從不放棄。

7. Grumpy脾氣壞的：形容一個人容易生氣或不高興。

Don't talk to him when he's grumpy; he needs some time to cool off. 他情緒不佳時不要與他交談；他需要一些時間冷靜下來。

8. Cantankerous易怒且愛爭吵的：這個詞結合了易怒和愛爭吵的特質，通常形容一個人非常脾氣暴躁且喜歡與他人爭論。

The cantankerous old man yelled at the kids for playing near his yard. 這個易怒且愛爭吵的老人對著在他院子附近玩耍的孩子們吼叫。

9. Curmudgeon [kər'mʌdʒ.ən] 壞脾氣的老人或易怒的人（名詞）

The old man was known as a curmudgeon, always complaining about something. 那位老人以壞脾氣著稱，總是對某事抱怨不休。

10. Grouchy ['graʊ.tʃi] 脾氣暴躁的（形容詞）

He woke up feeling grouchy and didn't want to talk to anyone. 他醒來時感覺脾氣很差，不想和任何人說話。

Capacious是什麼意思？

Capacious是形容詞，指有大容量、寬敞的空間，可以容納許多物品或人。這個詞通常用來描述房間、箱子、車輛等具有大空間的東西。當你想要強調某個地方或物品非常寬敞，可以使用capacious來形容。

以英文短文舉例：

This library is so capacious, with tens of thousands of books and many cozy reading corners. Its capacious interior space attracts many readers who can seek knowledge in this tranquil environment.

這間圖書館是如此寬敞，擁有數以萬計的書籍和許多舒適的閱讀角落。它的capacious內部空間吸引了許多讀者，他們可以在這個寧靜的環境中尋找知

當你想要強調某個地方或物品非常寬敞，可以使用「capacious」這個詞來形容。

Capacious的英文應用及例句

1. The ballroom in the palace is incredibly capacious, able to accommodate hundreds of guests for grand events. 這座宮殿的舞廳非常寬敞，能夠容納數百名賓客參加盛大的活動。

2. The capacious trunk of the SUV allowed us to pack all our camping gear for the weekend getaway. 這輛SUV寬敞的行李

箱讓我們能夠將所有的露營裝備都裝進去，度過了周末的短途旅行。

3. The capacious auditorium was filled with enthusiastic students eager to listen to the guest speaker. 這個寬敞的禮堂坐滿了熱情洋溢、渴望聆聽嘉賓演講的學生們。

Capacious的同義詞以及例句

1. spacious寬敞的（形容詞）

This loft apartment is incredibly spacious, with high ceilings and plenty of room for furniture. 這個開放式空間的公寓非常寬敞，有足夠空間擺放家具。（Loft閣樓、倉庫空間、開放式空間的意思，是指在建築物中的閣樓或倉庫空間，通常位於頂層，具有高天花板和開放的設計。這個詞也可以用來形容類似的開放式空間，不一定非要在頂層，但具有高天花板和少量的隔間。Loft apartment是指設計成開放式空間的公寓，通常包括高天花板、大窗戶和少量的內部隔間。這種公寓設計常見於工業風格的建築中，並強調開放感和現代感。）

2. Roomy寬敞的（形容詞）

The minivan is quite roomy, providing ample space for passengers and cargo. 這輛迷你貨車相當寬敞，提供了充足的空間供乘客和貨物使用。

3. Capable of holding a lot 能夠容納許多東西的

The storage unit is capable of holding a lot of items, making it perfect for our needs. 這個儲物單元能夠容納許多物品，非常適合我們的需求。

4. Roomful 擠滿了的房間（名詞）

The conference room was a roomful of eager participants, ready to discuss the project. 會議室擠滿了熱切的參與者，準備討論這個專案。

5. Ample充足的（形容詞）

The backyard provides ample space for gardening and outdoor activities. 後院提供充足的空間進行園藝和戶外活動。

與空間、數量相關的單字

plenteous、roomy、copious、profuse、commodious這些單字都與空間、數量或供應數量大或多有關，但細微的差異使它們在不同情境中有不同的適用性。以下是各個單字的意思及例句使用說明。

1. Roomy寬敞的，有足夠空間容納東西的。用來形容地方或物品有足夠的空間，但不強調極端的寬敞。

The living room in their new house is quite roomy, with plenty of seating for guests. 他們新房子的客廳相當寬敞，有足夠的座位供客人使用。

2. Plenteous豐富的，充足的，大量的。用來形容某物的「數量或供應」非常充足。

The garden yielded a plenteous harvest of fruits and vegetables this year. 這個花園今年豐收了大量的水果和蔬菜。

3. Commodious寬敞而舒適的，提供充足空間的。用來形容地方或物品提供舒適且充足的空間，通常有正面評價。

The hotel room was commodious, with a large bed and a

spacious bathroom. 這家酒店的房間很寬敞，有大床和寬敞的浴室。

4. Profuse極度豐富或大量的，通常指液體或東西的流出非常多。

用來形容某物過多或過量，有時可能帶有貶義。

After the heavy rain, there was a profuse flow of water in the river, causing flooding. 大雨過後，河流水量過多，導致洪水。

5. Copious大量的，豐富的，通常指資訊、筆記或數據非常多。用來形容大量的、充足的信息或數據。

She took copious notes during the lecture to help her study for the exam. 她在講座期間做了大量的筆記，以幫助她準備考試。

6. Capacious寬敞的，有大容量的，能容納許多東西的。用來形容地方或物品非常寬敞，能容納大量東西。

The capacious garage could fit three cars and still have room for storage. 這個寬敞的車庫可以容納三輛汽車，還有空間存放物品。

Capitulate｜屈服

Capitulate [kəˈpɪtʃ.ə.leɪt]（動詞）意指完全投降或屈服，通常出於無法繼續抵抗或達成妥協的情況。這個詞通常用來描述在戰爭、談判或爭執中，一方最終不得不放棄或接受對方的要求。

"Capitulate" (verb) means to surrender completely or yield, often due to an inability to continue resisting or reach a compromise. This word is typically used to describe situations in which one party in a war, negotiation, or dispute ultimately has to give in or accept the demands of the other.

來看一下「烏克蘭與俄羅斯長期衝突，烏克蘭堅持國家領土完整不屈服，毫不退讓」的短文，如何應用Capitulate在文章中：

In the conflict between Ukraine and Russia, Ukraine has never capitulated, steadfastly defending its territorial integrity and resisting with determination. This protracted conflict has witnessed the resilience and willpower of the Ukrainian people, who refuse to yield to external pressures and uphold their sovereignty. Despite facing numerous hardships and sacrifices, Ukraine has maintained its autonomy and continues to strive to protect the nation's independence. This story reflects people's unwavering belief in freedom and independence, and their willingness to fight for it to the end.

在烏克蘭和俄羅斯的衝突中，烏克蘭不曾屈服，堅決捍衛其領土完整，奮力抵抗。這場持久的衝突已經見證了烏克蘭人民的堅韌和意志，他們拒絕屈服於外部壓力，堅守自己的主權。儘管面臨許多困難和犧牲，但烏克蘭保持了其自主性，繼續為保護國家的獨立而努力。這個故事反映了人們對於自由和獨立的不可動搖信念，並願意為之奮鬥到底。

說明：Unwavering belief是「不動搖的信念」，意思是一種堅定、毫不動搖的信仰或信念，不論面臨多大的困難或挑戰，都不會改變或妥協的信念。

Capitulate應用及例句

1. After a long and intense negotiation, the two companies finally decided to capitulate and sign the merger agreement. 經過漫長而激烈的談判，這兩家公司最終決定屈服，簽署併購協議。

2. The general ordered his troops to fight to the last man and not capitulate to the enemy. 將軍命令部隊要戰至最後一人，不得向敵人投降。

3. Despite the resistance, the protesters eventually had to capitulate to the government's demands to maintain order. 儘管有抵抗，抗議者最終不得不屈服於政府為了維護秩序的要求。

Capitulate的同義詞及例句應用

1. Surrender（動詞）投降、屈服

The enemy forces had no choice but to surrender to the victorious army. 敵軍別無選擇，只能向勝利的軍隊投降。

2. Yield（動詞）屈服、讓步

Under pressure, the negotiators had to yield on some of their demands to reach a compromise. 在壓力下，談判代表們不得不在某些要求上做出讓步，以達成妥協。

3. Submit（動詞）屈服、提交

He was forced to submit to the authority's demands to avoid legal consequences. 為了避免法律後果，他被迫屈服於當局的要求。

這些詞都表示在壓力或困難面前屈服或投降，放棄原有的立場或堅持。

Succumb和Capitulate

雖然都表達屈服或投降的意思，但在用法和語氣上有一些不同之處。Succumb的意思是在面對壓力、疾病、誘惑等不利情況下失敗或屈服，通常帶有一種較無力或被迫的感覺。它不像Capitulate那樣明確地指涉到政治或戰爭上的投降，而更常用於形容個人或情感的屈服。以下是說明的例句

1. She succumbed to the temptation and ate the entire box of chocolates. 她屈服於誘惑，吃光了整盒巧克力。

2. Despite his best efforts, he succumbed to the illness and had to stay home. 儘管他盡力，他還是屈服於疾病，不得不留在家裡。

3. The company eventually succumbed to financial pressure and

declared bankruptcy. 這家公司最終屈服於財務壓力，宣告破產。

雖然Succumb和Capitulate都有一定的相似性，但它們的使用情境和語氣稍有不同，Succumb更常用於描述個人、情感或不利情況的屈服。

Cash cow｜搖錢樹

「搖錢樹」是一個常用的商業術語，它指的是一個業務或產品，能夠持續地產生高額利潤或現金流。這個詞彙的詞性是名詞，通常用來描述一個企業的核心收入來源，爲公司提供穩定的財務基礎。一個典型的現金奶牛是成熟的產品或服務，市場份額穩固，需求持續存在，並且不需要大量的投資或創新。

A "cash cow" is a commonly used business term that refers to a business or product that consistently generates high profits or cash flow. It is a noun and is typically used to describe a company's core source of income, providing a stable financial foundation for the company. A typical cash cow is a mature product or service with a solid market share, ongoing demand, and does not require significant investments or innovation.

閱讀一篇短文，瞭解Cash cow搖錢樹的使用方法：

Their technology startup, founded just a few years ago, has quickly become a cash cow in the competitive market. Their innovative product not only meets customer demands but also generates substantial profits. The rapid growth in user adoption has turned their initial investment into a lucrative venture. This cash cow enables them to reinvest in research and development, ensuring their continued success in the industry.

他們創立不久的科技新創公司，在競爭激烈的市場中迅速成為了一個搖錢樹。他們的創新產品不僅滿足客戶需求，還帶來可觀的利潤。用戶採用速度的快速增長，將他們最初的投資變成了一個有利可圖的事業。這個搖錢樹使他們能夠重新投資於研發，確保他們在該行業中的持續成功。

Cash cow的例句及應用

1. The smartphone industry's cash cow is often their flagship model, which consistently brings in substantial profits. 智慧手機產業的搖錢樹通常是他們的旗艦機，持續帶來可觀的利潤。

2. For many fast-food chains, their classic burger offerings serve as the cash cow, ensuring a steady income stream. 對許多快餐連鎖店來說，他們的經典漢堡提供穩定的收入，成為搖錢樹。

3. In the entertainment industry, streaming services have become the cash cows, driving revenue growth for major studios. 在娛樂業中，串流媒體服務已成為搖錢樹，推動了主要影視公司的收入成長。

Cash cow近似意涵的同義詞說明及應用

1. Money-spinner金錢創造者，指能夠持續產生大量金錢或利潤的事物。

   The successful book series turned into a money-spinner for the author and the publishing company. 這系列書的成功為作者和出版公司帶來了大量金錢。

2. Cash generator現金製造機，指能夠產生大量現金或收入的事物。

Their real estate investments have become a cash generator, providing a steady income stream. 他們的房地產投資已成為現金製造機，提供穩定的收入流。

3. Profit machine利潤機器，指能夠持續產生高額利潤的事物。

The company's flagship product has turned into a profit machine, driving their financial success. 公司的旗艦產品已變成了一臺利潤機器，促進了財務的成就。

4. Moneymaker賺錢機會，指能夠賺取大量金錢的事物或機會。

Investing in the stock market can be a moneymaker if you make informed decisions. 如果您做出明智的決策，投資股市可以成為一個賺錢的機會。

Circumlocution｜拐彎抹角

Circumlocution [ˌsɜr.kəm.loʊˈkjuː.ʃən] 拐彎抹角、婉轉迂迴的說話方式，故意不說出真心話，是一個多義的英文單字，通常指的是用冗長或迂迴的方式表達一個概念，而非直接明瞭地說出來。這個詞通常被當作修辭手法的一部分，用於創造戲劇性或文學性的效果，但有時也可能是因為不願意或不敢直接表達某事而使用。在書寫、演說、或對話中，Circumlocution 可以使語言更生動有趣，但有時也可能讓溝通變得模糊不清。

Circumlocution is a polysemous English word that typically refers to expressing a concept in a lengthy or indirect manner, rather than stating it directly. This term is often used as part of a rhetorical device to create dramatic or literary effects but can also be employed when one is hesitant or unwilling to express something directly. In writing, speeches, or conversations, Circumlocution can make language more vivid and engaging, but at times, it may also lead to unclear communication.

說明：Polysemous [pəˈlɪs.ɪ.məs] 是一個術語，指的是一個詞語具有多重不同但相關的意義或解釋。這意味著同一個詞語可以在不同的語境中具有不同的含義，而這些含義之間可能有一定的聯繫或相關性。

看看「牡羊座不喜歡拐彎抹角」一文，如何應用
circumlocution到文章之中：

Being forthright and outspoken characterizes the Aries personality.
They are inherently straightforward, conducting conversations
and handling matters in a direct manner. They prefer to express
their thoughts clearly and unequivocally, avoiding any form of
circumlocution or hesitation. Impatience is a trait, as they desire
immediate understanding from others, disliking the idea of
beating around the bush and wasting time

耿直、坦率是牡羊座的個性，他們天生就是直腸子，講話、
辦事直來直往，想說什麼直接說明，不喜歡拐彎抹角，更不
會吞吞吐吐！他們不喜歡等待，恨不得第一時間就讓對方懂
自己的意思，不想要繞很多圈浪費時間！

閱讀一篇有關「說話什麼時候應該婉轉迂迴」的文章，一起
來瞭解Circumlocution 的使用：

Circumlocution, the art of talking in circles, can be both
frustrating and fascinating. It's a skill mastered by some to avoid
direct answers or elongate conversations needlessly. In diplomatic
discourse, circumlocution is often used to navigate sensitive
subjects gracefully. However, in everyday communication, clarity
is key. Embracing simplicity over circumlocution can lead to
more effective and efficient exchanges of ideas.

迂迴曲折，一種以迂迴的言語藝術，有時令人沮喪，有時卻
引人入勝。有些人精通此道，以避免直接回答或不必要地拉
長對話。在外交對話中，婉轉曲折通常用於優雅地處理敏感

話題。然而，在日常溝通中，清晰明瞭至關重要。選擇簡潔而非拐彎抹角，能夠實現更有效率的想法交流。

Circumlocution 的例句應用

1. She was a master of circumlocution, never giving a straight answer to even the simplest questions. 她是迂迴大師，即使對最簡單的問題也不願給出直接答案。

2. The politician used circumlocution to avoid addressing the controversial issue during the press conference. 政治家在記者招待會上迂迴婉轉，避免談論有爭議的問題。

3. Instead of admitting his mistake, he resorted to circumlocution and excuses. 他不承認自己的錯誤，而是選擇了迂迴和找藉口。

Circumlocution的同義詞片語以及相應例句

1. Evasion（名詞）逃避，規避

   He used evasion to avoid answering the question directly. 他用逃避的方式來迴避直接回答問題。

2. Indirectness（名詞）迂迴，不直接

   Her communication style often involves unnecessary indirectness. 她的溝通風格常常涉及不必要的迂迴。

3. Beating around the bush（片語）拐彎抹角，不講重點

   Stop beating around the bush and get to the point. 別再拐彎抹角了，講重點吧。

4. Circumvention [ˌsɜr.kəmˈvɛn.ʃən]（名詞）規避，迴避

   Their circumvention of the rules was not appreciated by the

authorities. 他們對法律的規避行為未受到當權者的欣賞。

5. Verbiage ['vɜr.bi.ɪdʒ]（名詞）冗詞，累贅的言辭

His speech was filled with unnecessary verbiage. 他的演講充斥著不必要的冗詞。

Express in a roundabout way與 Circumlocution

在某種程度上有相似之處，都表示以迂迴或不直接的方式表達觀點。然而，它們的用法略有不同。Circumlocution是一種「語言風格」的描述，而express in a roundabout way則可以用於更廣泛的情境，不僅僅限於語言風格。

Circumlocution強調一種語言或說話的風格，通常指的是「故意」使用冗長或拐彎抹角的方式，以避免直接回答或說明。

Instead of giving a straightforward answer, he resorted to circumlocution, leaving us confused. 他沒有直接回答，而是採用迂迴的方式，讓我們感到困惑。

Express in a roundabout way可以更廣泛地用於描述任何以不直接或迂迴的方式表達觀點，不一定要和語言風格有關。

She expressed her dissatisfaction with the project in a roundabout way, hinting at its flaws without directly criticizing it. 她以迂迴的方式表達對這個專案的不滿，暗示了它的缺陷，而沒有直接批評它。

Clickbait
| 標題黨、釣魚式標題

Clickbait作名詞或動詞，誘餌式標題，又稱釣魚式標題、標題黨，是一個常見的網絡用語，指的是那些用來吸引人點擊的標題、圖片或內容及標題黨的意思。這些內容通常以誇大、誤導或挑逗的方式來引起注意，但實際內容可能不如所言。這種策略常見於社交媒體、新聞網站和影音平臺，目的是增加流量和廣告收入。

"Clickbait" is a common internet term referring to titles, images, or content designed to attract clicks. These materials often use exaggeration, misinformation, or provocative elements to grab attention, but the actual content may not live up to the hype. This strategy is frequently employed on social media, news websites, and video platforms to boost traffic and advertising revenue.

英文例句應用如下

1. The clickbait headline promised an incredible story, but the article was disappointingly dull. 那個釣魚標題許諾一個難以置信的內容，文章卻令人失望乏味。

2. She couldn't resist clicking on the clickbait thumbnail, only to find it was a misleading advertisement. 她無法抵抗點了釣魚式的縮圖，結果發現那只是一個誤導性的廣告。

3. Many news websites rely on clickbait to boost their online readership, often sacrificing quality journalism. 許多新聞網站

以釣魚式點擊來增加線上讀者，往往犧牲了高品質的報導。

4. Clickbait（當動詞時的例句）

指使用釣魚點擊的行為，通常指故意創造引人點擊但內容卻不如預期的情況。

Some websites engage in clickbaiting to boost their traffic, even if it means sacrificing content quality. 有些網站為了增加流量，甚至不惜犧牲內容品質而採用「標題釣魚」的手法。

Clickbait釣魚式在英文文章中如何使用：

"Clickbait" refers to sensational headlines or content designed to attract attention and clicks online. These eye-catching titles often exaggerate or mislead, luring users to click. While they generate traffic, the actual content may disappoint. Clickbait tactics are commonly used on social media, news sites, and video platforms to boost engagement and revenue. In today's digital landscape, distinguishing genuine information from clickbait is essential for informed decision-making and responsible media consumption.

「標題黨」是指那些設計來吸引注意和點擊的轟動性標題或內容。這些引人注目的標題常常誇大或誤導，誘使使用者點擊。雖然它們能夠帶來流量，但實際內容可能令人失望。在社交媒體、新聞網站和影片平臺上，廣泛使用「釣魚式點擊」策略，以提高參與度和收益。在今日的數位世界中，區分真實資訊和「釣魚式點擊」對於明智決策和負責任的媒體消費至關重要。

Clickbait（標題黨）英文同義詞及說明

1. Sensationalism （名詞）聳人聽聞，指以引起極大興趣或刺激感官為目的內容。

   The headline's sensationalism was obvious, designed to grab attention without delivering substantial information. 這個標題的聳人聽聞性質是顯而易見的，旨在吸引注意力，但未提供實質訊息。

2. Hype（名詞）炒作，指通常是誇大的言論或宣傳，旨在激發興趣或期望。

   The hype surrounding the product launch turned out to be mostly empty promises. 圍繞產品發布的炒作大多都是空洞的承諾。

3. Sensationalistic（形容詞）帶有聳人聽聞特性的，指傳媒或內容的強調刺激或戲劇性成分的。

   The sensationalistic news coverage of the event exaggerated the facts and created unnecessary panic. 對事件的聳人聽聞新聞報導誇大了事實，引起了不必要的恐慌。

Clickbait和Buzzword

它們是兩個不同的詞語，有不同的意義和使用情境。分別用於描述不同的概念和情境。

Clickbait（釣魚點擊、標題黨）是指使用具有吸引力但通常是誇大或不誠實的標題或內容，以引誘網絡用戶點擊連結，通常是為了增加流量或廣告收入Clickbait通常出現在網絡文章、社交媒體帖子、新聞標題等地，旨在引起人們的好奇心，但往往不能兌現承諾。

The website's clickbait headline promised shocking revelations, but the actual article was disappointing. 該網站的點擊誘餌標題預示了驚人的承諾，但實際內容令人讓人失望。

Buzzword（熱門詞語）是指在特定時期或領域中變得流行的詞語或短語，通常是由於其廣泛使用或被廣泛討論而變得熱門。Buzzwords通常出現在行業、政治、科技等領域，用來描述特定的概念、趨勢或技術，但有時被過度使用而失去原義。

In the tech industry, "AI" has become a buzzword, with many companies claiming to use artificial intelligence in their products. 在科技行業中，「人工智慧」已成為一個熱門詞語，許多公司聲稱在其產品中使用人工智慧。

The politician's speech was filled with buzzwords like "innovation" and "progress" but lacked concrete policy proposals. 這位政治家的演講充滿了「創新」和「進步」這樣的熱門詞語，但缺乏具體的政策提議。

Copacetic｜令人滿意的

Copacetic [,koʊpə'sɛtɪk]（形容詞）平順、順利、令人滿意的
Copacetic通常用來形容事物處於一種非常良好、令人滿意的
狀態，沒有問題或困難。你可以在輕鬆或幽默的情境下使用
它，前提是對話對象知道你在開玩笑或使用非正式的語言。
像是友人對你說How's your dining today? 你可以這樣說：

1. I'm dining copacetically, thanks! The food is delicious, and the company is great. 我正愉快地用餐，謝謝！食物很美味，而且同伴也很棒。

2. It's copacetic! I've got my favorite meal, and I'm enjoying every bite. 一切都很美好！我正在享受我最喜愛的一餐，每一口都很享受。

3. Our food is absolutely copacetic. The ambiance is romantic, and the food is top-notch. 我們的食物是絕對令人滿意。氛圍很浪漫，食物也是頂級的。

來看一下copacetic在短文中的應用：
Today's birthday party went quite copacetic; all the guests had a great time, and there were no unexpected mishaps. The atmosphere was harmonious, the food delicious, the music captivating – everything was just perfect. The host felt very satisfied because everything went smoothly without a hitch.
今天的生日派對進展得相當令人滿意copacetic，所有來賓都玩得非常開心，沒有任何意外事件。氣氛和諧，食物美味，音樂動聽，一切都是如此完美。主人感到十分滿足，因為一切都順利無阻。

再閱讀一篇「大巨蛋啟用品質讓人大致滿意」一文，學習copacetic在文章中的應用：

The visit of the Yomiuri Giants to Taiwan for exhibition games, attracting over 60,000 fans over the weekend, was generally copacetic, overshadowing minor facility issues like leaks and a stalled escalator. These ①glitches, criticized by city counselors across party lines, prompted apologies from Farglory and a response from Mayor Chiang Wan-an, who pledged a comprehensive review to prevent future occurrences. Despite the ②hiccups, the historic full house on the second day marked a significant achievement, with Farglory attributing the leaks to air conditioning ③strain and promising seat changes and ongoing reviews for affected spectators.

讀賣巨人隊來台舉行展覽賽，週末吸引超過6萬球迷，整體而言相當令人滿意，蓋過了設施小問題如漏水和手扶梯故障等的影響。這些小缺陷遭到跨黨派議員的批評，促使遠雄表達歉意，並得到市長蔣萬安的回應，他承諾將進行全面檢討以防止未來發生類似情況。儘管有小插曲，第二天滿場的歷史性成就標誌著重大成就，遠雄將漏水歸咎於空調負擔並承諾對受影響觀眾進行座位更換和持續檢討。

說明：①glitches名詞，小故障或問題。文中指場館出現的小問題，如漏水和手扶梯停擺等。The new software has a few glitches that need to be fixed. 這個新軟件有一些小故障需要修復。②hiccups名詞。打嗝或小問題或障礙。這邊指的是舉辦展覽賽過程中遇到的小問題或障礙。Despite a few hiccups in the planning phase, the event was a success. 儘管在計劃階段遇到了一些小問題，該活動還是成功了。③strain名詞。壓力、負擔。指的是由於空調負荷過重而導致的壓力或負擔，引起漏水。The constant strain on the bridge eventually led to its collapse. 對橋梁持續的施壓最終導致了它的崩塌。

Copacetic例句的應用

1. The project's progress has been copacetic so far, and we're on track to meet our deadlines. 這個專案的進展目前很順利，我們正在按計劃完成工作。

2. Despite a few minor setbacks, overall, our vacation was copacetic, and we made wonderful memories. 儘管有些小挫折，總的來說，我們的度假是令人滿意的，我們留下了美好的回憶。

3. The negotiation between the two companies went copacetic, resulting in a mutually beneficial partnership. 兩家公司之間的談判進展順利，達成了互惠互利的合作夥伴關係。

Copacetic的同義字、近似字詞片語

1. Satisfactory令人滿意的，形容詞

The results of the project were quite satisfactory. 這個專案的結果相當令人滿意。

2. Smooth sailing一路順風，片語

The journey has been smooth sailing so far. 這段旅程迄今一

路順風。

3. Hunky-dory一切正常，形容詞

Don't worry; everything is hunky-dory now. 別擔心，現在一切都正常。

4. A breeze輕而易舉

Finishing that task was a breeze. 完成那項任務輕而易舉。

5. Picture-perfect如畫般完美，形容詞

Their wedding was picture-perfect, with clear skies and beautiful decorations. 他們的婚禮如畫般完美，天空晴朗，裝飾精美。

6. A walk in the park輕鬆愜意，片語

Completing this assignment was a walk in the park for me. 對我來說，完成這項作業簡直輕鬆愜意。

7. Ticking all the boxes符合所有要求，片語

The new employee is really ticking all the boxes in terms of productivity and teamwork. 這位新員工在生產力和團隊合作方面真的符合所有要求。

8. On cloud nine心情非常愉快，片語

After receiving the promotion, she's been on cloud nine. 獲得晉升後，她一直心情非常愉快。

Corroborate｜證實

Corroborate [kəˈrɒb.ə.reɪt]
（動詞）證實、確認、證明

當我們需要提供證據或證明某事的真實性時，通常會使用 corroborate。表示我們通過提供額外的訊息或證據，來強化或確認某個主張或說法的正確性。

如何在「科學實證研究及驗證」的短文中應用Corroborate：

In the world of science, evidence plays a crucial role. Scientists continually seek to corroborate their hypotheses through rigorous experimentation. This means conducting experiments multiple times to ensure consistency in the results. When different research teams can independently corroborate the same findings, it strengthens the scientific community's confidence in the validity of those discoveries. The process of peer review also helps corroborate the quality and accuracy of research papers before they are published. Overall, the scientific method relies on the ability to corroborate results, leading to advancements in our understanding of the natural world.

在科學界，證據扮演著極為關鍵的角色。科學家不斷通過嚴謹的實驗來證實他們的假設。這意味著多次進行實驗，以確保結果的一致性。當不同的研究團隊可以獨立證實相同的發現時，它增強了科學界對這些發現的有效性的信心。同行評審的過程也有助於<u>證實</u>研究論文的質量和準確性，然後才能發表。總的來說，科學方法依賴於<u>證實</u>結果的能力，從而推動我們對自然界的理解不斷前進。

Corroborate的例句及應用

1. The witness's testimony corroborated the defendant's alibi, proving he was not at the crime scene. 證人的證詞證實了被告的不在犯罪現場，證明了他的不在場證明。

2. Scientific studies are essential to corroborate the effectiveness of a new medicine before it can be approved for public use. 新藥被批准供公眾使用之前，科學研究對於證實其有效性至關重要。

3. The fingerprints found at the crime scene corroborated the suspect's presence and involvement in the burglary. 如在犯罪現場發現的指紋證實了嫌疑犯的存在和參與了竊盜案。

Corroborate的同義詞及例句說明

1. Confirm（動詞）確認：確定某事的正確性或真實性
The DNA test confirmed the suspect's identity. DNA測試確認了嫌疑人的身分。

2. Substantiate（動詞）證實：提供證據或證明某事的真實性
The research findings substantiate the theory proposed by the scientist. 研究結果證實了科學家提出的理論。

3. Validate（動詞）驗證：確定某事的有效性或合法性
The certificate will validate your qualifications for the job. 這張證書將驗證您的資格是否符合這份工作的要求。

4. Authenticate（動詞）鑑定：確認某物的眞實性或眞實來源

The expert was called in to authenticate the ancient artifact.

專家被召來鑑定這個古代文物的眞實性。

Crestfallen ｜ 垂頭喪氣

Crestfallen [ˈkrɛstˌfɔː.lən]（形容詞）垂頭喪氣的

是一個用來形容人感到極度失望、沮喪或灰心喪志的詞語。
當一個人經歷了一次沒有達到期望的事件或受到打擊，他們
可能會感到crestfallen。這個詞通常用於形容個人的情感和表
情，表現出他們的失望和挫折。

Crestfallen (adjective) is a word used to describe a person who
feels extremely disappointed, disheartened, or discouraged.
When someone experiences an event that doesn't meet their
expectations or faces a setback, they may feel crestfallen. This
word is typically used to describe an individual's emotions and
facial expressions, reflecting their disappointment and frustration.

閱讀Crestfallen在一篇短文「運動跳水選手從垂頭喪氣到意
氣風發」的文章：

Four years ago, he was crestfallen after his dismal performance
in the diving event at the Olympics. The disappointment weighed
heavily on his shoulders, and he knew he had let down his
country and himself. However, this year has been a complete
turnaround. He dazzled the world with his exceptional dives,
earning gold and leaving everyone in awe.

四年前，在奧運會的跳水比賽中，他表現不佳，讓他垂頭喪
氣。失望的情緒沉重壓在他心頭，他知道自己辜負了國家和
自己。然而，今年的情況完全不同。他以出色的跳水表現令

全世界爲之驚嘆，贏得了金牌，讓所有人都讚嘆不已。

Crestfallen應用例句

1. She felt crestfallen when she didn't get the job she had interviewed for. 她沒有得到她面試的工作，感到非常失望。

2. After hours of practice, the team was crestfallen to lose the championship game. 經過幾個小時的練習，球隊在錦標賽比賽中輸掉，感到非常灰心。

3. He was crestfallen when his art exhibition received no positive reviews. 當他的藝術展覽沒有得到任何正面評價時，他感到非常沮喪。

Crestfallen的同義字詞和片語

1. Dishearten（動詞）失去信心、沮喪
   She was disheartened by the constant criticism of her work. 她對於工作不斷地受批評感到沮喪。

2. Dejected（形容詞）沮喪、消沉
   After failing the exam, he walked out of the classroom looking dejected. 考試不及格後，他沮喪地走出了教室。

3. Dismayed（動詞）受挫、灰心
   They were dismayed by the sudden cancellation of their vacation plans. 他們因渡假計畫突然取消而感到挫折。

4. Downcast（形容我詞）垂頭喪氣的
   His downcast expression revealed the disappointment he felt. 他垂頭喪氣的表情顯示出他的失望。

5. Broken-hearted（形容詞片語）心碎的、傷心的

She was truly broken-hearted when her beloved pet passed away. 當她心愛的寵物過世時，她真的傷心欲絕。

6. Deflated（動詞）洩氣的、無精打采的

After the team's defeat, their spirits were deflated. 在球隊失利後，他們的士氣像洩了氣一般。

7. Blue（形容詞）情緒低落的、沮喪的

She has been feeling blue ever since her best friend moved away. 自從她最好的朋友搬走後，她一直感到情緒低落。

8. Let down（動詞片語）讓人失望、辜負

The team's poor performance in the final game let down their fans. 球隊在決賽中表現不佳，讓球迷們感到失望。

9. Despondent（形容詞）絕望的、洩氣的

She became despondent when her efforts to find a job proved futile. 當她的尋找工作的努力毫無結果時，她變得絕望。

10. Heartbroken（形容詞片語）心碎的、痛心的

He was heartbroken when he discovered that his childhood home had been destroyed. 當他發現自己的童年家園被摧毀時，他感到心碎。

11. Miserable（形容詞）悲慘的、痛苦的

The rainy weather made her feel miserable throughout the weekend. 謝整個週末下雨的天氣讓她感到非常痛苦。

12. Crushed（動詞）壓垮、使心情沮喪

The news of his best friend's betrayal crushed him emotionally. 得知最好朋友的背叛消息使他感到在情感上壓垮。

13. Frustrated（形容詞）感到挫敗的、失望的

His repeated attempts to fix the broken computer left him frustrated. 他反復嘗試修理壞掉的電腦，最終讓他感到沮喪。

14. Let a person down（片語）讓人失望、辜負

Promising more than you can deliver can often let a person down. 承諾超過自己能夠實現的事情通常會讓人失望。

15. Saddened（動詞）感到悲傷的、使人傷心

The news of the accident saddened everyone in the community. 事故的消息使社區中的每個人都感到悲傷。

Crestfallen和Chapfallen

兩個詞都表達了一種失望或沮喪的情緒，chapfallen則較為少見。

Crestfallen常用來形容因失望、挫敗或不如預期的結果而感到非常沮喪和傷心的狀態。常描述因期望未達成或遭遇不幸而感到的情緒低落。

After hearing the bad news, she was crestfallen and could hardly speak. 聽到那個壞消息後，她感到非常沮喪，幾乎說不出話來。

Chapfallen也表示失望或沮喪，但這個詞在現代英語中的使用比較少見。它更多地與面部表情（尤其是下垂的下唇）相關，從而表達失望或不滿的情緒。

He looked chapfallen when he found out that he hadn't won the prize. 當他得知自己沒有贏得獎品時，他看起來非常失望。

crestfallen（垂頭喪氣的）的反義詞、詞語和片語

1. Triumphant（形容詞）得意洋洋的、充滿勝利感的

   After winning the championship, she felt triumphant and proud. 贏得冠軍後，她感到得意洋洋和自豪。

2. Elated（形容詞）高興的、興高采烈的

   The news of his promotion left him elated and excited. 升職的消息讓他感到高興和興奮。

3. Ecstatic（形容詞）狂喜的、非常高興的

   She was ecstatic when she received the birthday party invitation. 她收到生日派對的邀請時非常高興。

4. Overjoyed（形容詞）非常快樂的、興高采烈的

   They were overjoyed to hear the news of their engagement. 他們聽到訂婚的消息時非常快樂。

5. On cloud nine（片語）非常開心、情緒極好

   After their team's victory, they were on cloud nine for days. 在球隊勝利後，他們高興了好幾天。

6. Upbeat（形容詞）樂觀的、情緒高昂的

   Her upbeat attitude helped motivate the team to achieve their goals. 她樂觀的態度幫助激勵了團隊達成目標。

7. Jubilant（形容詞）歡欣鼓舞的、狂喜的

   The crowd was jubilant as they celebrated their team's championship win. 觀眾在慶祝他們的球隊贏得冠軍時非常歡欣鼓舞。

8. Radiant（形容詞）光彩照人的、煥發的

   She looked radiant on her wedding day, filled with happiness. 她在婚禮當天看起來光彩照人，充滿了幸福。

9. Euphoric（形容詞）非常快樂的、幸福至極的

Winning the lottery left him feeling euphoric for weeks. 中獎使他連續好幾周都感到非常快樂幸福。

10. Over the moon（片語）情緒極好、非常高興

She was over the moon when she received the news of her promotion. 她得知升職消息後情緒極好。

11. Blissful（形容詞）幸福的、快樂的

Their honeymoon in the tropical paradise was a blissful experience. 在熱帶天堂度蜜月是一次極幸福的經歷。

12. Uplifting（形容詞）令人振奮的、提升情緒的

The inspiring speech was truly uplifting for the audience. 那個鼓舞人心的演講對觀眾來說真的很振奮。

13. Exhilarated（形容詞）興高采烈的、精力充沛的

After the successful concert, the band members were exhilarated.成功的音樂會後，樂隊成員精力充沛並且興高采烈。

14. Radiate joy（片語）散發喜悅、流露快樂

She seemed to radiate joy as she celebrated her graduation. 她在慶祝畢業時似乎散發著喜悅。

15. Buoyant（形容詞）情緒輕鬆的、樂觀的

The success of the project left the team feeling buoyant about the future. 計畫的成功使團隊對未來感到樂觀。

16. High-spirited（形容詞）情緒高昂的、精神飽滿的

The children were high-spirited on their way to the amusement park. 孩子們在去遊樂園的路上情緒高昂。

Cut me some slack
放我一馬

Cut me some slack放我一馬

意指請求他人對自己表現出更多的寬容或耐心，不要對自己太嚴格或苛刻。這個表達通常用在個人希望得到別人的理解和寬恕的情境中，特別是當一個人面對壓力、挑戰或犯錯時，希望對方能給予一定的容忍空間，不要立即嚴厲批評或懲罰。

閱讀一篇cut me some slack新聞短文：

On Lunar New Year's Eve, Taipei's Mayor Chiang Wan-an, despite his busy schedule, has no plans for the holiday's second and third days, hoping to dedicate time to his family. He humorously pleads, "Cut me some slack," indicating a desire to avoid his wife's displeasure. Earlier, Chiang expressed his gratitude to the city's police and firefighters for their unwavering dedication during the festivities, ensuring Taipei's safety and security as they uphold peace throughout the holiday season.

在農曆新年除夕，儘管行程繁忙，臺北市長蔣萬安在春節初二及初三並無任何計畫，希望能專心陪伴家人。他幽默地請求：Cut me some slack放我一馬，顯示出他希望避免妻子不悅。此前，蔣萬安向城市的警察和消防員表達了感謝，感謝他們在節日期間不懈的奉獻，確保臺北的安全、保障，維持整個春節假期的平靜。

Cut me some slack的應用例句

1. I know I missed the deadline, but I've been sick all week. Cut me some slack, please. 我知道我錯過了截止日期，但我整個星期都生病了，請放我一馬吧。

2. He's still learning how to do it right, so cut him some slack if he isn't perfect at first. 他還在學習如何正確做這件事，所以如果他一開始不是那麼完美，就對他寬容些。

3. I've been really stressed out with everything going on. Could you cut me some slack on this assignment? 隨著所有事情的發生，我真的備感壓力。你能不能在這項任務上寬容點？

Cut me some slack相似意涵的例句

1. Be lenient with me對我寬容些：當希望別人在評價或對待自己時，能有更多的寬容和理解。

   I'm still learning, so please be lenient with me. 我還在學習階段，所以請對我寬容些。

2. Go easy on me對我手下留情：請求別人在批評或考核時不要太嚴厲。

   I'm new to this, so please go easy on me. 我對這個還不熟悉，所以請手下留情。

3. Give me a break給點喘息的機會：當需要從壓力或負擔下獲得暫時的解脫時。

   I've been working on this project for hours, give me a break. 我已經在這個專案上工作了好幾個小時了，給我點休息的時間吧。

4. Don't be too harsh on me別對我太嚴厲。

I did my best, so don't be too harsh on me. 我已經盡力了，所以別對我太嚴厲。

5. Show some mercy展現一些寬容、慈悲：當希望別人在對待自己的錯誤或失敗時能更加寬容。

I know I made a mistake, but show some mercy, please. 我知道我犯了錯，但請展現一些慈悲。

6. Take it easy on me對我放輕鬆一點：當需要別人在某事上不那麼嚴格或強硬時。

This is my first time performing, so take it easy on me. 這是我第一次表演，所以放輕鬆一點吧。

Cynosure ｜ 眾所矚目的焦點

Cynosure [ˈsaɪnəʃʊr] 中心、矚目的焦點、引人注目的對象，名詞）是指引領注意力的事物，通常因其獨特或吸引人的特點而成為眾人關注的焦點。這個詞彙常用來描述在一個場合、團體或領域中最引人注目的人或物。

Cynosure refers to something that captures attention, often due to its unique or captivating characteristics, becoming the center of attraction for people. This term is commonly used to describe the most prominent person or object in a particular setting, group, or field.

閱讀有關臺北101的介紹，學習Cynosure如何運用在短文中：Taipei 101, with its towering height and iconic design, stands as the cynosure of Taipei's skyline. This remarkable skyscraper, once the world's tallest, draws visitors and admirers from across the globe. Its innovative architecture seamlessly blends traditional and modern elements, making it a true cynosure of architectural brilliance. The breathtaking observatory on the 89th floor offers panoramic views that leave visitors in awe. Moreover, Taipei 101 has become a cynosure for cultural events and celebrations, such as the dazzling New Year's Eve fireworks display. It's a symbol of Taiwan's progress and a true cynosure for anyone exploring the city.

臺北101，以其高聳的高度和標誌性的設計，矗立在臺北天際線上，成爲萬衆矚目的焦點。這座令人驚嘆的摩天大樓曾經是世界上最高的，吸引了來自世界各地的遊客和愛好者。它創新的建築融合了傳統和現代元素，使其成爲建築燦爛的眞正焦點。位於第89層的壯觀觀景臺提供令人驚嘆的全景，讓參觀者讚嘆不已。此外，臺北101已經成爲文化活動和慶祝活動的焦點，如令人眼花繚亂的跨年煙火表演。它是臺灣進步的象徵，對於探索這座城市的任何人來說都是眞正的焦點。

Cynosure的例句及應用

1. The stunning fireworks display on New Year's Eve was the cynosure of the entire city's celebration. 新年前夕壯觀的煙火表演成爲整個城市慶祝活動的焦點。

2. In the world of fashion, the red carpet event is always the cynosure, with everyone eager to see what the celebrities are wearing. 在時尙界，紅地毯活動總是焦點，每個人都迫不及待地想看看名人們穿著什麼。

3. The newly unveiled architectural masterpiece became the cynosure of the architectural community, garnering praise and admiration from experts worldwide. 這座新揭幕的建築傑作成爲建築界的焦點，獲得了來自世界各地專家的讚譽和欽佩。

Cynosure的同義詞及例句

1. Focal Point焦點、中心（名詞）

The Eiffel Tower is the focal point of Paris. 艾菲爾鐵塔是巴黎的焦點。

2. Center of Attention關注的中心、焦點（名詞）

Her stunning performance made her the center of attention at the party. 她令人驚豔的表現使她成為派對的關注中心。

3. Highlight亮點、突出部分（名詞）

The fireworks display was the highlight of the event. 煙火表演是活動的亮點。

4. Showpiece精品、招牌產品（名詞）

The latest smartphone from that company is a real showpiece of technology. 那家公司的最新智慧手機是科技的精品。

5. Centerpiece中心裝飾、主要部分（名詞）

The floral arrangement served as the centerpiece of the dining table. 花卉擺設成為餐桌的中心裝飾。

以上詞彙都可以用來描述吸引人注意力的事物或人，並在不同情境中代表焦點或中心。

Cynosure和Bask in the limelight

雖然都與引人注目或吸引注意力有關，但它們的意思和使用情境略有不同。

Cynosure中心、萬眾矚目的焦點、引人注目的對象（名詞）是用來描述某個特定事物或人吸引大家的注意力，通常因其獨特或引人入勝的特點而成為焦點。它強調了某事物或某人在特定情境中的重要性和吸引力。

The new art exhibit became the cynosure of the art community due to its groundbreaking style and creativity. 這個新的藝術展因其開創性的風格和創意而成為藝術界的焦點。

Bask in the Limelight享受在聚光燈之下（片語）意味著享受被注意和受到讚譽的感覺，通常是因為成功、表現出色或處於公眾關注之中。這個片語強調的是個人或事物在公眾面前的表現和接受程度。

After winning the championship, the athlete basked in the limelight as fans cheered for their victory. 贏得冠軍後，這位運動員沈浸在聚光下，球迷為他的勝利歡呼雀躍。

Cynosure側重於描述事物或人在某一情境中成為焦點，而Bask in the Limelight則指的是享受被大眾眼光和讚譽的感覺，通常與成功或表現出色有關。

Deleterious｜有害的

Deleterious [ˌdelɪ'tɪərɪəs]（形容詞），用來描述對事物或健康有害的性質。常用來指稱那些可能對身體、環境或社會造成負面影響的事物或行為。這種影響可能是潛在的或直接的，總之都是不利的。Deleterious是一個警告性的詞彙，提醒我們要謹慎選擇行為和決策，以免產生有害後果。

"Deleterious" (adjective) is a term used to describe qualities that are harmful to something or someone. This word is often used to refer to things or actions that may have negative impacts on health, the environment, or society. These impacts can be potential or direct, but in any case, they are detrimental. In summary, "Deleterious" is a cautionary word that reminds us to choose our actions and decisions carefully to avoid harmful consequences.

閱讀短文「香菸有害，但你知道香氛也有害嗎？」學習將Deleterious運用到文章之中：

While many are aware of the deleterious effects of smoking on health, it's crucial to recognize that certain scented candles can also contain deleterious ingredients. These seemingly harmless candles often emit chemicals like benzene and toluene, which can be harmful when inhaled over time. Studies have linked long-term exposure to these substances with respiratory issues and even potential carcinogenic effects. Therefore, it's essential to exercise caution when using scented candles and opt for those made from natural, non-toxic materials to avoid unknowingly introducing deleterious elements into your indoor environment.

雖然許多人知道吸菸對健康有害，但關鍵是要認識到某些香氛蠟燭也可能含有有害成分。這些看似無害的蠟燭通常釋放出苯和甲苯等化學物質，長期吸入可能對健康造成危害。研究已經將長期暴露於這些物質與呼吸問題，甚至潛在的致癌效應聯繫起來。因此，在使用香氛蠟燭時要謹慎，最好選擇由天然、無毒材料製成的蠟燭，以避免不知不覺地引入有害元素到室內環境中。

Deleterious例句及應用

1. The deleterious effects of smoking on one's health are well-documented. 吸煙對健康有害的影響有充分的文獻證明。

2. The pollution from the factory had a deleterious impact on the nearby river, killing aquatic life. 工廠排放的污染對附近的河流造成了有害影響，導致水生生物死亡。

3. Excessive use of pesticides in farming can have deleterious consequences for the environment, including soil degradation and water pollution. 農業過度使用農藥可能對環境產生有害後果，包括土壤退化和水質污染。

Deleterious的同義詞及英文說明例句

1. Harmful（形容詞）有害的
Excessive exposure to UV radiation can have harmful effects on the skin. 過度暴露於紫外線輻射對皮膚有害。

2. Adverse（形容詞）不利的

The adverse weather conditions forced the event to be postponed. 不利的天氣條件迫使活動延期。

3. Detrimental [,detrɪ'mentl]（形容詞）有害的

The use of pesticides in farming can be detrimental to the environment. 農業中使用殺蟲劑對環境有害。

4. Damaging（形容詞）有損害的

The storm caused damaging winds and flooding in the area. 風暴在該地區引發了損害性的風勢和洪水。

5. Injurious（形容詞）有傷害的

The injurious effects of smoking on health are well-known. 吸菸對健康的傷害影響是眾所周知的。

6. Destructive（形容詞）破壞性的

The earthquake had a destructive impact on the city, causing widespread damage. 地震對城市造成了破壞性影響，導致廣泛的破壞。

7. Noxious ['nɒkʃəs]（形容詞）有害的

The noxious fumes from the factory posed a serious health risk to the workers. 工廠排放的有害煙霧對工人構成了嚴重的健康風險。

8. Toxic（形容詞）有毒的

he chemical spill resulted in toxic contamination of the river. 化學洩漏導致了河流的有毒污染。

9. Inimical [ɪ'nɪmɪkəl]（形容詞）敵對的

The inimical actions of the two nations led to a state of war. 兩國的敵對行爲導致了戰爭狀態。

10. Unfavorable（形容詞）不利的

The unfavorable conditions made it difficult for the crops to thrive. 不利的條件使作物難以茁壯成長。

Deprecatory
｜譴責／鄙視／輕蔑的

Deprecatory [ˈdeprəkətɔːri] 貶低的、責難的

（形容詞），描述指控、評論或言論中的蔑視或輕視性質。
常常用來表達對某個行為、言論或態度的不滿或譴責，暗示
著不尊重或不認同的情感。它是一種強烈的批評，通常伴隨
著道德或倫理上的指責。意味著對某事的輕視，並帶有蔑視
的態度。

"Deprecatory" is an adjective used to describe a disparaging or
contemptuous quality in accusations, comments, or remarks. This
word is often employed to express disapproval or condemnation
of a particular behavior, statement, or attitude, implying a lack
of respect or agreement. It represents a strong criticism, often
accompanied by moral or ethical censure. When this term is used
in discourse, it typically signifies disdain for something and may
carry a contemptuous attitude.

將Deprecatory運用在以下「美國等國發表聲明譴責中國經濟
威脅」一文，來看如何使用：

International media reports that the United States, Australia,
Canada, Japan, New Zealand, and the United Kingdom have
issued a joint statement condemning economic coercion and
non-market policies in trade and investment. Although China
was not explicitly named, a U.S. Trade Representative （USTR）

official stated prior to the release of the statement that China was the primary offender being <u>deprecatory</u>. He noted that China's decision to sever trade relations with Lithuania after Lithuania allowed the establishment of a Taiwanese representative office in 2021 serves as an example of economic coercion.

綜合國際媒體報導，美國、澳洲、加拿大、日本、紐西蘭和英國發表了一份聯合聲明，譴責貿易和投資中的經濟脅迫和非市場政策。雖然未明確提及中國，但美國貿易代表署（USTR）官員在該聲明發布前表示，中國是<u>被譴責的主要違法者，具有貶低性質</u>。他指出，中國於2021年允許立陶宛設立臺灣代表處後，切斷與立陶宛的貿易關係決定，就是經濟脅迫的一個範例。

Deprecatory的英文造句及應用

1. His deprecatory remarks about her work offended many colleagues. 他對她工作的貶低性評論冒犯了許多同事。

2. The deprecatory tone of the article suggested a lack of understanding of the subject matter. 文章中的貶低語氣暗示了對主題的理解不足。

3. She responded to his deprecatory comments with grace and professionalism. 她以優雅和專業的方式回應了他的輕蔑性的評論。

4. In his deprecatory comments, he belittled the efforts of the research team, which was quite demoralizing. 他在貶低性的評論中責難了研究團隊的努力，這對他們的士氣產生了負面影響。

Deprecatory的同義詞及例句請參考

1. Disparaging [dɪ'spærədʒɪŋ] 輕視的（形容詞）

   Her disparaging remarks about his achievements hurt his feelings. 她對他的成就發表的輕視性評論傷害了他的感情。

2. Contemptuous [kən'tɛmptʃuəs] 蔑視的（形容詞）

   He gave her a contemptuous look after her rude comment. 在她粗魯的評論後，他給了她一個蔑視的眼神。

3. Critical批判的（形容詞）

   The critical review of the book pointed out its flaws. 對這本書評指出了它的缺陷。

4. Derogatory [dɪ'rɒgətɔːri] 貶低的（形容詞）

   His derogatory comments about her appearance were hurtful. 他對她外貌的貶低性評論令人受傷。

5. Demeaning [dɪ'miːnɪŋ] 貶低的（形容詞）

   The demeaning treatment of employees led to low morale in the workplace. 對員工貶抑的對待導致職場上的士氣低落。

超級比一比 | Dilettante vs Layperson

Dilettante [ˌdɪlɪˈtænteɪ] 業餘愛好者

是描述某人對特定領域知識的詞語。Dilettante通常指的是一位對某一領域有著表面性了解或業餘愛好，但不具專業知識的人。

Layperson外行

Layperson則是一個更廣泛的詞，指的是那些在某領域缺乏專業知識的人，通常用於醫學或法律等領域。

Dilettante的應用

1. He dabbled in painting but was merely a dilettante, lacking the deep understanding of art. 他涉獵繪畫，但僅僅是一個業餘愛好者，缺乏對藝術的深刻理解。

2. While he claimed to be a wine expert, his knowledge was that of a dilettante, unable to distinguish between fine vintages. 雖然他自稱是一位葡萄酒專家，但他的知識只是業餘愛好者的水準，無法辨別優質的年分。

3. His friends considered him a dilettante in music because he could play a few simple tunes on the guitar but had no formal training. 他的朋友們認為他在音樂方面是一個業餘愛好者，因為他能彈奏一些簡單的吉他曲目，但並未接受過正規的培訓。

4. Although he dabbled in cooking as a dilettante, he never pursued it seriously as a career. 雖然他曾作爲一名業餘愛好者嘗試過烹飪，但從未認眞地把它當作職業追求。

Layperson的應用

1. The lawyer explained the complex legal terms in a way that even a layperson could understand. 這位律師以一種連外行都能理解的方式解釋了複雜的法律術語。

2. The doctor explained the medical procedure in simple terms so that even a layperson could understand it. 醫生以簡單的術語解釋醫療程序，以便一個外行也能理解。

3. It's important for a lawyer to be able to explain legal concepts to a layperson without using too much legal jargon. 對於律師來說，能夠以不使用過多法律術語的方式向外行解釋法律概念是很重要的。

Dilettante的同義詞

1. Amateur業餘者，指的是一個在特定領域缺乏專業知識或訓練的人，通常是出於興趣或愛好而參與的。
She's an amateur photographer who enjoys taking pictures in her free time. 她是一名業餘攝影師，喜歡在空閒時間拍照。

2. Novice新手，指的是一個在某領域或技能上缺乏經驗的人，通常是一個初學者。
He's a novice in the world of cooking and is still learning the basics. 他在烹飪世界中是一名新手，仍在學習基礎知識。

Layperson的同義詞

1. Non-expert非專家，指在某一特定領域不具專業知識或經驗的人。

   The book is written in a way that even non-experts can understand the complex scientific concepts. 這本書以一種即使非專家也能理解複雜科學概念的方式撰寫。

與知識、技能或經驗的程度有關的單字

1. Neophyte ['niːəfaɪt] 初學者：指剛開始學習或涉足某一領域的，通常對該領域的知識有限。用於描述那些在特定領域或技能上缺乏經驗且處於學習初期的人。

   She's a neophyte in the world of computer programming and is taking her first coding class. 她在電腦程式領域是一個初學者，正在上她的第一門程式課程。

2. Tyro初學者：可能稍微偏向自信，正在努力學習某領域或技能。用於描述那些對某一領域感興趣且正在積極學習的人。

   He's a tyro in the field of photography, but he's already showing a lot of potential. 他在攝影領域是一個初學者，但已經展現出很大的潛力。

3. Apprentice學徒：指正在接受專業指導並參與實際工作以獲得技能和知識的人。通常用於描述那些已經開始在特定行業或專業領域中接受訓練的人。

   He's working as an apprentice electrician to learn the trade from experienced professionals. 他正在擔任電工學徒，從有經驗的專業人士那裡學習這門行業。

4. Abecedarian [ˌæbɪˈsiːdɛəriən] 初學者：指連最基本的事物或知識都還不瞭解的初學者。通常用於形容那些對某一主題或領域的知識完全陌生的人。

As an abecedarian in chemistry, she didn't even know the periodic table's elements. 作為化學方面的初學者，她甚至都不了解周期表上的元素。

5. Inchoate [ɪnˈkəʊeɪt] [ˈɪnkoʊət] 未成熟的：尚未完全發展或成熟的事物或想法。用於描述那些處於初期階段，尚未完全成形或理解的事物或觀念。

His inchoate plan for the project lacked the details needed for execution. 他對於專案的初步計劃缺乏執行所需的細節。

Dissipate｜褪去

Dissipate [ˈdɪsɪpeɪt] 動詞，意指逐漸消散或消失。這個詞通常用來描述一種情感、能量或資源的消逝。當我們感到憤怒或擔憂時，如果我們冷靜下來，這種情感就會逐漸消散。同樣地，一個燃燒的火焰也會隨著時間的推移而逐漸減弱，最終消散於空氣中。

"Dissipate" is a verb that means to gradually disperse or disappear. This word is commonly used to describe the fading away of an emotion, energy, or resource. When we feel anger or worry, if we calm down, that emotion will dissipate over time. Similarly, a burning flame will also gradually weaken and eventually dissipate into the air.

閱讀一篇關於「隨著時間消逝怒氣逐漸消散」的短文，並瞭解一下：

Amidst the heated argument, tension hung heavy in the air. Harsh words were exchanged, and emotions ran high. But as time passed, the anger began to dissipate. Apologies were made, and forgiveness emerged like a calming breeze. It was a powerful reminder that even in the midst of conflict, the storm of emotions can eventually dissipate, making room for reconciliation and understanding.

在激烈的爭吵中，緊張感籠罩在空氣中。尖酸刻薄的言語交鋒，情緒高亢。然而，隨著時間的推移，憤怒逐漸消散。道歉提出了，寬恕如平靜的微風般出現。這是一個有力的提醒，卽使在衝突的間，情緒的風暴最終也會散去，爲和解和理解留下空間。

Dissipate例句應用

1. The tension in the room began to dissipate as people started to talk and share their thoughts. 房間內的緊張氛圍逐漸消散，因爲人們開始交談並分享他們的想法。

2. The heat from the hot coffee started to dissipate as it sat on the table. 熱咖啡的熱度隨著放在桌子上而逐漸消散。

3. After the storm, the dark clouds slowly dissipated, revealing a clear blue sky. 暴風雨過後，黑暗的雲朵逐漸散去，露出晴朗的藍天。

Dissipate的同義詞及例句

1. Disperse散布、分散（動詞）

   The crowd began to disperse after the event ended. 活動結束後，人群開始散去。

2. Scatter散開、分散（動詞）

   He accidentally knocked over the box, causing the contents to scatter all over the floor. 他不小心把盒子弄翻，導致內容物散落在地板上。

3. Evaporate蒸發、消失（動詞）

   The morning dew will evaporate once the sun rises. 早晨的露水會在太陽升起後蒸發掉。

4. Vanish消失、消散（動詞）

The magician made the rabbit vanish into thin air. 魔術師讓兔子在空中消失。

5. Dissolve溶解、解散（動詞）

Stir the sugar in hot water until it completely dissolves. 將糖攪拌在熱水中，直到完全溶解。

6. Fade褪色、變淡（動詞）

The colors of the painting began to fade over time due to exposure to sunlight. 畫作的顏色隨著時間暴露在陽光下而逐漸變淡。

7. Ebb衰退、退潮（動詞）

His enthusiasm for the project began to ebb as challenges arose. 隨著問題的出現，他對這個專案的熱情開始衰退。

8. Scatter分散、散開（動詞）

She used a fan to scatter the smoke away from the kitchen. 她用風扇把廚房裡的煙霧吹散。

9. Melt融化、消失（動詞）

The snow began to melt as the temperature rose above freezing. 隨著溫度升至攝氏零度以上，雪開始融化。

10. Evanesce逐漸消失、消逝（動詞）

His hopes of winning the competition seemed to evanesce as his performance faltered. 隨著他表現不佳，他期待贏得比賽的希望似乎逐漸逝去。

Divest｜撤資

Divest [dɪ'vɛst]（動詞）撤資、出售、轉讓或放棄權益、財產或投資之意。用於商業、金融和社會議題上，表示結束與某項資產或事務的關聯，通常是出於道德、財務或策略性的考慮。

來閱讀一篇關於中國經濟成長放緩及其他不利綜合因素，造成外資及企業紛紛撤資的現象學，一起來學及瞭解Divest在文章中應用的情境：

Concerns over China's economic outlook are driven by a combination of factors. The deceleration of the Chinese economy and unsatisfactory data are primary concerns. Additionally, the instability stemming from legal changes, the depreciation of the Renminbi, and insolvencies in the real estate sector have led to a wave of foreign divestment from Chinese stocks, accelerating capital withdrawals. Small and medium-sized enterprises also plan to divest or relocate investments, further exacerbating the vicious cycle of capital outflows.

對中國經濟前景的擔憂源於多種因素。中國經濟放緩和不滿意的數據是主要擔憂點。此外，法律變動帶來的不穩定性、人民幣貶值以及不動產業的破產，已導致外國加速撤資中國股票。小型和中型企業也計劃撤資或轉移投資，進一步加劇了資金外流的惡性循環。

Divest的應用實例

1. The company decided to divest its underperforming divisions to improve its overall profitability. 該公司決定出售表現不佳的部門，以提高整體獲利能力。

2. Many investors have divested from fossil fuel investments as part of their commitment to combating climate change. 許多投資者已經退出了化石燃料投資，作為他們對抗氣候變化的承諾的一部分。

3. The company decided to divest its overseas assets to focus more on its core business. 公司決定出售其海外資產，以更專注於其核心業務。

Divest的使用情境包括企業策略、環境保護和投資組合管理等領域，它強調了放棄或轉移資產的行動，以達到特定的目標或價值觀。

Divest同義詞及應用例句

1. Disinvest撤資（動詞）

   The company decided to disinvest from its overseas operations due to financial difficulties. 由於財務困難，該公司決定從海外業務中撤資。

2. Sell off賣掉（動詞片語）

   The investor chose to sell off their shares in the struggling tech company. 該投資者選擇賣掉他們在陷入困境的科技公司的股份。

3. Dispose of處置（動詞片語）

The government plans to dispose of its non-essential assets to reduce debt. 政府計劃處置其非必要資產以減少債務。

4. Liquidate清算（動詞）

The bankrupt company had to liquidate its assets to pay off creditors. 這家破產的公司必須清算其資產以償還債權人。

超級比一比 | Engender、 Effectuate、Transpire

Egender [ɪnˈdʒendər]

引發、引起（動詞），通常用來描述一個事物或情況所引起的特定情感或感受。

The tragic news seemed to engender a deep sense of sorrow among the community. 這則悲劇性的消息似乎在社區中「引發」了深刻的感傷。

Effectuate [ɪˈfektʃueɪt]

意指實現或使某事物生效，通常與實際行動和結果有關。

The manager wanted to effectuate changes in the company's policies to improve efficiency. 經理希望「有效實現」公司政策的變革，以提高效率。

Transpire [trænˈspaɪər]

意指「發生」或「逐漸展開」，通常與事件、情況或訊息的揭露有關。這個詞有時也用於指事件或情況逐漸變得清晰或明朗。

It will transpire in the meeting whether the project is approved or not. 在會議中將會揭曉該專案是否獲得批准。

閱讀一篇有關與城市綠化的實踐，讓社區引發生機，產生的共鳴的一篇文章，也來看看這三個字在文章中的運用：

In a bustling city, ambitious plans were set in motion to effectuate a greener future. The announcement of these initiatives quickly transpired across the community, sparking hope and excitement. The proposed changes aimed to engender a sense of environmental responsibility among its residents. As time passed, it became evident that small individual actions could collectively lead to significant progress.

在一個喧囂繁忙的城市中，野心勃勃的計劃已經啟動，以實現更為綠化的未來。這些倡議的宣布很快傳遍了整個社區，激起了希望和興奮。提出改變目的在引起居民對環境責任的意識。隨著時間的推移，人們逐漸意識到，個人的小行動可以共同帶來重大的進展。

Engender的同義詞

Generate、produce、evoke產生、引起的意思（動詞）

1. The surprising news story engendered a lot of discussion among the public. 這則令人驚訝的新聞故事引發了許多的大眾討論。

2. His kindness and generosity engendered a sense of gratitude in everyone he helped. 他的善心和慷慨引發了每個他所幫助的人心中的感激之情。

Transpire的同義詞

Occur、happen、take place發生（動詞）

1. The meeting is scheduled to transpire at 2PM. 會議預定於下

午兩點舉行。

2. It transpired that the missing documents were simply misplaced on the office desk. 眞相逐漸形成，遺失的文件只是被錯誤放置於辦公桌上。

Effectuate的同義詞

Achieve、accomplish、implement實現、完成（動詞）

1. The team worked tirelessly to effectuate the project's goals. 團隊不辭勞苦地努力實現了專案的目標。

2. The new policies were designed to effectuate positive changes in the organization. 這些新政策主要設計來實現機構中的積極變革。

Engross | 引人入勝

Engross（動詞）意指專注、全神貫注或吸引某人的注意力
當你在做某件事情時，如果你全神貫注，你就可以說你正在
「engrossed」。常常用來描述某人在閱讀一本引人入勝的書
籍、觀看一部精彩的電影或者參與一個有趣的活動時的狀
態。

Engrossed in the world of literature, I find solace in the pages of
books. Each word, a doorway to new adventures, engrosses my
mind and transports me to distant realms. It's as if time stands
still when I'm engrossed in a gripping story, and the worries of
the day fade away. Through books, I've learned to appreciate the
beauty of different cultures and eras. Reading is not just a hobby;
it's a passion that engrosses my heart and soul, enriching my life
in countless ways.

沉浸在文學的世界中，我在書中找到慰藉。每個字都是通往
一到新冒險的大門，專注吸引著我的心靈，帶我遨遊遙遠的
領域。當我沉浸在一個引人入勝的故事中時，似乎時間停滯
了，白晝的煩惱消逝無蹤。透過書籍，我學會欣賞不同文化
和時代的美麗。閱讀不僅僅是一個愛好，它是一種充滿激情
的事情，讓我全部的身心投入，豐富了我許多生活的面向。

Engross的例句應用

1. She was so engrossed in her favorite novel that she didn't notice the time passing by. 她對她最喜歡的小說如此全神貫注，她並沒有注意到時間的流逝。

2. During the captivating lecture, the audience was completely engrossed in the speaker's words. 在這場引人入勝的講座中，觀眾完全被演講者的話語所吸引。

3. The intricate details of the painting engrossed the art connoisseur, who couldn't take his eyes off it. 畫作的精細細節讓這位藝術鑑賞家全神貫注，他不禁對著畫作目不轉睛。（註：Connoisseur [ˌkɒnəˈsɜːr] 行家、鑑賞家，通常指的是在某一特定領域有高度專業知識和品味的人，能夠辨別、欣賞並評價該領域的作品或產品。）

Engross的同義詞及實例應用

1. Absorb吸收、全神貫注（動詞）

   The captivating movie absorbed her attention for the entire evening. 這部引人入勝的電影讓她整晚都全神貫注。

2. Immerse沉浸、專注於（動詞）

   She liked to immerse herself in the world of art by visiting museums regularly. 她喜歡定期參觀博物館，讓自己沉浸在藝術的世界中。

3. Engage參與、吸引（動詞）

   The interactive presentation engaged the audience and sparked lively discussions. 互動式的演示吸引了觀眾，引發了熱烈的討論。

4. Enthral迷住、使著迷（動詞）

The mesmerizing music enthralled the crowd, leaving them in awe. 那令人著迷的音樂使人群為之驚歎不已。

5. Captivate迷住、吸引（動詞）

Her storytelling skills never failed to captivate her young audience. 她的說故事技巧總能迷住年輕的聽眾。

Enthrall｜著迷

Enthrall是一個動詞，意指迷住、使著迷、吸引。這個詞常用於描述某物或某人對某事物感到極度吸引和著迷的情境。例如，當一本小說引人入勝，讓讀者完全沉浸其中時，我們可以說那本小說enthralls讀者。

"Enthrall" is a verb that means to captivate, fascinate, or attract. This word is commonly used to describe a situation where something or someone is deeply attracted and fascinated by something else. For example, when a novel is so engaging that it completely absorbs the reader, we can say that the novel "enthralls" the reader.

閱讀一篇有關「科目三」一文，瞭解enthrall的運用：

The dance video of "Subject Three" has gone viral online, enthralling numerous people who eagerly replicate its captivating moves and lively, amusing rhythm. This phenomenon has sparked a wave of events and competitions across various places, likely due to its eye-catching choreography and engaging beat.

「科目三」的舞蹈影片在網上走紅，吸引了許多人，他們急切地複製其迷人的動作和活潑有趣的節奏。這種現象在各個地方引發了一波波的活動和比賽，很可能是因為其引人注目的舞蹈編排和引人入勝的節拍。

說明：1. Go viral [ˈvaɪrəl] 指像病毒般傳染的迅速，在網路上流行或廣爲傳播的意思。The video of the dog playing piano went viral within hours of being posted online. 那隻狗彈鋼琴的影片在網上發布幾小時內就迅速走紅。2. Eye-catching choreography [kɔri'ɑːgrəfi] eye-catching是吸睛的意思，整個句子是指「引人注目的舞蹈編排」。The performance featured eye-catching choreography that captivated the audience. 這場演出有引人注目的舞蹈編排，深深吸引了觀眾。

Enthrall的例句應用

1. The magician's performance was so captivating that it enthralled the entire audience. 魔術師的表演如此迷人，以至於讓整個觀衆爲之著迷。

2. The beauty of the starry night sky never fails to enthrall me. 繁星點點的夜空之美總是能夠讓我深深著迷。

3. The melody of the music enthralls the listeners and takes them on a journey of emotions. 音樂的旋律迷住了聽衆，帶領他們走上情感之旅。

Enthrall的同義詞以及相關例句如下

1. Captivate迷住、著迷（動詞）
   Her performance on stage captivated the audience. 她在舞臺上的表演迷住了觀衆。

2. Fascinate迷住、著迷（動詞）
   The mysterious story fascinated me from beginning to end. 這個神祕的故事從頭到尾都讓我著迷。

3. Enchant使著迷、陶醉（動詞）

The beautiful scenery of the forest enchanted us all. 森林的美麗景色使我們所有人都陶醉了。

4. Mesmerize迷住、催眠（動詞）

The magician's performance mesmerized the entire audience. 魔術師的表演催眠了全部的觀眾。

5. Glamour迷人的魅力（名詞）

The movie star possessed a special glamour that drew people to her. 這位電影明星擁有一種特殊的迷人魅力，吸引了人們的關注。

Epiphany｜頓悟／靈感

Epiphany [ɪˈpɪfəni]（名詞）是一個重要的詞彙，指突然的靈感或領悟，通常伴隨著對某個問題或情況的深刻理解。這種瞬間的領悟能夠改變一個人的觀點，引導他們朝著更好的方向前進。

Epiphany（noun）is an important term referring to a sudden inspiration or realization, often accompanied by a profound understanding of a particular issue or situation. This momentary insight can change a person's perspective and guide them towards a better direction.

閱讀下面的這篇科學報導「有沒有發現洗澡的時候反而更容易有靈感或是頓悟呢？」來看看Epiphany如何應用在文章中：

Many people have similar experiences; they often experience an epiphany while taking a shower. Apart from the sheer pleasure of showering and the release of dopamine in the brain, showering provides an undisturbed environment. Furthermore, our minds automatically enter the "Default Mode Network" (DMN), somewhat akin to a computer's standby mode. Interestingly, the brain is more active in the DMN mode than during focused work, making it more conducive to triggering our epiphanies.

許多人都有類似的經驗，在洗澡時常常會突然領悟到一些事情。除了洗澡本身令人愉悅且有多巴胺釋放之外，洗澡提供了一個無干擾的環境。此外，我們的大腦會自動進入「預設模式網路」（Default Mode Network，DMN），有些類似電腦的待機模式。有趣的是，在DMN模式下，大腦的活躍程度比專注工作時更高，更容易引發我們的頓悟。

Epiphany的英文範例

1. The author had a crucial epiphany while writing the novel, allowing him to unravel the mystery of the story. 那位作家在寫小說時突然有了一個重要的靈感，讓他能夠解開故事的謎團。

2. She had a significant epiphany about her life direction and decided to pursue her dreams. 她在思考時人生方向，時突然有了一個重大的領悟，而決定追求自己的夢想。

3. After years of researching the problem, the scientist finally reached an important epiphany, potentially solving a long-standing puzzle. 在研究問題多年後，科學家終於有了一個重要的靈感，有望解決一個長久存在的難題。

Epiphany同義字詞及實例應用

1. Revelation啟示（名詞）

The discovery of ancient scrolls was a revelation that changed our understanding of history. 古代卷軸的發現是一個改變我們對歷史理解的啟示。

2. Realization認識、領悟（名詞）

Her realization of the importance of time management led to increased productivity. 她對時間管理重要性的認識增加了生產力。

3. Insight洞察力、見識（名詞）

His deep insight into human behavior made him an excellent psychologist. 他對人類行為的深刻洞察力使他成為優秀的心理學家。

4. Enlightenment啟迪、啟發（名詞）

The teachings of the wise guru brought enlightenment to his followers. 智慧大師的教導為他的追隨者帶來了啟發。

這些詞彙都指的是某種突然的理解或領悟，可以改變人對某事的看法或理解。

Intuition 、Afflatus及Epiphany

儘管具有相似的意思，但仍有一些區別。以下是它們的意思、使用情境以及例句。

Intuition直覺

指的是基於直覺或本能而獲得的知識或理解，通常不需要明確的推理或分析。當某人有一種感覺或認知，但無法明確解釋為何有這種感覺時，就可以用直覺來形容。

She had an intuition that something was wrong with the project, even though all the data looked fine. 儘管所有數據看起來都沒問題，但她有一種直覺，認為該專案存在問題。

Afflatus [əˈfleɪtəs] 靈感、靈光乍現

指的是突然而來的靈感或創意的湧現，通常帶有一種神祕的或靈感的特質。這個詞通常用於藝術、文學或創造性領域，以描述突然而來的靈感的瞬間。

The artist felt a sudden afflatus and created a masterpiece in just one night. 藝術家突然感到一股靈光乍現，僅在一個晚上就創作出了一件鉅作。

Epiphany 頓悟，靈光乍現

指突然的洞察、理解或領悟，通常是對複雜問題或情境的深刻認識。可以用於各種情境，通常用於描述在思考或研究中突然達到的明確理解。

After years of research, the scientist had an epiphany that led to a groundbreaking discovery. 經過多年的研究，這位科學家有了一個頓悟，引領他取得了突破性的發現。

Esoteric | 深奧

Esoteric [ˌesəˈterɪk]是一個形容詞，意指深奧或神祕的，通常用來形容那些不容易理解或只有少數人能夠理解的事物。這個詞語源於希臘文的esōterikos，最初是指內部或祕密的知識。在今天的用法中，它可以用來描述一些專業領域的知識、神祕的傳統或祕密的儀式。通常暗示著這些知識或事物只有一小部分人能夠理解或接觸。

"Esoteric" is an adjective that means deep or mysterious, usually used to describe things that are not easily understood or understood only by a few. The word comes from the Greek "esōterikos," originally referring to inner or secret knowledge. In today's usage, it can be used to describe specialized knowledge in certain fields, mysterious traditions, or secret rituals. "Esoteric" often implies that this knowledge or thing is understood or accessed by only a small number of people.

來看看esoteric短文中的應用：

Exploring the world of mathematics can be both exhilarating and daunting. Within this vast landscape lies a multitude of esoteric and abstruse theories and equations. These mathematical concepts may appear intimidating at first, with their complex symbols and intricate relationships. However, as one delves deeper into this realm, a sense of awe and wonder begins to emerge. The beauty of mathematics lies not only in its precision but also in its ability to unveil the hidden patterns of the universe. Embracing the challenge of deciphering these esoteric mathematical truths can lead to profound insights and a deeper appreciation of the world around us.

探索數學的世界既令人振奮又令人望而卻步。在這廣闊的領域中存在著眾多深奧而晦澀的理論和方程式。這些數學概念一開始可能看似嚇人，具有複雜的符號和錯綜複雜的關係。然而，當人深入研究這個領域時，一種敬畏和驚奇開始湧現。數學之美不僅在於其精確性，還在於其能夠揭示宇宙中的隱藏模式。擁抱解讀這些深奧的數學真理的挑戰可以帶來深刻的洞察和對我們對世界的更瞭解與欣賞。

Esoteric例句應用

1. His fascination with esoteric philosophy led him to study ancient texts that few others dared to explore. 他對深奧哲學的著迷使他研究了很少有人敢探索的古代文獻。

2. The ceremony was steeped in esoteric symbolism that only the initiated members of the secret society could decipher. 這個儀式充滿了深奧的象徵，只有這個祕密社團的發起成員才能解讀。（註：initiated member發起成員）

3. Her knowledge of esoteric healing practices made her a sought-after expert in the field of alternative medicine. 她對深奧的療癒治療方法的理解使她成爲了熱門的另類醫學領域的專家。（sought-after [sɔt 'æftər] 搶手的或受追捧的）

Esoteric的一些同義詞及例句

1. Obscure（艱澀的）難以理解的或不容易被發現的

   The obscure symbols in the ancient manuscript puzzled the scholars for years. 古老手稿中的艱澀難懂符號讓學者們困擾了多年。

2. Cryptic（神祕的）含有隱藏或祕密意義的

   His cryptic message left everyone wondering about its true meaning. 他的神祕訊息讓每個人都對其真正的含義感到好奇。

3. Abstruse（深奧的）難以理解或深度的

   The professor's lecture on quantum physics was so abstruse that only a few students could follow it. 教授關於量子物理的講座非常深奧，只有少數學生能夠理解。

4. Enigmatic（謎一般的）含有謎團或難以理解的

   The Mona Lisa's smile has always been enigmatic and intriguing to art enthusiasts. 蒙娜麗莎的微笑一直都是令藝術愛好者感到謎一般且引人入勝。

Encomium | 讚美

Encomium [ɛnˈkoʊmiəm]源自拉丁文,指的是一篇讚美詞或頌詞,用於表達對某人、某事或某物的高度讚譽和讚美。被用來形容精彩的演講、文學作品或者對特定成就的頒獎詞。在詞性上,它是一個名詞,可用於形容一份讚美的文學作品或演說。

"Encomium," derived from the Latin word "Ecomium," refers to a eulogy or panegyric, typically used to express high praise and admiration for someone, something, or an achievement. This term is commonly employed to describe splendid speeches, literary works, or awards given for specific accomplishments. Grammatically, it is a noun used to describe a piece of literary work or a speech that praises extensively.

來看一段在頒獎典禮,演員致詞讚美製作團隊的一篇短文,並瞭解encomium的運用:

The renowned award ceremony concluded with a heartfelt encomium to the production team behind the year's most outstanding film. The encomium, delivered by a distinguished actor, praised their unwavering dedication, artistic prowess, and tireless commitment to storytelling. It celebrated their ability to transcend boundaries and touch the hearts of audiences worldwide. This encomium encapsulated the profound impact of their collective efforts on the world of cinema.

著名的頒獎典禮在結束時以一份由傑出演員發表的深情讚美詞向該年度最傑出電影背後的製作團隊致敬。這份讚美詞稱讚了他們不懈的奉獻精神、藝術才華，以及對說故事孜孜不倦的承諾。它讚美了他們能夠超越界限，觸動全球觀眾的能力。這份讚美詞概括了他們團隊集體努力對電影界的深遠影響。

說明：1. Heartfelt眞心的描述對某人或某事的感情或關心。2. Unwavering（堅定不移的）表示持續堅定和不動搖，不受外界干擾。用來描述信念、承諾或堅持。3. Encapsulate [ɛnˈkæpsjuleɪt]（包含，概括）是一個動詞，表示將某事物或概念包含在內，簡潔地表達或摘要，通常是將大量資訊或想法總括到一種更簡單、易於理解的形式中。

Encomium的英文例句

1. The encomium delivered at the award ceremony for her lifetime achievements moved the audience to tears. 在頒獎典禮上爲她終身成就所作的讚美詞感動了觀眾。

2. The book received widespread acclaim, with critics hailing it as an encomium to the human spirit. 這本書廣受讚譽，評論家稱其爲對人類精神的讚美。

3. The President's encomium for the nation's healthcare workers acknowledged their dedication and sacrifice during the pandemic. 總統對國家醫護人員的讚美讓大人認識到了醫療人員在大流行期間的奉獻和犧牲。

4. Her encomium for his generosity was heartfelt. 她對他的慷慨表示由衷的讚美。

Encomium的同義詞

1. Panegyric [ˌpænəˈdʒɪrɪk] 讚美的（形容詞）

   The panegyric speech praised the achievements of the company. 這篇讚美的演講讚揚了公司的成就。

2. Laudation讚美（名詞）

   The laudation of the artist's work was well-deserved. 對藝術家作品的讚美是實至名歸的。

3. Tribute讚美詞（名詞）

   The tribute to the fallen soldiers was a moving ceremony. 對陣亡士兵的讚美詞是一個感人的儀式。

這些以上的詞彙都是用來表達讚美或贊美的，通常用於描述對某人、某事或某物的高度讚賞和欣賞。

超級比一比 | Fathom vs Unfathom vs Unfathomable

Fathom [ˈfæðəm]

（動詞）用來表示理解、掌握或測量某事物的深度或理解程度。它也可以指測量水深的的意思。

Unfathom [ʌnˈfæðəm]

（動詞）指「探究」難以理解或深不可測的事務的意思。
（形容詞）Unfathomable [ʌnˈfæðəməbl] 深不可測的、難以理解的。當我們面對某些事物或情況，難以理解其深度或範圍時，就可以使用Unfathom。

Unfathomable的應用範例

1. The complexity of the human mind is unfathomable, as it holds emotions and thoughts that are beyond measurement. 人類心靈的複雜性是難以理解的，它包含了無法測量的情感和思想。

2. The vastness of the universe is truly unfathomable; we can only grasp a fraction of its mysteries. 宇宙的廣闊是真正難以測量的；我們只能理解其中一部分的奧祕。

3. The depth of his knowledge on the subject is unfathomable; he seems to know everything about it. 他對這個主題的知識與理解深不可測；他似乎知道一切。

Unfathom的應用範例

1. It can be challenging to unfathom the motives of a person who acts in such mysterious ways. 要探究一個以如此神祕方式行事的人的動機可能會很具挑戰性。

2. He tried to unfathom the reasons behind her sudden departure, but the mystery remained unsolved. 他試圖探究她突然離去的原因，但這個謎團仍然未解。

3. It took years of research to unfathom the true potential of this groundbreaking technology.要探究這項突破性技術的真正潛力需要多年的研究。

4. The detective's goal was to unfathom the motive behind the crime, digging deep into the suspect's background and actions. 這名刑警的目標是探究犯罪背後的動機，深入挖掘嫌疑人的背景和行為。

Fathom的應用範例

1. I can't fathom why he would make such a decision. 我無法理解他為什麼會做出這樣的決定。

2. The diver needed to fathom the depth of the underwater cave. 潛水員需要測量水下洞穴的深度。

3. Her kindness and generosity were so immense that it was difficult to fathom the depth of her compassion. 她的善良和慷慨是如此巨大，以至於難以理解她的同情心有多深。

4. The scientist spent years trying to fathom the mysteries of the universe through research and experimentation. 這位科學家花了多年的時間通過研究和實驗試圖理解宇宙的奧祕。

看看這篇文章如何將Fathom瞭解、Unfathomable深不可測的和Unfathom探究應用在文章裡：

Title: Unfathomable Mysteries: Unraveling the Formation of the Universe and the Secrets of Black Holes

標題：深不可測的奧祕：揭開宇宙的形成以及黑洞的祕密

The cosmos, with its vast expanse of stars, galaxies, and celestial wonders, holds a wealth of knowledge waiting to be uncovered. Scientists and astronomers have long embarked on a quest to fathom the origins of the universe and delve into the unfathomable depths of black holes.

宇宙，以其廣闊的星星、星系和天體奇觀，蘊藏著等待被揭開的知識寶藏。科學家和天文學家長期以來一直在探索宇宙的起源，深入研究黑洞深不可測的奧祕。

The journey to understand the formation of the universe is an intellectual odyssey. It involves peering back in time, unraveling the cosmic microwave background radiation, and theorizing about the primordial conditions that birthed everything we know. The enormity of this task is truly unfathomable, as it challenges the limits of human comprehension.

理解宇宙的形成之旅是一場智慧的冒險。它涉及回望過去，解開宇宙微波背景輻射的謎團，並對形成我們所知的一切的原始條件進行理論化。這一任務的巨大性實在是難以想像，因為它挑戰了人類理解的極限。

說明：1. Odyssey名詞，一場冒險性的旅程或探索，通常伴隨著挑戰和發現；2. Peer Back動詞片語，回顧，追溯到過去意思；3. Primordial形容詞，意指原始的，最早的，存在於宇宙或地球形成初期的。

One of the most enigmatic cosmic phenomena is the black hole, a celestial entity so dense that not even light can escape its gravitational grasp. Unfathomable in its nature, black holes have fascinated scientists for decades. They are cosmic mysteries, and exploring them is akin to unlocking the secrets of the universe itself.

最神祕的宇宙現象之一是黑洞，一個天體實在是太密集，以至於連光都無法逃離其引力。黑洞的本質難以捉摸，數十年來一直吸引著科學家的注意。它們是宇宙的神祕，探索它們就像是解鎖宇宙本身的祕密。

Through advanced technology and mathematical models, scientists have made strides in understanding black holes. Yet, much of their inner workings remain uncharted territory. They continue to fathom the complexities of black holes' event horizons, singularities, and the mind-bending effects of spacetime curvature.

通過先進的技術和數學模型，科學家在理解黑洞方面已經取得了重大進展。然而，它們的內部運作仍然是未知的領域。科學家繼續探究黑洞的事件穹界、奇異點以及時空曲率所產生的令人難以置信的效應。

說明：1. Uncharted Territory未知領域，未經探索的地區或領域。2. Mind-bending令人難以理解的，具有極大挑戰的3. Black Hole's Event Horizon，又稱事件穹界，是一種時空的曲隔界線。是黑洞周圍的區域，其中重力場強到足以阻止光線逃逸的區域。4. Curvature曲率，指的是曲線或表面的彎曲程度。

In conclusion, the quest to unfathom the origins of the universe and the depths of black holes is a journey that challenges the limits of human understanding. These mysteries are truly unfathomable, and as scientists continue to probe these enigmas, they inch closer to unraveling the secrets that have captivated humanity for generations.

總之，探究宇宙的形成和黑洞的深度是一場挑戰人類理解極限的旅程。這些奧祕確實深不可測，而隨著科學家繼續探索這些謎團，他們正逐漸解開吸引人類世代的祕密。

Unfathomable的同義詞及例句

1. Incomprehensible [ˌɪnkɑːmprɪˈhɛnsəbəl] 難以理解或解釋的、無法理解的、深不可測的

   The advanced mathematics textbook was filled with incomprehensible equations. 那本高等數學教材充滿了難以理解的方程式。

   The intricacies of quantum mechanics can be incomprehensible to those without a physics background. 對於沒有物理背景的人來說，量子力學的複雜性可能難以理解。

2. Inscrutable [ɪnˈskruːtəbəl] 難以揣測的、難以捉摸或理解

的、難以預測的

The expression on her face remained inscrutable, giving no hint of her true emotions. 她臉上的表情一直難以揣測，沒有透露她真正的情感。

3. Abstruse [æb'struːs] 深奧的、深度理解的、晦澀難懂的

The professor's lecture on astrophysics was so abstruse that only a few students could follow it. 教授有關天文物理學的講座非常深奧，只有少數學生能夠理解。

4. Enigmatic謎一般的、神祕或令人困惑的、充滿謎團的

The ancient artifact discovered in the tomb was truly enigmatic, leaving archaeologists puzzled. 在墓穴中發現的古代文物確實充滿謎團，讓考古學家感到困惑。

5. Cryptic神祕的、隱晦或神祕的，不容易理解的

The message he left behind was cryptic and required deciphering to understand its meaning. 他留下的訊息很神祕，需要解讀才能理解其意義。

6. Mysterious神祕或難以解釋的，不容易被理解的

The old mansion on the hill had a mysterious aura that attracted the curiosity of the townspeople. 山上的古老大宅散發著神祕的氛圍，吸引了鎮上居民的好奇心。

7. Unknowable無法知曉或理解的，無法預測的

The future is unknowable, and we can only prepare for it to the best of our abilities. 未來是無法知曉的，我們只能盡力為它做好準備。

8. Perplexing [pər'plɛks]令人感到困惑或不知所措的

The sudden disappearance of the aircraft remains a perplexing mystery for investigators. 飛機的突然失蹤對調查人員來說仍然是一個令人困惑的謎團。

Unfathom的同義詞及例句

1. Investigate（動詞）調查、探究

The detective was called in to investigate the mysterious disappearance of the valuable painting. 這位偵探被招喚來調查那幅珍貴畫作的神祕失蹤。

2. Probe（動詞）深入探查

The journalist decided to probe into the politician's financial dealings to uncover any potential corruption. 這位記者決定深入探查政治家的財務交易，揭露任何潛在的貪腐行為。

3. Research（動詞）研究、調查

The team will research the historical documents to learn more about the origins of the ancient civilization. 團隊將研究歷史文件，以了解古代文明的起源。

4. Inspect（動詞）檢查、審查

The building inspector will inspect the construction site to ensure it meets safety regulations. 建築檢查員將檢查施工現場，以確保其符合安全規定。

5. Scrutinize（動詞）仔細檢查、詳細審查

The lawyer will scrutinize the evidence to build a strong case for the defense. 律師將仔細檢查證據，以建立強有力的辯護案件。

6. Explore（動詞）探索、研究

The archaeologists plan to explore the ancient ruins in search of artifacts from the past. 考古學家計劃探索古代遺址，尋找過去的文物。

7. Survey（動詞）調查、勘察

The geologists will survey the landscape to identify potential areas prone to landslides. 地質學家將調查地形，以識別可能易受山崩影響的區域。

8. Delve（動詞）深入探討

The historian will delve into ancient manuscripts to uncover forgotten historical events. 這位歷史學家將深入研究古老的手稿，以揭示被遺忘的歷史事件。

9. Investigate（動詞）調查、研究

The detective is tasked with investigating the series of burglaries in the neighborhood. 這名偵探負責調查社區內一系列的侵入住宅竊盜案。

Fathom的一些同義詞和片語

1. Comprehend（動詞）理解

It took me a while to comprehend the complex instructions. 我花了一段時間才理解這些複雜的指示。

2. Grasp（動詞）把握，理解

It's challenging to grasp the concept of quantum physics without a strong background in science. 如果沒有堅實的科學背景，理解量子物理的概念是有挑戰性的。

3. Understand（動詞）理解

I want to understand your perspective on this matter. 我想理

解你在這個問題上的看法。

4. Wrap One's Mind Around（片語）理解或接受困難的概念

It took me some time to wrap my mind around the idea of time travel. 我花了一些時間才理解時間旅行的概念。

5. Cognize（動詞）認知

He needed time to cognize the implications of the new scientific discovery. 他需要時間來認知這一新科學發現的含義。

6. Apprehend（動詞）理解，領悟

The students quickly apprehended the concept after the teacher's explanation. 在老師的解釋之後，學生們很快理解了這個概念。

7. Get the Hang of（片語）掌握，理解

It may take a while, but you'll eventually get the hang of playing the guitar. 可能需要一些時間，但最終你會掌握彈吉他的技巧。

8. Get a Handle On（片語）掌握，理解

It took some time, but I finally got a handle on the project's requirements. 花了一些時間，但我終於掌握了這個項目的要求。

9. Apperceive（動詞）感知，領會

She had a deep ability to apperceive the subtleties of art that others often missed. 她有深刻的感知能力，常常能領會到其他人經常忽略的藝術細節。

10. Get the Drift（片語）理解大意

Even though I didn't catch every word, I got the drift of their conversation. 雖然我沒聽懂每個字詞，但我理解了他們對話的大意。

這些同義詞和片語提供了不同的方式來表達理解Fathom、探究Unfathom、深不可測的Unfathomable意思，具體選擇取決於你要表達的情境和語境。希望這些字及詞彙能夠有一定的瞭解。

Feign │ 假裝／僞裝

Feign（動詞）是一個有趣的單字，意思是假裝或僞裝。當我們說一個人feigns時，他們正在假裝某種感覺、情感或行爲，通常是出於某種目的，可能是爲了保護自己或避免某種情境。這個詞可以在不同情境下使用，無論是在日常生活中還是在文學作品中。

Feign的例句及應用

1. She feigned surprise when she saw the surprise party, even though she knew about it all along. 她看到驚喜派對時假裝驚訝，儘管她早就知道這件事。

2. The actor had to feign sadness for the role, and he did it so convincingly that it brought tears to the audience's eyes. 這位演員爲了角色必須裝出悲傷，他演得如此逼眞，讓觀衆眼中充滿了淚水。

3. He tried to feign indifference when she mentioned her new job, but deep down, he was genuinely happy for her. 當她提到她的新工作時，他試圖假裝不在乎，但內心深處，他眞的爲她感到高興。

閱讀以下「間諜僞裝情緒」的短文：

In the world of espionage, the ability to feign emotions and intentions is a critical skill. Spies often need to feign surprise, anger, or even affection to deceive their adversaries. It's a high-stakes game of psychological manipulation.

在間諜的世界，偽裝情感和意圖的能力至關重要。間諜經常需要假裝驚訝、憤怒，甚至是情感，以欺騙他們的對手。這是一場高風險的心理操控遊戲。

Feign同義詞及例句

1. Pretend（動詞）假裝

    She liked to pretend that she was a detective solving mysteries.
    她喜歡假裝自己是一名解謎的偵探。

2. Simulate（動詞）模擬

    The flight simulator can simulate various weather conditions.
    飛行模擬器可以模擬各種天氣狀況。

3. Sham（動詞）偽裝

    He shammed illness to avoid going to school. 他假裝生病以避免上學。

4. Counterfeit（動詞）偽造

    They were arrested for counterfeiting money. 他們因偽造貨幣而被逮捕。

5. Fabricate（動詞）捏造

    He tried to fabricate an alibi to escape suspicion. 他試圖捏造不在場證明以躲避懷疑。

這些同義詞都有類似的意思，即假裝或虛偽地表現某種情感或行為。通常取決於上下文和語境。這邊要提出一些單字來比較一下，Malinger裝病、Shirk閃避／卸責、Swing the lead

偷懶裝病、Attitudinize做作，雖然都涉及到一種僞裝或虛僞的行爲，通常是爲了避免責任或引起注意。但在使用情境和細微差異方面略有不同。

其他同義詞解釋和例句

1. Malinger [mə'lɪŋgər]（動詞）裝病或假裝生病，通常是爲了逃避工作、責任或義務。用來描述一個人故意裝病以避免做某事，通常帶有貶義。

   He's been malingering to avoid going to school this week. 他這週一直在裝病，以避免上學。

2. Shirk（動詞）逃避、推卸（責任、工作等）指一個人試圖避免或躲避應該做的事情，也可以用來指責某人不履行其責任。

   She always tries to shirk her responsibilities at home. 她總是試圖逃避在家的責任。

3. Swing the lead（俚語）假裝生病或裝病以逃避工作或責任，類似於malinger。通常在非正式或口語語境中使用，描述某人故意裝病。

   He's been swinging the lead again to get out of doing his chores. 他又在裝病，以躲避做家務。

4. Attitudinize（動詞）做作地擺出姿態或態度，試圖吸引注意或表現自己。用來形容那些刻意表現、做作、裝腔作勢的態度行爲。

   She likes to attitudinize in front of the camera, pretending to be someone she's not. 她喜歡在鏡頭前做作地扭捏作態，假裝成她不是的樣子。

5. Feign（動詞）假裝、僞裝。描述一個人故意假裝某種感覺、情感或行爲，通常是爲了出於某種目的，和其他詞語有相似之處。

She feigned surprise when she saw the surprise party, even though she knew about it all along. 她在看到驚喜派對時假裝驚訝，儘管她早就知道這件事。

Flabbergasted｜目瞪口呆

Flabbergasted ['flæbɚ͵gæstɪd] 目瞪口呆的
（形容詞）意指極度驚訝或震驚到無法言喻的狀態。用來描述當人們遇到感到驚奇、不可思議或無法置信的事情時的情感。

閱讀一篇時事有關老人看到阿拉伯風的比基尼感到「目瞪口呆的」報導，並且了解flabbergasted的運用方式：

In a restaurant, a well-known woman was photographed wearing a complete black bikini, but what truly left everyone flabbergasted was her choice of attire - a loose, sheer Arabian-style pants. Even two elderly ladies in the distance couldn't believe their eyes. The original poster thought it was lingerie, only to discover it was casual wear. This unexpected fashion choice left netizens commenting in amazement, with statements like, "I wouldn't be surprised if people start wearing just pasties when going out," emphasizing the sheer audacity and "Zingy" nature of the situation.

在一家餐廳，一位知名女性被拍攝穿著一套完整的黑色比基尼，但真正讓所有人目瞪口呆的是她的穿著選擇——一條寬鬆、透明的阿拉伯風格長褲。就連遠處的兩位年長婦女也難以置信。原PO以為這是情趣內衣，但才發現這是休閒服。這出奇不意的時尚選擇讓網友驚嘆不已，他們紛紛評論，例如「如果人們外出只貼胸貼，我也不會感到意外」，強調了這種大膽和令人驚豔的「Zingy」情境。

說明：這句話中的Pasties指的是一種小型遮蓋乳頭的胸貼或稱Nipple pasties或Nipple stickers，通常由薄而粘性的材料製成，用於遮蓋乳房的部分。

Flabbergasted例句及應用

1. When she heard that she had won the lottery, she was absolutely flabbergasted. 當她聽到自己中了彩券時，她完全驚呆了。

2. The magician's incredible tricks left the audience flabbergasted. 魔術師令觀眾感到不可思議的表演讓大家感到震驚。

3. I was flabbergasted when I saw the size of the birthday cake; it was enormous! 當我看到生日蛋糕的大小時，我感到非常震驚，它太大了！

Flabbergasted的同義詞及應用例句

1. Astonished（形容詞）驚訝的

   He was astonished to find a hidden treasure in his backyard. 他驚訝地發現了自己後院的一個隱藏寶藏。

2. Amazed（形容詞）驚奇的

   The stunning view from the mountaintop left us all amazed. 山頂上的壯觀景色讓我們都感到驚奇。

3. Stunned（形容詞）目瞪口呆的

   The unexpected news left her completely stunned. 這個意外的消息讓她完全目瞪口呆。

4. Dumbfounded（形容詞）傻住的

His incredible magic trick left the audience dumbfounded. 他不可思議的魔術讓觀眾都傻住了。

5. Gobsmacked形容詞。極度驚訝或震驚。I was absolutely gobsmacked when I heard he had won the lottery.當我聽說他中了彩票，我完全嚇呆了。

6. Horripilation（名詞）毛骨悚然。The eerie music caused horripilation as we walked through the haunted house.當我們走過鬼屋時，那陰森的音樂讓我們感到毛骨悚然。

這些詞都可以用來描述類似的情感，即極度的驚奇、震驚或目瞪口呆，與flabbergasted有相似的詞性和意思。

Flabbergasted和Astounded

在意思上非常相似，都表示極度驚訝、吃驚或震驚的狀態。它們可以互換使用，但有些微細的語義差異。

Flabbergasted較常用於口語，通常帶有一些幽默或輕聳的語法。它強調了某人受到突如其來的驚訝而感到困惑或不知所措。Flabbergasted常翻譯爲「吃驚」或「大吃一驚」。
When I found out I won the lottery, I was absolutely flabbergasted! 當我發現我中了彩券，我眞的是完全吃驚！

Astounded較正式，強調對驚訝之事的嚴肅和驚歎。Astounded翻譯爲「震驚」或「感到驚奇」。
I was astounded by the beauty of the sunset over the ocean. 我對大海上的夕陽美景感到驚奇。

Flummox ｜困惑啊！

Flummox ['flʌməks] 動詞，困惑、迷惑、使混亂。通常在當某人或某事情使人感到困惑、不知所措時使用這個詞。

I walked into the room and was utterly <u>flummoxed</u> by the sight before me. There, inside the fish tank, was a Corgi dog, happily paddling around among the fish. My mind couldn't grasp how this adorable canine had ended up in a watery enclosure meant for fish. The Corgi, unfazed by my bewilderment, continued to wag its tail and playfully chase the fish, creating a scene that left me completely perplexed.

我走進房間，看到眼前的景象讓我感到非常困惑。在魚缸裡，有一隻柯基狗，快樂地在魚兒中游來游去。我的腦海無法理解這隻可愛的狗狗是如何進入這本應該是魚兒的水池的。這隻柯基似乎對我的困惑毫不在意，繼續搖尾巴，愉快地追逐著魚兒，讓我感到完全不知所措。

說明：1. Paddle（動詞）在水中行走或划動，通常用手或腳來划動水面，如游泳或划船。2. Bewilderment（名詞）困惑，指感到迷惑或不知所措的狀態，不明白發生的事情或情況。3. Unfaze（動詞）鎮靜、不受影響，指在面對困難、壓力或挑戰時保持冷靜或不受干擾。4. Perplex（動詞）使困惑，指使人感到困惑或疑惑，難以理解或解釋的情況。

Flummox例句及應用

1. The unexpected twist in the plot completely flummoxed the audience, leaving them in awe. 劇情中出現的意外轉折完全讓觀眾感到困惑，讓他們感到驚嘆。

2. The complex instructions flummoxed the new employees, leaving them unsure of what to do. 複雜的指示使新員工感到困惑，讓他們不確定該做什麼。

3. Her detailed explanation of the scientific theory left me utterly flummoxed; I couldn't grasp a word of it. 她對科學理論的詳細解釋讓我完全感到困惑，我一句話都不懂。

Flummox相似意涵同義詞及相應例句

1. Baffle困惑：To confuse or perplex someone.

   The complicated math problem baffled the students. 這個複雜的數學問題讓學生感到困惑。

2. Bewilder迷惑：To cause someone to become puzzled or confused.

   The sudden change in plans bewildered her. 計畫的突然變化讓她感到迷惑。

3. Confound混淆：To cause surprise or confusion by acting against expectations.

   His ability to speak five languages confounded everyone at the conference. 他能說五種語言讓會議上的每個人都感到困惑。

4. Perplex使困惑：To cause someone to be puzzled or confused.

   The complex instructions perplexed the participants. 複雜的指示使參與者感到困惑。

Foible｜怪癖

Foible ['fɔɪbəl]（缺點或怪癖）是一個有趣且多義的單字。這個詞通常用作名詞，指的是一個人的小缺點或怪癖，這些特點可能使他們與他人不同，但也增添了一些個性。舉例來說，有人可能有一個迷戀收集糖果紙的怪癖，這就是他們的 foible。

"Foible" is an intriguing and versatile word. This term is typically used as a noun, referring to a person's minor flaw or quirk, characteristics that may set them apart from others but also add some personality. For example, someone might have a foible of being obsessed with collecting candy wrappers.

閱讀一篇有關怪癖的英文短文：

Everyone has a <u>foible</u>, a quirky aspect of their personality that makes them unique. It's those <u>foibles</u> that add flavor to our lives and make us interesting. Whether it's a love for collecting vintage postcards or a tendency to hum when deep in thought, these little idiosyncrasies set us apart. Embracing our <u>foibles</u> can lead to self-acceptance and even endear us to others. So, let's celebrate these charming imperfections that make each of us one of a kind.

每個人都有個怪癖，這是他們個性中獨特的一面。正是這些怪癖為我們的生活增添了風味，讓我們變得有趣。無論是熱愛收集復古明信片還是在深思熟慮時嗡嗡作聲，這些小的特點使我們與眾不同。擁抱我們的怪癖可以帶來自我接受，甚至讓我們變得討人喜歡。因此，讓我們慶祝這些迷人的不完美之處，這些使我們每個人獨一無二的特質。

說明：1. Idiosyncrasy [ˌɪdioʊˈsɪŋkrəsi] 特質：指一個人或事物獨特的特點或行為模式，通常是因為他們的性格或背景而產生的。2. Quirk怪癖：指一個人或事物的奇特或不尋常之處。3. Endear to讓人喜愛，意思是使某人對你感到親近、喜愛或產生好感。

Foible的應用例句

1. His foible for always wearing mismatched socks made him stand out in the crowd. 他總是穿不搭配的襪子的怪癖使他在人群中顯眼。

2. Sarah's foible for rearranging furniture in her house every week was well-known among her friends. 莎拉每週都要重新布置家中家具的怪癖在朋友間非常有名。

3. Despite his foible of constantly losing his keys, he was a brilliant scientist renowned for his discoveries. 儘管他有常弄丟鑰匙的怪癖，但他是一位以發現聞名的傑出科學家。

Foible的同義字詞及例句

1. Eccentricity [ɛkˈsɛntrɪk] 古怪（名詞）
   Her eccentricity shines through in her choice of clothing. 她在服裝的選擇中表現出古怪之處。

2. Quirk怪癖（名詞）
   One of his quirks is always wearing mismatched socks. 他的

一個怪癖是總是穿不搭配的襪子。

3. Peculiarity奇特之處（名詞）

The peculiarity of that town is its unusual architecture. 那個城鎮的奇特之處在於它不尋常的建築。

4. Oddity奇特（名詞）

The oddity of his behavior often puzzled people. 他行為的奇特經常讓人感到困惑。

5. Idiosyncrasy特質或個人特徵，指某人特有的行為方式或思想。（名詞）

His taste for bizarre clothing is just an idiosyncrasy. 他對奇異服裝的喜好只是一種個人特質。

超級比一比 | Fortitudinous vs hellbent

Fortitude（名詞）

Fortitudinous [fɔːrˈtɪtjʊdɪnəs] 堅韌不拔的。用於形容人的堅強或不屈不撓的特性。指的是在面對困難、危險或逆境時所展現的堅韌和勇氣。這個詞彙強調一個人在面對逆境時的毅力和堅持不懈的態度。在生活中，我們常常需要展現出 Fortitude，以克服生活中的種種挑戰，並堅持追求自己的目標。

Fortitude的應用例句

1. She showed great fortitude in battling a serious illness and never gave up hope. 她在對抗嚴重疾病時表現出巨大的堅韌，從未放棄希望。

2. The soldiers' fortitude in the face of enemy fire was truly remarkable. 士兵們在敵火面前的堅毅表現令人印象深刻。

3. Facing financial difficulties, they demonstrated incredible fortitude by working tirelessly to support their family. 面對財務困難，他們通過不懈的努力工作，支撐家庭，展現了不可思議的堅韌。

Fortitude的同義詞

1. Courage勇氣（名詞）

Her courage in the face of danger inspired everyone around her. 她面對危險的勇氣激勵了身邊的每個人。

2. Resilience韌性（名詞）

The resilience of the community after the natural disaster was truly remarkable. 自然災害後社區的韌性令人印象深刻。

3. Bravery勇敢（名詞）

His bravery in the face of adversity earned him a medal of honor. 他在逆境中的勇敢獲得了榮譽勳章。

4. Grit毅力（名詞）

She showed incredible grit in pursuing her dreams despite many setbacks. 儘管多次挫折，她在追求夢想時展現了不可思議的毅力。

5. Steadfastness堅定（名詞）

His steadfastness in his beliefs made him a respected leader. 他對信仰的堅定使他成為一位受人尊敬的領袖。

Fortitudinous和Hellbent

Fortitudinous同義字詞為steadfast、Resolute，強調形容人的堅強或不屈不撓的特性。例Her fortitudinous approach to life's challenges was truly inspiring. 她面對生活挑戰時的堅韌態度真的很鼓舞人心。

Hellbent執著的、堅決要做某事，不顧一切後果的決心。同義字詞有persistent、tenacious。He was hellbent on winning the race, regardless of the risks. 他不顧一切風險，決心要贏得比賽。使用時應注意文章內容，選擇情境上合適的文意表達。

Frenemy｜亦敵亦友

Frenemy是一個結合了朋友和敵人的詞彙，用來形容那些表面上看似朋友，但實際上可能對你不利或有競爭關係的人，亦敵亦友的意思。

Frenemy is a term that combines (friend) and (enemy). It is typically used to describe people who appear to be friends on the surface but may actually work against your interests or have a competitive relationship with you. The word's part of speech is a noun.

一起閱讀以下「亦敵亦友究竟怎麼辦？」短文，來看看這個字彙的應用：

A "frenemy" is like a puzzle with missing pieces. On the surface, they seem like friends, sharing smiles and secrets. Yet beneath the facade lurks a sense of rivalry, like two chess players locked in a silent battle. They may applaud your successes but secretly harbor envy. This intricate relationship often leaves you questioning motives and loyalties. It's a delicate dance of camaraderie and competition, where trust is as fragile as glass. Navigating the world of frenemies requires astute perception and a heart guarded against unexpected betrayals.

Frenemy就像一個缺少拼圖的謎題。表面上，他們似乎是朋友，分享微笑和祕密。然而，在這外表之下潛藏著一種競爭感，就像兩位國際象棋選手在一場無聲的較量中。他們可能會對你的成功鼓掌，但暗地裡懷有嫉妒之心。這種錯綜複雜的關係常常讓你質疑別人的動機和誠信。一種充滿友情和競爭的微妙交織，信任如同玻璃一樣脆弱。在處理亦敵亦友的世界中，需要敏銳的洞察力和一顆警惕受到背叛的心。

Frenemy的應用例句

1. She's my frenemy at work – always acting friendly, but secretly trying to outdo me. 她是我工作中的亦敵亦友－總是表現得友好，但祕密嘗試超越我。）

2. It's hard to trust someone who constantly behaves like a frenemy. 很難相信那些行為不斷在表現上亦敵亦友的人。

3. Our frenemy relationship has caused more stress than support. 我們亦敵亦友朋友關係帶來的壓力比支持還多。

其他朋友相關的字彙

1. Antagonist敵對者：指在故事、競賽、或衝突中的對立角色。通常用於文學、戲劇或競賽中，描述主要角色的敵對反派。

   In the novel, the antagonist plotted to overthrow the hero and seize power. 在小說中，反派角色密謀推翻英雄並奪取權力。

2. Comrade同志、同伴：強調共同目標、價值觀或身分的人。通常用於政治、軍事或團體背景中，表示彼此之間的互相扶持和共同努力。

   We fought alongside our comrades in the battle for freedom.

我們和同志們一起在爭取自由的戰鬥中奮鬥。

3. Frenemy亦敵亦友：指的是複雜的人際關係，其中友情和
   敵意交織在一起。

I thought we were friends, but she turned out to be a frenemy, always trying to one-up me. 我以為我們是朋友，但她原來是個假朋友（敵人），總是試圖超越我。（註：One-up作為動詞使用時，是試圖超越或勝過他人。它可以用在形容詞或動詞，指在某個特定的情況或領域裡，一個人嘗試比另一個人做得更好，以此獲得優勢或認可。He tries to one-up me. 他總是試圖做得比我更好。）

Frivolous｜輕浮

Frivolous [ˈfrɪvələs]（形容詞）輕浮的、不嚴肅的、草率的。
通常用來形容行為或言談缺乏認真或重要性的情境。

閱讀一篇有關「禮儀師言詞輕浮造成的後過」短文，來看
frivolous在文章中應用：

In an episode of "Trembling Words," an etiquette expert recounted a chilling tale of a colleague who, while preparing a body for a funeral, made frivolous comments to the deceased. Mockingly instructing the corpse to "keep your hands to yourself," his light-heartedness was met with astonishment by his peers. Despite the funeral proceeding smoothly, he found himself mysteriously paralyzed the following day, unable to even leave his bed, an ailment that confounded doctors for a month. Etiquette expert emphasized the importance of respecting the deceased, warning against the consequences of treating such matters with levity.

在《震震有詞》節目中，一位禮儀專家回憶了一位同事在為葬禮準備遺體時，對亡者發表輕率的評論的驚悚故事。他嘲諷地指示遺體「保持你的手在自己身上」，他的輕鬆態度讓同事們感到驚訝。儘管葬禮順利進行，他卻在第二天神祕地癱瘓，連床都離不開，這是一種讓醫生們困惑了一個月的病症。禮儀專家強調尊重亡者的重要性，警告對待此類事務應避免輕率。

說明：1. etiquette expert禮儀專家。2. recounted [rɪˈkaʊntɪd] 回憶、敘述（動詞）。3. levity [ˈlɛvɪti] 輕率、輕浮（名詞）。His levity in such a serious meeting was deemed inappropriate by many. 他在如此嚴肅的會議中的輕浮被許多人認為是不恰當的。

Frivolous例句應用

1. He was criticized for his frivolous attitude during the important business meeting. 他在重要的商務會議上因其輕浮的態度而受到批評。
2. Her frivolous spending habits left her in financial trouble. 她不謹慎的花費習慣讓她陷入了財務困境。
3. Making jokes about such a serious topic is quite frivolous. 對於這般嚴肅的話題開玩笑是相當不合適的。

Frivolous表示某人或某事缺乏適當的認真態度或重要性，常常用來批評不負責任、不認真的行為或言談。

四個詞語分析

Flippant輕率的、Giddy昏頭的、Frolicsome嬉鬧的及Frivolous輕浮（率）的，都具有某種形式的輕率或不認真意味，但它們在使用情境和語氣上有些差異。

Frolicsome [ˈfrɑːlɪksəm]（形容詞）表示某人或某物活潑、快樂、喜歡嬉戲的性格。用來描述playful或joyous的情境。
The children were in a frolicsome mood as they played in the

park. 孩子們在公園裡嬉戲，情緒高昂。

Flippant（形容詞）表示某人輕率、不認真，通常涉及對重要或嚴肅事物的不適當對待。
His flippant comments during the meeting offended some of the participants. 他在會議中的輕率評論冒犯了一些參與者。

Giddy（形容詞）表示某人感到頭昏眼花、充滿興奮或混亂，通常涉及情感或生理狀態。
She felt giddy with excitement when she won the competition. 當她贏得比賽時，她感到興奮得頭昏眼花。

Frivolous（形容詞）與前三者有些相似，表示不認真、輕浮，但通常更強調缺乏重要性或價值。
Making jokes about the tragedy was seen as a frivolous response. 對於這個悲劇開玩笑被視為一種不重視的反應。

上述這些詞語都有一種輕率的意思，但使用情境和語境可以區分。Frolicsome通常描述開心、愉快，而Flippant不當態度地對待重要事物，Giddy則強調情感或生理狀態上的快速變化，frivolous則是輕浮的意思。

Gasconade｜自吹自擂

Gasconade [ˌɡæskəˈneɪd] 誇耀（動詞／名詞）：指誇大、吹噓自己的成就或能力，通常帶有自負和自吹自擂的含義。這個詞語源於法語，最早在19世紀出現在英語中。有時，人們會過分誇大自己的才華或成就，以吸引注意或贏得贊譽，但這種行爲常常被視爲虛僞或不眞誠。

Gasconade (verb/noun) refers to the act of exaggerating or boasting about one's achievements or abilities, often with a sense of self-importance and self-promotion. This word originated from French and first appeared in English in the 19th century. Sometimes, people may excessively inflate their talents or accomplishments to garner attention or praise, but such behavior is often seen as insincere or disingenuous.

閱讀一篇「自誇自擂」的短文，一起來瞭解Gasconade的意義及應用方式：

Gasconade, often driven by a need for validation, can be detrimental to genuine connections. People who constantly gasconade about their achievements risk alienating others. Authentic relationships thrive on humility and shared experiences rather than empty boasts. It's important to recognize that actions speak louder than words. Instead of gasconading, one should focus on demonstrating their abilities and virtues through their deeds. True admiration comes from those who witness sincerity and competence in action, not from those who merely self-promote. So, let actions be the testament of one's worth, for they speak far more eloquently than gasconade ever could.

自吹自擂，通常出於對肯定的需求，可能對眞誠的連結造成損害。不斷吹噓自己的成就的人可能會疏遠他人。眞誠的關係需要建立在謙遜和共同經歷之上，而不是空洞的自誇。重要的是要認識到，行動勝過言辭。與其自吹自擂，不如專注於通過行動展示自己的能力和美德。眞正的敬佩是來自那些行爲見證到眞誠和能力的人，而不是那些僅僅自我推銷的人。因此，讓行動成爲一個人價值的證明，因爲它們遠比自吹自擂更能明顯的表達。

Gasconade的應用及例句

1. He couldn't stop gasconading about his supposed wealth, but no one believed his extravagant claims. 他無法停止吹噓他所謂的財富，但沒有人相信他誇張的陳述。

2. Jane's constant gasconade about her intelligence and achievements annoyed her coworkers. 珍對她的智慧和成就不斷自吹自擂，讓她的同事感到惱怒。

3. Instead of gasconading, he preferred to let his actions speak for themselves and earn respect genuinely. 他不喜歡吹噓，寧願讓行動說話，眞誠地贏得尊重。

Gasconade的同義詞字詞及英文示例

1. Boast（動詞）吹噓自己的成就或能力

FancyEnglish 精湛英文II

She loved to boast about her expensive car. 她喜歡吹噓她昂貴的汽車。

2. Brag（動詞）自誇或誇大地談論自己的成就

He would often brag about his golfing skills. 他經常會自誇自己的高爾夫技巧。

3. Swagger ['swæɡər]（動詞）趾高氣揚，自信地行動或說話，以顯示自己的優越感

He swaggers around the office as if he's the boss. 他在辦公室裡趾高氣揚，彷彿他是老闆一樣。

4. Vaunt（動詞）盛讚或自吹自擂自己的品質、成就或財富

She would vaunt her designer wardrobe at every opportunity. 她會在每個機會都吹噓她的設計師衣櫃。

5. Exaggerate（動詞）過分誇大或描述，通常是爲了使故事更有趣或引人注目

He tends to exaggerate the difficulty of his job to impress others. 他傾向於誇大他的工作困難度，以給人留下深刻印象。

6. Show off（動詞）炫耀，爲了吸引注意而展示自己的東西或技能

She always shows off her latest gadgets to her friends. 她總是向朋友炫耀她的最新小玩意。

7. Oversell（動詞）過度誇大或吹噓，通常是爲了銷售產品或吸引關注

The salesperson tends to oversell the benefits of the product. 這名銷售員傾向於過分吹噓產品的優勢。

8. Cock-a-hoop（形容詞）形容某人因自己的成就或情況而

洋洋得意或自鳴得意

He's been cock-a-hoop ever since he got that promotion. 自從他獲得晉升以來，他一直洋洋得意。

上述詞語都具有類似的含義，都指涉及吹噓、自誇或誇大事實的行為，可以用來描述類似的行為，即過分強調、誇大或自誇。

Gaslight & PUA
英文是什麼意思

Gaslight動詞，給他人洗腦、情勒。是心理虐待的一種形式，指的是故意操縱、洗腦他人，使其懷疑自己的判斷力或感知。Gaslight這個詞來自1944年的一部同名電影，講述了一名丈夫試圖讓他的妻子相信她瘋了的故事。

"Gaslight" is a verb that means to manipulate or brainwash others, often used in the context of psychological abuse. It refers to the deliberate manipulation and brainwashing of someone to make them doubt their judgment or perception. The term "Gaslight" originates from a 1944 film of the same name, depicting a husband's attempts to convince his wife that she is going insane.

而PUA（Pick Up Artist），或稱「搭訕藝術家」，源自美國，起初是一種搭訕技巧的指南。然而這術語現今已轉變成一種危險趨勢，透過心理學的手段，包括心理洗腦、情感操控和威脅等，來迫使對方順從。這種行為和Gaslighting連結，意即精心策劃的心理操控，目的是扭曲對方的現實感知，使其感到困惑和不安。這種手法不僅具有潛在的危險性，遊走法律邊緣，也與倫理道德相衝突，應該受到嚴格檢視與譴責。

On the other hand, PUA（Pick Up Artist）, also known as "搭訕藝術家" in Chinese, originated in the United States as a guide to flirting techniques. However, this term has evolved into a dangerous trend where psychological tactics, including gaslighting, emotional manipulation, and threats, are used to coerce compliance from others. This behavior is linked to gaslighting, which involves calculated psychological manipulation aimed at distorting the target's perception of reality, leading to confusion and distress. These methods are not only potentially harmful and legally questionable but also ethically conflicting and should be closely examined and condemned.

Gaslighting的影響可能非常嚴重，受害者可能會失去自我認同，甚至患上精神疾病。如果您認為自己或您認識的人可能正在遭受 Gaslighting，請尋求專業幫助。

The impact of gaslighting can be severe, as victims may lose their sense of self-identity and even develop mental health issues. If you suspect that you or someone you know may be experiencing gaslighting, seeking professional help is strongly recommended.

來看看一篇Gaslight的應用文章：

In a series of thousand-word essays, the singer's wife touches upon marital issues that serve as poignant reminders for women to reflect upon and hold close to their hearts. When she exposes her celebrity husband's propensity for "emotional blackmail" (also known as gaslighting), it becomes a powerful catalyst for individuals to contemplate whether they've ever unknowingly fallen into a cycle of control or manipulation within their own marriages and intimate relationships.

歌手的妻子在一系列千字長文中觸及了婚姻議題，這些言辭深刻提醒著女性反思並牢記在心。當她揭露她的名人丈夫傾向於「情緒勒索」（也被稱為煤氣燈效應）時，這成為一個強大的催化劑，讓人們思考是否曾在自己的婚姻和親密關係中不自覺地陷入了控制或操控的循環中。」

Gaslight的英文例句

1. She tried to gaslight her coworker by insisting that she had already completed the project, even though she hadn't started it. 她試圖讓同事自我催眠，堅稱她已經完成了該計畫，即使她尚未開始。

2. The manipulative boss used gaslighting tactics to make his employees question their own abilities, making them more dependent on him. 那位有操控欲的老闆以使員工自我懷疑手法，讓他的員工懷疑自己的能力，達到他們更依賴他的目的。

3. Sarah's partner attempted to gaslight her by insisting that she had agreed to something she clearly hadn't, causing a rift in their relationship. 莎拉的伴侶試圖情勒她，堅稱她已經同意了明顯她沒有同意的事情，造成了他們關係的裂痕。

4. Jane realized that her ex-boyfriend was trying to gaslight her into believing that she had been the one at fault in their failed relationship. 珍意識到她的前男友試圖讓她自我懷疑，將他們之間失敗關係的責任歸咎於她的目的。

Gaslight & PUA英文是什麼意思　　187

Gaslight同義詞和片語及相應的例句

1. Brainwash（動詞）洗腦

   The cult leader attempted to brainwash his followers with his ideology. 那個教派領袖試圖用他的意識形態來洗腦他的追隨者。

2. Emotional Manipulation（片語）情感操控

   She was a victim of emotional manipulation in her toxic relationship. 她在惡性關係中成為了情感操控的受害者。

3. Psychological Abuse（片語）心理虐待

   The therapist recognized signs of psychological abuse in the client's history. 心理治療師在客戶的病史中辨識出了他心理受虐待的跡象。

4. Mind Games（片語）心理戰

   He played mind games with his opponents to gain a strategic advantage. 他和對手玩心理戰，以獲得戰略優勢。

5. Emotional Exploitation（片語）情感剝削

   He was accused of emotional exploitation by taking advantage of her vulnerability. 他被指控因利用她的脆弱性而進行情感剝削。

6. Mental Abuse（片語）心理虐待

   Mental abuse can leave long-lasting scars on a person's psyche. 心理虐待可以在一個人的心靈上留下持久的傷痕。

7. Control Tactics（片語）控制手法

   She recognized his control tactics and decided to break free from the relationship. 她識破了他的控制手法，決定從關係中解脫出來。

這些詞彙和片語都可以用來描述一個人企圖在關係中操控、剝削或虐待他人的心理或情感，試圖操控、欺騙或控制他人的行為，類似於Gaslight的意涵。

Grandiloquent & Pompous
| 誇誇其談

今天來介紹兩個意思接近的單字，有相似的意思，但不完全一樣。

Grandiloquent [ˈɡrændɪˌloʊkwənt]

指的是言辭華麗、誇張、浮誇而大言不慚的，通常是為了讓自己聽起來更重要或更有權威，但有時可能顯得虛偽或過分。這個詞強調言詞的浮誇和華麗性質。

1. The politician's grandiloquent speech was filled with elaborate metaphors and lofty language but lacked substance. 這位政治家華麗的演講充滿了精心編排的比喻和高調的言辭，但缺乏實質內容。

2. Her grandiloquent descriptions of her achievements left everyone in the room rolling their eyes. 她對自己成就的浮誇描述讓房間裡的每個人都翻白眼。

3. His grandiloquent speech at the conference was filled with complex vocabulary and lofty expressions, but it lacked substance. 他在會議上的華麗演講充滿了複雜的詞彙和浮誇的表達，但缺乏實質內容。

4. Sarah's grandiloquent claims about her accomplishments were met with skepticism by her colleagues, who preferred modesty over arrogance. 莎拉對自己成就所做的誇大宣稱引起了同事們質疑，他們寧願選擇謙遜而非傲慢。

Pompous ['pɑːmpəs]

形容一種自以為是、自大、愛炫耀及自命不凡的自己的態度或言行。這個詞強調個人的自負和愛顯示自己的特徵,通常以一種令人討厭或不悅的方式表現出來。

1. The pompous professor constantly boasted about his academic achievements, making it hard for his students to connect with him. 這位自負的教授經常吹噓他的學術成就,使得他的學生難以與他建立聯繫。

2. His pompous demeanor made it difficult for anyone to approach him without feeling intimidated. 他自大的態度讓任何人都難以接近他而不感到受到威脅。

3. The manager's pompous insistence on his own ideas led to a lack of collaboration within the team. 經理對自己想法的自以為是的堅持導致團隊缺乏合作。

4. She couldn't stand his pompous boasting about his possessions and accomplishments. 她無法忍受他對於自己財產和成就的自吹自擂。

Grandiloquent的同義詞及應用例句

1. Grandiose ['græn,dʒoʊs](形容詞)誇大的、宏偉的
   His grandiose plans for the project exceeded the budget. 對於這項專案,他宏大計畫已超出了預算。

2. Bombastic [bɑːmˈbæstɪk](形容詞)浮誇的
   His speech was filled with bombastic words that lacked substance. 他的演講充滿了華而不實的言辭。

3. Pretentious [prɪˈtɛnʃəs](形容詞)矯揉造作的

Her pretentious use of complex language made the article difficult to understand. 她刻意使用複雜的語言，使文章難以理解。

4. Ornate [ɔːr'neɪt]（形容詞）華麗的

The novel was written in an ornate style that was characteristic of the 19th century. 這部小說以19世紀特有的華麗風格寫成。

5. Florid ['flɔːrɪd]（形容詞）過分修飾的

His florid prose was admired for its poetic beauty but criticized for its lack of clarity. 他那過分修飾的散文因其詩意之美而受到讚賞，但也因缺乏清晰度而遭到批評。

6. Rhetorical [rɪ'tɔːrɪkəl]（形容詞）修辭的

The politician's rhetorical skills were evident in his persuasive speeches. 這位政治家的修辭技巧在他的說服性演講中顯而易見。

7. Overblown [ˌəʊvə'bləʊn]（形容詞）誇張的

The overblown language in the article made it seem more dramatic than it really was. 文章中誇張的語言讓它看起來比實際情況更戲劇化。

8. Highfalutin [ˌhaɪfə'luːtɪn]（形容詞）高調的、做作的

He always speaks in such highfalutin terms that it's hard to understand his real point. 他總是用高調的語彙說話，很難理解他的真正觀點。

9. Magniloquent [mæg'nɪləkwənt]（形容詞）說大話的、誇大的

His magniloquent speech was full of grand promises with little substance. 他那說大話的演講充滿了華而不實的承諾。

10. Turgid ['tɜːrdʒɪd]（形容詞）膨脹的、冗長僵化的、困難複雜的、不流暢的

The turgid style of the book made it a difficult and unenjoyable read. 這本複雜風格的書使得閱讀變得困難又不愉快。

請注意，Grandiloquent的同義詞可能因上下文而略有不同，但這些詞彙都帶有描述誇大、浮誇或自我吹噓的意涵。

來看一下這一篇短文如何運用Grandiloquent及Pompous：

The speaker's grandiloquent language was unbearable, as he continuously used exaggerated vocabulary and flashy descriptions, making himself appear extremely self-aggrandizing. His pompous demeanor exacerbated this impression, as he came across as arrogantly certain of his own correctness. However, the audience was not interested in such a speech; they preferred to listen to genuine and practical discourse. Therefore, the speaker's grandiloquent and pompous style ultimately did not win people's support and resonance.

這位演講者的浮誇的言辭令人難以忍受，他不斷使用浮誇的詞藻和華而不實的描述，讓人覺得他極度自吹自擂。他的自負的態度也加劇了這種印象，他一副自以爲是的樣子，好像自己是唯一正確的人。然而，聽衆們對這樣的演說並不感興趣，他們更傾向於聆聽眞誠和實用的言談。所以，這位演講者的浮誇的和自負的風格最終並未贏得人們的支持和共鳴。

Groove | 自己舒適的節奏

Groove [gru:v]（名詞）指物理上的長條形凹槽；在音樂上指一種吸引人的節奏或感覺；在非正式用法中，表示找到自己的舒適節奏或狀態。

閱讀Find Your Own Groove找到人生節奏一文：

Finding your own groove in life is like tuning into your favorite song. It's not about conforming to others' expectations, but rather discovering what makes your heart sing. Sarah, a young artist, spent years trying to please her parents by pursuing a career in law. However, her true passion lay in painting. The day she decided to embrace her art, she found her groove. She realized that life's melody becomes harmonious when you dance to your own rhythm, not someone else's.

在人生中找到自己的節奏就像是調到你最喜歡的歌曲。這不是爲了遵循他人的期望，而是發現讓你內心歌唱的東西。莎拉，一位年輕的藝術家，花了多年時間試圖通過追求法律職業來討好她的父母。然而，她眞正的熱情在於繪畫。在她決定擁抱自己的藝術那天，她找到了自己的節奏。她意識到，當你按照自己的節奏跳舞，而不是別人的，生活的旋律就會變得和諧。

Groove的英文例句及應用

1. The carpenter cut a groove into the wood for the drawer's track. 那位木匠在木頭上切了一條凹槽用於抽屜的軌道。

2. This song has a really cool groove that makes you want to dance. 這首歌有一個非常酷的節奏，讓你忍不住想要跳舞。

3. Once you get into the groove of studying, it becomes easier and more enjoyable. 一旦你進入學習的節奏，它變得更容易且更有樂趣。

Groove的同義字詞及例句

1. Rhythm ['rɪðəm] 節奏（名詞）

   He struggled to keep up with the rhythm of the dance class. 他努力跟上舞蹈課的節奏。

2. Beat [biːt] 節拍（名詞）

   She tapped her foot to the beat of the music. 她隨著音樂的節拍輕敲著腳。

3. Riff [rɪf] 指爵士或流行音樂中的短小而引人入勝的旋律或重複段落（名詞）

   The guitarist played an impressive riff that caught everyone's attention. 吉他手演奏了一段令人印象深刻的旋律，吸引了所有人的注意。

4. Sync（synchronization）[sɪŋk] 同步（名詞或動詞）

   The dancers were perfectly in sync with the music. 舞者們與音樂完美同步。

5. Cadence ['keɪdəns] 韻律，節奏（名詞）

   The poet's unique cadence gave a musical quality to her reading. 詩人獨特的韻律給她的朗讀增添了音樂質感。

6. Tempo ['tempoʊ] 速度，節奏（名詞）

The conductor slowed the tempo to create a more dramatic effect. 指揮家放慢了速度，營造出更戲劇性的效果。

His words are
a self-fulfilling prophecy
｜一語成讖

The prophecy has come true.和The prediction has come to pass. 意思就是「預言成眞」。His words turned out to be prophetic. 和 His words came back to haunt him. 他的話後來應驗了。His words were a self-fulfilling prophecy.他的話自己成眞了。都有一言成讖的意思。

來閱讀一篇有關「馬雲對支付寶的預言一語成讖」的報導：
The Chinese government has always been highly vigilant towards tech giants, fearing that their excessive expansion could threaten national security and social stability. As a result, increased regulatory scrutiny on the tech industry has raised concerns. Jack Ma once predicted difficulties for Alipay and stated that he would offer up his company to the government if needed. Now, as the Chinese government intensifies its regulatory grip on the tech sector, his statement is seen as a self-fulfilling prophesy.
中國政府一直對科技巨頭保持著高度警惕，擔心其過度擴張會威脅到國家安全和社會穩定，因此對科技行業的監管力度加強，引發了關注。馬雲曾預言支付寶會遇到困難，並曾表示如果政府需要，他可以將自己的企業「送給國家」。如今，隨著中國政府加強對科技行業的監管，這一言論被視爲「一語成讖」。

各種「一語成讖」的說法及應用

1. The prophecy has come true.

   After years of warnings, the prophecy has come true; the ancient city was discovered under the sands. 經過多年的預言，這預言終於成眞了；古代城市被發現埋藏在沙子之下。

2. The prediction has come to pass.

   As the economist had feared, the prediction has come to pass, and the market crashed. 正如經濟學家所擔憂的，這預測終於實現，市場崩盤了。

3. His words turned out to be prophetic.

   His words turned out to be prophetic when the new product completely changed the industry. 當新產品徹底改變了整個行業時，他的話證明是預言成眞。

4. His words came back to haunt him.

   After the scandal, his earlier denials of wrongdoing came back to haunt him. 在醜聞爆發後，被自己早先否認的不當行爲所反噬。

5. His words were a self-fulfilling prophecy.

   His constant fear of failure was a self-fulfilling prophecy when he finally gave up. 他對失敗的不斷恐懼最終究一語成讖，最終放棄。

6. An offhand comment that proves to be prescient.

   At the family dinner, Mark made an offhand comment that they should buy stock in the small tech startup, a suggestion that proved to be prescient when the company's value skyrocketed two years later. 在家庭晚餐時，馬克隨口說說他們應該買進那家小型科技新創公司的股票，這個建議在兩年後當公司價值暴漲時，證明是先見之明的。

Hush the buzz ｜掃興

Hush動詞，使安靜、制止聲響。

hush the buzz

意思是「使喧鬧聲平靜下來」、「使議論聲停止」。

The crowd was buzzing with excitement, but the announcer hushed the buzz and asked for quiet before making the big announcement. 群眾因興奮而議論紛紛，但主持人讓喧鬧聲平靜下來,在宣布大事前要求大家安靜。

可以用來表示「掃興」，形容某個行爲或情況將一個原本熱鬧、活躍的氛圍變得安靜或沉悶。以下是一些例子：

1. The news of the scandal hushed the buzz of the party. 醜聞的消息讓這個聚會掃了興。

2. The party was in full swing until Mrs. Smith entered the room and hushed the buzz with her stern look.派對正歡樂進行中，直到史密斯夫人進入房間，用她嚴厲的眼神讓氣氛降溫。

3. The unexpected arrival of her parents hushed the buzz of the party. 她父母的意外到來讓派對掃了興。

4. As soon as the manager started discussing work, he completely hushed the buzz of the office gathering.當經理開始談論工作時，他完全讓辦公室聚會的熱鬧氣氛掃了興。

5. The DJ tried to hush the buzz with some slow songs, but the crowd wasn't having it and demanded more upbeat music. DJ 試著用一些慢歌降低派對的熱鬧氣氛，但人群不接受，要求更多快節奏的音樂。

buzz-husher

指用來消除嗡嗡聲或其他噪音的裝置或設備，通常用於電子產品，例如揚聲器、電視機和電腦。The new buzz-husher in my headphones has really improved the sound quality. 我的新耳機的嗡嗡聲消除器真的改善了音質。

buzz-husher也可以當作掃興的人

1. The party was ruined by the buzz-husher who kept complaining about the food. 派對被那個一直抱怨食物的掃興鬼給毀了。

2. The buzz-husher at the meeting kept interrupting and derailing the conversation. 會議上掃興的人一直打斷和破壞談話。buzz-husher 可以翻譯為「掃興鬼」、「掃興的人」、「樂趣破壞者」。

除了hush the buzz，還有其他掃興的說法

1. kill the mood破壞氣氛

   I'm sorry to kill the mood, but I have to go. 不好意思破壞氣氛，我得走了。

2. rain on someone's parade澆熄某人的興致

   Don't rain on my parade! I just got a new job! 別掃興！我剛

剛得到一份新工作！

3. burst someone's bubble戳破某人的幻想

I'm so sorry to burst your bubble, but the concert is sold out.
我很抱歉讓你掃興，演唱會已售罄。

4. pop someone's balloon打破某人的希望

I hate to pop your balloon, but I don't think you're going to
win the lottery. 我很不想掃興／打破你的希望，但我認為
你不會中樂透。（pop作動詞時有爆裂意思。）

5. spoil someone's fun破壞某人的樂趣

I'm sorry to spoil your fun, but we have to go home now. 不
好意思讓你掃興／破壞了你的興致，我們現在要回家
了。

6. put a damper on things澆冷水

He put a damper on things by telling a really bad joke. 他講了
一個很爛的笑話，澆冷水了。（Damper名詞原本意思是
控制流量用的閥門或閘門。）

7. put a downer on things搞砸事情

She put a downer on things by talking about her ex-boyfriend.
她講了她前男友的事情，搞砸了事情很掃興。（downer
名詞，鎮靜劑或是只使人情緒低落事務。）

8. put a wet blanket on things澆熄熱情

He put a wet blanket on things by being so negative. 他太消
極了，澆熄了熱情很掃興。

I'm running on fumes
| 精疲力盡

I am running on fumes是一個俚語表達，意指一個人或事物已經非常疲憊、耗盡精力或資源，幾乎無法繼續前進。這個詞語通常用來形容極度疲憊或耗盡的狀態，彷彿剩下最後一絲力量。

"I am running on fumes" is an idiomatic expression that means a person or thing is extremely tired, depleted of energy, or resources, and can hardly continue. This phrase is often used to describe a state of extreme exhaustion, as if there's only a tiny bit of energy or resources left.

閱讀一篇描寫「馬拉比賽竭盡全力」的一篇短文，看看如何運用I am running on fumes.到文章之中：

As the marathon race day draws near, I can't help but feel a mix of excitement and nervousness. Months of training, countless early morning runs, and a strict diet regimen have all led to this moment. It's a journey that has pushed my physical and mental limits. I know that when I stand at the starting line, I'll be running on fumes, relying on sheer determination and the support of fellow runners and spectators. The grueling miles ahead will test my endurance, but the finish line beckons with a sense of accomplishment that makes every step worth it.

隨著馬拉松賽日的臨近，我不自禁地感到興奮和緊張交織。幾個月的訓練，無數次的清晨跑步和嚴格的飲食計劃都是為了這一刻的來臨。這是一段讓我挑戰身體和心理極限的旅程。我知道當我站在起跑線上，我將會精疲力竭，只能單純靠著毅力、選手及觀眾的支持。前方路途的艱困將考驗我的耐力，但終點線的呼喚是一種成就感，使每一步都變得有價值。

I'm running on fumes例句應用

1. After working two jobs and taking care of her family, she felt like she was running on fumes. 在做了兩份工作並照顧家人後，她感覺自己筋疲力盡。

2. The marathon runner was running on fumes as he approached the finish line. 那名馬拉松選手接近終點時已經體力幾乎耗盡。

3. Our project deadline is tomorrow, and we're still working late into the night. At this point, we're definitely running on fumes. 我們的計畫截止日期是明天，我們仍在深夜加班工作。現在，我們真的是筋疲力盡了。

I'm running on fumes的同義字詞或片語

1. Exhausted（形容詞）精疲力盡的
   After the long hike, I was completely exhausted. 長途徒步後，我完全精疲力盡。

2. Running on empty（片語）幾乎耗盡了
   After the long road trip, the car was running on empty, and

we needed to refuel. 長途自駕遊之後，車子幾乎耗盡了油，我們需要加油。

3. Out of steam（片語）沒有精力

I've been working all day, and now I'm completely out of steam. 我整天都在工作，現在我完全沒有精力了。

4. Drained（形容詞）精疲力盡的

After the intense workout, I felt drained of energy. 經過激烈的運動，我感到精疲力盡。

5. Worn out（形容詞）疲憊不堪的

She's been working long hours, and she looks completely worn out. 她一直工作很長時間，看起來完全疲憊不堪。

6. Lassitude ['læs.ɪ.tju:d]（名詞）疲倦，無力

After the marathon, she felt an overwhelming sense of lassitude. 馬拉松賽後，她感到極度疲倦和無力。

7. Knackered ['næk.əd]（形容詞）非常疲憊的，筋疲力盡的（主要在英國英語中使用）

I'm absolutely knackered after working all weekend. 經過整個週末的工作，我完全筋疲力盡了。

8. Fatigue [fə'ti:g]（名詞）疲勞，疲乏

The long journey caused considerable fatigue among the crew. 長途旅行使得船員們感到相當疲勞。

9. Wearying ['wɪər.i.ɪŋ]（形容詞）使人疲倦的，令人厭煩的

The constant noise from the construction site was a wearying presence in our lives. 來自建築工地的持續噪音是我們生活中令人疲倦的存在。

10. Enervating ['ɛn.ər.veɪ.tɪŋ]（形容詞）使人衰弱的，使人失

去活力的

The hot and humid climate was enervating, leaving us all feeling drained. 炎熱潮濕的氣候令人衰弱，讓我們都感到精疲力盡。

11. Sap（動詞）逐漸削弱，耗盡（某人的體力或決心）

Weeks of hard work had sapped his strength. 數週的辛勤工作消耗了他的體力。

12. Sapping ['sæp.ɪŋ]（Sap的現在分詞形態）逐漸削弱體力或決心的

The endless meetings were sapping his energy, making it hard to focus on actual work. 無休止的會議正在消耗他的精力，使他難以專注於實際工作。

這些詞語和片語都用來形容極度疲憊或耗盡的狀態，可以替換 I'm running on fumes 以豐富語言表達。

超級比一比 | Imbroglio vs Entanglement

您也有這樣的「糾葛」嗎？網路上常有人問究竟要不要幫剛的小朋友取得一個耳熟能詳的名字，或是菜市場名字？順口、好記、又方便書寫但是很菜市場、很罕見或是有諧音究竟好不好？終究各說各話、莫衷一是。

Do you also find yourself in such an "imbroglio"? Online, there's a frequent debate about whether to give newborns a familiar name or one that sounds more like it's from a traditional market. Names that are easy to pronounce, memorable, and convenient to write, but at the same time, very commonplace, rare, or with puns – are they good or not? Ultimately, there are various opinions and no consensus .

Imbroglio [ɪmˈbroʊl.jo]

（名詞）用來描述一種複雜、混亂的局面，「糾葛」的意思。特別是涉及誤會、爭議或困難的情況。形容政治混亂或僵局就可說成political imbroglio。

Due to the political impasse in the parliament, where no party holds a majority, the situation regarding the election of the Speaker of the House has become even more of an "imbroglio", with the circumstances growing increasingly unclear among the parties. 由於國會三黨不過半的政治僵局，使得各黨對於國

會議長推選的情勢更加混沌不明。（imbroglio通常用來形容政治、社會、或個人關係中的複雜困難情況。）

Imbroglio的例子和應用

1. The political imbroglio complicated the peace negotiations. 政治上的混亂、糾葛使和平談判更加複雜。

2. They found themselves in an imbroglio after misunderstanding each other's intentions. 在誤解彼此的意圖之後，他們發現自己陷入了一個困難、糾葛中。

3. The legal imbroglio delayed the project for several months. 法律上的爭議導致該計畫延遲了數月。

和imbroglio相同意涵的字詞

1. Quagmire（名詞）泥沼之意，比喻困境或難以擺脫的情況
   The legal case quickly turned into a quagmire, with no easy solution in sight. 這個法律案件迅速變成了一個泥沼，看不到可以容易的解決辦法。

2. Muddle（名詞）混亂，指情況或思想混亂，缺乏條理
   The project was in a muddle due to poor management. 由於管理不善，這個計畫陷入了混亂中。

3. Entanglement（名詞）糾纏或糾結，指複雜的或難以解決的關係或情況
   Their business entanglement lasted for years, making it difficult to separate their assets. 他們的業務盤根錯節持續多年，使得分離資產變得困難。

4. Predicament（名詞）困境

She found herself in a predicament when she lost her job and couldn't pay her bills. 當她失業並且無法支付賬單時，她發現自己處於一個困境中。

5. Plight（名詞）困境，與predicament同義

The plight of the refugees touched the hearts of many people. 難民的困境 感動了許多人的心。

6. Conundrum（名詞）難題

Solving the budget issue was a conundrum for the committee. 解決預算問題對委員會來說是一個難題。

7. Knot（名詞）糾結，複雜且難以解開的問題或情況

The negotiations became a complex knot, with each party having conflicting interests. 談判變成了一個複雜的糾結，彼此的利益都互相衝突。

與Entanglement同義字詞

1. Snarl（名詞）纏結，通常指交通或其他形式的阻塞、混亂

The accident caused a huge snarl in rush hour traffic. 這起事故在尖峰時段造成了嚴重的交通堵塞。

2. Tangle（名詞）纏繞

The fishing lines got into a tangle, making it difficult to use them again. 釣魚線纏在一起，使得再次使用變得困難。

3. Knot（名詞）比喻複雜且難以解開的問題或情況

The story was a complex knot of events and characters that was hard to unravel. 這個故事是一個由事件和人物構成的複雜糾結，很難解開。

4. Intertwine交織、緊密相連或相結合（動詞）

Their fates seemed to intertwine, leading them to meet in the most unexpected places. 他們的命運似乎緊密相連，讓他們在最意想不到的地方相遇。

Imbroglio和Entanglement的差異

雖然這兩個字詞都描述了複雜或困難的情況，但它們的使用情境略有不同。Imbroglio通常用來指一個特別複雜且尷尬的爭議或混亂狀態，常常涉及誤解和衝突。它強調的是情況的混亂和錯綜複雜的性質。Entanglement則更廣泛地指任何形式的糾纏或糾結，不一定涉及爭議或混亂，但強調的是事情或關係之間難以分清、複雜交錯的情況。

Imbroglio爭議或混亂

The political imbroglio became more complicated with each passing day, involving multiple parties and various hidden agendas. 隨著時間的推移，這場政治爭議變得越來越複雜，涉及多個政黨和各種隱藏的議程。

Entanglement糾結或牽扯

Her entanglement in the company's affairs made it difficult for her to maintain an objective perspective. 她在公司事務中的牽扯使她難以保持客觀的視角。

Inadvertent | 不經意

Inadvertent [ɪnˈædvɚtənt]

形容詞，意指不經意的、無意的、不小心的、疏忽的。這個詞常常用來形容某事或行為是在無意中發生或沒有預先計劃的情況下發生的。在日常生活中，我們都可能犯下不小心的錯誤，這些錯誤通常是因為缺乏警覺性或未注意到細節而產生的。要避免這些無心的過失，我們需要更加謹慎和細心。

The word "inadvertent" is an adjective that means unintentional, accidental, or careless. This term is often used to describe something or an action that occurs without prior planning or in an unintended manner. In our daily lives, we all may make inadvertent mistakes, which typically result from a lack of awareness or not paying attention to details. To avoid these unintentional errors, we need to be more cautious and attentive.

看一篇關於「不經意的日常動作，可能造成失明的後果」的文章，來看看如何在文章中出現及應用：

A physician highlights three inadvertent actions in daily life that may lead to increased intraocular pressure, damaging the optic nerve, and potentially causing blindness. These actions include:

1. Inadvertent Constipation: Chronic constipation can result in elevated internal pressure, affecting intraocular pressure. Regular intake of dietary fiber and staying hydrated can prevent this condition.

2. Wearing Tight Neckties: Cinching neckties too tightly can impede blood flow, potentially raising eye pressure over time. Opting for looser neckwear is advisable.

3. Overconsumption of Water（>300 ml at Once）: Drinking excessive water in a single sitting can temporarily spike intraocular pressure. It's better to space out fluid intake throughout the day.

一位醫師指出了日常生活中三個不經意的動作，可能會導致眼內壓升高，損害視神經，並可能導致失明。這些動作包括：

1. 不經意的便祕：長期便祕可能會導致體內壓力升高，影響眼內壓。定期攝取食物纖維並保持足夠的水分攝入可以預防這種情況。

2. 打緊領帶：過緊領帶可能會阻礙血液流動，潛在地會使眼內壓隨著時間上升。選擇鬆散的領帶是明智的選擇。

3. 過多飲水（一次超過300毫升）：一次性過多飲水可能會暫時性地提高眼內壓。最好分散一天中的飲水量。

說明：1. Intraocular [ˌɪntrəˈɑːkjələr] 指的是與眼球內部相關的事物或過程。2. Cinch緊縮、收緊，通常指的是繫緊、固定或加固某物，使其更牢固或更緊密。3. Space out water intake 分散水分的攝取，意指在一天內均勻地分配水的飲用量，不要一次性喝很多水。有助維持身體水分平衡和健康。

Inadvertent的例句及應用

1. She made an inadvertent mistake by sending the wrong email to the client. 她犯了一個不小心的錯誤，把錯誤的郵件發

送給了客戶。

2. The inadvertent slip of the hand caused the glass to shatter on the floor. 手不小心一滑，導致玻璃在地板上碎裂。

3. His inadvertent comment offended some of his colleagues during the meeting. 他在會議中不小心的評論冒犯了一些同事。

Inadvertent的同義詞及例句解釋

1. Unintentional（意外的）指不是有意的，發生在無意之間
   Her unintentional remark offended some people at the party. 她無意中的言論冒犯了派對上的一些人。

2. Accidental（意外的）表示某事是偶然發生的，不是故意的
   The broken vase was an accidental result of the cat knocking it over. 破裂的花瓶是貓意外打翻的結果。

3. Unplanned（未計劃的）指某事情沒有提前計劃或預期
   Their unplanned road trip turned out to be a great adventure. 他們沒有計劃的公路旅行變成了一場精彩的冒險。

4. Haphazard[ˈhæp͵hæzəd]（無計劃的）表示某事物缺乏秩序或計劃，隨意的意思
   The haphazard arrangement of the furniture made the room look chaotic. 傢俱的隨意擺放讓房間看起來混亂不堪。

5. Desultory無計劃的，雜亂無章的
   Her reading was desultory—she jumped from one book to another without finishing any. 她的閱讀非常雜亂無章——她從一本書跳到另一本，卻沒有完整地讀完任何一本。

這些同義詞都描述了某事或行爲是在無意間發生或不是事先計劃的情況下發生的，類似於Inadvertent。

Unpremeditated、Casual和Inadvertent

在某些情境下可能有相似之處，但仍有些微意差異，Unpremeditated指的是未經事先考慮的，casual指的是隨意的或輕鬆的，而Inadvertent則強調無意間或不經意的、偶發的發生。以下是各個單字的說明：

Unpremeditated無預謀的

表示某事情是無計劃或無預謀的，未經事先考慮或策劃。通常指某個行動或決策是出於即興或未經思考的，並非特意計劃的。His unpremeditated response to the question surprised everyone in the room. 他對問題的即興式的回應讓房裡的每個人都感到驚訝。

Casual偶然的、隨便的

表示某事情是不經過深思熟慮、不特意的、隨意的，通常指輕鬆或不正式的性質。可以用於描述行爲、交談或關係的性質，表明它們不是嚴肅或正式的。Their casual meeting at the café turned into a deep conversation about life. 他們在咖啡廳的偶然相遇演變成了一場關於生活的深入對話。

Inadvertent不經意的

表示某事情是無意間或疏忽地發生的，通常指無意的、不經意的或不小心的行動。通常用於描述某事或行爲是在無意中發生，而不是有計劃的。Her inadvertent comment offended her colleague, even though she didn't mean to. 她的不經意評論冒犯了她的同事，即使她並不是有意的。

Inimical 敵意／對立

Inimical（形容詞）意思是敵意的，是一個用來描述事物或情況不利於、有害於、對立或敵對的詞語。這個詞常常用於表達一種對某事物或情況的強烈不滿或反感。

來看一下inimical在短文的運用：

This storm has had a tremendously <u>inimical</u> impact on our plans, to the point where it can be considered highly detrimental. This weather has truly been hostile to our activities, impeding our progress.

這場風暴對我們的計劃造成了極大的<u>不利影響</u>，可以說是極為不利的。這種天氣真的對我們的活動極具敵意，阻礙我們的進展。

Inimical應用及示例

1. The inimical remarks made by the competitor during the conference were meant to undermine our reputation. 競爭對手在會議期間發表的敵意的言論意思是在破壞我們的聲譽。

2. His inimical attitude towards teamwork hindered the project's success. 他對團隊合作的對立態度阻礙了計畫的成功。

3. The harsh economic conditions proved to be inimical to small businesses struggling to survive. 嚴苛的經濟環境證實對那些奮鬥求生存的小企業是有害的。

Inimical的同義字詞片語和例句說明

1. Adverse（形容詞）不利的、有害的

   The adverse weather conditions forced us to cancel the outdoor event. 不利的天氣狀況迫使我們取消了戶外活動。

2. Hostile（形容詞）敵對的、敵意的

   Their hostile response to our proposal was unexpected. 他們對我們提案的敵意反應出乎意料。

3. Unfavorable（形容詞）不利的、不順利的

   The unfavorable economic conditions led to job cuts. 不利的經濟狀況導致了裁員。

4. Detrimental（形容詞）有害的、不利的

   Smoking is detrimental to your health. 吸菸對健康有害。

5. Harmful（形容詞）有害的、危害的

   Exposure to harmful chemicals can be dangerous. 暴露於有害化學物質可能會危險。

6. Destructive（形容詞）破壞性的、毀滅性的

   The hurricane caused destructive damage to the coastal area. 颶風對沿海地區造成了毀滅性的破壞。

7. Unfriendly（形容詞）不友好的、敵對的

   The competitor's tactics were unfriendly and aggressive. 競爭對手的策略不友好且具有攻擊性。

8. Counterproductive（形容詞）適得其反的、事與願違的

   His constant interruptions during the meeting were counterproductive to our productivity. 他在會議中不斷打斷是對我們的工作效率適得其反的。

9. Damaging（形容詞）損害的、有害的

The scandal had a damaging effect on the company's reputation. 醜聞對公司的聲譽造成了損害。

這些詞語和片語都可以用來描述有害的、不利的、或敵對的情況，根據不同的語境和語氣選擇適當的詞語可以使語言表達更加豐富和精確。

Inimical、Deleterious和Noxious
雖然有一定的相似性，都可以描述有害的事物，但有些微不同的意義和使用情境

Inimical（形容詞）不利於、有害的、對立的、敵對的
通常用於描述一個情況或事物對某事物或目標具有對立或敵意，但不一定表示直接的有害性。The inimical relationship between the two companies led to intense competition. 兩家公司之間的敵對關係導致了激烈的競爭。

Deleterious [ˌdɛləˈtɪriəs]（形容詞）有害的、有害健康的
主要用於描述對健康、環境或一個系統造成有害影響的情況，更強調有害的效果。The deleterious effects of smoking on lung health are well-documented. 吸菸對肺部健康的有害的影響已有充分的記錄。

Noxious（形容詞）有害的、有毒的、令人不悅的

用來描述有害、有毒或令人反感的事物，通常強調其有毒性或對人類或環境的不利影響。The chemical spill released noxious fumes into the air. 化學洩漏釋放了有毒氣體到空氣中。

這三個詞語都涉及有害的概念，但它們的語境和強調的點有所不同。根據具體的情境，可以選擇使用最適合的詞語以更準確地傳達意思。

Innocuous｜無傷大雅

Innocuous [ɪ'nɒkjuəs] 形容詞。無害的、無傷大雅，形容某事物不會造成傷害或不會引起爭議。例如The innocuous appearance of the man belied his true intentions. 那個男人看似無害的外表掩蓋了他眞正的意圖。

innocuous在「潮水退了，民調誤差影響政黨信譽」一文的應用：

As the tide recedes after the election, the essence of the matter becomes clearer. There is a certain discrepancy between the poll results and the actual election results. Although the poll error is well-known and also innocuous, it seeds the feeling of being deceived in the people's hearts by covering up the unfavorable factors, leaving a perfidious impression, which may belie the party's credibility and trustworthiness.

選後潮水退去，事情的本質愈發清晰。民調結果與實際選舉結果存在一定的差異。儘管民調有誤眾所皆知也「無傷大雅」，但爲了掩蓋不利因素，種下民眾心中被欺騙的種子，給人留下「背信棄義」的印象，可能會造成政黨的信譽及信任度「受到質疑」。

說明：1. Perfidiousness [pər'fɪdiəsnəs] 缺乏誠信、不忠誠或背信棄義的意思。如His perfidious actions betrayed the trust of his closest friends, leaving them shocked and disillusioned. 他的

背叛行為辜負了他最親密朋友的信任，使他們感到震驚和幻滅。2. Belie [bɪˈlaɪ] 掩蓋或給出與真相相反的印象；使人誤解之意。Her calm demeanor belied the turmoil she was feeling inside.她平靜的外表掩蓋了她內心的不安。

Innocuous的應用例句

1. The comment was intended to be innocuous, but it unintentionally offended some members of the audience. 那個評論原本是無傷大雅的，但無意中冒犯了一些觀眾。

2. Despite its innocuous appearance, the plant is actually highly toxic if ingested. 儘管這種植物看起來無害，但如果吞食實際上是有劇毒的。

3. She thought the joke was innocuous, but it caused an unexpected uproar in the office. 她認為那個玩笑話是無害的，但它在辦公室引起了無預期的騷動。

Innocuous的同義詞

1. Harmless（形容詞）無害的

Despite its large size, the animal is completely harmless to humans. 儘管體型很大，這種動物對人類完全無害。

2. Benign（形容詞）良性的，和善的

The tumor was found to be benign, much to the patient's relief. 腫瘤被確診為良性，這讓病人鬆了一口氣。

3. Inoffensive（形容詞）無冒犯的，無害的

He prefers inoffensive humor that doesn't hurt anyone's feelings. 他偏好不會冒犯到人情感的幽默。

4. Nonthreatening [ˌnɑnˈθrɛtənɪŋ]（形容詞）不構成威脅的

He has a nonthreatening manner that makes everyone feel at ease. 他的舉止不具威脅性，讓每個人都感到輕鬆自在。

Insouciant｜漫不經心

Insouciant [ˌɪnˈsuːsɪənt] 漫不經心，一個精彩的單字，指的是某人對事情漠不關心或不在乎的態度。這個詞通常用作形容詞，描述一個人的態度或行為。

"Inscouciant" is a fascinating word that describes someone's attitude of being indifferent or unconcerned about things. This word is typically used as an adjective to depict a person's demeanor or behavior.

閱讀短文「公部門對於城市停車位不足規劃漫不經心」，學習insouciant在文章中如何應用：

Government officials displayed an insouciant attitude towards parliamentary inquiries regarding the inadequate urban parking facilities. Despite crucial questions raised by lawmakers concerning the improvement of city transportation and parking, these officials seemed utterly indifferent. They failed to provide concrete plans or solutions, offering casual responses and lacking a serious approach to the issue. Such insouciance is irresponsible for both residents and urban development. The government should take these concerns seriously, devise practical strategies to address the shortage of parking spaces in the city, and ensure the quality of life for citizens and the sustainability of the city.

政府官員對於議員質詢有關城市停車位不足的規劃表現得漫不經心。儘管議員提出了關於改善城市交通和停車的重要問題，這些官員似乎對此毫不在乎。他們未能提供明確的計劃或解決方案，只是隨意回答，缺乏對問題的認真對待。這種漫不經心的態度對於居民和城市的發展都是不負責任的。政府應該認真對待這些問題，制定可行的策略，以解決城市停車位不足的問題，確保市民的生活品質和城市的可持續發展。

Insouciant的應用例句

1. When we asked her about the exam tomorrow, she just smiled insouciantly, as if she wasn't worried at all. 當我們問她關於明天的考試時，她只是漫不經心地笑了笑，好像一點也不擔心。

2. His insouciant attitude towards his responsibilities often leads to problems at work. 他對工作責任的漫不經心態度經常導致問題。

3. Despite the looming deadline, Sarah remained insouciant and continued to relax at the beach. 儘管截止日期迫在眉睫，莎拉仍然漫不經心，繼續在海灘上放鬆。

4. Even in the face of criticism, the artist maintained an insouciant demeanor and continued to create his unique works. 即使面對批評，這位藝術家仍然保持著漫不經心的態度，繼續創作他獨特的作品。

Insouciant涵義近似的同義字詞及例句

1. Nonchalant [ˈnɒnʃələnt]（形容詞）冷漠的：表示冷漠或漠不關心的態度。

   He gave a nonchalant shrug when asked about his performance, as if it didn't matter to him. 當問及他的表現時，他冷漠地聳了聳肩，好像對他來說無所謂。

2. Indifferent [ɪnˈdɪfərənt]（形容詞）無動於衷的：表示對某事物漠不關心或無感的態度。

   The politician appeared indifferent to the concerns of the citizens, which caused dissatisfaction among voters. 這位政治家對市民的關切顯得漠不關心，引起了選民的不滿。

3. Unconcerned（形容詞）不關心的：指的是對某事物不在意或不關心的狀態。

   She seemed entirely unconcerned about the impending storm, continuing her picnic as if nothing were wrong. 她對即將來臨的暴風雨顯得毫不在意，繼續野餐，好像什麼都沒發生。

4. Casual [ˈkæʒuəl]（形容詞）隨意的：表示不拘束、隨意或不正式的。

   His casual approach to the interview surprised the panel, as they expected a more serious demeanor. 他對面試的隨意態度讓評審小驚訝，因爲他們預期他會更嚴肅。

5. Apathetic（形容詞）冷淡的：表示缺乏興趣或熱情，對事情冷漠無感。

   The audience's apathetic response to the performance disappointed the actors. 觀衆對表演的冷淡反應讓演員們感

到失望。

6. Unmindful（形容詞）不在意的：表示不注意、不關心的。

He seemed unmindful of the consequences of his actions, which caused trouble for others. 他似乎不在意他行爲的後果，這給別人帶來了麻煩。

7. Insensitive（形容詞）不敏感的：表示對他人感受缺乏敏感，漠視情感。

Her insensitive remarks hurt his feelings deeply. 她少一條筋的言論深深傷害了他的感情。

8. Dispassionate [dɪsˈpæʃənət]（形容詞）表示冷靜、不受情感影響的。

In her role as a judge, she maintained a dispassionate demeanor when making decisions. 在她擔任法官的角色中，她在做出決定時保持冷靜的態度。

9. Detached（形容詞）超然的：表示超然於情感之外，不參與或不投入。

He remained detached from the heated argument and chose not to get involved. 他對激烈的爭論保持超然，選擇不參與其中。

10. Desultory [ˈdɛs.əl.tɔːr.i]（形容詞）散漫的，無計畫或目的性的，隨意的

His desultory attempts at finding a job didn't yield much success. 他那漫不經心的找工作嘗試沒有取得成功。

11. Lackadaisical [ˌlæk.əˈdeɪ.zɪ.kəl]（形容詞）無精打采的，不感興趣的，懶散的

Her lackadaisical approach to studying resulted in poor grades. 她那無精打采的學習態度導致了成績不佳。

12. Offhand [ˌɔːfˈhænd] 卽興的，隨便的，不經意的

（形容詞）He gave me an offhand answer that didn't really solve the problem. 他隨便給了我一個答案，並沒有真正解決問題。

（副詞）She mentioned it offhand, but it caught everyone's attention. 她隨口一提，但卻引起了大家的注意。

上述的詞語都可以用來表達對事物漠不關心、冷淡、不在意、漫不經心或不受情感影響的態度，具體選擇取決於上下文和所要表達的感覺。

Intoxication levels
│ 酒醉程度的英文應用

酒精還會促進體內的多巴胺（Dopamine）分泌讓大腦快樂，但也常常酒醉intoxication失控發生問題，甚至斷片引發犯罪。依照不同酒醉程度，從輕微至斷片分別是Tipsy（微醺）開始，上升到Buzzed（微醉）、Ebrious ['iː.bri.əs]（醉酒）、Drunken（醉酒）、Sloshed [slɒʃt]（很醉）、Hammered（酩酊大醉）、Black out（斷片／昏迷）。

酒醉程度用英文應用

1. Tipsy微醺：輕微的醉意，感覺愉快但仍然清醒
   After a glass of champagne, she was feeling a bit tipsy. 喝了一杯香檳後，她感覺有點微醺。

2. Buzzed微醉：比微醺更明顯
   He was just buzzed enough to sing karaoke. 他喝得微醉，剛好夠膽上臺唱卡拉OK。

3. Ebrious ['iː.bri.əs] 酒醉：較正式醉酒的用詞，描述明顯的醉酒狀態
   His ebrious demeanor was noticeable at the dinner. 他在晚餐上明顯醉態畢露。

4. Drunken酒醉：明顯的醉酒，可能包括行為失控
   Her drunken laughter filled the room. 她醉酒的笑聲充滿了整個房間。

5. Hammered酩酊大醉：非常醉，行為和判斷力受到嚴重影響He got hammered at the bar and couldn't even stand up. 他在酒吧喝得爛醉，甚至站不起來。

6. Black out斷片、昏迷：極醉酒

She drank so much that she blacked out and couldn't remember anything the next day. 她喝得太多，導致昏迷失憶，第二天什麼都不記得了。

I blacked out after drinking too much at the party. I don't remember anything after that. 我喝醉了，在派對上失憶了。我從那以後什麼也記不起來了。

其他形容酒醉程度的字詞

1. Sloshed [slɒʃt] 英語俚語，意為喝醉了。通常用來描述一個人喝了很多酒，以至於他或她無法站立、說話或思考清楚

I got sloshed at the party last night. I can't remember a thing. 我昨晚在派對上喝醉了。我什麼也記不起來了。

2. Plastered嚴重醉酒，幾乎失去所有控制

After the party, he was completely plastered and couldn't even walk straight. 派對結束後，他醉得一塌糊塗，甚至走不了直線。

3. Wasted爛醉如泥：極度醉酒，幾乎失去意識

She drank so much at the bar last night that she ended up totally wasted. 她昨晚在酒吧喝了太多酒，最終醉得不省人事。

超級比一比 | Lackadaisical vs Obsequious

Lackadaisical（形容詞）：漫不經心的、懈怠的

用來描述人或事物的狀態或態度。當某人或某事表現出缺乏動力、興趣或精神，對任務或工作不積極時，可以使用這個詞來形容。

1. His lackadaisical attitude towards his studies led to poor grades. 他對學業的漫不經心態度導致了差勁的成績。

2. The team's lackadaisical performance in the first half of the game cost them the victory. 球隊上半場的懈怠表現使他們失去了勝利。

3. We can't afford to have a lackadaisical approach to this project; we need to be fully committed. 我們不能對這個計畫採取漫不經心的態度；我們需要全情投入。

Obsequious（形容詞）：巴結的、奉承的

用來描述人或他們的行為，通常涉及過分的奉承或討好。當某人過分巴結或奉承他人，以獲取好處、權力或利益時，可以使用這個詞。

1. The obsequious waiter constantly hovered around the wealthy customer, eager to fulfill every request. 那位巴結的服務生一直在富有的客戶周圍晃來晃去，渴望滿足每一個要求。（註：Hover around ['hʌvər ə'raʊnd] 用於描述輕盈

地移動或保持在某個位置附近繞行，也可以形容人的行為，特別是當他們似乎不安或猶豫不決時。The helicopter hovered around the building, searching for a safe place to land. 直升機在大樓周圍盤旋，尋找一個安全的降落地點。）

2. Her obsequious behavior towards her boss was so transparent that it made her colleagues uncomfortable. 她對老闆的奉承行為如此顯而易見，以至於讓她的同事感到不自在。

3. The politician was known for being obsequious to those in power, always seeking their favor. 這位政治人物以對權力人士巴結奉承而聞名，總是尋求他們的青睞。

閱讀一篇短文關於描寫職場兩種不同類型個性的人如何在面對職場工作及人際關係，看看如何運用lackadaisical和obsequious做出描述及建議：

In a corporate setting, it's not uncommon to encounter individuals with starkly different attitudes. Some employees approach their tasks with a lackadaisical attitude, showing little enthusiasm or commitment to their work. They often procrastinate on deadlines and seem disinterested in the company's goals. Such lackadaisical behavior can hinder productivity and teamwork.

在企業環境中，遇到態度截然不同的人是很常見的。有些員工對待工作持有一種漫不經心的態度，對工作缺乏熱情或承諾。他們經常延遲工作期限，似乎對公司的目標不感興趣。這種漫不經心的行為可能會妨礙生產力和團隊合作。

On the other hand, there are those who employ an obsequious

demeanor to climb the corporate ladder. These individuals constantly flatter their superiors, seeking every opportunity to curry favor and gain preferential treatment. While this approach may yield short-term benefits, it can lead to resentment among colleagues who perceive it as insincere and opportunistic.

另一方面，有些人使用巴結奉承的態度來攀爬企業階梯。這些人不斷地奉承他們的上級，尋求每一個機會討好並獲得特殊待遇。雖然這種方法可能會帶來短期的好處，但它可能會引起同事的不滿，認爲這種行爲不眞誠且機會主義。

說明：Curry favor是一個片語，意思是試圖討好或取悅某人，通常是出於自己的私人利益或爲了贏得對方的好感而行動。例如，如果某人試圖通過奉承、讚美或其他方式來取悅老闆以爭取升遷，可以說他正在curry favor。

In a balanced workplace, it's essential to strike a middle ground, where employees are <u>neither lackadaisical nor obsequious</u>. Instead, they should be motivated and committed to their tasks, while also maintaining genuine and respectful relationships with their colleagues and superiors.

在平衡的工作場所中，重要的是要找到一個折衷的方式，員工既不懈怠也不巴結。相反，他們應該對工作充滿動力和承諾，同時與同事和上級保持眞誠和尊重的關係。

Lackadaisical（漫不經心的、懈怠的）的同義詞

1. Indifferent（形容詞）冷漠的，指對事物缺乏興趣或情感的態度。

His indifferent attitude towards the project showed in his lack of effort. 他對這個項目的冷漠態度反映在他的不努力上。

2. Apathetic（形容詞）無感情的、冷淡的，缺乏熱情或情感的狀態。

The apathetic response from the audience disappointed the performers. 觀眾的冷淡反應讓演出者感到失望。

Obsequious的同義詞

1. Sycophantic（阿諛奉承的）指一種過分奉承和諂媚的態度。形容詞

The sycophantic employee constantly praised the boss in the hope of gaining favor. 這位阿諛奉承的員工不斷讚美老闆，希望獲得好感。

2. Fawning（諂媚的）指一種過度諂媚和奉承的行為。形容詞

Her fawning behavior towards the celebrity made her seem insincere. 她對名人的諂媚行為使她顯得不真誠。

Unctuous vs. Obsequious

Unctuous和Obsequious都表示一種不真誠或虛偽的態度，但Unctuous更強調表面虛偽，而Obsequious更強調巴結和奉承。

Unctuous['ʌŋkʃuəs]（形容詞）油腔滑調的
形容一種過分、虛偽或不真誠的表現，通常帶有虛情假意或矯揉造作。His unctuous praise of the boss didn't fool anyone; it

was clear he was just trying to gain favor. 他對老闆的矯揉造作的讚美並沒有矇騙任何人，顯然他只是想討好。

Obsequious（形容詞）巴結的、奉承的
指一種過分巴結或奉承的態度，通常出於希望討好或獲得別人的好意或贊同。Her obsequious behavior towards her supervisor was quite evident; she constantly sought approval and attention. 她對主管的巴結行為非常明顯；她不斷尋求批准和關注。

Lukewarm vs. Lackadaisical

Lukewarm和Lackadaisical都表示冷淡或不積極的態度，但Lackadaisical更強調懈怠和漫不經心。以下分別說明它們的意思和使用情境。

Lukewarm（形容詞）溫吞的
指冷淡或不熱情的態度或反應，通常表示對某事物缺乏興趣或投入度不高。The audience's lukewarm response to the performance disappointed the actors. 觀眾對表演的冷淡反應讓演員們感到失望。

2. Lackadaisical（形容詞）漫不經心的、懈怠的
指一種懈怠、無精打采、漫不經心的態度或行為，通常表現出缺乏動力或興趣。Her lackadaisical approach to her studies resulted in poor grades. 她對學習的漫不經心態度導致了差劣的成績。

Lackadaisical vs desultory vs insouciant

Lackadaisical、Desultory和Insouciant這三個字詞都有「漫不經心」的意思，但每個詞強調的方面略有不同。

Lackadaisical無精打采的，不感興趣的
強調的是缺乏熱情和動力，給人一種懶散或不在乎的感覺。
His lackadaisical approach to the project resulted in poor-quality work. 他對於這個專案的無精打采的態度導致工作品質不佳。

Desultory指缺乏計劃、目的或連貫性，隨意而沒有系統的
The meeting was desultory and unproductive, with no clear agenda. 會議散漫且無成果，沒有明確的議程。

Insouciant則是指無憂無慮、不關心或不在乎的態度
Despite the looming deadline, he remained insouciant and relaxed.
儘管截止日期迫在眉睫，他依然保持著漫不經心和放鬆的態度。

Lackadaisical強調缺乏熱情或動力的態度，Desultory強調缺乏計劃或目的的不連貫性，而Insouciant則強調不在乎的態度。這些字都涉及到一種不那麼積極或關注的態度，但它們各自強調的焦點有些許不同。

Make a veiled attack
指桑罵槐

Veil（名詞）指面紗、帷幕或覆蓋物，用來的薄布。

Veiled（形容詞）表示隱藏的、不明顯的或間接的，其意思是指含蓄的、不直接表達的，常用來形容話語或批評。

Make a veiled attack（片語）間接或隱晦地進行攻擊或批評。即指桑罵槐之意，如In his speech, the mayor made a veiled attack on his rival's policies. 在他的演講中，市長指桑罵槐批評了對手的政策。

Make a veiled attack在競選場域政治攻防中短文的應用：

The politician made a veiled attack on his opponents, accusing them of perfidious tactics. He criticized the astroturf movements, claiming they undulated public opinion with uncouth methods.政治人物指桑罵槐地指責對手使用卑鄙的策略。他批評了那些帶風向的假輿論，聲稱使用拙劣的手段來控制民意的波動。

1. The politician made a veiled attack這個片語在文中表示間接或隱晦地批評對手。指桑罵槐的意思。

2. Perfidious背信棄義的、卑鄙的。在文中用來形容對手的策略是不誠實和不值得信賴的。

   The spy was known for his perfidious behavior, betraying his own country. 這名間諜因其不忠的行爲而聞名，背叛了自

己的國家。

3. Astroturf這是一種比喻用法，指代那些製造假風向、假輿論的活動。

The campaign was accused of creating astroturf support to mislead the public. 該活動被指控帶風向、輿論來誤導大眾。

4. Uncouth指行爲粗魯、不文雅的。文中用來形容用於操縱公衆輿論的方法是粗俗和不合適的。

His uncouth remarks during the meeting shocked all the attendees.他在會議期間的粗魯言論震驚了所有與會者。

5. Undulate指波浪般起伏。文中用來比喻公衆輿論的波動或變化。

The curtains undulated in the wind, creating a calming effect. 窗簾隨風波動，營造出一種平靜的效果。

來看看make a veiled attack的例句

1. During the meeting, the manager made a veiled attack on his team's performance, hinting at their lack of progress without directly saying it. 在會議中，經理對他團隊的表現進行了隱晦的批評，暗示了他們進展的缺乏，但沒有直接說出來。

2. The politician's speech contained a veiled attack against her opponents, cleverly disguised as general commentary. 這位政治人物的演說指桑罵槐批判了她的對手，並且巧妙地僞裝成一般評論。

3. In her article, the writer made a veiled attack on the

government's policies, using irony and satire. 在她的文章中，作者用諷刺和嘲諷對政府的政策進行了間接的批判。

Make a veiled attack的同義字詞片語

1. Insinuate（動詞）暗示，間接地表示。通常用來指含蓄地表達批評或不滿。

   He didn't openly criticize his colleague but insinuated that the work was not up to standard. 他沒有公開批評他的同事，但暗示了工作沒有達到標準。

2. Throw shade（俚語片語）間接地批評或蔑視某人，通常以輕蔑或諷刺的方式。

   The celebrity didn't directly insult her rival, but she did throw shade with her sarcastic comments. 這位名人沒有直接侮辱她的對手，但她的諷刺評論確實含有蔑視之意。

超級比一比 | Mercurial vs Mercury Retrograde

Mercurial（形容詞）用來形容人或事物變化多端、反應快速、情緒多變、或不穩定的特質。

來看一段醫學的報導有關淋巴癌號成為「變化多端」的腫瘤，看看將如何將Mercurial在應用在文章內：

In Taiwan, approximately 3,000 new cases of lymphoma are diagnosed each year. Many celebrities and entrepreneurs have also been affected by lymphoma. Lymphoma falls under the category of cancers with extremely high diagnostic and treatment complexities. It can manifest in various organs and tissues within the body, often leading to confusion with other diseases. Careful discrimination in diagnosis is essential, earning it the nickname "the mercurial tumor."

在臺灣，每年約有約3,000例淋巴癌的新病例被診斷出來。許多名人和企業家也受到淋巴癌影響。淋巴癌屬於診斷和治療極其複雜的癌症之一。它可以在身體的各個器官和組織中表現出來，常常容易與其他疾病混淆。在診斷時需要非常謹慎的鑑別，因此被稱為「多變的腫瘤」。

Mercurial的例句應用

1. Her mercurial personality made it difficult to predict how she

would react to different situations. 她多變的個性讓人難以預測她對不同情況的反應。

2. The stock market can be quite mercurial, with prices fluctuating rapidly. 股市可能變動迅速，價格波動大。

3. His mercurial moods often left his friends feeling unsure about how to approach him. 他多變的情緒經常讓朋友們感到不確定應該如何接近他。

Mercurial同義詞及例句應用

1. Unpredictable不可預測的、變化多端的

Her moods are as unpredictable as the weather. 她的情緒變化如同天氣一般難以預測。

2. Fickle善變的：形容人或情況容易變化，不穩定

The stock market can be quite fickle, with prices fluctuating rapidly. 股市可能相當善變，價格波動迅速。

3. Capricious反覆無常的：形容某人或某事隨心所欲地變化

The capricious nature of the wind made sailing a challenge. 風的反覆無常性使得航行變得具有挑戰性。

4. Volatile不穩定的：描述容易快速變化或爆發的狀態

The volatile chemicals required careful handling. 這些不穩定的化學品需要小心處理。

5. Erratic不規則的：指的是行為或運動缺乏規律性

His erratic driving made other motorists nervous. 他不規則的駕駛讓其他駕駛者感到緊張。

6. Wayward任性的，不易控制的

Despite the efforts to guide him, the wayward teenager

continued to make poor decisions. 儘管試圖引導他，這個任性的少年還是繼續做出錯誤的決定。

Mercury Retrograde水逆

Mercurial這個詞來自於Mercury的名字，最初指的是與Mercury水星之神相關的事物。後來，它的意義擴展爲形容那些變化快速、難以預測或智慧的特質，這與水星神的特性相符。

星座運勢中常提到的「水逆」被稱爲Mercury Retrograde。指水星看似在天空中逆行的現象，從地球觀察時，水星似乎是在向相反方向移動。在占星學中，水星逆行被認爲會影響通訊、旅行、合約和技術等方面，常常與混亂和誤解相關聯。

來看一下有關「水逆」Mercury Retrograde的影響一文：

What should we do when faced with Mercury Retrograde? The term "Mercury Retrograde" often appears when things don't go smoothly, and many people use it as an explanation for all sorts of misfortunes. In reality, retrograde motion is not exclusive to Mercury, and planets don't actually move backward – it's all just an optical illusion observed from Earth. Astrology experts have commented on this phenomenon: "Mercury Retrograde brings chaos, forcing us out of our comfort zones, but it also leads to new experiences and changes, which are not about right or wrong." Astrology suggests that during Mercury Retrograde, the key is to maintain a positive and relaxed attitude. If you encounter disagreements in communication with friends or colleagues, try to take a step back, or approach the situation with a more tolerant mindset. If you experience some setbacks during the retrograde period, there's no need to attribute all problems to Mercury Retrograde.

當我們遇到水逆時該如何應對呢？「水星逆行」這個詞似乎總在不順利時出現，許多人甚至用它來解釋一切不如意。實際上，「逆行」並非水星獨有的現象，而且行星本身並未真正倒退，這一切不過是從地球上觀察到的錯覺。專家對於水星逆行的現象有這樣的見解：「水星逆行帶來混亂，迫使我們離開熟悉的舒適圈，但同時也開啟了新的體驗與變化，這與好壞無關。」星座學指出，在水逆期間，保持積極且放鬆的心態是關鍵。如果在與朋友或同事溝通時出現分歧，嘗試後退一步，或者採取更包容的態度去面對。如果你在水逆期間遇到了些小挫折，也不必把所有問題都歸咎於水星逆行哦。

1. Mercury Retrograde [ˈmɜːrkjʊri ˌrɛtroʊˈɡreɪd] 水星逆行
   Many people blame Mercury Retrograde for their communication issues. 許多人將他們的溝通問題歸咎於水星逆行。

2. Misfortunes [ˈmɪsfɔːrtʃənz] 名詞（複數）不幸的意思
   She overcame many misfortunes to achieve her goals. 她克服了許多不幸來達成她的目標。

3. Optical illusion [ˈɑːptɪkəl ɪˈluːʒən] 名詞，視覺錯覺
   The artwork creates an optical illusion, making flat surfaces appear three-dimensional. 這件藝術作品創造了一種視覺錯

覺，使平面看起來像是三維的。

4. Attribute ['ætrɪˌbjuːt] 歸因於

He attributed his success to hard work and dedication. 他將自己的成功歸因於努力工作和奉獻。

Myopia | 近視度數怎麼說？

近視myopia [maɪˈoʊpi]

一種視力障礙，患者看遠處不清楚，但看近處清楚。近視的度數通常用屈光度diopters [ˈdaɪəp.tərz] 來表示。屈光度為負數表示近視，為正數表示遠視。I am nearsighted with -5.00 diopters in both my left and right eyes.或I have a myopia of -5.00 diopters in both eyes. 我有近視左右眼各500。

散光astigmatism [əˈstɪgməˌtɪzəm]

一種視力障礙，患者看任何距離的物體都會模糊。散光的度數通常也用屈光度來表示。散光的屈光度可以是正數也可以是負數。近視、散光的度數都是用diopters表示。近視度數以diopters表示，並且是負數。例如-5.00 diopters代表近視500度。散光可以是正數或負數，例如-1.00 diopters代表某種程度的散光，而+1.00 diopters也代表散光，但方向不同。I have astigmatism of -1.00 diopter in my left eye and -1.50 diopters in my right eye. 散光左眼100度，右眼150度。

問人家視力可以這樣表達

How is your vision?

How good is your eyesight?

How nearsighted are you?

What is your nearsightedness?

Nip in the bud 防患於未然

Nip in the bud這個片語直譯為「在發芽中掐斷」，意指在問題或狀況剛開始出現時就及時處理，以防它發展成更嚴重的問題。這個表達用於強調預防措施的重要性，旨在避免未來的麻煩或困難。通常用來描述對初期小問題的迅速和決定性的解決，以避免事態惡化。

閱讀「警方為防患於未然，春節假期間邀宴、尾牙、春酒活動多，為避免酒駕，提醒民眾將加強取締酒駕，不要以身試法」一文，一起來瞭解nip in the bud在文章中的應用：

With the Lunar New Year holiday approaching, festivities like banquets, year-end parties, and spring drinks are abundant. To nip the issue of drunk driving in the bud and prevent potential tragedies, the police are issuing a stern reminder to the public. They emphasize that enforcement against drunk driving will be intensified before and after the Spring Festival. The message is clear: do not test the law by drinking and driving. It's a proactive measure to ensure the safety and well-being of everyone during this celebratory season.

隨著農曆新年假期的來臨，宴會、尾牙、春酒等活動頻繁。為了防患於未然防止酒駕問題發生並避免潛在的悲劇，警方發出嚴正的提醒。強調春節前後將加強對酒駕的取締工作。訊息很清楚：不要因酒駕而以身試法。這是一項積極的措施，旨在確保在這個慶祝季節期間，每個人的安全與福祉。

Nip in the bud的應用例句

1. The manager decided to nip the conflict in the bud before it escalated into a bigger issue. 經理決定在衝突升級成更大問題之前就將其掐滅。

2. It's important to nip such bad habits in the bud to ensure they don't become ingrained. 重要的是要在這些壞習慣固化之前及時遏止它們。

3. The government took measures to nip the economic downturn in the bud. 政府採取措施在初期就遏制經濟衰退。

4. Teachers should take immediate action when they detect a tendency to cheat among students, to nip it in the bud. 發現學生有作弊的傾向時，老師應該立即採取措施，防止這種行為惡化。

5. Upon noticing signs of low morale among employees, the company immediately organized team-building activities to nip the problem in the bud. 公司在發現員工士氣低落的跡象時，立刻組織團隊組織活動，以防問題進一步發展。因此及時的預防措施可以避免問題的蔓延和加劇。

和Nip in the bud類似意涵的字詞片語

以下詞彙和片語在不同情境下都是被用來描述預防、避免、拖延或結束不希望發生的事件的策略。

1. Cut off at the pass：提前阻止。意思是指在問題發展到更嚴重階段之前阻止或攔截它。通常用於策略性地提前阻止某事發生。

   The teacher cut off the argument at the pass by separating the two students before the situation escalated. 老師通過在情況升級之前將兩個學生分開,提前阻止了爭論。

2. Squelch:指迅速壓制或結束(通常指聲音、言論或活動)。用於表達迅速結束或消除不需要或不希望的事物。

The principal squelched the rumors by addressing the entire school with the truth. 校長透過向全校講述真相,迅速平息了謠言。

3. Preempt:以先發制人的行動來防止或解決問題。在預見到可能的問題或挑戰時採取行動。

The company preempted potential legal issues by reviewing their policies in advance. 公司先發制人提前審查政策,預先防止了可能的法律問題。

4. Stall:拖延時間或進程,使發展暫時停止。用於暫時阻止事情進展,以獲得更多時間進行處理。

The negotiation team stalled the talks to get more time to consider the new proposal. 談判團隊拖延談判,以獲得更多時間考慮新提案。

5. Head off:提前阻止或避免(問題或困難)的發生。在問題發生之前採取措施避免它。

The quick response of the emergency team headed off a disaster. 快速反應小組的快速響應避免了一場災難。

A stitch in time saves nine. 小洞不補,大洞痛苦

A stitch in time saves nine和nip in the bud都強調了預防措施的重要性,意指在問題初期就進行處理可以避免後期更大的

麻煩或成本。不過,這兩個表達的著重點有些許不同。

A stitch in time saves nine傳達的是及時解決小問題可以避免未來需要更大規模修補的觀念,這句諺語通常用於強調修補或維修的及時性,以防小裂縫變成大洞。

nip in the bud則更直接地指在問題或行為剛開始形成時就將其消除,強調的是防止問題成長或擴大的必要性。

本篇說明了及時處理小問題a stitch in time saves nine和在問題萌芽時期就阻止其發展nip in the bud的重要性,儘管兩者都強調預防的價值,但應用的範疇和情境略有不同。

Nonplus | 不知所措

Nonplus ['nɑːnplʌs] 動詞，使困惑，使不知所措

Nonplussed是Nonplus的過去式和過去分詞，來看一篇對簡報時一片寂靜感到困惑時一文的應用：

When Emily presented her innovative idea at the meeting, she was nonplussed by the silence that followed. She had expected questions, maybe even some skepticism, but not this quiet contemplation. It was as if her colleagues were so taken aback by the novelty of her proposal that they were at a loss for words. This moment of silence, though initially unsettling, turned out to be a sign of deep consideration.

當艾米莉在會議上提出她的創新想法時，隨之而來的寂靜讓她感到困惑。她本以為會有問題，甚至可能有些懷疑，但沒有想到會是這樣的沉思靜默。就好像她的同事們被她提案的新穎性所震撼，以至於無言以對。這一刻的沉默，雖然起初令人不安，卻成為了深思的象徵。

1. Taken aback感到驚訝或困惑，通常因為意料之外的事情發生。如She was taken aback by the unexpected gift from her colleague.她對同事送的意外禮物感到驚訝。
2. At a loss for words不知道該說什麼。When he proposed, she was so surprised that she was at a loss for words.當他求婚時，她驚訝到說不出話來。

3. Unsettling形容詞。令人不安的，引起緊張或不舒服的感覺。The strange noise in the middle of the night was quite unsettling.半夜裡的奇怪聲音相當令人不安。

Nonpluss的英文例句及應用

1. The complex math problem nonplussed most of the students in the class. 複雜的數學問題讓班上大多數學生感到困惑。
2. She was completely nonplussed by his sudden decision to quit his job. 他突然決定辭職，讓她完全不知所措。
3. The unexpected question nonplussed the speaker during the interview. 那個意料之外的問題在面試中讓發言人感到困惑。
4. The lawyer's aggressive cross-examination nonplussed the witness. 律師的咄咄逼人的盤問讓證人感到不知所措。

與Nonplus同義的字詞或片語

1. Bewildered迷惑的，困惑的（形容詞）

   The complex instructions left him completely bewildered. 那些複雜的指示讓他完全迷惑不解。
2. Perplexed困惑的，不解的（形容詞）

   She was perplexed by the sudden change in his attitude. 他態度的突然改變讓她感到困惑。
3. Baffled困惑不解的，無法理解的（形容詞）

   The detective was baffled by the lack of evidence in the case. 偵探對於這個案件缺乏證據感到困惑。
4. Confounded困惑的，糊塗的（形容詞）

He was confounded by the complicated rules of the game. 他對這個遊戲複雜的規則感到困惑。

5. Flummoxed ['flʌməkst] 困惑的，擾亂的（形容詞）

The unexpected question flummoxed the candidate during the interview. 面試中的意料之外的問題讓應試者困惑不已。

6. Disconcerted 不安的，窘迫的（形容詞）

She was disconcerted by the sudden attention she received. 她對自己突然受到的注意感到不安。

7. Puzzled 迷惑的，困惑的（形容詞）

The child looked puzzled when he couldn't find his toy. 當那個孩子找不到他的玩具時，他看起來很困惑。

8. Stumped 困惑的，難倒的（形容詞）

The teacher's question stumped the entire class. 老師的問題讓全班學生都感到困惑。

9. Dumbfounded ['dʌm,faʊndɪd] 驚呆的，說不出話的（形容詞）

They were dumbfounded by the unexpected announcement. 他們對那個出乎意料的公告感到驚呆。

10. At a loss 不知所措，茫然（片語）

After the sudden change of plans, everyone was at a loss for what to do next. 在計劃突然改變後，大家都很茫然不知道接下來該做什麼。

Opprobrium | 譴責

Opprobrium公開譴責、恥辱或社會上的厭惡感

名詞，用來描述對某人或某事的強烈譴責或厭惡，通常是因為他們的行為或觀點違背了道德、社會規範或公衆的期望。

閱讀一則關於聯合國譴責北韓試射飛彈的短文，來瞭解這個字Opprobrium扮演的角色：

North Korea has once again violated relevant United Nations Security Council resolutions, posing a grave threat to international peace and stability. The Foreign Ministry strongly condemns this and reiterates its opprobrium. We call on North Korea to adhere to the relevant United Nations Security Council resolutions.

北韓再度違反了聯合國安理會相關決議，對國際和平與穩定構成嚴重威脅。外交部對此表示嚴正譴責，並再次要求北韓遵守聯合國安理會相關決議。

Opprobrium的應用實例

1. The politician faced widespread opprobrium after being caught in a corruption scandal. 這位政治人物因被捲入貪污醜聞後受到廣泛的譴責。

2. The company's decision to lay off thousands of employees without notice drew opprobrium from labor unions and the public.公司決定在沒有提前通知的情況下解僱成千上萬名

員工，引來了工會和民眾的譴責。

3. His offensive comments on social media led to a storm of opprobrium, with many people condemning his behavior. 他在社交媒體上的攻擊性的言論引發了一陣譴責風暴，許多人譴責他的行為。

Opprobrium的同義字詞、例句

1. Censure ['sɛnʃər] 譴責（名詞／動詞）

The public censure of the politician's unethical behavior was widespread. 對政治人物不道德行為的公開譴責在群眾間廣泛傳播。

2. Reproach [rɪ'proʊtʃ] 責備（名詞／動詞）

Her reproach for missing the important meeting was well-deserved. 她因缺席重要會議而受到的責備是理所當然的。

3. Disapproval不贊成（名詞）

The decision to cut funding for education met with widespread disapproval. 削減教育經費的決定面對到普遍的不贊成。

4. Vilify ['vɪlɪ,faɪ] 誹謗或詆毀（動詞），通常指的是惡意地評價或中傷某人或某事。

The tabloid newspaper is known for its tendency to vilify celebrities with baseless accusations. 這家小報慣用以毫無根據的指控來誹謗名人。

5. Castigate ['kæstɪgeɪt] 嚴厲指責或嚴厲批評（動詞），通常是因為某人的錯誤或不當行為。

The coach castigated the player for his unsportsmanlike

conduct on the field. 教練對球場上沒有運動家精神的球員進行了嚴厲的批評。

6. Denunciation [dɪ,naʊnsɪ'eɪʃn] 公開譴責或譴責（名詞），通常與正式的聲明或公告相關聯。

The denunciation of the dictator's human rights abuses came from various international organizations. 對獨裁者侵犯人權的譴責來自多個國際組織。

7. Execrate 痛恨或詛咒（動詞），通常表示對某人或某事的極度厭惡。

Many people execrate the war for its devastating impact on innocent civilians. 許多人對戰爭造成無辜平民衝擊深感厭惡。

8. Excoriate [ɛks'kɔːrieɪt] 嚴厲批評或斥責（動詞），通常針對某人的行爲或表現進行尖銳的批評。

The film critic excoriated the director for the lackluster screenplay and uninspired performances. 電影評論家對導演平淡的劇本和乏味的演出進行了嚴厲的批評。

9. Lambast ['læmbæst] 嚴厲指責或抨擊，通常是因爲某人的錯誤或不當行爲。像是新聞評論家對政治家的表現進行了嚴厲的抨擊。

The journalist lambasted the government's handling of the crisis as inadequate and poorly planned. 記者抨擊政府對危機的處理不足和計劃不周。

10. Upbraid [ʌp'breɪd] 公開譴責或責難，通常指的是以口頭方式對某人表達不滿或不滿。

She upbraided her friend for breaking the promise they had made. 她因朋友違背了他們的諾言而加以責難。

Parochial perspective
｜狹隘觀點

Parochial [pəˈroʊkiəl] 狹隘

形容詞，用來描述那些過分關注狹隘、局部事物，而忽略了更廣泛、開放的觀點或全球視野的人或事物。這個詞通常帶有貶義，指的是缺乏開放思維和文化多元性的態度。

"Parochial" is an adjective used to describe individuals or things that are overly concerned with narrow, local matters and overlook broader, more open-minded perspectives or a global outlook. This term often carries a negative connotation, indicating a lack of open-mindedness and cultural diversity.

Parochial的例句應用

1. His parochial perspective made it difficult for him to understand the differences between cultures, leading to challenges in international affairs. 他狹隘的觀點讓他難以理解不同文化之間的差異，因此在國際事務中遇到了困難。

2. The residents of that small town are almost indifferent to global issues, with their interests largely confined to their own community, demonstrating an extreme parochial attitude. 那個小鎮的居民對於全球議題幾乎不關心，他們的興趣主要限於自己的社區，顯示出了一種極度狹隘的態度。

3. Companies with a parochial mindset may miss out on opportunities in the international market because they cannot adapt to the needs of different cultures and markets. 僅具狹隘思維的企業可能會錯失在國際市場上的機會，因爲他們無法適應不同文化和市場的需求。

Parochial的同義字詞及例句應用

1. Narrow-minded（形容詞）狹隘的、心胸狹窄的

   His narrow-minded views on immigration hindered constructive discussion. 日他狹隘的移民觀點妨礙了建設性的討論。

2. Provincial（形容詞）鄉村的、地方性的

   Her provincial attitude prevented her from embracing diverse cultures. 她的地方性態度使她難以接納多樣的文化。

3. Insular（形容詞）島嶼的、與外界隔絕的

   Their insular mindset isolates them from global trends and innovations. 他們的島嶼思維使他們與全球趨勢和創新隔絕。

4. Myopic（形容詞）目光短淺的、缺乏遠見的

   His myopic approach to business strategy led to missed opportunities. 他對業務目光短淺的策略導致錯失機會。

這些同義詞都用來形容那些過分關注狹隘、局部事物而忽視更廣泛、開放的觀點或全球視野的人或事物。

Perspicacious｜敏銳

Perspicacious [ˌpɜrˌspɪˈkeɪʃəs]

形容詞，形容一個人具有敏銳的洞察力和理解力。這個詞彙源於拉丁語的perspicax，意味著透徹的或聰明的。一個perspicacious的人能夠快速而準確地理解複雜的情況，他們具有卓越的觀察力，能夠洞悉事情的本質。

"Perspicacious" is an adjective used to describe a person with keen insight and understanding. This word derives from the Latin "perspicax," meaning perceptive or clever. A perspicacious individual can quickly and accurately grasp complex situations, possessing outstanding observational skills to discern the essence of things.

閱讀一篇如何應用Perspicacious到文章中：

A perspicacious individual possesses a remarkable ability to comprehend intricate situations swiftly. This trait extends beyond mere insight; it encompasses an innate talent for discerning concealed patterns and subtle nuances. In professional contexts, a perspicacious leader can identify opportunities within adversity, making astute decisions. In personal relationships, a perspicacious friend offers guidance without the need for elaborate explanations. Overall, perspicacity proves an invaluable asset, augmenting one's capacity to navigate the complexities of life.

敏銳的個體擁有出色的能力，可以迅速理解複雜的情況。這種特點不僅僅是洞察力，還包括一種天生的才華，可以識別隱藏的模式和微妙的細微差異。在職業環境中，敏銳的領袖能夠在逆境中找到機會，做出明智的決策。在人際關係中，敏銳的朋友能夠提供指導，而無需繁瑣的解釋。總的來說，敏銳性是一項無價的資產，增強了個體應對生活複雜性的能力。

Perspicacious的例句及應用

1. Mary's perspicacious analysis of the market trends allowed her to make profitable investments. 瑪麗對市場趨勢的敏銳分析使得她能夠進行有利可圖的投資。

2. The detective's perspicacious deductions led to the swift resolution of the mysterious case. 這位偵探敏銳的推理致使神祕案件的快速解決。

3. With his perspicacious understanding of human behavior, John excelled in his career as a psychologist. 憑借他對人類行為的敏銳理解，約翰在心理學家職業中表現出色。

4. The perspicacious detective solved the case by noticing a small but crucial piece of evidence that everyone else had missed. 敏銳的偵探透過注意到一個微小但關鍵的證據，解開了這個案件，而其他人都忽略了。

Perspicacious的同義詞

1. Astute [əˈstuːt]形容詞，機敏的

   Her astute observations always reveal the heart of any

problem. 她敏銳的觀察總是能揭示問題的核心。

2. Sagacious [sə'geɪʃəs]形容詞，睿智的

The sagacious leader made decisions that benefited everyone. 這位睿智的領導者做出了對所有人都有益的決策。

3. Insightful ['ɪnsaɪtfl]形容詞，有洞察力的

Her insightful analysis provided a new perspective on the issue. 她富有洞察力的分析為這個問題提供了新視角。

4. Shrewd [ʃruːd]形容詞，精明的

He is known for his shrewd business tactics. 他以其精明的商業手腕而聞名。

5. Keen [kiːn]形容詞，敏銳的

She has a keen mind for details. 她對細節有敏銳的頭腦。

6. Acute [ə'kjuːt]形容詞，敏銳的

He has an acute sense of smell. 他有非常敏銳的嗅覺。

7. Perceptive [pər'sɛptɪv]形容詞，有洞察力的

Her perceptive comments were appreciated by all. 她富有洞察力的評論受到大家的讚賞。

8. Discerning [dɪ'sɜːrnɪŋ]形容詞，有辨識力的

A discerning reader can always tell when an author has not done their research. 一個有辨識力的讀者總能辨別出作者是否做足了研究。

9. Clear-sighted [ˌklɪr'saɪtɪd]形容詞，眼光清晰的

His clear-sighted approach to problem-solving is admirable. 他解決問題的清晰眼光令人欽佩。

10. Quick-witted [ˌkwɪk'wɪtɪd]形容詞，機智的

Her quick-witted response defused a tense situation. 她機智

的回應化解了一個緊張的局面。

Perspicacious、Agile和Adroit的比較

Perspicacious（敏銳的）、Agile（靈活的）和Adroit（熟練的）意思有所不同，它們表示不同的特質和能力。

Perspicacious（有洞察力的）指的是一個人能夠敏銳地觀察、理解和洞察事物的本質，通常用來形容一個人的智慧和洞察力。

She is perspicacious and can easily see through people's intentions. 她很有洞察力，能夠輕鬆洞悉別人的意圖。

Agile（靈活的）則表示一個人或事物能夠快速、靈活地適應變化、移動或執行任務，通常用來形容身體或思維的靈活性。

The gymnast's agile movements on the balance beam were impressive. 那名體操選手在平衡木上的靈活動作令人印象深刻。

Adroit（熟練的）則表示一個人具有熟練或巧妙的技巧，能夠靈活地應對各種情況。

His adroit handling of the difficult situation impressed everyone. 他巧妙地處理困難的情況讓所有人印象深刻。

超級比一比 | Phubbing vs Petextrians

當代社會中，手機的過度使用或在不當場合使用手機的現象日益普遍。新興詞彙如phub[fʌb]、phone zombie、smombi ['smɑːmbi]及Petextrian [pɛ'tɛkstrɪən] 均反映了人們對手機的高度依賴。雖然手機爲我們的生活帶來許多便利，但同時也容易讓人沉迷其中，而忽視現實世界的存在。

Phub

phone-snubbing的縮寫，意指在社交場合專注於手機，而忽略他人的行爲。可以被稱爲「低頭滑手機族」「手機冷落」或「手機冷落症」。Phubbing意思是忽視身邊的人，過度專注於手機。

1. During dinner, my brother was phubbing, completely ignoring our conversation. 吃晚餐時，我弟弟一直在低頭滑手機，完全不理會我們的對話。

2. I felt so isolated when my friends started phubbing at the party. 當我的朋友們在派對上開始當低頭族時，我覺得非常的孤單。

3. Phubbing during meetings is considered unprofessional behavior. 在會議中當低頭族被認爲是不專業的行爲。

Phone zombie

這一詞用來指稱那些在公共場合埋頭於手機，對周遭人事物毫不關心的人。

1. A phone zombie almost bumped into me on the sidewalk. 一個手機殭屍差點在人行道上撞到我。

2. The subway was full of phone zombies this morning. 今天早上地鐵裡滿是手機殭屍。

3. Being a phone zombie can be dangerous while crossing the street. 當手機殭屍穿越馬路時可能很危險。

Smombie（smartphone zombie）

由smartphone和zombie（殭屍）組合而成，形容那些使用智慧型手機時，對周圍環境毫無察覺的人。這些人常常低頭看手機，不顧交通、人群或其他障礙物，因此容易造成危險。該詞最早於2012年由英國心理學家Derek Thompson提出。隨著智慧型手機的廣泛普及，這一現象引發了社會廣泛關注，多國推出宣導活動，提醒人們避免成為Smombie。

1. Smombies often cause delays on busy sidewalks. 智慧手機殭屍經常在繁忙的人行道上造成延遲。

2. I nearly collided with a smombie who wasn't looking up from their phone. 我差點和一個沒有抬頭離開手機的智慧手機殭屍撞上。

3. Cities are now designing special lanes for smombies to walk safely. 城市正在設計專門的行人道讓智慧型手機殭屍安全行走。

Petextrian

由pedestrian 和text組合而成，指那些在走路時使用手機或其他電子設備的人。這一新造詞用來描述走路時分心的行人，這種行為可能導致交通事故或其他危險情況。

1. Petextrians often miss traffic signals, leading to dangerous situations. 邊走邊用手機的行人常常忽視交通號誌，導致危險。
2. The intersection is always crowded with petextrians during rush hour. 在尖峰時間，那個路口總是擠滿了邊走邊用手機的行人。
3. As a driver, it's hard to anticipate the movements of petextrians. 作為一名駕駛者，很難預測邊走邊用手機的行人的動作。

以上這些詞彙都反映了現代科技對日常行為的影響。

Prerogative｜特權

Prerogative是一個名詞，指的是某人的特權或特別權力，通常是根據地位、職位或權威而來的權力。這個詞通常用來描述高層管理者、政府官員或其他具有特殊權力的人所擁有的權利，這些權利可以超越一般人的權限，例如決策、掌握資源或做出重大決定。

關於現代社會厭惡特權的一篇英文短文，一起來閱讀看看Prerogative在文章中的應用：

In society, people often harbor disdain for the abuse of prerogative. When those in positions of power exploit their prerogatives, it leads to inequality and frustration among the populace. Such actions erode trust in institutions and sow the seeds of unrest. People yearn for fairness, where prerogatives are exercised judiciously for the greater good, rather than personal gain. It is imperative for leaders to recognize that with prerogative comes responsibility – a responsibility to serve the people and uphold justice. Only through a fair and equitable exercise of prerogative can a society truly thrive.

在社會中，人們常常對特權的濫用感到厭惡。當掌握權力的人濫用他們的特權時，這導致了社會的不平等，並引起了民眾的不滿。這樣的行為侵蝕了對機構的信任，並埋下了動盪的種子。人們渴望公平，希望特權被明智地行使，用於大眾的利益，而不是個人私利。領袖必須認識到，特權伴隨著責任–一種爲民眾服務並維護正義的責任。只有通過公平和公正的特權行使，社會才能眞正繁榮。」

Prerogative的例句

1. The CEO's prerogative allowed him to make the final decision on the merger. 總裁的特權允許他對公司合併事宜做出最終決定。

2. It is within the president's prerogative to pardon individuals convicted of certain crimes. 總統有權赦免被判犯有特定罪行的個人。

3. The mayor's prerogative as the city's leader gives her the authority to allocate the budget. 作爲市長，她擁有分配預算的權力，這是她的特權。

Prerogative同義字詞及應用

1. Authority權威、權力

   The manager has the authority to make decisions about the project. 經理有權力來決定該計畫的事宜。

2. Privilege特權

   Access to the VIP lounge is a privilege reserved for premium members. 進入貴賓休息室是獨家供高級會員享有的特權。

3. Entitlement權利

   Every citizen has the entitlement to free education. 每位公民都有享受免費教育的權利。

4. Discretion 審酌權

The judge used his discretion when sentencing the defendant.
法官在判處被告時行使了他的裁量權。

5. Privilege 特權

Being able to work from home is considered a privilege in
many companies. 在許多公司中，能夠在家工作被視為一
種特權。

6. Right 權利

Freedom of speech is a fundamental right in democratic
societies. 言論自由是民主社會中的一項基本權利。

7. Supremacy 至高無上

The king's supremacy was unquestioned during his reign. 國
王統治期間的至高無上地位毫無爭議。

8. Dominance 優勢

The company's dominance in the market has led to its success.
公司在市場上的優勢地位促成了它的成功。

上述的這些同義字詞和片語都描述了某人擁有的權力或特殊
地位，可以在特定情境下使用，以表示類似的概念。

Prudent | 謹慎

Prudent ['prudənt] 謹慎的

（形容詞）描述了一種謹慎和謹慎小心的特質。當我們說一個人是prudent時，我們指的是他們在做決策或行動時非常謹慎和明智，通常避免冒險或衝動。這種特質在財務管理、投資決策以及風險管理方面特別重要。

"Prudent" is an adjective that describes a quality of being cautious and careful. When we say someone is "prudent," we mean that they are very cautious and wise in their decision-making or actions, typically avoiding risks or impulsiveness. This trait is particularly important in financial management, investment decisions, and risk management.

來閱讀一篇有關「政府謹慎財政政策強化了國家財政韌性」的財經新聞短文，瞭解Prudent的應用：

In a recent financial development, the government's prudent fiscal policies have garnered praise from economists. Their careful management of public funds during uncertain economic times has proven to be effective in maintaining stability. By avoiding excessive spending and prioritizing essential investments, the government has ensured resilience in the face of economic challenges. This prudent approach to fiscal responsibility has resulted in increased confidence among investors and citizens alike, setting a positive course for the nation's financial future.

最近的財經消息顯示，政府<u>謹慎</u>的財政政策受到經濟學家的讚譽。在經濟不確定性時期，政府對公共資金的謹慎管理已被證明在維持穩定方面非常有效。通過避免過度支出並優先考慮重要投資，政府確保了在經濟挑戰面前的韌性。這種財政責任的<u>謹慎的</u>做法增強了投資者和市民的信心，爲國家的財政未來設定了積極的方向。

Prudent的例句及應用

1. She was prudent with her savings, always setting aside a portion of her income for emergencies. 她在儲蓄方面很謹慎，總是把一部分收入用於應急情況。

2. The CEO's prudent approach to expanding the business ensured its long-term stability and growth. CEO對擴展業務的謹慎方法確保了其長期穩定和增長。

3. It's prudent to conduct thorough research before making any major investment decisions. 在做出重大投資決策之前進行充分的研究是明智的。

Prudent的同義詞及實例

1. Cautious（謹慎的）指行動或決策時小心謹慎，以避免風險或錯誤

   She took a cautious approach to investing her savings. 她在投資儲蓄時採取謹慎的方法。

2. Sensible（明智的）指做事明智，考慮周全，不輕率

   It's sensible to wear a helmet while riding a bike for safety. 騎自行車時戴安全帽是明智的，爲了安全考慮。

3. Judicious（明智的）指明智地考慮選擇，以獲得最佳結果

The manager made a judicious decision to invest in research and development. 經理明智地決定投資於研發領域。

4. Pragmatic（實際的）指重視實際和有效的解決辦法，不受理論或理想主義的干擾。

Her pragmatic approach to problem-solving led to practical solutions. 她實際的解決問題方法導致了實際的解決方案。

5. Wary（謹慎的）指對可能的危險或問題保持警覺，謹慎小心

He was wary of strangers approaching him in the dark alley. 他對陌生人在黑暗的小巷中接近保持警覺。

6. Conservative（保守的）指傾向於選擇保守或傳統方法，不願冒險。

The company followed a conservative investment strategy to minimize risks. 公司採用保守的投資策略，以降低風險。

7. Circumspect（謹慎的）指在做決策或行動之前仔細考慮和評估情況

He was circumspect in his response, choosing his words carefully. 他在回應時謹慎小心，仔細挑選措辭。

8. Scrupulous ['skru:pjʊləs]（一絲不苟的、有道德原則的）

He is known for his scrupulous attention to detail in his work. 他以工作中對細節的一絲不苟而聞名。

Prudent、Punctilious、Meticulous的使用情境及差異

雖然這三個詞彙都與謹慎和細心有關，但它們的意思有些微區別，Prudent強調的是在行動和決策上的智慧和謹慎，Punctilious更強調對細節的嚴謹和規範，而Meticulous則強調在執行任務時的極端細致和精確。這幾個同義詞都描述了謹慎和明智的特質，通常表現為在行動和決策中考慮風險、避免冒險或衝動，以達到更好的結果。

Prudent ['prudənt] 謹慎的，明智的
當形容一個人在做決定時謹慎且考慮周全。It is prudent to save money for unexpected expenses. 為了未預見的開支儲蓄是明智的。

Punctilious [pʌŋk'tɪliəs] 一絲不苟的，謹慎細心的
描述一個人對細節非常謹慎且遵循嚴格規範。Her punctilious attention to detail made her an excellent editor. 她對細節的一絲不苟使她成為一位出色的編輯。

Meticulous [mə'tɪkjələs] 極其仔細的，小心翼翼的
用來形容一個人非常注重細節，做事非常小心謹慎。He is meticulous in his work, ensuring every aspect is perfect. 他在工作中小心翼翼，確保每個環節都完美。

超級比一比 | Prudery vs Rectitude

Prudery偽善

Prudery ['pru:dəri] 名詞，指一種偽善或過度謹慎的行為，特別是在性方面。這個詞通常用來形容那些過分拘謹、害羞或過於保守的人，他們可能對性話題感到極度不舒服，甚至會因此感到害羞或過度反應。英文例句的應用：

1. Her prudery made it difficult for her to have an open and honest conversation about relationships. 她的偽善使她難以就相關問題進行坦白和誠實的對話。

2. His prudery prevented him from attending the art exhibit, fearing it might contain explicit content. 他的偽善讓他不敢參加藝術展覽，擔心其中可能包含露骨的內容。

3. The prudery of the older generation often clashes with the more liberal views of the younger generation. 老一輩的過度謹慎的觀念常常與年輕一代自由的觀點發生衝突。

Rectitude正直

Rectitude ['rɛktɪtu:d] 名詞，表示正直和誠實的品質。這個詞通常用來形容那些秉持高度道德標準，遵守道義規範的人，他們在行為和決策中嚴格遵循正確的原則。正直和Rectitude可以建立信任並維護組織的道德價值觀。英文示例如下：

1. Her rectitude and unwavering commitment to honesty earned her the respect of her colleagues. 她的正直和對誠實的堅定承諾贏得了同事們的尊敬。

2. The company's success can be attributed to the rectitude of its founder, who always made ethical decisions. 公司的成功應歸功於其創辦人的正直，他始終做出道德正確的決策。

3. In times of crisis, a leader's rectitude and moral compass become even more crucial in guiding the team's actions. 在危機時刻，領導者的正直和道德帶領團隊的行動變得更加關鍵。

閱讀In the Name of AI: Rectitude and Prudery 「以AI之名的正直與偽善」的文章之中如何運用這兩個單字：

The future development of AI holds infinite possibilities, but it also comes with moral and ethical issues. Some individuals harness AI in the pursuit of what they deem as justice, yet do so by profiting from warfare, a manifestation of Prudery. On the other hand, some are accused of Prudery for participating in AI development. For instance, figures like the billionaire Elon Musk have joined scientists and industry experts in urging a halt to the development of powerful AI systems, awaiting the establishment of relevant regulatory standards, demonstrating Rectitude.

However, while vocal about the dangers of AI on one hand, these same individuals invest substantial resources in AI development for electric vehicles, a phenomenon that can be seen as Prudery. Experts also remind us that the world of tomorrow requires leaders of Rectitude who can make judicious use of AI to prevent its abuse. The line between Rectitude and Prudery in the application of AI may be a fine one, but the key lies in how we choose to wield the power of AI.

以AI之名的正直與僞善-AI的未來發展具有無限可能性，但也伴隨著道德和倫理議題。一些人借助AI來實現所謂的正義，卻是透過戰爭賺取財富，這種行爲可說是Prudery（僞善）的一種體現。另一方面，有人因爲參與AI發展而被指責爲僞善，例如，像富豪馬斯克曾與科學家和業內人士一同呼籲暫停開發強大的AI系統，等待相關監管規範的制定，這種舉動則展現了Rectitude（正直）的特質。

然而質疑一方面大聲疾呼AI危險的同時，卻在爲電動車的AI開發投入大量資金，這種現象相當具有僞善性質。

也有專家也提醒我們，未來世界需要正直的領導者，他們能夠適切地使用AI，避免濫用。AI的應用界限可能只在一線之隔，關鍵在於如何選擇以AI之名行事。

Prudery的同義詞

1. Hypocrisy（僞善）指表面虛僞，言行不一致，不眞誠的行爲

   Her hypocrisy was evident when she criticized others for the same behavior she engaged in. 她的僞善在於批評同樣的行爲時變得明顯。

2. Sanctimoniousness（假裝聖潔）指一種假裝虔誠或道德高尚的行爲

   His sanctimoniousness was evident in his constant moralizing and holier-than-thou attitude. 他的假聖潔在他不斷的道德講道和高人一等的態度中變得明顯。

Rectitude（正直）的同義詞

1. Integrity（誠實正直）指堅守道德原則，誠實正直的品質

His integrity and honesty in business dealings earned him a reputation for trustworthiness. 他在商業交易中的誠實正直爲他贏得了值得信賴的聲譽。

2. Virtue（品德、端正行爲）指道德上的優點或品質

Her virtuous actions and kindness towards others set a positive example for everyone. 她端正的行爲和對他人的善心爲大家樹立了一個正面的榜樣。

Pulchritude｜內外兼具的美人

Pulchritude是一個不太常見的詞彙，它指的是美麗和吸引力。這個詞通常用來描述人或事物的外貌之美。Pulchritude是名詞，形容詞是Pulchritudinous，表示美麗和吸引力的特質。

"Pulchritude" is a rarely used word that signifies beauty and allure. This term is typically employed to describe the physical beauty of a person or object. "Pulchritude" is a noun that represents the qualities of beauty and attractiveness.

這個詞彙帶有一種深沉的美感，它不僅僅是外表的吸引力，更包括了內在的迷人特質，可以說是內外兼具。當我們用這個詞來形容一位人士時，我們不僅在談論他們的外貌，還在強調他們的獨特魅力和吸引力，這種吸引力往往來自於他們的自信、智慧和個性的魅力。Pulchritude也是一個提醒著我們，美不僅僅是外表，更是一種內在的魅力，一種吸引人的氛圍。

來看一篇有關內外兼修的美女，是怎麼運用Pulchritude：

I once had the privilege of witnessing the epitome of pulchritude. She was a vision of beauty, both inside and out. Her exterior was graced with delicate features, a radiant smile, and eyes that sparkled like stars. Yet, it was her inner pulchritude that truly mesmerized me. Her kindness and grace were as captivating as her appearance, radiating warmth and sincerity. In her presence, one couldn't help but be drawn to the harmony of her character and physical allure. She was a living testament to the profound beauty that can exist within a person, leaving an indelible impression on all who crossed her path.

有一次，我有幸目睹了美的典範。她是一位內外兼具的美人。她的外貌充滿著精緻的特徵，一個燦爛的微笑，和閃爍如星星的眼睛。然而，真正讓我著迷的是她內在的美。她的善良和優雅像她的外表一樣令人著迷，散發出溫暖和真誠。在她的陪伴下，人們無法不被她性格和外貌的和諧所吸引。她活生生地證明了一個人內在的深刻美麗，對所有遇到她的人都留下了難以磨滅的印象。」

Pulchritude的應用及示例

1. Her pulchritude was evident to everyone at the party. 她的美麗顯而易見，每個參加派對的人都能感受到。

2. The pulchritude of the sunset over the ocean left us speechless. 夕陽在海上的美麗讓我們目瞪口呆。

3. His pulchritude went beyond his physical appearance; it was his charisma and kindness that truly made him attractive. 他的吸引力不僅僅體現在外表，更在於他的魅力和善良，這才使他真正具有吸引力。

Pulchritude的同義詞及例句

1. Beauty美麗（名詞）

Her beauty was undeniable, captivating everyone who saw her. 她的美麗不容置疑，吸引了所有看到她的人。

2. Attractiveness吸引力（名詞）

His attractiveness went beyond his looks; his charisma was magnetic. 他的吸引力不僅僅體現在外表，他的魅力是磁性的。

3. Loveliness可愛（名詞）

The loveliness of the countryside was breathtaking. 鄉村的可愛令人驚嘆。

4. Glamour迷人（名詞）

The glamour of the movie star captivated the audience. 電影明星的迷人吸引了觀眾。

5. Elegance優雅（名詞）

Her elegance in dress and demeanor was admired by everyone. 她在服裝和舉止上的優雅受到了所有人的欽佩。

除了詞性不同之外，有一些相似之處，但它們在意思和使用情境上仍有些許不同，Pulchritude指美貌過人，而Exquisite則更側重於事物的高度精緻和品質，也可以用來形容人的優雅。Suave則用來形容人的文雅和風度。

Pulchritude美麗／美貌（名詞）

指的是美麗和吸引力，通常用來描述人或事物的外貌之美
Her pulchritude was evident to everyone in the room. 她的美麗對房間裡的每個人都是明顯的。

Pulchritudinous 貌美的（形容詞）

Her pulchritudinous appearance drew the attention of everyone in the room. 她美麗的外表吸引了房間裡每個人的注意。

Exquisite 精緻（形容詞）

表示非常精緻、優雅和精細，通常用於形容事物的品質或工藝或是美女高尚、優雅的美

The craftsmanship on the antique vase was exquisite. 古董花瓶的製作工藝很精緻。

Her exquisite beauty, with its delicate features and graceful demeanor, left everyone in awe. 她的優雅美麗，擁有精緻的容貌和優雅的風度，讓每個人都讚嘆不已。

Suave 溫文儒雅（形容詞）

指人的舉止或風格充滿文雅和自信，通常用來形容一個人的社交技巧和風度。

His suave demeanor made him a charming host at the party. 他的溫文儒雅的舉止使他成為派對上迷人的主人。

超級比一比 | Purloin vs Peculate

Purloin與Peculate都是竊取，都涉及到不當取得財物的行為，但在用法和涵義上有些不同。讓我們來分別討論這兩個詞：

Purloin [pɜːrˈlɔɪn]

動詞，指的是祕密或偷偷地偷竊或盜取某物，通常是在未被察覺的情況下。這個詞強調偷竊行為的隱祕性和不正當性。

Peculate[pekjuleɪt]

動詞，意指以不正當的方式占有或挪用他人的財產，尤其是在管理或負責的職位上。這個詞通常用來描述官員、管理人員或信任職位濫用權力，挪用公款或財產的情況。

在法律上，Purloin與Peculate都是指取得財物的不當行為，但它們有不同的使用情境。Purloin更偏向於描述私下的、小規模的偷竊行為，如偷竊店內的商品或他人的財物，而peculate則涉及更嚴重的行為，通常是指在管理或官職中濫用權力，挪用公共資金或資產。儘管如此，這兩個詞都表達了不誠實和不道德的行為，都應受到法律制裁。

In legal terms, both "purloin" and "peculate" refer to the improper acquisition of property, but they have different contexts of use. "Purloin" leans towards describing private, small-scale theft, such as stealing goods from a store or someone else's property, while "peculate" involves more serious misconduct, typically referring to the misuse of power in a managerial or official capacity to embezzle public funds or assets. Nonetheless, both words convey dishonest and unethical behavior and should be subject to legal consequences. 說明：Embezzle[ɛmˈbɛzəl] 動詞，挪用公款、盜用之意，如The accountant was found to have embezzled thousands of dollars from the company. 這位會計被發現從公司挪用了數千美元。

Purloin的例句

1. He managed to purloin some office supplies from the supply room without anyone noticing. 他成功地偷竊了一些辦公用品，而沒有人注意到。

2. The art thief attempted to purloin a priceless painting from the museum, but security caught him in the act. 這名藝術賊試圖從博物館偷竊一幅無價的畫作，但保全在行動中抓到了他。

3. He managed to purloin confidential documents from the company's safe, jeopardizing the security of sensitive information. 他成功地竊取了公司保險箱中的機密文件，危及了敏感訊息的安全。

4. He was caught trying to purloin his colleague's ideas and present them as his own during the team meeting. 在團隊會議期間，他試圖竊取同事的想法，然後以自己的名義提出，但被發現了。

Peculate例句

1. The treasurer was found to have peculated a significant amount of funds from the organization's accounts over the years. 財務主管被發現多年來從組織的帳戶挪用了大筆資金。

2. The corrupt official was found guilty of peculating public funds for his personal use, leading to his arrest and prosecution. 那名貪污的官員因挪用公款供個人使用而被判有罪,導致他被逮捕和起訴。

3. The company's accountant was suspected of peculating funds, so a thorough audit was conducted to uncover any financial irregularities. 公司的會計被懷疑挪用資金,因此進行了徹底的審計以揭示任何財務不正常情況。

Peculate通常用在竊用/挪用財產,Purloin是偷取、竊取,下面文章中有關官員挪用公款的文章,一起來看看這兩個單字的意思上有沒有不同:

In a small town, there was a scandal when it was discovered that the mayor had attempted to peculate public funds for a luxurious vacation. The town's residents were shocked by the audacity of the mayor's plan. However, before he could fully execute his scheme, an anonymous whistleblower leaked the information to the press. This act of exposing the corruption prevented the mayor from successfully peculating the funds. It was a reminder that even those in positions of power could not easily purloin public resources for personal gain.

在一個小鎮上，一個醜聞曝光了，當時發現市長企圖挪用公共資金度過奢華的假期。該鎮的居民對市長計劃的大膽程度感到震驚。然而，在他完全實施計劃之前，一名匿名告密者將信息洩漏給了新聞界。這一揭露貪污行爲的舉動阻止了市長成功挪用資金。這提醒人們，即使是擁有權力的人也不能輕易地爲了個人利益而竊取公共資源。

說明：1. Audacity（名詞）大膽、魄力、冒失，通常指在挑戰或冒險方面的勇氣或無畏精神。例：He had the audacity to propose this bold plan. 他有足夠的勇氣來提出這個大膽的計劃。2. Whistleblower名詞，吹哨者或是揭發者，通常指那些揭示組織或政府不法行爲或不正當活動的人。

Purloin同義詞

1. Steal（動詞）意指偷竊或盜取財物

   He attempted to steal the priceless artwork from the museum. 他試圖偷竊博物館的無價藝術品。

2. Filch（動詞）意指祕密偷竊或偷偷取走

   She managed to filch some cookies from the jar without anyone noticing. 她成功地偷竊了罐子中的一些餅乾，而沒有人注意到。

3. Pilfer ['pɪl.fər]（動詞）偷竊（尤指小物件或不貴重的東西）

   Someone has been pilfering from the petty cash. 有人一直從小額現金中偷竊。

Peculate同義詞

1. Embezzle（動詞）意指挪用資金或財產，通常是指官員或管理人員的不當行爲

   The corrupt official was found guilty of embezzling funds from the organization. 貪污的官員被判有罪，因爲他從機構中挪用資金。

2. Misappropriate（動詞）意指不當使用或挪用資產或資金

   He was accused of misappropriating company funds for his personal expenses. 他被指控挪用公司資金支付個人開支。

3. Defraud（動詞）意指欺詐性地取得財物或資金

   The scam artist defrauded investors out of millions of dollars. 詐騙藝術家欺詐投資者數百萬美元。

4. Defalcate ['diː.fæl.keɪt]（動詞）挪用，盜用（尤指公款）

   The accountant was found to have defalcated thousands of dollars from the company. 查出那位會計從公司挪用了數千美元。

Quiddity | 本質

Quiddity [ˈkwɪdəti] 名詞，指某事物的本質或特性，通常用於討論一個事物最重要、最本質的特點。這個詞通常在哲學、文學或討論某事物的特性時使用，以強調該事物最核心的特質。

Quiddity, as a noun, refers to the inherent nature or essence of something, often used in philosophical or deep discussions to delve into the fundamental characteristics that define an object, concept, or idea. It represents the core, unique quality that makes something what it truly is, setting it apart from other things. Philosophers and thinkers frequently explore the quiddity of various subjects, seeking to understand their fundamental truths and significance in our understanding of the world.

本質，作爲一個名詞，指的是某事物的固有本質或特性，通常在哲學或深入探討中使用，以深入探究定義一個物體、概念或想法的基本特徵。它代表了使某物眞正成爲自己的核心、獨特品質，使其與其他事物區分開來。哲學家和思想家經常探討各種主題的實質，力求理解它們的基本眞理以及它們對我們對世界的理解的重要性。

Quiddity英文應用的實例

1. The quiddity of a good detective is their keen ability to observe details others might miss. 一位優秀的偵探的本質在於他們敏銳的觀察力，可能被其他人忽略。

2. In literature, the quiddity of a character often defines their role in the story. 在文學中，一個角色的本質通常決定了他們在故事中的角色。

3. Philosophers have debated the quiddity of human existence for centuries. 哲學家們幾世紀來一直在討論人類存在的本質。

Quiddity同義詞及運用

1. Essence（本質）名詞

   The essence of a good story is its ability to captivate the reader. 一個好的故事本質在於它能夠吸引讀者。

2. Nature（性質）名詞

   The nature of a diamond is its exceptional hardness and brilliance. 鑽石的性質在於它卓越的硬度和光澤。

3. Core（核心）名詞

   Teamwork is at the core of any successful project. 團隊合作是任何專案成功的關鍵。

4. Substance（實質）名詞

   The substance of her argument was based on thorough research. 她的論點實質上基於深入的研究。

5. Inherent Quality（固有品質）名詞

The inherent quality of the old house was its charm and character. 這座老房子的本質特色是它的迷人和個性。

Quiddity和 Quintessence

這兩個單字雖然意涵上有一定的相似性，但意思有些不同，在使用情境上也有區別。Quiddity強調某事物的本質，而Quintessence更強調某事物的代表性或典型特點。

Quiddity

指的是某事物的本質或固有特性，通常用於深入討論事物的核心特點，強調該事物最重要、最本質的特點。常見於哲學或深入分析時，用來討論某事物的真正本質。

The quiddity of human existence has been a subject of philosophical debate for centuries. 人類存在的本質已經成為幾個世紀以來哲學辯論的主題。

Quintessence

指的是某事物的最純粹、最完美、或最典型的表現，通常用來形容某物代表或具有最典型特點的特性。常用於讚美或形容某物具有出色的特性，並代表著最高水準。

Her kindness and compassion were the quintessence of human goodness. 她的善良和同情是人類善良的典範。

超級比一比 | Remiss vs Amiss

Remiss疏忽、不盡責任的（形容詞）

通常用來形容某人或某事因疏忽或不盡責而未能履行其責任或義務。

1. He was remiss in completing his assignments, leading to poor grades. 他對功課的完善有所疏忽，導致成績不佳。
2. The manager was remiss in checking the safety procedures, and that led to an accident. 經理在安全檢查程序方面有所疏忽，導致了一次事故。
3. It would be remiss of me not to thank you for your hard work. 如果我不感謝你的辛勤工作，那就是我的疏忽。

Amiss錯誤的、不正確的（形容詞或副詞）

通常用來指出某事物或情況不正確、有問題或不如預期。

1. There is something amiss with this computer; it keeps freezing. 這臺電腦有些問題，它一直凍結。
2. Her suspicion that something was amiss turned out to be true when she discovered the missing money. 她對些事感到不對勁的懷疑在她發現錢不見時被證實了。
3. The recipe went amiss when I accidentally added salt instead of sugar. 我不小心加了鹽而不是糖，食譜出了錯。

來閱讀一篇「避免疏忽犯錯」的短文

When a person is <u>remiss</u> in their work, failing to detect issues, it's a serious mistake. This negligence can lead to things going awry, much like abrasive sandpaper damaging a surface. However, at times, people may display temerity, ignoring risks due to overconfidence. Such reckless behavior can be as soporific as a hypnotic, lulling them into a dangerous unconscious state until problems arise. Hence, in handling matters, we should exercise caution, avoiding abrasive actions, and not being <u>amiss</u> by disregarding potential issues due to undue confidence.

當一個人在執行工作時<u>疏忽大意</u>，未能發現問題，這就是他犯了一個嚴重的<u>錯誤</u>。這種疏忽可能會導致事情出現問題，正如粗糙的沙紙可能會損壞表面一樣。然而，有時候，人們可能會因爲過於膽大妄爲，而忽視了風險。這種魯莽行爲有時像催眠劑一樣，讓人陷入危險的無意識狀態，直到事情出現問題。因此，在處理事情時，我們應該謹愼小心，避免粗糙的舉動，並不要因過度自信而忽略了可能的錯誤。

說明：1. Go awry：出現錯誤、不按計劃進行、走上歧途，通常用於描述計劃、事情或情況未能如預期地發展，出現問題或走上錯誤的方向。2. Soporific：（形容詞）催眠的、令人昏昏欲睡的，通常用來形容能引起睡意或無聊的事物，例如一部沉悶的電影或一場無趣的演講。3. Hypnotic：（形容詞）催眠的、引人入勝的、迷人的，通常用來形容某物或某事能引起注意力集中、迷住人或讓人感到陶醉的特質。4. Temerity：（名詞）魯莽、膽大妄爲、無畏，用來描述某人敢於冒險或做出大膽行爲，有時帶有一定的冒險精神或無謀。5. Abrasive：粗糙的、刺激的、令人不悅的，用來形容某物或某人的行爲，可能引起摩擦、不適或不快，就像砂紙表面一樣。

Remiss的同義詞

1. Negligent（形容詞）不注意的、疏忽的

   She was negligent in her duties, causing problems for the team. 她在職責上疏忽大意，對團隊造成了問題。

2. Careless（形容詞）粗心的、馬虎的

   His careless attitude led to mistakes in the project. 他的粗心態度導致了項目中的錯誤。

Amiss的同義詞

1. Wrong（形容詞）錯誤的、不正確的

   There's something wrong with this machine; it's not functioning properly. 這臺機器有問題，它無法正常運行。

2. Incorrect（形容詞）不正確的、錯誤的

   The information in the report is incorrect and needs to be revised. 報告中的信息是錯誤的，需要修訂。

Reprehensible │ 應受譴責

Reprehensible應受譴責的，形容詞。常用來描述那些道德上或倫理上不應被接受的行為或行為者。一個被認為reprehensible的行為可能引起公憤，並可能產生負面的後果，例如法律處罰或社會排斥。

"Reprehensible," which means "deserving of blame," is an adjective. This word is often used to describe actions or individuals that are morally or ethically unacceptable. Behavior considered "reprehensible" can provoke public outrage and may lead to negative consequences such as legal penalties or social ostracism.

來看一則最近發生事件，有關臺北建案因施工不愼導致鄰近房屋倒塌、下陷，事件受到政府及各界譴責的一則新聞，順便來學一下「應受譴責」的運用：

A construction company in Taipei City, Taiwan, was involved in a construction project in the Zhongshan District of Taipei City. Unfortunately, due to their negligence, nearby residential buildings tilted and sank. However, following the incident, the company's management did not promptly appear to explain the situation to the public, nor did they engage in communication and coordination regarding the housing issues of the affected residents. City government officials consider this irresponsible behavior by the construction company to be reprehensible. They believe that such an attitude warrants severe penalties. As a result, the Taipei City government intends to pursue legal means to address the situation.

臺北市某建設公司在臺北市中山區進行工程建設時出現了不慎事件，導致附近的民宅傾斜下陷。然而，事故發生後，該公司的管理層未能及時出面解釋情況給公衆，也未就受影響的居民住房問題進行溝通和協調。市政府官員認爲這種建設公司的不負責任態度是應受譴責的。他們認爲這樣的態度應該受到嚴厲懲罰。因此，臺北市政府打算採取法律手段解決這個問題。

Reprehensible的實例及應用

1. His reprehensible actions, such as cheating on the exam, led to his expulsion from school. 他應受譴責的行爲，例如考試作弊，導致他被學校開除。

2. The company's reprehensible business practices, including fraud, resulted in a major scandal. 該公司應受譴責的商業行爲，包括詐騙，導致了一場重大醜聞。

3. Engaging in discriminatory behavior based on race is morally reprehensible and goes against our values of equality. 基於種族進行歧視性的行爲在道德上是應受譴責的，並違背了我們的平等價值觀。

Reprehensible的同義字詞及應用

1. Blameworthy應受譴責的，形容詞。描述行爲或情況應該受到譴責或指責

His blameworthy actions resulted in financial losses for many. 他應受譴責的行為導致許多人財務損失。

2. Repugnant[rɪ'pʌgnənt] 令人厭惡的，形容詞。形容引起強烈反感或厭惡的事物或行為

   His behavior at the party was repugnant, and it offended many guests. 他在派對上的行為令人厭惡，冒犯了許多賓客。

3. Censurable應受譴責的，形容詞。指責或譴責不當的行為

   The censurable actions of the company's executives led to a public outcry. 公司高層的應受譴責行為引起了公眾的強烈抗議。

4. Disgraceful可恥的，形容詞。形容令人感到恥辱或羞愧的行為

   His disgraceful conduct during the event embarrassed everyone present. 他在活動期間的可恥行為讓在場的每個人感到尷尬。

這些同義詞都用來表示某事或某人的行為應受譴責，但它們可能在語境中帶有稍微不同的語感或強調。

比較關於責罵的單字

Reprehensible和Reproachable、Scoldable、Rebukable、Reprimandable意涵上相似但有些微差異。它們都用來表示某事或某人的行為是值得指責或譴責的，但在語感上略有不同。

Reproachable值得責難的

也表示行為值得責難,但它可能稍微更寬泛,可能不一定涉及到極端的道德問題,但仍然不被認為是正確或合適的。

Her rudeness at the meeting was reproachable, and it created a negative atmosphere. 她在會議上的粗魯行為是值得責難的,並且造成了負面氛圍。

Scoldable值得責罵的

通常指的是某人的行為或言談可以被他人責罵或指責,但未必涉及到嚴重的道德或倫理問題。這個詞通常用來形容比較輕微或一般的責難行為。

His rudeness during the meeting was scoldable, and his colleagues criticized him for it. 他在會議期間的粗魯行為是值得責罵的,他的同事批評了他。

Rebukable值得指責的

指的是行為或言談可以被指責或責難,但也不一定涉及到極端的道德問題。這個詞的語感較中性,可用於各種情境。

Her repeated lateness to work was rebukable, and her supervisor had a talk with her about punctuality. 她屢次遲到上班是值得指責的,她的主管與她談了談守時性。

Reprimandable值得受到譴責的

指的是某事或某人的行為或言論可能需要受到指責或批評,但未必是道德上的錯誤。強調了一種可以接受的批評或指責。

Reprehensible｜應受譴責

His behavior at the meeting was reprimandable because he interrupted others frequently. 他在會議上的行爲值得受到譴責，因爲他經常打斷別人。

Reprehensible應受譴責的
通常更強調行爲的嚴重性，可能涉及到更嚴重的道德或倫理問題，或者引起更強烈的譴責感。
The embezzlement of company funds is reprehensible, and it will lead to legal consequences. 挪用公司資金是應受譴責的行爲，將導致法律後果。

Reproachable、Scoldable和Rebukable用於比較輕微的責難行爲，而Reprimandable則表示言行值得譴責或批評，但Reprehensible更強調行爲的嚴重性和道德問題。

Safeguard Human Rights：
The Pillars of Justice
捍衛人權：正義的支柱

在閱讀以下文章前先來看一下美國人身自由重要權利的說明及一些文章中的重要單字：

1. Right to legal counsel合法法律代理權：指任何被指控犯罪的人都有權獲得合法的法律代理人，以協助他們應對刑事訴訟或法律問題。

2. Miranda rules [mɪˈrændə] 米蘭達規則：一個法律原則，要求在對嫌犯進行拘留和盤問時，警方必須在特定情況下向其宣讀其權利，包括保持沉默和請求律師的權利。

3. Habeas corpus [ˈheɪbɪəs] [ˈkɔːrpəs] 人身保護令：是一種法律程序，允許被拘留的人向法院提交申請，要求法院檢查他們是否合法拘留，並釋放他們，如果他們的拘留是非法的。

4. Due process of law法律正當程序：一個法律原則，確保在法律程序中，每個人都受到平等和公平的對待，並且有機會為自己辯護。

本文重要單字說明

1. Paramount至關重要的（形容詞）
2. Cornerstone基石、基礎（名詞）
3. Derive from源自、來自於（動詞片語）通常用於解釋一個事物或概念的根本來源或原因。

4. Self-indiscriminate自我指控的、自白的（形容詞）

5. Retain保留、保持（動詞）

6. Undue government interference不當的政府干預

7. Judicial impartiality司法中立性

8. Double jeopardy重覆起訴

9. Undue infringement不當的侵犯

10. Collectively集體地、共同地（副詞）

11. Indispensable不可或缺的、必不可少的（形容詞）

In today's society, the protection of human rights is regarded as a paramount challenge. Ensuring that individuals are treated fairly within the legal system and that justice is upheld is a fundamental principle of a just society. In this article, we will explore four crucial legal principles that support the protection of human rights: the "Right to Legal Counsel," the "Miranda Rule," "Due Process," and "Habeas Corpus." These principles are the cornerstones of preserving human dignity and rights and are essential in any legal system.

在當今社會中，保護人權被視爲一個極端重要的挑戰。確保個人在法律體系中受到公平對待，並維護正義，是一個公正社會的基本原則。在本文中，我們將探討支持保護人權的四個至關重要的法律原則：「法律援助權利」、「米蘭達規則」、「正當程序」和「人身保護令」。這些原則是保護人類尊嚴和權利的基石，無論在哪個法律體系中都是至關重要的。

Right to Legal Counsel法律援助權利

The "Right to Legal Counsel" is a cornerstone of human rights protection. It ensures that defendants in criminal proceedings have the right to hire an attorney to represent them, whether through their own means or provided by the government as legal aid. This right ensures that individuals are not left defenseless within the legal system, promoting legal fairness and equality.

「法律援助權利」是保護人權的基石之一。它確保在刑事訴訟中的被告有權聘請律師代表他們，無論是通過自己的資金還是由政府提供法律援助。這個權利確保個人不會在法律體系中無助無援，促進法律公平和平等。

Miranda Rule米蘭達規則

The "Miranda Rule" derives from a 1966 United States Supreme Court decision in "Miranda v. Arizona." This principle guarantees that, in criminal proceedings, when law enforcement detains a suspect and conducts an interrogation, they must inform the suspect of their rights. The core elements of the Miranda Rule include:

「米蘭達規則」源自1966年美國最高法院在「米蘭達訴亞利桑那州案」中的判決。這一原則確保在刑事訴訟中，當執法機構拘留嫌疑人並進行審問時，他們必須告知嫌疑人他們的權利。米蘭達規則的核心要點包括：

①The right to remain silent: A detained individual has the right to remain silent and is not obligated to provide any self-incriminating statements to the police.

①保持沉默的權利：被拘留的個人有權保持沉默，不必對警方提供任何自白陳述。

②The right to an attorney: A detained individual has the right to retain an attorney and to have legal representation present during questioning.

②聘請律師的權利：被拘留的個人有權聘請律師，並在審問期間有法律代理人在場。

③Warnings: Law enforcement must inform the detained individual that anything they say can be used against them in court and that if they cannot afford an attorney, one will be provided for them.

③警告：執法機構必須告知被拘留的個人，他們所說的一切都可以在法庭上作爲證據，並且如果他們無法負擔律師費用，將提供公共辯護律師。

The purpose of the Miranda Rule is to protect the self-incrimination rights of the detained, ensuring that they are aware of their rights during police interrogations and can exercise them appropriately. 米蘭達規則的目的是保護被拘留者的自我指控權，確保他們在警方審問期間知曉自己的權利，並能夠在法律代理的陪同下適當地行使這些權利。

Due Process正當程序

"Due Process" is a legal principle that ensures individuals are treated fairly and lawfully within the legal process and are protected from undue government interference. In the context of personal freedom, this principle includes various crucial rights, such as the right to be informed of charges, the right to a public trial, the right to a fair hearing, judicial impartiality, protection against double jeopardy, the prohibition of unlawful searches and seizures, and the right to legal representation. Due Process guarantees the fairness of the judicial process and safeguards defendants from unjust criminal charges and punishments.

「正當程序」是一個法律原則，確保個人在法律程序中受到公平和合法的對待，並免受政府的不當干預。在個人自由的背景下，這一原則包括多個重要方面的權利，如被告的通知權、公開審判權、公平聆訊權、法官的中立性、防止重覆起訴的權利、禁止非法搜索和扣押，以及法律代理的權利。正當程序保證了司法過程的公平性，並保護被告免受不公平的刑事指控和處罰。

Habeas Corpus人身保護令

"Habeas Corpus" is an essential legal principle aimed at protecting an individual's personal freedom from undue infringement. This principle allows individuals who are detained or imprisoned to petition a court to review the legality of their detention, including examining the presence of proper arrest warrants or detention justifications. Habeas Corpus ensures that the government adheres to legal procedures when detaining individuals, prevents unlawful detention, and ensures the respect of detainees' rights.

「人身保護令」是一個重要的法律原則，旨在保護個人的人身自由免受不當侵犯。這一原則允許被拘留或監禁的個人向法院申請審查其拘留的合法性，包括檢查是否存在適當的逮捕令或拘留理由。人身保護令確保政府在拘留個人時遵守法律程序，防止非法拘留，並確保尊重被拘留者的權利。

In the United States legal system, there are also other prominent personal freedom rights, including freedom of speech, religious freedom, freedom of the press, the right to assemble and demonstrate, limitations on searches and seizures, and the right to bear arms, among others. These rights are safeguarded by the United States Constitution and related laws, providing critical protections for individual liberties.

在美國的法律體系中，還有其他一些重要的人身自由權利，包括言論自由、宗教自由、新聞自由、集會和示威權利、對搜索和扣押的限制以及擁有和攜帶武器的權利，等等。這些權利在美國憲法和相關法律中得到確保，為個人自由提供了關鍵保障。

In conclusion, these legal principles and personal freedom rights collectively form a robust foundation for safeguarding human rights. They ensure that individuals are treated fairly within the legal system and protect them from undue interference and deprivation. In a just society, these principles and rights are indispensable, representing core values of the rule of law and human rights. We should cherish and uphold these principles to ensure that everyone can enjoy fairness and justice.

總之，這些法律原則和人身自由權利共同構成了捍衛人權的堅實基礎。它們確保個人在法律體系中受到公平對待，並保護他們免受不當的干預和剝奪。在一個公正的社會中，這些原則和權利是不可或缺的，代表了法治和人權的核心價值。我們應該珍惜並捍衛這些原則，以確保每個人都能享有公平正義。

Sass ｜ 挑釁、頂嘴

Sass [sæs]

作為名詞時，則指無禮的言語或態度。

作為動詞時sass意指無禮地回話或回嘴，挑釁之意。

Don't sass me則是在告誡或警告對方不要以無禮的頂嘴或嘴硬的方式說話。說這句話的人通常是覺得對方的言語方式太過無禮或挑釁，希望對方改正態度,以更有禮貌和尊重的方式說話。像是Don't sass me, kid. I'm not in the mood. 小子別頂嘴，我現在沒心情。

來看一下Sass在「網紅找碴爆發衝突」一文的應用：

Media details a conflict between live streamer Toyz and YouTuber Chao Ge at Chao Ge's restaurant. The polemic began over food quality and escalated into a physical altercation, resulting in Toyz's hospitalization. Chao Ge was arrested for assault. The conflict was triggered by an exchange regarding nationality. Some netizens condemn Chao Ge's violent reaction, while others blame Toyz for sassing and deserving the outcome for 5nitpicking. 媒體報導直播主Toyz與YouTuber超哥之間的衝突引發關注。事件起因是對超哥餐廳醋飯品質的爭議，再因言語交鋒最終演變成肢體衝突，導致Toyz受傷並住院。超哥被警方以傷害罪逮捕。有網友譴責超哥的暴力反應，也有酸民指責Toyz挑釁，被認為找碴被打活該。

1. Polemic [pəˈlɛmɪk] 爭端，用來描述激烈的或爭議性的爭論

   His latest book has caused quite a polemic among scholars. 他最近的書在學者間引起了激烈的爭論。

2. Altercation [ˌæl.təˈkeɪ.ʃən] 指口頭爭吵或衝突

   The two politicians were involved in a heated altercation during the debate. 這兩位政治家在辯論中發生了激烈的爭吵。

3. Netizens [ˈnɛt.ɪ.zən]

   Netizens expressed their opinions on the new policy through social media. 網民透過社交媒體對新政策表達了他們的看法。

4. Sassing [ˈsæs.ɪŋ] 口出狂言、無禮的回話

   The student was reprimanded for sassing the teacher. 這名學生因對老師出言不遜而受到斥責。

5. Nitpicking [ˈnɪt.pɪk.ɪŋ] 吹毛求疵，找碴之意

   Instead of appreciating the overall effort, he wasted time nitpicking. 他沒有欣賞整體努力，反而浪費時間吹毛求疵。

Sass的例句應用

1. Don't you dare sass me, young lady! 別對我無禮，小姐！

2. I don't tolerate that kind of sassing in my classroom. 我不允許課堂上有那種挑釁的行為。

3. She always has a sassy comeback ready whenever someone tries to insult her. 每當有人想侮辱她的時候,她都會馬上提出無禮的回應。

Sass的同義詞及應用

1. Talk back（片語）頂嘴，回嘴

   The student got in trouble for talking back to the teacher. 那名學生因為對老師頂嘴而遭到處罰。

2. Lip（名詞）原本是嘴唇的意思，也可當作無禮的話，頂嘴

   He got a detention for giving the teacher lip during class. 他因為上課時對老師頂嘴而被留校察看。

3. Mouth off（片語）粗魯、放肆地說話

   He is always mouthing off to his parents and getting into trouble. 他總是對父母放肆地說話，並因此惹上麻煩。

Scalper｜黃牛

Scalper黃牛、Be snapped in no time秒殺、Ticket touting黃牛行為、Ticket scalping搶票，這些詞彙通常與票券轉售有關，尤其是針對音樂會、體育比賽或劇院表演等活動的門票。

Scalper黃牛

這是指那些購買活動票券後，為了賺取利潤而以高於原價轉售的人。在許多地區，這種做法可能是非法的。

Fans are often advised not to buy tickets from scalpers due to the risk of fraud. 粉絲們經常被建議不要向黃牛購票，因為存在欺詐風險。

Be snapped up in no time 秒殺

形容某件事物（如門票）非常受歡迎，一上市就迅速被購買一空。這種情況常見於熱門活動的門票，進而創造轉售市場。

Baseball fans need to act fast, as the championship game tickets will be snapped up in no time once they go on sale, missing the chance to witness this historic moment would be a regret. 棒球迷手腳要快，冠軍賽的票一開賣將會立即被搶購一空，錯過見證這歷史時刻的機會將會成為遺憾。

「秒殺」還可以這樣表達Be gone in a flash╱Be snapped up in no time╱Flash Sale or Instant Sellout：

1. The tickets for the Taylor Swift concert were snapped up in no time, so I had to buy from a scalper. Taylor Swift的演唱會門票馬上就被搶光了，所以我只好從黃牛那裡買。

2. The tickets for the Ed Sheeran concert were gone in a flash, so I couldn't get any. Ed Sheeran的演唱會門票一轉眼就沒了，所以我沒買到。

3. The new smartphone model was an instant sellout, disappearing within seconds of release. 手機一推出就秒殺，幾秒鐘內銷售一空。

4. During the flash sale, prices were so low that products sold out immediately. 在秒殺銷售期間，價格低廉，產品立刻售罄。

Ticket touting黃牛行爲

指的是以高於面值的價格非法銷售活動票券的行爲。

1. Ticket touts often sell tickets at much higher prices outside the venue. 黃牛經常在場地外以高很多的價格銷售門票。

2. Many events now use electronic tickets to combat ticket touting. 許多活動現在使用電子票以打擊黃牛。

Scalping Tickets╱Ticket Scalping搶票行爲

指搶票購買後再以高價轉售票券的行爲。通常這些票券是從正規渠道（如票務網站）購得，然後在黑市或通過其他非正式渠道以更高的價格出售，從中賺取差價。

1. Many fans were disappointed because ticket scalping led to sold-out concerts. 許多粉絲因為搶票行為導致演唱會門票售罄而感到失望。

2. The artist criticized ticket scalping, saying it prevents real fans from attending shows. 這位藝術家批評搶票行為，表示它阻止了真正的粉絲參加演出。

搶票（Scalping Tickets）的英文，可以加上illegal（非法）或unethical（不道德）等形容詞，來強調這種行為的負面性。
Many fans were disappointed because illegal ticket scalping led to sold-out concerts.

搶票和黃牛行為在世界各地都存在，並引起了人們的反感，就禁止或限制搶票和黃牛行為《文化創意產業發展法》規定，非供自用，購買運輸、遊樂票券而轉售圖利者，處票面金額定價10至50倍罰鍰。搶票和黃牛行為對消費者和市場都造成了負面影響。搶票行為除了會使門票價格上漲，扭曲了市場價格Distorted market prices，讓消費者的權益受到侵害。

超級比一比｜Scrappy vs Eristic

Scrappy

一詞有多個含義，具體的意思可能因上下文而異，有「鬥志旺盛的」正面的意思，也有負面「好鬥的」意思，另外還有「不連貫的」意思。

鬥志旺盛的Positive Meaning

表示一個人充滿決心、毅力和積極性，通常在面對困難或挑戰時仍然堅定不移。通常用於描述某人在不斷努力克服困難或實現目標時，表現出堅韌和積極性。

1. Despite facing numerous setbacks, she remained scrappy and determined to succeed. 儘管面臨了眾多挫折，她仍然充滿鬥志，決心成功。

2. The scrappy boxer never gave up, even when he was clearly the underdog. 這位好鬥的拳擊手從不放棄，即使明顯處於劣勢。

3. His scrappy attitude and relentless work ethic earned him the promotion. 他的好鬥態度和不懈的工作道德使他獲得了晉升。

好鬥的Negative Meaning

表示一個人或動物容易生氣，願意與他人或其他動物爭鬥或發生衝突。通常用於描述具有攻擊性或好鬥特質的個體。

1. The scrappy dog aggressively barked at any stranger who approached the house. 那隻好鬥的狗對任何接近房子的陌生人都會有攻擊性地吠叫。

2. Their scrappy rivalry led to frequent arguments and conflicts in the workplace. 他們之間的好鬥競爭導致了工作場所經常爭吵和衝突。

3. He has a scrappy nature, often getting into fights over minor disagreements. 他性格好鬥，經常因小爭論而發生爭吵。

不連續的Discontinuous

表示某物或某過程存在間斷或不連貫的特點。通常用於描述事物或情況中出現的斷裂或不連貫性。

1. The scrappy road was full of potholes, making the drive uncomfortable. 那條坎坷的道路上充滿了坑洞，讓駕車不舒適。

2. His scrappy speech lacked coherence, jumping from one topic to another. 他的演講不連貫，話題跳來跳去，缺乏連貫性。

3. The project progress has been scrappy, with frequent delays and interruptions. 專案進展不順，經常出現延誤和中斷。

Eristic

用來形容一種好辯論或爭論的特性，通常伴隨著挑釁和爭辯的傾向。這個詞有時帶有貶義，因為指的是追求爭論而非解決問題的人。例如，某人可能被形容為Eristic，因為他喜歡在社交場合挑起爭論，而不是建設性地參與討論。

eristic的英文示例

1. Their eristic behavior at the family gathering turned a peaceful dinner into a heated argument. 他們在家庭聚會上的好辯行為將一頓平靜的晚餐變成了激烈的爭論。

2. Instead of offering solutions, he often resorts to eristic tactics to undermine his colleagues' ideas.他經常不提供解決方案，而是採用好辯的策略來瓦解同事的想法。

Scrappy vs. Eristic

Scappy指出於追求某種目標或立場的熱情，通常用於形容「個人特質」。She's a scrappy debater, always willing to defend her opinions vigorously. 她是個好鬥的辯論者，總是樂意堅決地捍衛她的觀點。

Eristic強調「爭辯的技巧」，通常指的是一種愛辯論、引發爭議或採用反駁的方法。這個詞可能帶有貶義，說明某人可能經常使用矛盾或不誠實的辯論手法。His eristic style of arguing often frustrated those who sought genuine discussions. 他那種爭辯的風格常常讓那些希望進行真正討論的人感到沮喪。

也就是說，Scappy強調個人的好鬥精神及態度，Eristic則更關注好辯論或好爭辯的方式和技巧，有時可能帶有貶義的意味。

In a scrappy debate competition, participants often employ eristic tactics to win arguments. Scrappy individuals are known for their tenacity and determination, which can be both admirable and challenging. Eristic behavior, on the other hand, involves engaging in heated and argumentative discussions without seeking common ground.

以積極的態度參加辯論比賽，常使用爭辯性策略，試圖贏得爭論。鬥志旺盛的人以其堅持不懈和毅力而聞名，這既令人欽佩，也有挑戰性。另一方面，辯論的行為涉及參與激烈和爭論性的討論，而不是尋求共同立場。

看完上文的短文，對Scrappy、Eristic有深層的瞭解了嗎？

Shtick │ 獨特風格

Shtick [ʃtɪk] 噱頭、招式、技巧

這個字讓世界變得有趣、多元，也常常是成爲一個人的「風格」。它通常用來指喜劇演員的獨特風格或噱頭，也就是一個人的識別度。Shtick可以是任何東西，從身體動作到口頭禪到經常出現的笑話。它是讓人與眾不同和可識別的東西。著名的shtick例子像卓別林的墨鏡、鬍鬚和雪茄；麥克傑克遜的舞步及嗓音。

來看一下Shtick在形容總統候選人的風格短文中的應用：

Each Taiwanese presidential candidate has their own unique shtick that appeals to and garners support from voters. For instance, Lai Ching-te: a political self-discipline, refusing to accept compromises in gray areas, stubbornly sticking to what's good. Ko Wen-je: speaks his mind and doesn't play by the book, attracting young, centrist voters and some latent KMT supporters. Hou You-yi: iron-fisted governance with a background in the police force. Terry Gou: a business tycoon with successful cross-strait wealth accumulation experience, likely appealing to voters seeking economic growth. All these are identifiable "styles" covered by their shtick.

臺灣總統候選人有也各自「獨特風格」Schtick足以讓選民青睞及支持，像是賴清德：政治上的自律，不接受灰色地帶的妥協，擇善固執；柯文哲：快人快語，不按牌理出牌，吸引年輕中間選民及一些隱性的國民黨支持者；侯友宜：鐵腕施政，有警界背景；郭台銘：商業強人，有在兩岸成功致富的經驗，可能吸引一些追求經濟發展的選民。這些都是Schtick涵蓋的可資識別的「風格」。

Shtick的實例應用

1. His comedic shtick involves a lot of physical humor. 他的喜劇風格包括大量的肢體幽默。

2. The musician's shtick is to combine classical and electronic music. 這位音樂家的特色是將古典和現代音樂結合。

3. She is known for her shtick of impersonating famous celebrities. 她以模仿著名名人的特點。

4. The chef's shtick is to infuse traditional dishes with modern flavors. 這位廚師的特點是將傳統菜肴注入現代風味。

5. The comedian's shtick is a mix of observational humor and witty one-liners. 喜劇演員的幽默風格結合了觀察生活中的幽默和機智的俏皮話。

Shtick可以用來描述一個人所知的「特定技能」或「才能」，即使它不是喜劇性質的。例如，一個籃球運動員以他的招牌過人動作而聞名，或一個歌手以他獨特的音域而聞名。

Shtick通常指好事，使你在人群中脫穎而出並變得有趣、特別而難忘。但是，Shtick被過度的操弄，若過度依賴，仍會造成預測和無聊反效果。在具體應用時的語境中，像是銷售人員會使用Shtick來說服客戶購買產品；政治人物會使用Schtick來贏得選民青睞；小朋友也可以使用Schtick來獲得父母、師長及同學的關注。

與Shtick相近的同義詞

1. Gimmick [ˈɡɪmɪk]名詞，一種為了吸引注意、娛樂或達到特定目的而使用的獨特方法

   The magician's gimmick was so clever that the audience couldn't figure out how he did the trick. 那位魔術師的噱頭非常巧妙，觀眾都無法猜出他是如何做到那個戲法的。

2. Antic [ˈæn.tɪk]名詞，滑稽的、古怪的或奇特的行為

   The clown's antics made all the children laugh. 小丑的滑稽動作讓所有小孩都笑了。

3. Quirk [kwɜːrk]名詞，一種獨特的、個人特有的行為或習慣

   Her quirk of always wearing a hat regardless of the weather was well-known among her friends. 她不論天氣如何都要戴帽子的怪癖在她的朋友中是眾所周知的。

4. Trait [treɪt]名詞，特徵

   Her most notable trait is her unwavering optimism. 最顯著的特徵是她那不屈不撓的樂觀。

5. Idiosyncrasy [ˌɪdioʊˈsɪŋkrəsi]名詞，習性

   One of his idiosyncrasies is that he always writes in green ink. 他的一個習性是他總是用綠色墨水寫字。

6. Peculiarity [pɪˌkjuːliˈærəti]名詞，特性

Her peculiarities make her stand out in a crowd. 她的特性讓她在人群中脫穎而出。

7. Foible [ˈfɔɪbl] 小缺點、怪癖

His only foible is his lack of punctuality. 他唯一的小缺點是不守時。

8. Eccentricity [ˌɛksɛnˈtrɪsɪti] 名詞，怪異

His eccentricity is well known in the artistic community. 他的怪異在藝術界是眾所周知的。

9. Mannerism [ˈmænərɪzəm] 名詞，矯揉造作的行為

His speech is full of mannerisms that make him unique. 他的講話中充滿了獨特的矯揉造作行為。

Sedentary | 久坐

Sedentary ['sedn,teri] 久坐的，形容詞。常用來描述那些長時間坐在辦公桌前或螢幕前的人，缺乏運動的生活方式。久坐的生活方式可能導致健康問題，如肥胖和心臟疾病。要避免久坐，我們應該每隔一段時間站起來活動一下。

"Sedentary," which means "sitting for extended periods," is an adjective. This word is often used to describe individuals who spend prolonged hours sitting at their desks or in front of screens, leading a lifestyle lacking physical activity. A sedentary lifestyle can result in health issues such as obesity and heart disease. To avoid prolonged sitting, it is advisable to get up and move around periodically.

Sedentary的應用及例句

1. I have a sedentary job that requires me to sit at a computer for eight hours a day. 我有一份久坐的工作，每天需要在電腦前坐八個小時。

2. Sedentary activities like binge-watching TV shows can be detrimental to your health if not balanced with exercise. 像連續觀看電視劇這樣的久坐活動，如果不與運動相平衡，可能對你的健康有害。

3. To combat the sedentary lifestyle, I've started taking short walks during my breaks at work. 為了對抗久坐的生活方式，我已經開始在工作休息時間散步一下了。

Sedentary的同義詞及運用

1. Inactive不活躍的，形容詞。用來形容缺乏運動或行動的狀態

   His inactive lifestyle led to weight gain. 他不活躍的生活方式導致體重增加。

2. Idle閒置的、無所事事的，形容詞。描述沒有工作或活動的狀態

   During the weekend, he preferred to be idle and relax at home. 週末時，他寧願無所事事的在家放鬆。

3. Deskbound緊守辦公桌的，形容詞。形容那些長時間坐在辦公桌前的人

   Many office workers have a deskbound lifestyle, which can lead to health problems. 許多上班族有緊守辦公桌的生活方式，這可能導致健康問題。

4. Lethargic [ləˈθɑːrdʒɪk] 無精打采的，形容詞。形容人感到缺乏活力或精神不振的狀態

   After a long flight, I felt lethargic and needed some rest. 長途飛行後，我感到無精打采，需要休息一下。

Sinecure │ 高薪閒差

Sinecure ['saɪnɪkjʊr] 名詞，是閒職或閒差的意思。一個有趣的單字，它通常用來指代一個輕鬆且無需付出多少努力的職位或工作。這種職位通常有高薪水，但工作內容卻相對簡單。這些工作可能需要一些基本的監督或出席會議，但通常並不需要太多的實際工作。這種情況下，人們經常用Sinecure來形容這種輕鬆的職位，而其他人可能會感到不公平，因為他們必須付出更多的辛勞。

"Sinecure" is an interesting word that is often used to refer to a position or job that is easy and requires little effort. These positions typically come with high salaries, but the job duties are relatively simple. They may involve some basic supervision or attending meetings, but generally do not require much actual work. In such cases, people often use "sinecure" to describe these cushy positions, while others may feel it's unfair because they have to put in more effort.

一篇短文描述年輕人嚮往的高薪閒差一篇短文的分析，並來了解Sinecure如何在文中運用：

Young people today often aspire to secure a sinecure, a position that offers high pay and minimal effort. They seek careers where they can enjoy the perks of a comfortable lifestyle without the burden of strenuous work. This desire for sinecures is driven by a desire for work-life balance and financial stability. However, it's essential to strike a balance between ambition and meaningful contributions to society. While sinecures may seem appealing, they may not provide the sense of fulfillment that comes from challenging and purposeful work.

年輕人今天通常渴望著找到一份閒差sinecure，一個既能提供高薪又要求最少努力的職位。他們追求能夠享受舒適生活方式的職業，而不必背負繁重的工作壓力。對閒差的渴望源於對工作與生活平衡和財務穩定的渴望。然而，在野心和對社會的有意義貢獻之間需要取得平衡。儘管閒差可能看似吸引人，但它們可能無法提供來自具有挑戰性和有意義工作的滿足感。」

說明：Perk是一個俚語詞，通常指的是特殊福利、額外好處或附加待遇。這些待遇通常是公司或組織提供給員工或成員的，以增加他們的工作滿意度或提供額外的價值。一些常見的例子包括公司提供的免費午餐、健身房會籍、靈活的工作時間、或者是其他福利待遇。Perk也可以指一個人或事物的特點或特色，使其在某方面更加吸引人或特別。這個詞通常用來描述某種額外的好處或特殊的優勢。

Sinecure的例句應用

1. The CEO's job was more of a sinecure than actual work, as most of the day-to-day operations were handled by the senior management team. CEO的工作更像是一個閒差，因為大部分日常運營由高階管理團隊負責。

2. His appointment as the head of the committee seemed like a

sinecure, as he rarely had to make any decisions. 他被任命爲委員會主席似乎是一個閒職，因爲他幾乎不需要做出任何決定。

3. Many employees were frustrated with the perceived sinecures given to certain individuals in the company while they had to work long hours to meet deadlines. 許多員工對公司中某些人被認爲是閒差感到挫折，自己卻爲了趕上截止期限而必須加班工作。

Sinecure相關的同義字詞片語及應用

1. Cushy Job：舒適的工作

He landed a cushy job at a tech company where he barely had to work overtime. 他在一家科技公司找到了一份舒適的工作，幾乎不用加班。（註：Cushy舒適的、輕鬆的，形容詞。用來形容一個工作或情境很輕鬆、無壓力的，通常指工作較爲輕鬆且令人感到舒適。）

2. Plum Position：優越的職位

She was offered a plum position as the head of marketing, with an attractive salary package. 她被提供了一個優越的市場部主管職位，附帶有吸引人的薪資待遇。

3. Sweetspot Job：最佳職位

Finding the sweetspot job that combines passion and a good income is a dream for many. 找到結合熱情和高收入的最佳職位對許多人來說都是一個夢想。

4. Easy Street：中文意思是輕鬆的道路（通向成功或幸福）

He thought that getting a degree would put him on easy street, but he soon realized it required hard work. 他認爲獲得學位會讓他走上輕鬆的道路,但他很快就意識到這需要努力工作。

5. Gravy Train:容易獲得成功或財富的途徑

Some people believe that investing in cryptocurrencies is a quick ticket to the gravy train, but it can be risky. 有些人認爲投資加密貨幣是通往財富的快捷途徑,但這可能具有風險。

6. Snap Job:輕鬆的工作

After years of hard work, he finally found a snap job that allowed him to enjoy life more. 經過多年的努力,他終於找到了一份輕鬆的工作,讓他能夠更多地享受生活。

7. Plush Position舒適的職位

Landing a plush position in a prestigious law firm was her ultimate career goal. 在一家著名的律師事務所找到一個舒適的職位是她的最終職業目標。(註:Plush豪華的、舒適的,形容詞。用來形容東西或地方非常舒適、豪華,通常指具有高級感或高品質的設計和設施。)

8. Golden Opportunity黃金機會

Joining the startup at its early stage proved to be a golden opportunity for him, as the company later became highly successful. 加入新創公司是對他來說一個黃金機會,因爲該公司後來非常成功。

超級比一比｜Slip of tongue vs Off-the-cuff remarks vs Ad hockery

「口誤」是人類語言的一種常見現象，尤其選舉的時候常有政治人物口誤引發議論，口誤雖然沒有重大的影響，但卻可以反映出人類的心理和行為。例如，有些人經常說錯話、用錯字，則這可能反映出他們的注意力不集中、記憶力衰退或是反應出內心世界。

這讓我想到歷史上一個著名口誤，第一個登陸月球的太空人阿姆斯壯Neil Armstrong他原本在月球打算說That's one small step for a man, one giant leap for mankind.（這是個人的一小步，但卻是全人類的一大步），但他實際上說的是That's one small step for man, one giant leap for mankind. 遺漏了 "a" 。這個a導致了一些理解上的紊亂（究竟要指個人的一小步？還是人類的一小步？）有些人認為Armstrong是口誤，但有人卻因只是在傳輸中音訊問題。無論Armstrong實際說了什麼，他的成就仍然是人類歷史上最偉大的時刻之一。

英文中的口誤表達意思相近，但不完全相同

1. Slip of the tongue口誤：指不經意間說錯話，通常是由於疏忽或無意的誤發音
2. Off-the-cuff remarks即興發言：指未經準備或即興的發

言，可能未經深思熟慮

3. Misstatement誤述：指不正確或錯誤的陳述，可能是故意或非故意的

4. Verbal blunder言語失誤：指在說話過程中的錯誤，通常是不小心的

5. Faux pas失態：在社交或公共場合不合適或失禮的言行

6. Gaffe失言：在社交或公共場合的明顯錯誤或失誤

7. Freudian slip佛洛伊德口誤：通常指無意間透露出真實想法的言語失誤

8. Verbal misstep言語錯誤

「口誤」相關在英文句子中的應用

1. Slip of the tongue口誤

   In his speech, the politician meant to commend the staff's hard work but instead, due to a slip of the tongue, he accidentally thanked them for their "hardly working". 在他的演講中，這位政治家原本想讚揚工作人員的辛勤工作，但由於一時口誤，他不小心感謝了他們的「幾乎沒在工作」。

2. Off-the-cuff remarks即興發言

   Her off-the-cuff remarks about company policy during the interview were surprisingly candid. 她在面試中對公司政策的即興發言出奇地坦率。

3. Misstatement誤述

   The CEO's misstatement about the product's capabilities led to confusion among customers. CEO對產品能力的誤述導致顧客感到困惑。

4. Verbal blunder言語誤失

His verbal blunder during the speech caused embarrassment among his supporters. 他在演講中的言語失誤讓支持者感到尷尬。

5. Faux pas [ˌfoʊ ˈpɑː] 言行失當

The host made a faux pas when he asked the guest about her age. 主人在問客人年齡時犯了一個失言。

Wearing jeans to the formal event was a major faux pas. 在正式場合穿牛仔褲是一個重大的失態。

6. Gaffe [gæf] 失言

The politician's gaffe during the debate was widely criticized in the media. 政治家在辯論中的失言在媒體中受到廣泛批評。

這裡要說明ad hockery的用法及意思。經常口誤的原因之一是即興脫稿演出，Ad hockery可以理解為臨時拼湊或即興處理的方式。這通常用來形容在缺乏計劃或結構的情況下，用一種即興、隨機拼湊的方式解決問題或應對挑戰。和上述Off-the-cuff remarks（即興發言）指未經準備或即興的發言，可能未經深思熟慮，ad hockery比較強調事務處理上的即興，和口語的即興使用情境及解釋方式不同。

"Ad hockery" refers to an approach or solution that is improvised, makeshift, or cobbled together without much planning or structure. It's often used in a somewhat critical way to describe a situation where things are being handled in a disorganized, reactive manner rather than through careful planning and consideration.

Ad hockery在句子中的應用

1. The company's approach to problem-solving was often criticized as ad hockery, lacking in strategic thinking. 這家公司解決問題的方法常被批評爲即興式處理，缺乏戰略思維。

2. In the face of the crisis, their ad hockery led to more confusion than solutions. 面對危機，他們即興處理的做法導致了更多的混亂而非方案的解決。

3. The project's progress was hindered by constant ad hockery, with no clear long-term strategy. 該計劃的進展因不斷的即興應對而受阻，缺乏明確的長期策略。

4. Due to the lack of formal procedures, the team resorted to ad hockery to meet the deadline. 由於缺乏正式程序，團隊不得不採用臨時拼湊處理的方法來趕上截止日期。

Slake │ 滿足你的渴望

Slake是一個動詞，意思是「滿足」或「解渴」。這個詞通常用來描述對渴望或需求的滿足，或者消除某種欲望的過程。"Slake" is a verb, and its Chinese meaning is滿足or解渴。This word is commonly used to describe the satisfaction of desires or needs or the process of quenching a particular craving.

閱讀一篇文章有關蘋果iPhone 15發布新機的主題報導「Wanderlust」，準備滿足所有果粉的慾望，及slake在文中的應用：

The theme "iPhone 15 Launch: Wonderlust" embodies Apple's aspirations and pursuit for their new iPhone. "Wonderlust" combines "Wonder" and "Lust," suggesting that Apple aims to slake users' desires with astonishing features and experiences through the new iPhone 15. This term encapsulates Apple's commitment to slaking the tech enthusiasts' cravings, delivering innovative marvels and fulfilling their expectations during the launch event.

主題「iPhone 15發布會：Wonderlust」象徵著蘋果對於新iPhone 的期望和追求。Wonderlust結合了Wonder（驚奇）和Lust（渴望），暗示著蘋果希望透過新iPhone 15來滿足使用者的渴望，提供令人驚奇的功能和體驗。展現了蘋果致力於滿足科技愛好者的渴求，在發布會上呈現創新的奇蹟，滿足他們的期望。

說明：1. Embody體現：表示將某個觀念、特質、或思想具體化或體現在具體事物中，使之具體表現出來。2. Encapsulate包含：表示將多個元素或概念包含或總結在一個簡潔的形式或描述中，以便更清晰地傳達信息。舉例來說，像是一個簡短的報告可能encapsulates一個長期研究的主要發現，將其總結成一個簡明的陳述，以方便理解和分享。

Slake運用實例

1. After a long hike in the scorching sun, a cold glass of water can slake your thirst like nothing else. 在烈日下長途跋涉之後，一杯冰冷的水無與倫比地滿足了你的口渴。

2. She tried to slake her curiosity about the mysterious old book by finally opening it and reading its pages. 她試圖透過打開這本神祕的古書並閱讀其中的內容，來滿足她對它的好奇心。

3. The delicious meal at the restaurant was enough to slake our hunger and leave us completely satisfied. 餐廳裡的美味餐點足以滿足我們的飢餓，讓我們感到完全滿足。

Slake同義字詞片語及英文例句

1. Quench（動詞）解渴、滿足、熄滅

   Drinking a glass of cold water can quench your thirst on a hot day. 在炎熱的一天，喝一杯冰水可以解渴。

2. Sate [seɪt]（動詞）使飽足、滿足

   The lavish buffet at the party sated everyone's appetite. 派對上豐盛的自助餐使每個人都飽足了。

3. Appease（動詞）平息、安撫、滿足

He tried to appease her anger with an apology. 他試圖用道歉來平息她的憤怒。

4. Assuage [əˈsweɪdʒ]（動詞）緩和、安慰、滿足

A warm cup of tea can assuage a sore throat. 一杯熱茶可以緩解喉嚨痛。

這些詞都是用來描述滿足需求、欲望或渴望的行為，並可以根據上下文選擇使用。

Satiate和Slake

具有相似的意思，但使用情境和語氣上可能有些微的差異。

Satiate

意味著完全滿足或過度滿足某人的需求、渴望或飢餓。它通常指的是達到一種極致或過量的飽足感。當你吃飽到無法再吃更多的食物，或者當你滿足一個深刻的渴望時，可以使用這個詞。

After the Thanksgiving dinner, I was so satiated that I couldn't eat another bite. 感恩節大餐後，我吃得飽到無法再吃下一口。

Slake

意味著滿足或解渴，但通常強調的是消除渴望或緩解口渴的感覺，可能不一定達到完全飽足。

The refreshing lemonade helped slake my thirst on a hot summer day. 在炎熱的夏天，清涼的檸檬汁幫助我解渴。

satiate通常指的是完全滿足，而slake則更強調渴望或需求的部分滿足。它們的選擇取決於具體的情境和所要表達的程度。

Smug｜自以爲是／沾沾自喜

Smug（形容詞）意指一種自以爲是或沾沾自喜的自滿態度的意思，通常伴隨著對自己的成就或看法感到過於滿意，並且可能表現出對他人不夠尊重的特徵。這種態度往往不受歡迎，因爲它可以顯示出缺乏謙遜和謙虛。

Smug的例句及應用

1. She had a smug smile on her face after winning the award, which rubbed some people the wrong way. 她在贏得獎項後臉上掛著一個自鳴得意的微笑，這讓一些人感到不悅。

2. His smug attitude about his intelligence made it difficult for others to engage in meaningful conversations with him. 他對自己的智慧表現出自滿的態度，讓其他人難以與他進行有意義的對話。

3. Instead of being smug about his success, he remained humble and grateful for the support he received from his team. 他沒有因爲成功而自以爲是，而是保持謙卑，對他的團隊給予的支持感到感激。

In social settings, a "smug" attitude can be a real turn-off. When someone appears overly self-satisfied, it often creates an uncomfortable atmosphere. People prefer humility and genuine interactions over someone who seems too pleased with themselves. Being humble and open to different perspectives can foster better relationships and more meaningful conversations. So, it's essential to avoid coming across as "smug" if you want to connect with others effectively.

在社交場合中，一種「自滿」的態度可能會令人反感。當某人表現出過於自滿時，通常會創造一種不舒適的氛圍。人們更喜歡謙卑和真誠的互動，而不是看起來過於自得的人。保持謙虛並對不同的觀點持開放態度可以促進更好的人際關係和更有意義的對話。因此，如果您想有效地與他人建立聯繫，避免顯得「自滿」是很重要的。

Smug同義詞和例句

1. Conceited（形容詞）自負的、自大的

   She's so conceited that she believes she's always right. 她非常自負，認為自己總是對的。

2. Arrogant（形容詞）傲慢的、驕傲的

   His arrogant behavior alienated his colleagues at work. 他傲慢的行為使他在工作中疏遠了同事。

3. Self-satisfied（形容詞）自滿的、自得的

   After completing the project, he had a self-satisfied grin on his face. 完成項目後，他臉上露出了自滿的笑容。

4. Smirking（Smirk動詞，通常用作形容詞Smirking）嘲笑的、嘻嘻偷笑的

   He had a smirking expression when he heard about his rival's failure. 當他聽到對手的失敗時，他露出了一個嘲笑的表情。

5. Cocky自大的、驕傲的（形容詞）

His cocky attitude makes it hard to work with him. 他的自大態度讓人難以與他合作。

6. Complacent（形容詞）自滿的、滿足的

Their complacent attitude towards their success may hinder further growth. 他們對自己的成功的自滿態度可能會妨礙進一步的成長。

上述同義詞都指稱一種自以為是或自滿的態度，通常帶有傲慢或自大的特徵。它們可以根據具體語境來選擇使用，以表達類似的含義。

Soporific │ 昏沉沉

Soporific這個詞通常用來形容那些能夠引起睡意或昏昏欲睡的事物。它是一個形容詞，通常用於描述令人感到無聊、乏味或令人困倦的東西。當我們說某個活動或場景是「睡藥」時，意味著它缺乏足夠的刺激或興奮，可能會讓人感到想要入睡。

"Soporific" is a term typically used to describe things that induce sleepiness or drowsiness. It is an adjective often used to characterize something as boring, dull, or tiring. When we say that an activity or a scene is "soporific," it means that it lacks sufficient stimulation or excitement and may make people feel like falling asleep.

Soporific英文例句及應用

1. The professor's monotone lecture was so soporific that half the class struggled to stay awake. 教授單調的講座如此乏味，以至於一半的學生勉強保持清醒。

2. The slow, droning music in the spa had a soporific effect on the guests, lulling them into a state of relaxation. 水療中緩慢而單調的音樂對客人有著催眠的效果，使他們進入一種放鬆的狀態。

3. The long, tedious meeting became a soporific ordeal for everyone in the conference room. 冗長而乏味的會議對會議室中的每個人來說成了一場催眠的折磨。

Soporific的同義詞以及示例

1. Hypnotic催眠的（形容詞）

   The soft, soothing music had a hypnotic effect on the audienc. 柔和舒緩的音樂對觀眾有著催眠的效果。

2. Sedative鎮靜劑（名詞）

   The doctor prescribed a sedative to help the patient sleep. 醫生開了一種鎮靜劑來幫助病人入睡。

3. Drowsy昏昏欲睡的（形容詞）

   The warm, dimly lit room made me feel drowsy. 溫暖、昏暗的房間讓我感到昏昏欲睡。

4. Sleep-inducing催眠的（形容詞）

   The boring lecture was almost sleep-inducing. 那個無聊的講座幾乎令人想入睡。

5. Lethargic無精打采的（形容詞）

   After the heavy meal, I felt lethargic and couldn't stay awake. 吃完大餐後，我感到無精打采，難以保持清醒。

6. Stultifying令人感到沈悶的（形容詞）

   The repetitive tasks at work were stultifying, and I longed for something more engaging. 工作中反覆的任務令人感到沈悶，我渴望著更有趣的事情。

7. Soporose ['soʊpəroʊs] 催眠的（形容詞）

   The soporose atmosphere in the library made it difficult to concentrate on studying. 圖書館中的催眠氛圍讓專心讀書變得困難。

8. Narcotic麻醉的（形容詞）

   The medication had a narcotic effect, causing the patient to feel drowsy. 這種藥物有麻醉效果，讓病人感到昏昏欲睡。

9. Yawning打哈欠的（形容詞）

The endless meeting with no breaks left everyone feeling yawning and fatigued. 沒有休息的無休止會議讓每個人都感到打哈欠和疲憊。

10. Lulling使人安靜的（形容詞）

The lulling sound of the rain outside made it difficult to stay alert while studying. 外面雨水的使人安靜的聲音讓我在學習時難以保持警覺。

這些同義詞都與Soporific有著相似的意思，用來形容能夠引起睡意、昏昏欲睡、或令人感到困倦的事物或情境。

超級比一比 | Sore loser vs Gracious winner

Sore loser是一個用來形容那些在失敗後表現出極端不滿或惡劣情緒的詞語。這個詞語中的loser指的是失敗者,而sore則表示疼痛或不適。一個sore loser通常是指那些無法接受失敗、可能會生氣、抱怨或對其他人感到不滿的人。這種行為通常被認為是不成熟和不適當的。

A "sore loser" is a term used to describe those who exhibit extreme dissatisfaction or negative emotions after experiencing a defeat. In this term, "loser" refers to someone who has failed, while "sore" indicates discomfort or distress. A "sore loser" is typically someone who cannot accept defeat and may become angry, complain, or harbor resentment towards others. Such behavior is often considered immature and inappropriate.

Sore loser應用例句

1. He was such a sore loser after losing the game that he refused to shake hands with the winning team. 他輸掉比賽後表現得非常不滿,拒絕和獲勝隊伍握手。

2. She became a sore loser when her project was not selected for the competition, criticizing the judges and the winning entries. 當她的專案未被選中參賽時,她成為了一個愛發牢騷的輸家,批評評委和獲獎作品。

3. Instead of being a sore loser, he decided to learn from his mistakes and improve for the next match. 他決定不當一個輸家而發牢騷,而是決定從自己的錯誤中學習,爲下一場比賽做出改進。

4. He's such a sour loser; he sulks for hours after a loss. 他真是個不爽快的輸家,輸掉比賽後會生悶氣好幾個小時。

Sore loser的同義字詞或片語及例句

1. Poor sport中文意思是差勁的運動家

She acted like a poor sport when she didn't win the race. 她輸了比賽後表現得像個差勁的運動家。

2. Graceless loser不謙遜的輸家

Her behavior at the awards ceremony showed that she's a graceless loser. 她在頒獎典禮上的行爲顯示她是個不謙遜的輸家。

3. Bitter loser心情不好的輸家

He became a bitter loser after losing the championship match. 在輸掉冠軍賽後,他變得心情不好的輸家。

Sore loser的反義字詞或片語可以用Gracious winner

1. 勝者不驕(形容詞短語)

She's a gracious winner, always congratulating her opponents. 她是個優雅的贏家,總是祝賀她的對手。

2. 接受失敗(動詞片語)

He gracefully accepted defeat and offered a handshake to his opponent. 他優雅地接受了失敗，並向對手伸出了握手。

3. 友善的競爭者（名詞片語）

He's known as a gracious competitor, always encouraging others and showing sportsmanship. 他以友善的競爭者而聞名，總是鼓勵別人，表現出運動家精神。

這些反義字詞或片語描述了能夠接受失敗、表現出友好和尊重的態度，與Sore loser相反，後者指的是無法接受失敗並表現出不滿或惱怒的人。

Sportsmanship的應用

1. His sportsmanship shone through even in defeat, as he congratulated his opponent and shook hands with a smile. 即使在失敗時，他的運動家精神仍然閃耀，他祝賀了對手，微笑著握手。

2. The coach emphasized the importance of sportsmanship, reminding the team that showing respect to their rivals was as crucial as winning. 教練強調了運動家精神的重要性，提醒球隊，對競爭對手表示尊重與贏得比賽同樣重要。

3. She displayed exceptional sportsmanship by helping her competitor when they got injured during the game, putting fair play above winning. 她展現了卓越的運動家精神，當比賽中對手受傷時，她幫助了對手，將公平競爭置於勝利之上。

Sportsmanship的同義字詞或片語

1. Fair play公平競爭（名詞片語）

   Fair play is the foundation of any sportsmanship. 公平競爭是任何運動家精神的基石。

2. Good sportsmanship良好的運動家精神（名詞片語）

   Displaying good sportsmanship is essential for fostering a positive sports environment. 展現良好的運動家精神對於營造積極的體育環境至關重要。

3. Sports ethics體育倫理（名詞片語）

   Teaching sports ethics to young athletes helps them understand the importance of sportsmanship. 教導年輕運動員體育倫理有助於他們理解運動家精神的重要性。

與Sportsmanship反義字詞或片語

1. Poor sportsmanship差勁的運動家精神（名詞片語）

   His display of poor sportsmanship after losing the match was disappointing. 在輸掉比賽後他展現出的差勁的運動家精神讓人失望。

2. Unfair play不公平競爭（名詞片語）

   Engaging in unfair play goes against the principles of sportsmanship. 參與不公平競爭違反了運動家精神的原則。

3. Unsportsmanlike conduct不遵循運動家精神的行為（名詞片語）

   The referee penalized the player for his unsportsmanlike conduct on the field. 裁判因球場上該選手的不遵循運動家

精神行為而對其處以懲罰。

希望這些詞語和片語用於描述運動中的道德和行為，有助於大家在區分適當的運動家精神行為和不適當的行為的應用。

Staycation ｜宅度假

Staycation（名詞）是一個由stay（停留）和vacation（假期）組合而成的詞語，是國內旅遊或居家旅遊的意思。這指的是在家鄉或附近地區度過休假，而不是前往遠方的目的地。Staycation的概念源於減少旅行成本，減少環境影響，或者在受限的情況下維持休閒生活方式。

Staycation (noun) is a word formed by combining "stay" and "vacation." It refers to spending a holiday in your hometown or nearby area rather than traveling to a distant destination. The concept of Staycation originated from reducing travel costs, minimizing environmental impact, or maintaining a leisurely lifestyle under restricted circumstances.

藉著疫情後宅度假的興盛文，來看Staycation要怎麼應用：

"Staycation" is a new term that emerged due to the COVID-19 pandemic in 2019. It originates from the lockdown measures implemented by various countries in response to the outbreak. Since people couldn't leave their hometowns for an extended period, they opted to stay in local hotels for a vacation experience. With a lack of foreign tourists, Staycation became a crucial revenue source for hotels, helping cover operational costs. Consequently, hotels started offering discounts to attract guests.

Staycation「宅度假」是一個由於2019年COVID-19大流行而出現的新詞。它源於各國針對疫情實施的封鎖措施。由於人們長時間無法離開自己的故鄉，他們選擇在當地的酒店度過假期。由於缺乏外國遊客，Staycation「宅度假」成為酒店的重要收入來源，有助於支付運營成本。因此，酒店紛紛推出優惠來吸引客人。

Staycation的例句

1. This summer, we opted for a Staycation and explored the beautiful landscapes of our hometown. 今年夏天，我們選擇了宅度假，探索了我們家鄉的美麗風景。
2. Staycation not only saved us money but also reduced the fatigue of long-distance travel. 國內旅遊不僅節省了我們的錢，還減少了長途旅行的疲勞感。
3. During our Staycation, we enjoyed local cuisine and culture. 在留宅度假期間，我們享受了當地美食和文化。

Staycation的同義詞及示例

1. Immersive Vacation沉浸式假期，一種全身心投入當地文化和環境的度假方式
   We had an immersive vacation in Italy, learning to cook pasta and speaking with the locals. 我們在意大利度過了一個沉浸式假期，學習做義大利麵並與當地人交談。
2. Hometown Tour家鄉之旅，在自己的家鄉或故鄉探索新奇之處的旅遊
   This weekend, we're going on a hometown tour, revisiting all

our favorite childhood spots. 這個週末，我們將進行一次家鄉之旅，重溫所有我們童年喜愛的地方。

3. Local Getaway本地度假，在附近地區度過假期，不必長途旅行

We decided on a local getaway for the long weekend, booking a cozy cabin in the nearby mountains. 我們決定在這個長週末本地度假，在附近的山區預訂了一間舒適的小屋。

這些同義詞都描述了一種在家鄉或附近地區度過假期的方式，而不是前往遠方的旅行。

Suave & Deferential
優雅、殷勤

Suave優雅的（形容詞）

描述一個人或事物充滿風度和優雅。這詞彙常用於形容一個人的外表、舉止或言談，通常指其溫文爾雅、有教養。優雅的表現可以贏得他人的讚美和喜愛，讓人留下深刻印象。

"Suave" is an adjective that describes a person or thing as possessing grace and elegance. This term is often used to characterize one's appearance, behavior, or speech, typically implying refinement and sophistication. A suave demeanor can garner praise and endearment from others, leaving a lasting impression.

Suave「優雅／文雅的」應用

1. His suave attire and polished manners made him the center of attention at the party. 他優雅的服裝和精緻的舉止使他成為派對的焦點。

2. Her suave speech and confident delivery captivated the audience.
她優雅的演講和自信的表達吸引了觀眾的注意。

3. The suave design of the luxury car reflected the manufacturer's commitment to elegance and quality. 這輛豪華汽車的優雅設計反映了製造商對高雅和品質的承諾。

Deferential恭敬的（形容詞）

用來形容一個人或態度表現出尊敬、殷勤和恭敬。這詞通常用來描述某人對權威、長輩或他人的尊重和服從。恭敬的態度顯示出對他人的尊重和禮貌。

"Deferential" is an adjective used to describe a person or attitude that displays respect and deference. This term is typically used to depict someone's respect and obedience towards authority figures, elders, or others. A deferential attitude demonstrates respect and courtesy toward others.

Deferential的應用

1. The employee's deferential behavior towards his supervisor earned him a promotion. 員工對主管的恭敬態度讓他獲得了升遷。

2. In many cultures, it is customary to be deferential to elders and show them great respect. 在許多文化中，對長輩表示恭敬並尊重他們是一種慣例。

3. The student's deferential response to the teacher's feedback demonstrated his willingness to learn and improve. 學生對老師的回饋表現出恭敬，顯示了他學習和進步的意願。

閱讀一篇An Evening of Charismatic Elegance充滿魅力的優雅之夜，將這兩個單字運用在的文章中描述及營造氛圍：

In the heart of the city, there's an upscale restaurant renowned for its suave ambiance and deferential service. This establishment seamlessly blends suave aesthetics with deferential attitudes, offering a unique experience.

在城市的中心，有一家以其優雅的氛圍和殷勤的服務而聞名的高檔餐廳。這家餐廳巧妙地融合了優雅的美學和殷勤的態度，提供了一種獨特的體驗。

Upon entry, a charismatic host, oozing charm and warmth, sets the tone. His suave manner and impeccable etiquette ensure every guest feels cherished. As the evening unfolds, the charismatic chef showcases culinary mastery. Each dish, not just delicious but presented with suave flair, pays deference to the diner's palate.

一位充滿魅力且充滿溫暖的迎賓主持人在入口處為您定下了基調。他的優雅舉止和無可挑剔的禮儀確保每位客人都感到尊重。隨著夜幕的降臨，充滿魅力的大廚展示了烹飪的嫻熟。每道菜不僅美味，而且呈現出優雅的風采，尊重飲食者的味蕾。說明：1. Impeccable etiquette意指無可挑剔的禮儀或無懈可擊的行為標準。是一個表示高度禮貌和尊重的詞組。2. Ooze動詞，慢慢流出或滲出，指液體或物質從一個地方慢慢流動或滲漏出來。oozing charm and warmth意味著主人散發著迷人和溫暖的魅力，一種形容方式。3. Palate味覺或口味，通常指的是一個人的味覺感受或口味喜好。

The waitstaff, equally suave and deferential, tend to every need with grace and precision. Their impeccable etiquette, from wine service to menu suggestions, fosters genuine hospitality. This suave and deferential experience centers on creating an upscale haven. The ambiance, service, and cuisine unite to transport diners to a world of refined elegance and charisma.

服務人員同樣優雅且殷勤，以優雅和精確度滿足了每個需求。他們的無可挑剔的禮儀，從倒酒到菜單建議，培養了真正的好客之道。這種充滿魅力和殷勤的體驗是爲了要創建一個高檔的休憩庇護場所。氛圍、服務和美食融爲一體，將飲食者帶入了一個精緻優雅和魅力十足的世界。

As the night ends, patrons depart with memories of a truly special experience. This restaurant reminds us that amidst hurried interactions, suave elegance and genuine deference still have a place, crafting an unforgettable dining adventure.

夜幕降臨，客人帶著一個真正特別的體驗離開。這家餐廳提醒我們，在匆忙的互動中，優雅的禮儀和真誠的殷勤仍然有其存在的空間，營造了一個難以忘懷的用餐冒險。

Suave的同義詞

1. Polished精緻的，高雅特質的（形容詞）

   Her polished manners and eloquent speech impressed everyone at the event. 她的精緻舉止和雄辯演講令活動上的每個人都印象深刻。

2. Sophisticated精緻的，具有精湛和高雅的意涵（形容詞）

   The restaurant's sophisticated decor and menu appealed to a discerning clientele. 該餐廳精緻的裝潢和菜單吸引了有眼光的客戶。

3. Elegant優雅的，高雅的（形容詞）

   She wore an elegant gown to the formal event, looking

Suave & Deferential 優雅、殷勤　　347

stunning. 她穿著一件優雅的禮服參加正式活動，看起來令人驚豔。

4. Dapper整潔雅致的（形容詞）

He appeared at the party looking very dapper in a tailor-made suit.他穿著定做的西裝出現在派對上，看起來非常整潔雅致。

Deferential（恭敬）的同義詞

1. Respectful尊重的（形容詞）

The students were always respectful towards their wise and caring teacher. 學生們對他們聰明而關心的老師總是表示尊重。

2. Obedient聽話的，順從的（形容詞）

The dog was highly obedient, following its owner's commands without hesitation. 這隻狗非常聽話，毫不猶豫地遵從主人的命令。

3. Courteous有禮貌的（形容詞）

His courteous response to criticism demonstrated his professionalism. 他對批評的禮貌的回應顯示了他的專業素養。

Swing the lead
｜老闆來了還「偷懶」

Swing the lead是一個俚語表達，意指故意偷懶、拖延工作或裝病以逃避責任。通常在形容某人不誠實或懶惰的情境下使用。 This is an idiomatic expression that means to pretend to be ill or avoid work.

來看看經濟學人的報導一份研究指出未來公司老闆可以透過AI看你是不是裝病偷懶的文章中，如何運用Swing the lead：
According to The Economist, research conducted at the Indian Institute of Technology reveals that AI can effortlessly detect whether someone is trying to "swing the lead" by faking illness through voice audio analysis. When humans have a cold, their vocal patterns undergo changes. By analyzing extensive speech data using sophisticated algorithms, employers can now determine if an employee is genuinely sick. Therefore, employers can easily expose attempts to "swing the lead" and deceive. It's essential to remember that if employees fail to follow the legally prescribed leave procedures, they are still engaging in absenteeism. 根據《經濟學人》報導，印度理工學院的研究顯示，人工智慧可以輕鬆地通過聲音分析來檢測是否有人試圖想裝病來逃避工作。當人們感冒時，他們的聲音模式會發生變化。通過使用複雜的算法分析大量的語音數據，雇主現

在可以確定員工是否眞的生病。因此，雇主可以輕鬆地揭示
試圖裝病偷懶的企圖和欺騙行爲。重要的是要記住，如果員
工未按法定的請假程序執行，他們仍然在參與曠職行爲。
說明：Absenteeism曠職，指的是員工未按照工作時間表或法
定請假程序出勤，而是缺席工作。

Swing the lead的例句及應用

1. She's been swinging the lead all week, pretending to be too
   sick to come to work. 她整個星期都在故意偷懶，假裝生
   病不來上班。

2. The students were caught swinging the lead when they claimed
   they couldn't complete their assignments because of a sudden
   computer malfunction. 學生們聲稱由於電腦突然故障，無
   法完成作業，但他們被抓到是故意偷懶。

3. Don't trust him; he's always trying to swing the lead and avoid
   his responsibilities. 不要相信他；他總是企圖故意裝病偷
   懶，避免負起責任。

Swing the lead意指故意偷懶、拖延工作或裝病以逃避責任，
通常在形容某人不誠實或懶惰的情境下使用。

相同意思的英文單字或短語

1. Malingering [məˈlɪŋɡərɪŋ] 故意裝病：指某人故意假裝患病
   以避免工作或責任。

   He's been malingering for days, claiming he's too sick to
   come to work, but I think he's just trying to avoid his

responsibilities. 他已經裝病好幾天了，聲稱病得厲害無法上班，但我認為他只是試圖逃避他的責任。

2. Feigning illness假裝生病：表示某人故意裝出生病的狀態，通常是為了躲避某事。

She was feigning illness to skip the team meeting, but her colleagues saw through her act. 她假裝生病以逃避團隊會議，但她的同事看穿了她的做作。

3. Playing sick假裝生病：類似於feigning illness，表示故意裝病以逃避職責

He's just playing sick to avoid doing his share of the project work. 他只是假裝生病，以避免完成他在專案工作中應該分擔的工作。

4. Shirking one's duties逃避職責：這是一個正式詞語，指不履行工作或職責

His constant shirking of duties is becoming a problem in the workplace. 他一直在規避職責，這已經成為工作場所的問題。

Tenable／Untenable
｜可行不可行？！

Tenable是一個形容詞，指的是一個觀點、立場或計劃在一定情況下是合理且可接受的。這個詞通常用來評估一個主張或計畫的可行性和合理性。

"Tenable" is an adjective that refers to an argument, position, or plan that is reasonable and acceptable under certain circumstances. This word is often used to assess the feasibility and soundness of a claim or plan.

而Untenable是形容詞，是指的是一個立場、論點、或情況不可不可行的。這個詞通常用來描述一個觀點或局勢在某些方面是站不住腳的，或者無法被合理辯護。

"Untenable" is an adjective that refers to a position, argument, or situation that cannot be reasonably or sustainably supported. This word is often used to describe a standpoint or situation that is weak in some aspects or cannot be reasonably defended.

一起來看Tenable可行的、Untenable不可行的在「發展小型核電廠可行與否」的一篇時事報導，如何應用：

Following the renowned entrepreneur's suggestion to establish small-scale nuclear power plants as part of the energy development strategy, even though he issued a prompt apology, some still find this proposal <u>less tenable</u>. Environmental groups argue that apart from considering Taiwan's reality and aligning with global decarbonization trends, it's crucial to first understand Taiwan's geological environment. On the other hand, some scholars support the notion that Taiwan can support the development of small modular reactors. However, others view it as <u>untenable</u> and unfeasible from the perspective of seismic safety risks.

在知名企業家提出將小型核能發電廠納入能源發展策略後，儘管他迅速道歉，但仍有人認為這個提議較<u>不可行</u>。環保團體指出，除了需考慮臺灣的現實情況和全球減碳趨勢外，更重要的是要首先了解臺灣的地質環境。另一方面，一些學者支持臺灣發展小型模組化反應爐的觀點。然而，其他人從地震安全風險的角度來看，認為這個提議<u>不可行</u>也不切實際。」

Tenable的例子

1. His proposal is tenable in terms of budget. 他提出的方案在預算方面是可行的。

2. This argument has sparked widespread debate in the scientific community but remains tenable. 這個論點在科學界引起了廣泛的爭議，但仍然是可接受的。

3. Given the current economic conditions, is this business plan still tenable? 考慮到目前的經濟狀況，這個商業計劃是否還能維持下去？

Untenable的應用及示例

1. His argument is widely regarded as untenable in the scientific community. 他的論點在科學界被廣泛視爲不可行的。
2. Given the current economic conditions, this plan is untenable. 在當前的經濟情況下，這個計劃是不可行的。
3. His position becomes untenable when confronted with facts. 他的立場在面對事實時變得不堪一擊。

Tenable的同義詞

1. Feasible可行的

   The proposed project is feasible given the available resources. 考慮到現有資源，這個提議的計畫是可行的。

2. Viable可行的

   The business idea is financially viable and has great potential. 這個商業點子在財務上是可行的，並具有巨大潛力。

Untenable的同義詞

1. Unfeasible不可行的，無法實現的

   The plan was deemed unfeasible due to budget constraints. 由於預算限制，這個計劃被認爲是不可行的。

2. Unsustainable不可持續的，無法維持的

   The rapid deforestation in that region is leading to an unsustainable loss of biodiversity and is harming the ecosystem. 該地區的快速森林砍伐正在導致不可持續的生物多樣性損失，並對生態系統造成傷害。

Terricolous
陸生及各種生態介紹

Terricolous [ˌterəˈkɑːləs]（陸生的）是一個形容詞，用來描述生長在陸地上的生物或植物。這個詞通常用來區分陸地生物和水生生物，特別是在生態學和生物學研究中。地球上有許多種地生的生物，從微小的昆蟲到巨大的樹木，都可以被描述爲Terricolous，因爲它們在陸地上扎根或生長。

"Terricolous" is an adjective used to describe organisms or plants that grow on land. This term is commonly used to distinguish terrestrial organisms from aquatic ones, especially in the fields of ecology and biology. There are numerous terricolous organisms on Earth, ranging from tiny insects to towering trees, all of which can be described as terricolous because they root or grow on land.

英文例句

1. Many animals, like lions and elephants, are terricolous and roam the savannahs and forests. 許多動物，如獅子和大象，是地生的，它們在大草原和森林中漫遊。

2. Terricolous plants rely on soil for nutrients and water, unlike aquatic plants that grow in water. 地生植物依賴土壤提供營養和水分，不同於在水中生長的水生植物。

3. The terricolous ecosystem in this region is rich in biodiversity,

with various species coexisting in harmony. 該地區的地生生態系統物種多樣性豐富，各種物種和諧共存。

各種生態系生物如何以英文應用、造句以及應用

1. Predatory掠食性的–Predatory animals are carnivorous creatures that hunt and eat other animals for their sustenance.
   Lions are well-known for their predatory nature in the wild. 獅子以其在野外的掠食性質而聞名。

2. Reptile ['reptaɪl] 爬蟲類，爬行動物–Reptiles are cold-blooded vertebrates that include snakes, turtles, and lizards.
   The desert is home to various reptile species, such as rattlesnakes and iguanas. 沙漠是各種爬蟲動物的家園，如響尾蛇和鬣蜥。

3. Mammal哺乳類動物–Mammals are warm-blooded vertebrates that give birth to live young and typically nurse them with milk.
   Humans, dogs, and dolphins are examples of mammals. 人類、狗和海豚都是哺乳動物的例子。

4. Primate靈長類動物–Primates are a group of mammals that include humans, apes, and monkeys, known for their advanced cognitive abilities.
   Chimpanzees are among the closest relatives of humans in the primate family. 黑猩猩是靈長類動物中與人類最接近的親戚之一。

5. Amphibian兩棲類動物–Amphibians are vertebrates that can live both in water and on land, such as frogs and salamanders.

Frogs undergo a metamorphosis from tadpoles to adults, which is typical for amphibians. 青蛙從蝌蚪到成年青蛙的變態是兩棲動物的典型特徵。

6. Migratory遷徙的–Migratory animals are those that travel long distances seasonally, often for breeding or food.

Birds like swans and geese are known for their migratory behavior. 天鵝和雁等鳥類以其遷徙行為而聞名。

7. Carnivore肉食性動物–Carnivores are animals that primarily eat meat as their main source of nutrition.

Lions and tigers are examples of carnivorous predators. 獅子和老虎是肉食性掠食動物的例子。

8. Herbivore草食性動物–Herbivores are animals that primarily consume plants and vegetation.

Deer and cows are classic examples of herbivorous animals. 鹿和牛是草食性動物的典型例子。

9. Omnivore [ˈɑːmnɪvɔːr] 雜食性動物–Omnivores are creatures that eat both plants and meat, having a diverse diet.

Humans are considered omnivorous because they consume both plant-based and animal-based foods. 人類被認為是雜食性動物，因為他們食用植物和動物的食物。

10. Nocturnal [nɑːkˈtɜːrnəl] 夜行性的，夜間活動的– Nocturnal animals are active during the night and sleep during the day.

Owls are well-adapted to their nocturnal lifestyle, hunting for prey in the dark. 貓頭鷹很適應夜行生活方式，它們在黑暗中捕食獵物。

11. Aquatic水生的–Aquatic organisms or plants are those that live in water environments.

Fish are a classic example of aquatic animals. 魚是水生動物的經典例子。

12. Terrestrial [tə'restrɪəl] 陸生的–Terrestrial organisms or plants live on land, not in water.

Many terrestrial animals have adapted to life in forests and grasslands. 許多陸地動物已適應了生活在森林和草原中。

13. Rodent嚙齒類動物–Rodents are mammals characterized by continuously growing front teeth that they must gnaw on to keep at a reasonable length.

Rats and mice are common examples of rodents. 老鼠和家鼠是嚙齒動物的常見例子。

14. Marsupial [mɑːr'suːpiəl] 有袋目動物–Marsupials are mammals with pouches in which they carry and nurse their undeveloped young.

Kangaroos and koalas are iconic marsupials from Australia. 袋鼠和考拉是澳大利亞的標誌性有袋動物。

15. Scavenger ['skævəndʒər] 食腐動物–Scavengers are animals that primarily feed on dead or decaying organisms.

Vultures are well-known scavengers in the animal kingdom. 禿鷹在動物界中以其食腐特性而聞名。

16. Homoiothermal [ˌhoʊmɪoʊ'θɜːrməl] 恆溫的–Homoiothermal, also known as warm-blooded, refers to organisms that can regulate their body temperature internally. Birds and mammals are examples of homoiothermal animals.

鳥類和哺乳動物是恆溫動物的例子。

17. Cold-blooded冷血的–Cold-blooded organisms, or ectothermic animals, cannot regulate their body temperature internally and rely on external sources.

Snakes and lizards are cold-blooded reptiles. 蛇和蜥蜴是冷血爬行動物。

18. Invertebrate [ɪn'vɜːrtəbrət] 無脊椎動物–Invertebrates are animals that lack a vertebral column or backbone. 無脊椎動物是指缺乏脊椎或脊柱的動物。

Insects, mollusks, and jellyfish are examples of invertebrates. 昆蟲、軟體動物和水母都是無脊椎動物的例子。

19. Vertebrate ['vɜːrtəbrət] 脊椎動物–Vertebrates are animals with a well-defined vertebral column or backbone.

Fish, amphibians, reptiles, birds, and mammals are all vertebrates. 魚類、兩棲動物、爬行動物、鳥類和哺乳動物都是脊椎動物。

To throw a sprat to catch a herring | 拋磚引玉

「拋磚引玉」一種策略或手段，即通過先以一些基本的、不成熟的想法、作法，來激發出其他深入、更有價值的見解或方案。常用做自謙之詞。在英文裡可以這麼說To throw a sprat to catch a herring.

Sprat指的是一種小型鯡魚，而herring則指的是一種大型的鯡魚。在句子中，前面的sprat通常用來表示拋磚引玉的行動，而herring則用來表示要誘發更大的目標或利益。除了catch a herring的用法，也可以throw a sprat to catch a mackerel表示，意思是一樣的。

To throw a sprat to catch a herring.的實例及運用

1. At the meeting, the moderator threw a sprat to catch a herring by first putting forward a few suggestions, hoping to spark a brainstorming session to come up with solutions. 在會議上，主持人拋磚引玉先提出幾點建議，希望大家能激盪出解決方案。

2. Setting a precedent, the female celebrity threw a sprat to catch a herring by making a generous donation to charity, hoping it would inspire more people to join in and collectively

demonstrate their love and compassion. 女明星以身作則，
拋磚引玉地捐出一筆慷慨的愛心款項，她希望藉此激勵
更多人共襄善舉，一同展現他愛心和關懷。

超級比一比
Unctuous vs Fulsome

Unctuous（形容詞），用來描述某人或某物表現出過分的矯情或虛偽的特質，通常伴隨著過多的奉承或虛情假意。這個詞彙通常帶有貶義，因為它指涉著一種不眞誠的行為或言辭，常常讓人感到不舒服或反感。在各種社交場合中，過於Unctuous的表現往往不會受到歡迎，因為人們更傾向於眞誠和直接的互動。

閱讀一篇文章，看「矯情」Unctuous如何運用在文章中：
In social interactions, it's essential to strike a balance between courtesy and authenticity. Being excessively <u>unctuous</u>, marked by insincere flattery and over-the-top praise, often backfires. People tend to see through the facade and feel uncomfortable when faced with such behavior. True sincerity and straightforwardness are more appreciated in various situations, as they foster genuine connections. So, remember that an unctuous approach may yield short-term benefits, but it rarely leads to lasting trust and meaningful relationships.

社交互動中，保持禮貌和眞誠之間的平衡至關重要。過於「矯情」，即表現出不眞誠的奉承和過度的讚美，通常會適得其反。人們往往能看穿這種偽裝，並在面對這種行為時感到不舒服。在各種情境下，眞誠和坦誠更受歡迎，因為它們有助於建立真正的聯繫。因此，請記住，過度「矯情」的方法可能會帶來短期的好處，但很少能夠建立持久的信任和有意義的關係。

Unctuous的應用及例句

1. His unctuous compliments about my work made me uneasy, as I could tell he was just trying to gain favor. 他對我的工作讚美過分，讓我感到不安，我可以感覺到他只是想討好。

2. The politician's unctuous speech was filled with insincere promises and exaggerated praise for his accomplishments. 政治人物矯情的演說充滿了不誠實的許諾和對他的成就的誇大讚美。

3. She gave me an unctuous smile, but I knew she was only being nice to get a favor in return. 她給了我一個虛偽的微笑，但我知道她只是出於私心想要換取一個回報。

Unctuous的同義詞及例句說明

1. Sycophantic奉承的、諂媚的（形容詞）
   Her sycophantic behavior towards her boss was quite evident as she constantly praised him even when he made mistakes. 她對老闆的奉承行為非常明顯，即使老闆犯錯，她也經常讚美他。

2. Fawning阿諛奉承的（形容詞）
   The celebrity was surrounded by fawning fans who showered her with compliments and adoration. 這位名人被一群阿諛奉承的粉絲包圍，他們不停地讚美她並崇拜她。

3. Obsequious奉承的、順從的（形容詞）

The obsequious waiter was overly attentive, constantly refilling our glasses without us asking. 那位獻殷情的服務生過於細心，總是不停地為我們倒酒，即使我們沒有要求。

4. Groveling卑躬屈膝的、爬行的（形容詞）

He resorted to groveling to keep his job, apologizing profusely to his angry boss. 他不得不卑躬屈膝以保住工作，對著怒氣沖沖的老闆不停地道歉。（註：Profuse大量的、豐富的、慷慨的，用來形容某事物或某種情況非常充沛或過多。Apologize profusely深表歉意、誠摯道歉。）

5. Servile奴性的、順從的（形容詞）

The servile attitude of the employees towards the demanding manager created a tense work environment. 員工對於要求嚴格經理的奴性態度造成了緊張的工作環境。

6. Ingratiating 討好的，迎合的（形容詞）

His ingratiating smile was meant to win over the skeptical audience. 他那討好的微笑旨在贏得懷疑的觀眾的好感。

7. Unctuous 油腔滑調的，虛情假意的（形容詞）

The salesman's unctuous demeanor made us uncomfortable; his flattery felt insincere. 那位銷售員油腔滑調的態度讓我們感到不舒服；他的奉承感覺不真誠。

這些同義詞描述了一種過分奉承或虛情假意的特質，通常在社交或職業場合中使用，但都含有貶義。

Unctuous和Deferential

Unctuous意指過分矯情、虛情假意、油腔滑調、或表現出不誠實或不真誠的特質。通常帶有貶義，用來形容某人的行為讓人感到不真誠或不喜歡。

His unctuous flattery was obvious to everyone in the room. 他的虛情假意讚美對房間裡的每個人都很明顯。

Deferential意指殷勤、尊敬、恭敬、顯示對權威或長輩的尊重和禮貌。這個詞用來形容某人表現出尊重和順從的態度。

She always spoke to her elders in a deferential manner. 她總是以恭敬的方式對待年長者。

所以當我們在描述服務態度好且殷勤的waiter時，最合適的詞語是Obsequious。這個詞表示某人獻殷勤或過分諂媚，通常是為了取悅客人而表現出的服務態度。Deferential也可以用來形容尊重和恭敬的態度，但不帶有諂媚或過分殷勤的含義。Unctuous通常帶有貶義，描述一種虛情假意或不真誠的態度，通常不適用於形容良好的服務態度。所以在服務殷情的這個情境下，Obsequious最合適。

Unctuous和Fulsome

Unctuous [ˈʌŋkʃuəs] 矯情的，油腔滑調的，過分熱情的，假裝友善的。形容人做事過分熱情或諂媚，通常帶有貶義。

His unctuous manner made everyone uncomfortable. 他油腔滑調的態度讓每個人都感到不舒服。

Fulsome ['fʊlsəm] 指恭維過度得的。描述過分的讚美或表揚，可能被視爲不眞誠或過於誇張。

Her fulsome praise for the mediocre performance seemed insincere. 她對平凡的表現過分恭維在美似乎不太眞誠。

Unctuous指一個人的諂媚或做作態度，矯情的意思；而fulsome則常用來形容過分的讚美或恭維，這可能讓人感到不舒服或不誠實。這兩個詞彙在某些情況下可能有相似之處，但它們的重點和使用情境略有不同。

Unfaze | 泰然自若

Unfaze不爲所動（動詞），unfazed不爲所動的（形容詞），表示一個人在面對困難、壓力或挑戰時保持冷靜和自信，不受這些困難影響。能夠保持堅定和不受干擾，不被外部因素影響。不論遇到多麼大的困難，這種人都能夠保持冷靜，堅定前進。

"Unfaze" is a verb that signifies a person's ability to remain calm and confident in the face of difficulties, stress, or challenges without being affected by them. It means being able to stay resolute and undisturbed, unaffected by external factors. Regardless of how significant the challenges may be, such individuals can maintain their composure and continue steadfastly.

來看一篇與Unfazed有關的短文，順便學習如何運用：

In a world filled with distractions and temptations, the ability to stay unfazed is a rare and valuable trait. Those who possess this quality remain resolute in their goals, undeterred by the allure of instant gratification. They understand that the path to success is often paved with challenges and sacrifices, and they are willing to stay unfazed.

在充滿誘惑和讓人分心的世界中，能夠保持不爲所動的能力是一種珍貴的品質。擁有這種品質的人在他們的目標上保持堅定，不受即時滿足的吸引所動搖。他們明白通往成功的道路常常充滿挑戰和犧牲，並且願意保持不為所動。」

Unfaze應用及例句

1. Despite the unexpected setbacks, she remained unfazed and continued working towards her goal. 儘管遇到了意外的挫折，她仍然保持冷靜，繼續朝著她的目標努力。

2. His ability to stay unfazed under pressure makes him an excellent leader in high-stress situations. 他在壓力下保持不動搖的能力使他成為高壓情境中的出色領導者。

3. Even when faced with criticism and doubts, he remained unfazed and believed in his creative vision. 即使面對批評和懷疑，他仍然不為所動，相信自己的創意遠見。

當我們說到unfazed時，我們通常指的是某人在面對困難、壓力或挑戰時保持鎮定，不受影響的情況。

Unfazed的同義詞和片語

1. Unperturbed（形容詞）泰然自若的意思

   Despite the unexpected setback, she remained unperturbed. 儘管遇到意外的挫折，她保持鎮定不受影響。

2. Unflappable（形容詞）鎮定自若的

   He's known for being unflappable in high-pressure situations. 他以在高壓情況下保持鎮定而聞名。

3. Cool as a cucumber（片語）

   Even in a crisis, she's as cool as a cucumber. 即使在危機時

刻，她也鎮定自若。

4. Composed（形容詞）冷靜的

The speaker appeared composed and confident on stage. 演講者在舞臺上顯得冷靜自信。

5. Imperturbable（形容詞）不為所動的

His imperturbable demeanor makes him an excellent leader. 他不為所動的態度使他成為優秀的領袖。

6. Stoic（形容詞）堅忍的

Despite the chaos around him, he remained stoic and focused. 儘管周圍一片混亂，他保持堅忍和專注。

7. Unshaken（形容詞）不受動搖的

Hcr rcsolvc to succeed was unshaken by the obstacles in her path. 她成功的決心不受道路上的障礙所動搖。

8. Calm and collected（片語）冷靜沈著的

He stayed calm and collected during the intense negotiation. 在激烈的談判中，他保持冷靜和沉著。

9. Unruffled（形容詞）鎮定的

Despite the commotion, she remained unruffled. 儘管有喧囂，她依然鎮靜自若。

10. Aplomb [ə'plɑːm]（名詞）沉著自信

He handled the challenging situation with great aplomb. 他以極大的沉著自信處理了這個棘手的情況。

11. Phlegmatic [flɛg'mætɪk]（形容詞）冷靜的，不易激動的

Despite the chaos around him, he remained phlegmatic and focused. 儘管周圍一片混亂，他仍保持冷靜和專注。

Vicissitude | 變遷

Vicissitude是一個有趣且深具意義的單字，它主要是指生活中的變遷和變化，特別是那些不斷變動的狀況和狀態。這個詞可以用作名詞，指的是生活中的起伏變化，也可以用作動詞，表示變動或變化。Vicissitude提醒我們，生活中的變數是不可避免的，無論是好的還是壞的，我們都必須學會適應和應對它們。

"Vicissitude" is an intriguing and meaningful word that primarily refers to the changes and fluctuations in life, especially those ever-shifting circumstances and states. This word can be used as a noun, denoting the ups and downs in life, or as a verb, indicating variation or alteration. Vicissitude reminds us that variables in life are inevitable, whether they are good or bad, and we must learn to adapt and respond to them.

來看一篇有關「臺北城市發展變遷」短文，學習Vacissitude「變遷」如何應用：

Over the years, Taipei has undergone significant "vicissitudes" in its development. From its humble beginnings as a small trading post, the city has transformed into a bustling metropolis. The "vicissitude" of Taipei's skyline is evident, with modern skyscrapers now dominating the horizon.

This urban transformation has not only reshaped the city's physical landscape but also its cultural and economic identity. Taipei's transition from an agricultural society to a technology and finance hub exemplifies these "vicissitudes." Today, it stands as a global center for innovation and business.

However, amidst these changes, Taipei has managed to preserve its rich cultural heritage and traditions. The city's temples, historic districts, and vibrant street markets offer glimpses into its past, even as it embraces the future. The "vicissitude" of Taipei reflects its resilience and adaptability.

多年來，臺北在其發展中經歷了顯著的「變遷」。從一個小小的貿易站點謙卑的開始，這座城市已經轉變成一個繁華的大都市。臺北市天際線的「變遷」明顯可見，現代摩天大樓如今主導了地平線。

這種城市轉型不僅改變了城市的物理景觀，還改變了其文化和經濟特性。臺北從一個農業社會轉變爲一個科技和金融中心，這是這些「變遷」的例證。如今，它是全球創新和商業的中心。

然而，在這些變化之中，臺北設法保留了其豐富的文化遺產和傳統。這個城市的寺廟、歷史區和充滿活力的街頭市場讓人們窺見了它的過去，即使它迎接未來。臺北的「變遷」反映了其韌性和適應能力。

Vicissitude的應用及例句

1. The vicissitudes of the stock market can be unpredictable. 股市的變化多端往往難以預測。

2. She has experienced the vicissitudes of life, from poverty to success. 她經歷了生活的波折,從貧困到成功。

3. The vicissitude of weather in this region can be quite dramatic. 這個地區的氣候變化多端,變化劇烈。

Vicissitude的同義字詞或片語及示例

1. Fluctuation波動（名詞）

   The fluctuation in oil prices affects the global economy. 油價的波動影響全球經濟。

2. Variability變動性（名詞）

   The variability of weather in this region is well-known. 這個地區的天氣變動性是眾所周知的。

3. Alteration變化（名詞）

   The alteration of the original plan led to a better outcome. 原計劃的變化導致了更好的結果。

4. Transformation轉變（名詞）

   The transformation of the old factory into a modern art gallery was impressive. 將舊工廠轉變成現代藝術畫廊的改造令人印象深刻。

5. Shift轉變（名詞）

   There has been a significant shift in consumer preferences towards eco-friendly products. 消費者偏好朝向環保產品發生了顯著的變化。

6. Oscillation振盪（名詞）

The oscillation of the pendulum was used to measure time accurately. 鐘擺的振盪被用來精確測量時間。

7. Changeability易變性（名詞）

The changeability of market trends requires constant adaptation. 市場趨勢的易變性需要不斷的適應。

8. Instability不穩定性（名詞）

The political instability in the region has led to economic uncertainty. 該地區的政治不穩定導致了經濟不確定性。

9. Upheaval劇變（名詞）

The social upheaval of the 1960s brought about significant cultural changes. 20世紀60年代的社會劇變帶來了重大的文化變革。

10. Transition過渡（名詞）

The transition from analog to digital technology revolutionized communication. 從模擬到數字技術的過渡使通信獲得了革命性的變化。

11. Evolution演變（名詞）

The evolution of the internet has transformed how we live and work. 網路的演變改變了我們的生活和工作方式。

12. Flux變遷（名詞）

The constant flux of information can be overwhelming at times. 信息的不斷變遷有時可能令人不知所措。

13. Metamorphosis蛻變、變形（名詞）

The caterpillar's metamorphosis into a butterfly is a remarkable natural process. 毛毛蟲變形成蝴蝶是一個卓越

的自然過程。

14. Blip小波動或變動（名詞）

The sudden drop in sales was just a blip in the overall growth of the company. 銷售的突然下降只是公司整體增長中的一個小波動。

Vindictive | 報復

Vindictive是一個形容詞，意指報復心重的，通常指一個人擁有強烈的復仇心理，並願意采取行動來傷害或妨害那些曾對他們造成不滿或困擾的人。這種情緒常源於過去的衝突或爭執，而且可能導致長期的敵對關係。Vindictive的情境中，人們可能會尋求機會來報復，而不是嘗試解決問題或釋放怨恨。

"Vindictive" is an adjective that describes a person who is vengeful, often indicating someone with a strong desire for revenge and a willingness to take action to harm or hinder those who have caused them dissatisfaction or trouble. This emotion is typically rooted in past conflicts or disputes and may lead to long-standing hostile relationships. In a vindictive context, individuals may seek opportunities for retaliation rather than trying to resolve issues or let go of grudges.

Vindictive的應用例句

1. She was so vindictive that she plotted to ruin her ex-partner's career out of spite. 她如此報復心懷恨意，竟出於惡意策劃破壞她前任伴侶的事業。

2. His vindictive nature made it difficult for him to forgive those who had wronged him in the past. 他報復心重的天性讓他難以原諒那些曾在過去冤枉他的人。

3. The vindictive rivalry between the two companies led to a series of damaging lawsuits. 兩家公司之間的報復性競爭導致了一系列損害的訴訟案件。

Vindictive的同義字詞及例句

1. Revengeful報復心重的（形容詞）

   She is quite revengeful and never forgets a grudge. 她報復心重的，永遠不會忘記怨恨。

2. Retaliatory報復的（形容詞）

   The company took retaliatory action against its competitors. 該公司對競爭對手採取了報復行動。

3. Spiteful惡意的（形容詞）

   His spiteful comments hurt her feelings deeply. 他的惡意評論深深傷害了她的感情。

4. Malicious惡意的（形容詞）

   The malicious rumors about him were completely untrue. 關於他的惡意謠言完全不屬實。

5. Vengeful報仇心重的（形容詞）

   He harbored vengeful thoughts after the betrayal. 在受到背叛之後，他心懷報仇的念頭。

以上詞彙都指涉到一個人擁有報復心理或有意願採取行動來傷害他人的情感或性格特徵。

Wanderlust | 旅行狂熱者

Wanderlust名詞，指的是一種強烈的渴望去探索世界和旅行的慾望。用來形容對於未知地點、文化和冒險充滿好奇心的人。

"Wanderlust" is a noun that refers to a strong desire to explore the world and travel. This term is often used to describe individuals who are curious about unknown places, cultures, and adventures.

Wanderlust的應用及示例

1. Her inner wanderlust drove her to leave everything behind and embark on a thrilling journey around the world. 她內心深處的旅行狂熱驅使她放下一切，踏上了一場精彩的世界之旅。

2. The young photographer always seeks new shooting locations, and his wanderlust leads him to travel with his camera wherever he goes. 那位年輕的攝影師總是追求著新的拍攝地點，他對旅遊的狂熱讓他經常背著相機四處遊歷。

3. In this story, the protagonist's wanderlust leads him to search for a lost civilization in the jungle, unveiling an incredible adventure tale. 在這個故事中，主角對漫遊的狂熱驅使他在叢林中尋找失落的文明，揭開了一個驚人的冒險故事。

Wanderlust的同義字詞及例句

1. Roaming漫遊、流浪（名詞或動詞）

He had a strong desire for roaming the world. 他渴望漫遊世界。

2. Wander漫遊、遊歷（動詞）

She loved to wander through the picturesque countryside. 她喜歡漫遊於風景如畫的鄉間。

3. Travel Bug旅行癖（名詞，俚語）

Ever since he caught the travel bug, he can't stop exploring new places. 自從他染上旅行的癖好，他就停不下來探索新地方。

4. Nomadism遊牧生活（名詞）

Nomadism has been a way of life for generations in that region.在那個地區，遊牧生活已經是世世代代的生活方式。

Zingy party │ 激情派對

Zingy形容詞，令人振奮、活力奔放的，用於描述具有強烈的味道、刺激性或獨特性的飲食或情境。例如，一碗搭配辛辣醬汁的墨西哥炸玉米片可以被形容爲Zingy，因爲它們充滿了辛辣的風味和令人振奮的口感。這個詞也可以用來形容一場充滿活力和刺激的音樂會或派對。

"Zingy" is an adjective used to describe a stimulating and vivacious feeling or characteristic. This word is typically used to describe food, drinks, or situations when they have a strong flavor, excitement, or uniqueness. For example, a bowl of nachos with spicy sauce can be described as "zingy" because they are full of spicy flavor and an exhilarating texture. This term can also be used to describe an energetic and thrilling music concert or party.

來看看Zingy在文章中的應用：

Embrace the zingy spirit of life! Life is too short for dull moments. Infuse your days with enthusiasm and energy. Seek out zingy experiences that awaken your senses – from savoring spicy cuisine that tingles your taste buds to exploring new places that invigorate your soul. Surround yourself with zingy people who radiate positivity and excitement. Don't let monotony dampen your spirit; instead, let the zingy moments light up your journey.

With a zingy attitude, every day becomes an adventure, every challenge a chance to shine, and every encounter a source of inspiration. Live zingy, and watch life sparkle!"

擁抱生命的充滿活力精神吧！生命太短，不容許無聊的瞬間存在。注入你的日子充滿熱情和活力。追尋那些能喚醒你感官的刺激體驗——從品嚐能刺激你味蕾的辛辣美食到探索能振奮你靈魂的新地方。讓自己環繞在充滿正能量和興奮的人群中。別讓單調壓抑你的精神；相反，讓充滿活力的時刻照亮你的旅程。擁有充滿活力的態度，每一天都成為一次冒險，每一個挑戰都是一次發光的機會，每一次相遇都是一個靈感的源泉。活得充滿活力，看著生活閃耀吧！

讀一篇單字zingy在「貓貓、狗狗太活潑怎麼辦？」報導文的應用：

If your dogs and cats are too zingy, there are ways to manage their zestful energy. Ensure they get sufficient exercise every day, such as walks, playtime, or engaging indoor activities. Provide them with stimulating toys and mental challenges to keep their minds sharp. Basic training and routines help control their behavior. Encourage socialization with other pets to learn proper interaction. If the zinginess becomes a concern, consider seeking professional help from a pet behavior expert or veterinarian.

如果你的狗狗和貓貓過於活潑，有方法可以管理他們的充沛精力。確保他們每天都獲得足夠的運動，例如散步、遊戲時間，或參與有趣的室內活動。提供具有刺激性的玩具和智力挑戰，以保持他們的思維敏銳。基本的訓練和規律有助於控制他們的行為。鼓勵他們與其他寵物社交，學習適當的互動方式。如果過度的活潑成為問題，考慮尋求來自寵物行為專家或獸醫的專業幫助。

Zingy的例句

1. The zingy salsa with fresh cilantro and lime added a burst of flavor to the tacos. 新鮮香菜和萊姆調製的辣醬為墨西哥餅添加了一絲風味。

2. Her zingy dance moves on the dance floor caught everyone's attention and brought energy to the party. 她在舞池上的活力奔放的舞蹈動作吸引了所有人的注意，為派對帶來了活力。

3. The zingy atmosphere of the amusement park, with its bright lights and thrilling rides, made it a memorable experience for the visitors. 遊樂園充滿了亮燈和刺激的遊樂設施，營造出一種活力四溢的氛圍，讓遊客留下難忘的回憶。

Zingy的同義詞及示例

1. Vibrant（形容詞）充滿活力的

The city's nightlife is vibrant with music and dancing. 這個城市的夜生活充滿音樂和舞蹈。

2. Zesty（形容詞）充滿風味的

The zesty sauce added a burst of flavor to the dish. 那個充滿風味的醬汁為這道菜增添了風味。

3. Lively（形容詞）活躍的

The lively discussion at the meeting lasted for hours. 會議上

熱烈的討論持續了幾個小時。

4. Energetic（形容詞）充滿能量的

She's always so energetic and ready to take on new challenges.
她總是充滿活力，隨時準備迎接新的挑戰。

5. Invigorating（形容詞）令人振奮的

A walk in the fresh mountain air is invigorating. 在清新的山
區空氣中散步令人振奮。

Zingy和Vivacious

Zingy指一種充滿活力、刺激和活力的「感覺」。通常用來
描述一種明亮、有趣、令人振奮的「情感」或「氛圍」。強
調了一種讓人感到興奮、生氣勃勃的氛圍。

The salsa had a zingy flavor that made everyone want to dance.
這個莎莎醬有一種令人興奮的風味，讓每個人都想跳舞。

Vivacious形容詞，指「一個人」充滿活力、生氣勃勃、有活
力和快樂的特質。這個詞通常用來描述一個人的性格，強調
他們的快樂和充滿活力的本質。

She's a vivacious young woman who brings joy to everyone she
meets. 她是一位充滿活力的年輕女子，讓她遇到的每個人都
感到快樂。

Zingy更側重描述一種情境的感覺，而vivacious則是形容人充
滿活力、快樂和生氣勃勃的性格。

專文 │ Apple iPhone 15's Success: Key Factors to Watch 蘋果 iPhone 15 的值得觀察成功關鍵因素

蘋果iPhone 15擁有性能提升及品牌競爭力的關鍵因素，包括Type-C接口、相機升級、價格策略、客戶忠誠度、適應市場變化的能力以及解決環保問題的承諾。這些關鍵因素也將決定iPhone 15在競爭激烈的手機市場中的地位。來閱讀一下以下文章，來探討iPhone 15的命運吧！

閱讀之前先來瞭解以下幾個文章裡的提到重要的單字、詞語和片語的解釋、詞性以及單字的使用情境：

1. Crucial improvements關鍵性的改進，指對產品或情況的重要改進或升級。

   The crucial improvements in the new software update have made the app run much faster. 這次軟體更新中的關鍵改進使應用程序運行速度大大提高。

2. Titanium Alloy鈦合金，這個詞語意思指由鈦和其他金屬組成的合金，通常用於製造輕量且堅固的產品。

   The watchcase was made from a durable titanium alloy, ensuring its longevity. 錶殼是由耐用的鈦合金製成的，確保其使用壽命。

3. Persist堅持，持續（動詞）表示持續進行某種行爲或狀態，通常是在面臨困難或挑戰時。

She will persist in her studies, no matter how tough the coursework becomes. 無論課業變得多困難，她都會堅持學習。

4. Sustain Apple's streak of bestsellers維持蘋果的暢銷紀錄，這句話表示持續取得成功或保持某種紀錄，通常是指產品暢銷的紀錄。

The new product launch needs to sustain Apple's streak of bestsellers to meet investors' expectations. 新產品的推出需要維持蘋果的暢銷紀錄，以滿足投資者的期望。

5. Standout feature傑出的特點，意思指在眾多特點或功能中特別引人注目或出色的特點。

The standout feature of the new phone is its incredibly long battery life. 新手機的突出特點是其驚人的長電池壽命。

6. Appeal to吸引，訴求。這個動詞片語表示對某人或某事情感興趣或有吸引力。

The new fashion collection is designed to appeal to a younger audience. 這個新的時尚系列是設計來吸引年輕觀眾的。

7. Periscope-style zoom lens指潛望式變焦鏡頭，一種類似潛望鏡的設計，用於實現較長的光學變焦，通常在攝影和相機中使用。

The periscope-style zoom lens on the new smartphone allows for incredible zoom capabilities. 新智能手機上的潛望式變焦鏡頭允許令人難以置信的變焦功能。

8. 10x Zoom change 10倍變焦，指相機或光學設備能夠實現的10倍光學變焦能力。

The 10x zoom change in the camera greatly improves the ability to capture distant subjects. 相機中的10倍變焦大大提高了拍攝遠處主題的能力。

9. Caveat ['kævɪˌæt] 警告、注意事項（名詞），表示提醒或注意某件事情可能有潛在問題或風險。

The seller gave a caveat about the product's fragility, advising customers to handle it with care. 賣家對產品的易碎性提出了警告，建議顧客小心處理。

10. Discern about察覺，辨別（動詞片語）表示能夠看清或分辨某事物，通常用於形容對細節的敏銳感知。

She could discern about the subtle differences in the artwork that others might overlook. 她能夠察覺到藝術品中微妙的差異。

一起來閱讀以下本文：

In the rapidly changing world of smartphones, Apple's iPhone series maintains its leading position. Each new release generates anticipation as tech enthusiasts and analysts eagerly await groundbreaking features. The iPhone 15, especially the Pro and Pro Max models, stands out due to crucial improvements, such as its lightweight titanium alloy build, the shift to a Type-C interface, and remarkable camera enhancements. Yet, a fundamental question persists: Can the iPhone 15 sustain Apple's streak of best-sellers?

在快速變化的智能手機世界中，蘋果的iPhone系列一直保持著領先地位。每一次新的發布都引起愛好者和分析師的期待，他們迫不及待地等待著突破性功能的到來。iPhone 15，尤其是Pro和Pro Max型號，因其重要的改進而脫穎而出，包括其輕巧的鈦合金結構、轉向Type-C接口和印象深刻的相機增強功能。然而，一個根本性的問題仍然存在：iPhone 15是否能夠維持蘋果暢銷產品的紀錄？

The Type-C interface is a standout feature of the iPhone 15 Pro and Pro Max. Departing from the Lightning connector, this change aligns Apple with industry standards and promises lightning-fast data transfers at 20Gbps. This appeals to users relying heavily on smartphones for productivity and entertainment.

Type-C接口是iPhone 15 Pro和Pro Max的一個優秀特點。這一變化不僅使蘋果符合行業標準，還承諾20Gbps的超快數據傳輸速度。這對於那些極度依賴智能手機進行工作和娛樂的用戶來說非常吸引人。

Camera enthusiasts are delighted with the iPhone 15 Pro Max. Its periscope-style zoom lens delivers a potent 5x optical zoom. Coupled with a 48MP sensor featuring a 2x focal length conversion ratio（2x crop），Apple claims an effective 10x optical zoom range. This pushes Apple into direct competition with rivals like Samsung in smartphone photography, attracting photography enthusiasts.

相機愛好者對iPhone 15 Pro Max感到高興。其潛望式變焦鏡頭提供了強大的5倍光學變焦。再加上一個具有2倍焦距轉換率（2倍剪裁）的4800萬像素感測器，蘋果聲稱實現了有效的10倍光學變焦範圍。這使蘋果在智能手機攝影方面與三星等競爭對手直接競爭，吸引了攝影愛好者的關注。

However, a caveat exists - the iPhone 15 Pro Max starts at $1199, ranking among the priciest smartphones. Prospective buyers must weigh these impressive upgrades against the premium cost. In an intensely competitive market, consumers are becoming more discerning about their purchases, questioning whether the value justifies the price.

然而，需要考慮的一個問題是，iPhone 15 Pro Max的起價爲1199美元，位居最昂貴的智能手機之一。潛在買家必須權衡這些令人印象深刻的升級與高昂的價格之間的關係。在競爭激烈的市場中，消費者對於他們的購買變得更加挑剔，質疑價值是否合理。

The iPhone 15's success depends on factors beyond its features. Apple's dedicated customer base eagerly anticipates new releases, driving initial sales. Yet, challenges arise from Android competitors and lengthening smartphone upgrade cycles.

iPhone 15的成功取決於超出其功能的因素。蘋果忠實的客戶基礎迫不及待地期待著新產品的推出，這推動了初期銷售的增長。然而，來自Android競爭對手和不斷延長的智能手機升級週期帶來了挑戰。

Consumer sentiment is another aspect to monitor. Sustainability and environmental concerns are growing. Apple's adoption of the eco-friendly Type-C interface aligns with this trend. Addressing these issues and effectively communicating environmental efforts will affect the iPhone 15's appeal to eco-conscious consumers.

消費者情感是另一個需要關注的因素。可持續性和環境問題逐漸凸顯。蘋果採用環保的Type-C接口符合這一趨勢。如何有效地解決這些問題並傳達環境努力將影響iPhone 15對環保意識消費者的吸引力。

In conclusion, the iPhone 15 holds promise for ongoing sales success, thanks to its cutting-edge features. The Pro and Pro Max models offer remarkable camera capabilities and swift data transfers. Nonetheless, the steep price presents a hurdle, and competition evolves.

總之，由於其尖端功能，iPhone 15為持續的銷售成功提供了潛力。特別是Pro和Pro Max型號提供了卓越的相機功能和快速的數據傳輸。然而，高昂的價格是一個障礙，競爭也在不斷演變。

The smartphone industry is dynamic. Apple's ability to adapt to consumer preferences and market trends is pivotal for the iPhone 15's long-term success. As consumers weigh the upgrades against costs, close observation remains essential. Apple's loyal customer base and innovation capacity will shape the iPhone 15's fate in the fiercely competitive smartphone arena.

智能手機市場變化迅速。蘋果能否適應消費者偏好和市場趨勢對於iPhone 15的長期成功至關重要。當消費者權衡升級和成本時，仔細觀察仍然是必要的。蘋果忠實的客戶群和創新能力將塑造iPhone 15在競爭激烈的智能手機市場中的命運。

專文｜Taiwan's First Encounter with Deadly Bongkrekic Acid— Emphasizing the Importance of Food Safety and Storage Practices.
米酵菌酸毒素警訊：台灣首次發現！

寶林茶室中毒案重大發現，死者解剖驗出米酵菌酸Bongkrekic Acid為台灣首見。此毒素抑制粒腺體ATP功能，導致細胞失去能量。米酵菌酸常見於長時間發酵或泡發的食品，如穀物發酵製品及薯類製品。預防措施包括冷藏妥善保存，避免長時間室溫放置。目前對米酵菌酸中毒無特效解毒藥物，只能給予支持療法。衛福部正積極調查，以釐清真正死因，並加強食品安全管理。

In a pivotal discovery following the Polam Kopitiam poisoning case, autopsies of the deceased unearthed traces of ①Bongkrekic Acid, marking Taiwan's first encounter with this lethal toxin. Originating from Bongkrek bacteria, the poison disrupts② mitochondrial functions crucial for cellular energy, essentially starving cells of oxygen and nutrients. This acid is notably found in foods subjected to prolonged③ fermentation, including fermented grains and ④tubers, creating a breeding ground for the toxin in improperly stored foods. Despite the grave risk it poses, with mortality rates soaring between 30% to

100%, medical science has yet to find a specific ⑤antidote or ⑥suppressant, leaving supportive care as the only current treatment. This incident underscores the critical importance of strict food storage practices to prevent such dangerous outbreaks.

寶林茶室中毒案之後的一個關鍵發現，死者的驗屍中發現了米酵菌酸Bongkrekic Aci的痕跡，是台灣首次經歷這種致命毒素。這種毒素源自米酵菌酸，它會干擾細胞和能量相關線粒體mitochondrial功能，基本上會使細胞缺氧和養分。這種菌酸特別存在於經過長時間發酵的食物中，包括發酵的穀物和塊莖tubers，在不當存儲的食物中產生毒素的滋生地。儘管它帶來嚴重風險，死亡率在30％到100％之間飆升，醫學科學尚未找到特定的解毒劑antidote或抑制劑suppressant，目前唯一的治療方法是支持性療法。這一事件凸顯了嚴格食品儲存實踐的關鍵重要性，以防止此類危險的爆發。

① Bongkrekic /bɒŋˈkrɛkɪk/ Acid米酵酸菌，是一種毒素對人體極為致命，解剖死者時首次在台灣發現的致命毒素。

② Mitochondrial /ˌmaɪ.təˈkɑːn.drɪ.əl/ functions指粒線體作用：粒線體功能指的是粒線體在細胞內產生能量的過程，對於細胞的生存至關重要。Mitochondrial biogenesis is essential for energy production in cells. 線粒體生物生成對於細胞內的能量產生至關重要。

③ Fermentation /ˌfɜː.mɛnˈteɪ.ʃən/ 發酵，發酵是指微生物在無氧環境下有機物質產生，文中指長時間的發酵過程被認為是毒素出現在食物中的原因之一。The toxin present in the Polam Kopitiam is likely caused by the death-inducing

Bongkrekic Acid bacterium, produced by the fermentation of the rice product, Kway teow. 寶林茶室中的毒素很可能是由發酵的米製品板條產生的米酵酸菌造成的死亡。

④Tubers塊莖，像是蕃薯類，塊莖是植物的一種脹大的地下莖，用於儲存營養。

⑤Antidote解毒劑。文章強調目前醫學界尚未找到針對米酵酸菌中毒的特定解毒劑。Antidotes for snake bites are an essential part of a hiker's first aid kit. 蛇咬傷的解藥是徒步旅行者急救包中不可或缺的一部分。

⑥Suppressant抑制劑。抑制劑是指能夠減緩或阻止某些生理反應或病情。文中說明醫學上尚未找到可以直接對抗的藥物，目前只能提供支持性照護作為治療方式。The doctor prescribed a cough suppressant to help manage her symptoms. 醫生開了止咳抑制劑來幫助她控制症狀。

專文｜Scientists Nurture Mammoth Stem Cells, Edging Closer to Resurrecting the Prehistoric Giant. 科學家復活史前巨獸：向復育猛獁象幹細胞邁進！

科學家透過培育猛獁象的幹細胞，目標是要透過基因工程技術，將瀕危的亞洲象體細胞轉化爲類似猛獁象的特徵，這些幹細胞稱爲誘導性多功能幹細胞（induced pluripotent stem cell/iPSC）。這一過程不同於複製羊Dolly的直接複製技術，而是透過基因編輯讓亞洲象擁有猛獁象的特性，如毛茸茸的皮毛和小耳朵，挑戰在於開發人造子宮等技術。此項研究的潛在好處在於，透過復育猛獁象這類大型草食動物，可能有助於北極苔原生態系統的恢復，進而緩和氣候變遷。不過，這一復育過程面臨許多挑戰，包括倫理和技術難題。

Scientists are cultivating mammoth stem cells, specifically iPSCs, to potentially resurrect the extinct, ①tusked mammoth by editing the Asian elephant's ②genome, aiming for a mammoth-elephant hybrid. Unlike Dolly's cloning, this process involves gene editing for mammoth traits like woolly fur. This ③scalable effort suggests we might see real mammoths, whose ④grazing behavior could tramp down and compact the Arctic tundra, ⑤palliating climate change effects. However, challenges such as developing an artificial womb for gestation have ⑥come home to roost.

〔譯文〕科學家正在孕育猛獁象的幹細胞，特別是誘導性多能幹細胞iPSCs，希望能透過編輯亞洲象的②基因組，復活已經滅絕的①有獠牙的猛獁象，最終目標是培育出猛獁象——亞洲象的混合體。與複製羊Dolly不同的是，這個過程需要基因編程，以導入長毛等猛獁象特徵。這項③可擴充的技術暗示著我們可能有一天會看到真正的猛獁象，牠們的④覓食放牧的行為可以壓實苔原上的凍土，有潛力幫助⑤減緩氣候變化的影響。然而，像開發人工子宮等挑戰及難題仍然必須回頭面對。

①tusked形容詞，有獠牙的、有長牙的。猛獁象具有顯著的獠牙特徵。The tusked elephant charged out of the brush, startling the safari group. 長著長牙的大象從灌木叢中衝了出來，驚動了野生動物的觀賞旅行團。

②genome名詞，基因序列。指以亞洲象的遺傳物質，編輯及復育猛獁象。

③scalable /ˈskeɪ.lə.bəl/ 形容詞，可擴展的。指復育猛獁象的努力可以隨著需要進行擴大，暗示這項技術和過程有潛力被擴大應用。The software is designed to be scalable, accommodating growing user numbers without performance degradation. 該軟體被設計為可擴展的，可以在不降低性能的情況下容納越來越多的用戶。

④grazing名詞，放牧；牧草。描述猛獁象放牧的行為，可以使北極苔原更緊密，這對於生態系統具有重要影響。Grazing is a common practice in sustainable agriculture to maintain healthy grasslands. 放牧是可持續農業中維持健康草原的一種常見做法。

⑤palliate /ˈpæl.i.eɪt/ 動詞，減輕，緩和。指猛獁象放牧行爲對於氣候變遷影響，透過其自然活動能夠減緩氣候變化的效應。Hospice care aims to palliate pain and make patients comfortable in their final days. 安寧照護旨在緩解痛苦，讓病人在最後的日子裡感到舒適。

⑥come home to roost片語（問題、後果等）最終要回頭面對難題或結果。文章指開發人工子宮孕育胚胎等挑戰，最終仍必須面對及解決。Years of unhealthy eating have come home to roost, leading to serious health issues. 多年不健康的飲食習慣最終帶來了嚴重的健康問題需要面對。

專文 | Culinary Journey Beyond the Stars: The Space Michelin Dining Experience.
一生一次跨越星際的味蕾之旅：太空米其林用餐體驗！

想成名快報名喔！一生一次的極致的米其林太空饗宴。這趟太空米其林之旅的特殊設計之處在於，預定2025年底從佛羅里達州甘迺迪太空中心（Kennedy Space Center）發射展開，整趟旅行耗時6小時，每趟旅程將有6人在海拔10萬英尺的高度，乘坐碳中和的「海王星號太空船」，體驗平流層用餐。但旅程售價高達490,000美元，包括由米其林二星丹麥名廚Rasmus Munk準備的創意菜餚，以及觀賞地球日出及絕佳地球曲線視角。主廚的夢想是將美食、藝術和科學融合，透過僅有一生一次體驗，強調食物在人類生活中的核心地位，並提高對社會和環境問題的意識。餐廳用餐規定或限制主要體現在空間有限，部分食物須提前準備，且艙內僅配備小型廚房進行熱食加工和裝盤。在這趟太空之旅中，用餐者可以一邊享受美食，一邊俯瞰地球曲率所展現的壯觀景色。並提供Wi-Fi進行直播，這場直播極有可能吸引廣泛關注，令用餐者一夜成名啊。

Embarking on a culinary odyssey to the edge of space, the "Stratospheric Dining Experience" aboard the carbon-neutral Spaceship Neptune, designed by Space Perspective, sets a new pinnacle for luxury dining. Scheduled for a 2025 launch from the Kennedy Space Center in Florida, this six-hour journey costs $495,000 per ticket, offering a once-in-a-lifetime dining spectacle above 99% of Earth's atmosphere. This price not only reflects the ①bespoke, ②cutting-edge experience but also includes creative dishes prepared by two-Michelin-star Danish chef Rasmus Munk, renowned for his Alchemist restaurant. His dream intertwines ③gastronomy with art and science, aiming to spotlight food's pivotal role in human existence against the breathtaking backdrop of Earth's ④curvature. The strict space constraints aboard necessitate pre-preparation of several food components, yet a mini-kitchen allows for final touches. This exclusive experience, allowing diners to live-stream their meal, might just ⑤catapult them to viral fame, as they dine while gazing down upon the mesmerizing curve of the Earth.

太空Space Perspective公司所設計的「平流層饗宴體驗」將帶您踏上一趟豪華的美食太空之旅，登上碳中和的「海王星號」太空船，引領奢華用餐體驗達到新的巔峰。六小時的旅程預計於2025年從佛羅里達州的甘迺迪太空中心啟程，每張票價爲49.5萬美元，讓您在距地球大氣層99%以上的高空享受一生難忘的用餐奇觀。這個價格不僅反映了①客製化和②前衛的頂級體驗，還包含由丹麥米其林二星主廚拉斯穆斯‧穆克Rasmus Munk烹製的創意菜餚，他以其「鍊金術師餐廳」Alchemist restaurant而聞名。穆克的夢想是將③美食與藝術和科學融爲一體，以地球令人屏息地球的④彎曲弧度curvature爲背景，凸顯食物在人類生存中扮演的重要角色。

由於太空船艙內空間有限，必須提前準備一些食物材料，但小型的廚房仍可進行最後的烹調。這獨家體驗可以讓用餐者一邊享用美食，一邊俯瞰地球迷人的曲線，並可以透過直播分享用餐體驗，或許因此而⑤一炮而紅呢！

①bespoke形容詞，定制的，特製的。指這次太空米其林用餐體驗是為客戶量身定制的。Offering bespoke travel experiences, the agency caters to clients seeking unique adventures. 該旅行社提供客製化旅行體驗，迎合尋求獨特冒險的客戶。

②cutting-edge形容詞，最先進的，尖端的。They developed a cutting-edge smartphone with features not found in any other device. 他們開發了一款尖端科技的智慧型手機，具有其他工具所沒有的功能的。

③gastronomy名詞，美食學，烹飪藝術。指名廚Rasmus Munk將美食學與藝術和科學相結合，提升食物在人類生活中的重要性。He has a deep passion for gastronomy, constantly exploring new flavors and culinary techniques. 他對美食有著深厚的熱情，不斷探索新的美味和烹飪技術。

④curvature名詞，曲率、弧度，彎曲度。用餐可以從太空艙內看到的地球表面的彎曲弧度，突顯這次用餐體驗的獨特視角。The curvature of the Earth affects global navigation and satellite communication systems. 地球的弧度影響全球導航和衛星通信系統。

⑤catapult動詞，快速推進，使突然升高，文章指這種獨一無二的太空用餐體驗可能迅速提升參與者的知名度，使他

們快速成爲網絡紅人。The startup was catapulted into fame after receiving a major investment from a well-known venture capitalist. 新創公司在獲得一位著名風險投資家的重大投資後聲名大噪。

專文｜Musk vs OpenAI: A Legal Battle Over AI's Ethical and Open-Source Future
馬斯克、OpenAI奧特曼大鬥法：開源碼與AI未來之爭

AI大鬥法！誰眞的重視人類福祉Humanity？身爲OpenAI新創時期股東的馬斯克，在舊金山高等法院對OpenAI及其執行長Altman提訟，指控OpenAI背離了以「人類福祉」爲前提的非營利初衷。馬斯克還在X平台上批評OpenAI未公開原始碼，違背了對人類利益的承諾，並宣布將公佈更讓人信賴的Grok開源碼。然而，OpenAI的CEO Altman將馬斯克的訴訟描述爲毫無依據，專家們對於最初的投資協議也提出質疑，指出其缺乏約束力的正式合約，對訴訟的成立提出疑問。然而此案件仍凸顯了AI的發展、倫理和開源的問題，引發全球關注。

As an inchoate participant in OpenAI's journey, the ①daredevil mogul Elon Musk has launched a legal challenge against the company and its CEO, Sam Altman, in San Francisco. He accuses them of deviating from their ②altruistic, non-profit origins, which were supposed to prioritize human welfare. Musk ③deprecates OpenAI's decision to keep its code proprietary, asserting it goes against ④the grain of communal benefit, and in a move to ⑤whet the appetite for transparency, has open-sourced Grok's code himself. Altman and Musk trade barbs over this, with Altman branding Musk's legal action as ⑥errant nonsense, ⑦devoid of pecuniary or privity foundation. Experts are poised on the cusp of debate, wrestling with the question of the initial agreement's enforceability, given the absence of a ⑧cromulent, binding founding contract. This skirmish not only highlights the burgeoning ethical and open-source quandaries within AI's evolution but also garners widespread fascination.

作爲OpenAI發展歷程中早期參與者之一，①冒險家大亨伊隆‧馬斯克在舊金山對該公司OpenAI及其首席執行官阿爾特曼發起法律挑戰。他控告他們偏離了②無私的非營利宗旨，而該宗旨本應優先考慮人類福祉。馬斯克③譴責OpenAI決定對其代碼保密，聲稱這違背了④公共利益的原則，並且爲了⑤激起人們對透明的渴望，他自己開源了Grok的代碼。阿爾特曼和馬斯克就此唇槍舌劍，阿爾特曼將馬斯克的法律行動斥爲⑥胡言亂語，並稱其⑦缺乏經濟或利益基礎。鑑於缺乏⑧合理、正式、具有約束力的創始合約，專家們準備辯論最初協議的可執行性問題。這場爭執不僅凸顯了人工智慧發展過程中新興的倫理和開源難題，而且還引起了廣泛的關注。

①the daredevil mogul敢於冒險的企業大亨，指馬斯克Elon Musk。Known as a daredevil mogul, he regularly invests in high-risk, high-reward projects. 作爲一位敢於冒險的大亨，他經常投資於高風險、高回報的項目。

②altruistic形容詞，表示無私的、利他的。文中指OpenAI原本以非營利、優先考慮人類福祉的創始宗旨。The

billionaire's altruistic decision to donate half of his fortune to charity surprised many. 這位億萬富翁將一半財富捐給慈善事業的無私決定讓許多人感到驚訝。

③deprecates動詞，表示反對、貶低。馬斯克反對OpenAI的決定將其代碼保持專有，認為這違背了公共利益。Some members of the community deprecate the development of the new shopping center, fearing it will lead to increased traffic and pollution. 社區中的一些成員不贊成開發新購物中心，擔心這將導致交通和污染增加。

④the grain of communal benefit指符合或支持公共利益的本質或方向。馬斯克認為OpenAI應當公開其代碼，以符合人類共享的利益。The project was designed with the grain of communal benefit in mind, aiming to improve the lives of all residents. 這個計劃是以社區共同利益為出發點設計的，旨在改善所有居民的生活。

⑤whet動詞，挑起、激起、增強。whet the appetite for transparency激起了對透明度的渴望。透過開源Grok的代碼，馬斯克試圖增強人們對於透明度的期望。The preview of the upcoming movie was enough to whet the audience's appetite for more. 即將上映的電影預告足以激起觀眾對更多內容的渴望。

⑥errant nonsense荒謬無理。Altman認為馬斯克的法律行動毫無根據。In a world of errant nonsense, finding truth becomes a daunting task. 在一個充斥著離譜胡言的世界裡，尋找真相變成了一項艱巨的任務。

⑦pecuniary與金錢相關的；privity名詞，共同利益，特

定的知情權或參與關係。devoid of pecuniary or privity foundation 缺乏金錢或共同利益關係的基礎，意思是馬斯克的訴訟沒有基於金錢利益或特定的知情參與關係。

The judge imposed a pecuniary penalty on the company for violating environmental laws. 法官對該公司因違反環境的法律而處以金錢罰款。

⑧Cromulent形容詞，可接受的、合適的，合理的。given the absence of a cromulent, binding founding contract. 鑑於缺乏一個合理的、具有約束力的創始合約。His explanation was odd but perfectly cromulent, and everyone seemed to understand. 他的解釋雖然奇怪，但完全可接受，而且每個人似乎都能理解。

專文 | California Consumers Launch Antitrust Class Action Against Hermès Over Exclusive Birkin Bag Sales.
美加州消費者對愛馬仕Hermès獨家銷售策略，發起反壟斷集體訴

加州消費者對愛馬仕提起聯合壟斷的集體訴訟，控訴其綁賣柏金包與其他商品，依據《反壟斷法》提出訴求。愛馬仕透過特殊銷售手法，限制顧客直接購買柏金包，要求先購買其他商品以建立「購買歷史」，方可獲得購買機會，商店內不直接展售柏金包，爲了增加了其獨家性及吸引力。消費者質疑此策略反競爭和壟斷法的規範，尋求法律裁定禁制令與金錢賠償。

In California, consumers have launched a ①titillating legal battle against Hermès, coveting justice for what they perceive as a sought-after but unnervingly exclusive acquisition process for the famed Birkin bags. These plaintiffs allege that Hermès has ②foisted on them ③a panoply of ancillary products to ④inflate their purchase history, a strategy that runs afoul of ⑤the Sherman Act by creating a nugatory choice in luxury consumerism. This exclusive sales tactic piques curiosity yet frustrates many, as the chance to own a Birkin does not come from walking into a store but from an opaque selection process, devoid of any iota of transparency. Hermès's allure lies not just in the craftsmanship of its bags but also in the elusive status they confer, making each sale a testament to the buyer's loyalty and financial prowess. The lawsuit seeks not only ⑥injunctive relief to prohibit Hermès from continuing these practices but also ⑦pecuniary damages for consumers who have been economically affected by what they claim are anticompetitive tactics, advocating for fairer access luxury goods without the prerequisite of unrelated purchases.

在加州，消費者針對愛馬仕發起了一場①引人注目的法律戰，爭取他們認爲惡名昭彰的柏金包讓人難以捉摸的購買過程及待遇。原告指控愛馬仕②強迫他們購買③琳瑯滿目的產品來④擴充他們購買的歷史記錄，這種策略違反了⑤《謝爾曼法案》，因爲它在奢侈品消費中創造了一種無意義的選擇。這種獨家銷售策略既讓人好奇也讓許多人感到沮喪，因爲擁有柏金包的機會不是走進商店就能得到的，而是來自一個不透明的選擇過程，完全缺乏任何透明度。愛馬仕的吸引力不僅在於其包包的精湛工藝，還在於賦予的難以捉摸的地位，使每一次銷售都成買家忠誠度和財力的證明。該訴訟不僅尋求法院⑥禁制令，禁止愛馬仕繼續這些做法，而且還尋求⑦金錢賠償，用於那些聲稱反競爭行爲而受到經濟影響的消費者，主張在沒有額外的消費前提下更公平地獲取奢侈品。

①a titillating legal battle指這場訴法訴訟是一場挑動情緒法律
　　戰。The celebrity's divorce case turned into a titillating legal

battleground, with salacious details filling the headlines. 這位名人的離婚案變成了一場挑起興奮感的法律戰場，醜聞細節充斥著頭條新聞。

②foisted on強加於。文章指愛馬仕將一系列的附加產品強加給消費者。The salesman tried to foist on us some expensive products that we didn't need. 那位銷售員試圖強推我們一些我們不需要的昂貴產品。

③a panoply全套；大量。指愛馬仕在消費者購買包包前需購買的一大系列的附加產品。The museum's exhibit featured a panoply of artifacts from ancient civilizations. 博物館的展覽展示了來自古代文明的各式各樣文物。

④Inflate動詞，膨脹、增加或抬高。也可以用在比喻意義上，如價格、數量或價值的人為增加。The company was accused of trying to inflate its sales figures to attract more investors. 這家公司被指控試圖人為增加其銷售數字，以吸引更多投資者。The government's excessive printing of money is likely to inflate the currency and cause inflation. 政府過度印鈔很可能會導致貨幣膨脹和引起通貨膨脹。

⑤the Sherman Act美國反壟斷法律案，旨在禁止妨礙競爭的商業行為。The Sherman Act is a landmark federal statute in the United States that prohibits monopolistic practices and promotes competition. 謝爾曼法案Sherman Act是美國的一項標誌性聯邦法律，禁止壟斷行為並促進競爭。

⑥injunctive relief此處指訴訟尋求法院命令愛馬仕停止其被控的行為。The company sought injunctive relief to prevent their competitor from infringing on their exclusive rights. 該

公司尋求禁令救濟，以防止競爭對手侵害其專營權。

⑦pecuniary damages金錢上的損害賠償。The court awarded pecuniary damages to the plaintiff to compensate for the financial losses suffered due to the defendant's negligence. 法院判給原告金錢損害賠償，以彌補因被告疏忽造成的財務損失。

國家圖書館出版品預行編目資料

Fancy English精湛英文II／謝文欽著. --初版.--
臺中市：白象文化事業有限公司，2024.6
　　面；　公分
ISBN 978-626-364-332-1（平裝）
1.CST: 英語 2.CST: 讀本
805.18　　　　　　　　　　　113004940

Fancy English精湛英文II

作　　者　謝文欽
校　　對　謝文欽
發 行 人　張輝潭
出版發行　白象文化事業有限公司
　　　　　412台中市大里區科技路1號8樓之2（台中軟體園區）
　　　　　出版專線：（04）2496-5995　　傳眞：（04）2496-9901
　　　　　401台中市東區和平街228巷44號（經銷部）
　　　　　購書專線：（04）2220-8589　　傳眞：（04）2220-8505
出版編印　林榮威、陳逸儒、黃麗穎、水邊、陳婥婷、李婕、林金郎
設計創意　張禮南、何佳誼
經紀企劃　張輝潭、徐錦淳、林尉儒
經銷推廣　李莉吟、莊博亞、劉育姍、林政泓
行銷宣傳　黃姿虹、沈若瑜
營運管理　曾千熏、羅禎琳
印　　刷　基盛印刷工場
初版一刷　2024年6月
定　　價　450元

白象文化　印書小舖　PressStore　出版・經銷・宣傳・設計
www.ElephantWhite.com.tw　f 自費出版的領導者　購書 白象文化生活館